THE WAR ETERNAL

ALONG THE RAZOR'S EDGE

ROB J. HAYES

For Vicki and Korra
who kept me sane, fed, and walked.

PROLOGUE

My life began the day we lost the war.

I remember seeing the fire go out of Josef's eyes. I remember seeing my oldest friend give up and surrender. "Eskara, STOP! It's over. We've lost."

We were surrounded by enemies, standing atop the tallest tower of Fort Vernan. The city around us was chaos, a battle played out in the darkest shades of red. Beyond the city was a scorched ruin, fields turned black by fire and war.

"It's not over!" I screamed, a shard of ice forming in one hand while the other burst into green flame. "We can take them. We are the Emperor's Weapons." Oh, the overconfidence of youth, before the hammer and anvil of time and reality have beaten us into whatever shape society demands.

I remember twenty men and women surrounding us, though my memory is fuzzy from rage. Perhaps it was more like ten. Some were warriors with glowing armour, enchanted to deflect magic. Others were Sourcerers like Josef and I. Well, not quite like us. We were beyond them. In our prime. Each with five Sources lending us power.

"It's over," Josef said again, grabbing my arm and pointing.

Down below, on the field of battle I could see the two armies clashing; crashing against each other. Horns sounded over the din, echoing up to our ears. And I saw flags falling. The tell-tale blue blur of a Chronomancer darting between units, relaying the orders. Our soldiers laying down their arms.

Josef was right, the order had been given to surrender. It might not have reached us yet, so high up, but it would. After ten years of war the Orran empire was crumbling.

I didn't know it then, but the emperor was dead. While the battle raged at our door and I rained down five types of bloody hell upon our enemy, they had infiltrated the palace and ended the Orran bloodline once and for all.

"Stand down," ordered one of the Terrelan soldiers. His armour was silver with etched runes glowing pink. There was fear on his face, as well there should have been. I saw it there and smiled. We had already killed so many of his comrades. They were right to fear me.

The sky was on fire, blood red showing behind the grey clouds, lightning rippling overhead and thunder rattling the earth. A Meteomancer beating out a dramatic ending to the ten-year war.

There are times in life when it is wise to lay down and accept defeat. It is a lesson Josef learned early on in his life. I was, as always, the slower learner.

"No! I will not lay down and..." My mouth fumbled out a strangled cry as Josef hit me from behind, and the world went bright for a moment. The next thing I remember, I was down on my hands and knees, staring at stone the colour of ash. It was rough to the touch and cold despite the battle. I have always been attuned to temperature. Pyromancy was the first school I mastered and remains one of my most proficient.

When I looked up, I saw a woman rushing towards me, she wore Terrelan robes and her eyes glowed green with her magic. I felt a wave of hopelessness wash over me, quashing my will to fight.

Hands grabbed hold of me from behind and pulled me up to stare at the woman with the glowing eyes. She reached into a pouch hanging from her belt and pulled out a clump of brown weed. I clenched my jaw shut and struggled against the hands holding me, but I was not strong enough. My power lay in magic, not brute strength.

Fingers pushed into my cheeks so hard I felt them puncture the skin. They forced my mouth open and shoved the weed inside. Then there was a hand underneath my jaw, clamping my mouth shut. The taste was bitter and spicy all at once, so hot it burned my tongue and made my eyes water.

Too late, I thought to use magic. With a surge of power, I ignited my hands into searing green flame. Those holding me screamed and fell away. I leapt back to my feet just as the first wave of vertigo hit. The world turned upside down and then wobbled, finally righting itself with a violent shake. I was back on my hands and knees again, the green flame guttering out even as I watched.

You can't control the retching once it starts. Spiceweed is potent stuff. Within moments I was hacking up the contents of my stomach while struggling to breathe. My first Source hit the floor in pool of acidic vomit. It held a faint orange glow, already fading. I felt my connection to fire fade with it.

The second Source to go was my connection to the Other World. It was larger than the others with hard edges, and bringing it back up was beyond painful. Somewhere above, I knew the hellions I had summoned would tear free of their bondage and fly away. Unleashed monsters are a blight on the world, but a few monsters to hunt down are less dangerous than I with a Source in my stomach.

My last three Sources I vomited up as well, each with a sticky coating of blood. They were snatched away as soon as I retched them onto the floor. I was exhausted. Bringing up Sources has always been that way for me. It takes such effort, as though my body refuses to let go of the power even once it starts to hurt me. And it *has* hurt me. Many times.

I lay there on the rooftop of the tallest tower of Fort Vernan, in a pool of my own vomit and blood. Beaten. Stripped of my power. And so fucking angry! My hands were pulled behind my back and I felt rope wrap around them. A distant discomfort I barely registered as the misery of my defeat rose up to claim me.

At just fifteen years old, I had fought in the greatest war mankind has ever known. I had been one of Orran's most powerful Sourcerers, celebrated by our allies and feared by our enemies. I had helped bring prosperity to my emperor's lands, destruction to his foes. And now I was a prisoner, my power gone with my Sources. There was only one place the Terrelans would send a prisoner as valuable as I– the Pit.

CHAPTER 1

You may think it strange I start my story there, at the end of the great war. The truth is, my part in that war was small and insignificant; a few skirmishes, some fire in the night, one battle lost before it even began. I may have been there at the end, but I missed the great war. It's probably a good thing. The young and innocent are usually the first casualties of any conflict. Though I was already far from innocent.

Before that, I grew up sheltered in the Orran Academy of Magic. Food, lodgings, education; all was provided for me. It was not an easy life, never that. The training we Sourcerers are put through is a harrowing experience, especially for one as young as I. That's not to say I don't have some stories to tell about my time there. I was always in one type of trouble or another. I believe the tutors liked to describe me as *challenging*. Often a bad influence on others, especially Josef.

No, I start my story at the end of the war for good reason. I consider that the time where my life began in earnest. It was after the war, after everything had been taken from me, that I had to stand on my own for the first time. It was down in the Pit where I found a purpose for my existence, a reason for living. I'm not about to claim that retribution is a wholesome purpose, but then my life has never been that. Friend and enemy alike have long referred to me as the Corpse Queen, and it is a name I bloody well earned.

But I'm getting ahead of myself. I choose to start my story in the Pit. Down there, I was surrounded by monsters, some terran and some not. Down there, I made friendships that would last a lifetime, and enemies that would last even longer. I was raised in the luxury of the Orran Academy of Magic, but I grew up in the squalor of the Pit.

Three months into my incarceration, and I had fallen into a routine of sorts. I slept near Josef, as much for protection as for loyalty. We had been together since our first day at the Orran Academy of Magic and I loved him more than I ever did my own flesh and blood brother. Even after he helped the Terrelans capture me, I loved Josef. I know he did it to save our lives; we would have died up there on the tower if not for him stopping my retaliation. Even so, part of me hated him for the betrayal. I sometimes entertained dreams of smothering him in his sleep. I'll admit I was a little confused back then.

There is no true day or night cycle down in the Pit. At least not as far down as we worked. After three months of not seeing the sky, nor a single ray of natural light, I began to forget what they looked like. I tried to picture the sky in my mind every day and all I could see was rough-hewn rock lit by greasy lamplight. The world is a miserable place down in the Pit, but then prisons are not meant to be cheerful.

We worked, slept, and ate in shifts and I lost all sense of time. I relied on the internal clock of my body to wake me for work and learned early on not to be late. The foreman's punishments were particularly harsh, and the mouldy arsehole was not shy in handing them out.

Josef and I were assigned to different teams, though by sheer luck we kept the same shifts. At night we would curl up together, as we had many times back in the academy, and pull our dirty, threadbare blanket over us both. Everything down in the Pit is dirty, covered in layers of grease and rock dust. After a while I forgot what it was like to be clean. After just a little longer, I stopped caring. There are no mirrors down in the Pit for good reason.

I always woke just a little before Josef. Each morning— and I called them mornings for lack of a better term— I would wake and roll away from him. I would stare up at the rock above me and hate. Anger has always been one of my strongest passions. Some say it grants strength when reason and will fail. I think maybe those people are right. It granted me a fire burning inside when hope failed me. I didn't so much desire to escape, as I needed to visit my burning wrath upon all the bastards who had put me there. I had a great many enemies to kill, and most of them didn't even know I existed. There is little that is as maddening as being beneath the notice of those you wish to murder.

I hated the Terrelans, every single one of the fuckers, for putting me down in the Pit, for winning the war and even letting me live. I hated Prig, the rotten cunt of a foreman who drove our team deeper into the rock each day. I hated my team, broken workers for the most part, for not standing up and fighting Prig. I hated the cock-faced overseer, even to this day I don't know his name, for trying to break me once a week. I even hated Josef for helping in

7

my capture and for giving up. I could see in his eyes every day that he had given up. But I think most of all I hated my own damned self.

No! Most of all I definitely hated Prig.

"Up! Get up, scabs!" Prig bellowed, punctuating his order with a crack of his leather whip. Nasty things, whips, perfectly suited to inflict terror on a person as much as pain. I hate to admit it, but I came to dread the sound of that whip cracking. I wanted nothing more than to take it from him, shove it up his arse and drag it out through his mouth. Just a few months earlier I would have set the shit-sniffing bastard on fire for talking to me that way. Instead, I rushed to my feet and stood ready along with the rest of my team. Josef let out a groan and sat up, already rolling our blanket into a ball. He would find some little nook to hide it until we returned. It wasn't much, but the other inmates would happily steal nothing much. I've heard it said there is honour amongst thieves, but down in the Pit honour was a commodity worth shit. Down there, there was nothing so valuable as food and fear. Well, and shoes.

The whip cracked again and Josef cried out as it lashed a bloody trail along his leg. He scrambled backwards against the rough stone wall, clutching at the limb. I have found there is little in this world quite so horrible as a loved one's pain. It carries with it a certain hopelessness. A knowledge that there is nothing you can do but watch them suffer.

"Always sniffing around this one. Heh!" Prig snorted, a crooked grin revealing brown teeth. His rot-breath could have felled a particularly vicious tiger at twenty paces.

I took a step sideways, putting myself between Prig and Josef, and locked my knees, trying to stop the trembling in my legs. I have said fear was valuable commodity down in the Pit, and it was one Prig was rich in. I refused to add to his hoard of riches.

"Fuck you, Prig," I hissed. "He's not on your team. He can sleep wherever he likes."

Prig was not a small man and I was still a girl. He dwarfed me both in height and bulk and I had already learned the hard way, more than once, that he had no qualms beating a young girl. I think he enjoyed it as some men do. I think it made the rotten fucker feel powerful being able to dominate a woman, even one as young as I, and there were no others on his team. Without any Sources, without any magic, I had no way to stop him from doing whatever he pleased.

In a flash he was on me, a meaty fist slamming into my gut. I staggered, feeling air rush out my lungs and bile rise in my throat. I think I must have closed my eyes. It would not be the first nor last time Prig had beaten me unconscious. Fingers like iron wrapped around my throat, hauled me back to my feet and bashed me against the wall of the cavern. I smelled that rotten breath, so vile it made the urge to vomit even stronger. Honestly, it smelled like the bastard regularly dined on shit.

I struggled against the grip, clawing at the fingers digging into my neck. It's hard to describe the panic of suffocating. Prig had already driven the air from my lungs and his iron grip stopped me from breathing. I couldn't even make a sound as I struggled, pawing impotently at his hand, eyes goggling with terror. Prig was worse than

9

anything the Terrelans ever did to me. He made me helpless.

Just as my vision started to dim, Prig let go, dropping me to my knees in front of him. I gasped down air, clutching at my throat and shedding shameful tears onto the rock below. There were eight other people in the little cavern we slept in and not a single one of the fuckers helped me, not even Josef. I hated them for that, even as I realised I didn't blame them. Prig was chief of this little part of the world and he did not brook defiance. That didn't stop me from hating them though. I think, looking back now, I still hate them a little.

I felt a hand grip hold of my hair and my head was wrenched back forcing me to stare at Prig's leering face. "Just for that, cunt. You get to hold the marker." A violent shove sent me sprawling onto my back and Prig turned and strode away, cracking his whip against the floor. "Heel! All of you."

None of us hesitated to jump to his command; even I, still shaking, sobbing, and coughing. The shame of that terrified obedience burns me still. I spared a glance back towards Josef and he gave me a nod. His own shift would be starting soon enough, and his rot-brained foreman was almost as unpleasant as Prig. Almost.

To this day I still do not know the purpose of the Pit, Terrelan's largest prison sunk deep into the ground. The inmates spent their sentences digging and transporting rock to the surface. Then that rock is dumped elsewhere. We weren't mining, there were no seams of precious metal. I once heard of a team who found coal, but that tunnel was quickly collapsed and the team reassigned. It seems to me we were there simply to dig. What a fucking waste of time. I sometimes wonder if the purpose was to break us. To crush the prisoners' spirits. Maybe it was just punishment; never-ending, pointless toil down in the dark. The sure, unwavering knowledge that nothing we did or said meant a damned thing. A punishment worse than death. Irrelevance.

I guess I'll never know the truth since I eventually flooded the damned place and everyone in it. I sometimes imagine Prig drowning down in the Pit, struggling for air in the pitch-black, icy water flooding his lungs and dragging him down into a forgotten grave. Such thoughts bring a smile to my face even now. Age and wisdom have done nothing to quash my thirst for vengeance, even against those long dead. But even those we've vanquished leave their marks upon us, and Prig certainly left his on me.

Prig always marched us along at a quick pace, caring nothing for the strain it put us through. The foremen down in the Pit were inmates as much as their charges, but they had a better quality of life. Prig had his own bed and two real meals a day, not the gruel and mouldering bread the rest of us had to fight for. His boots were new, though certainly not shiny, and most amazingly of all, he had socks. It says a lot about the conditions we lived in that I dreamed of owning a pair of socks.

We passed other teams, and other inmates, trudging along in the greasy gloom. Some were also on their way to or from work, while others made their way down to the arena. I had yet to see the arena so early in my incarceration, but I had heard of it. Inmates slaughtered each other for the amusement of those in charge. Sometimes the gladiators were even pitted against other things, like creatures found down in the depths. What a fucking tragic waste of life. The Terrelans could have put a stop to the arena, but they didn't care. As long as the digging was done the bastards let those in charge run the other inmates as they saw fit. Those of us at the very bottom of the pecking order were always the ones to suffer most.

Our little tunnel where we dug our lives away was on the seventeenth level of the Pit. It was far enough down that we never saw sunlight, but not so far that we were at danger from the creatures that called solid rock their home. Those poor bastards who worked down in the deep depths were often driven mad by the things that they saw in the dark, or killed by the things they didn't see. We rode the wooden lift up, not because we had earned special treatment, but because our lazy fucking foreman hated stairs. It was a lucky day for us scabs, finding the lift not in use. Prig was far more generous with his whip the days he was forced to climb to work, as though it was somehow our fault he was a fat fucker.

The tools we used each day waited for us right where we had left them. Hammers, pickaxes, shovels, and a little wooden cart with rusted wheels that squealed like a pig on the butcher's block. I could feel my nerves fraying away every time that fucking cart moved. Prig could have done something about it, ordered a little oil to ease the grinding metal, but the noise did not bother him and he knew it bothered me so he kept it just as it was. That bastard was always so quick to jump on every torment he could find, no matter how little it might be. He lived to

12

make our misery more fucking miserable. Oh, I definitely hated Prig the most!

The marker was an iron spike, two feet long with the final quarter painted white. Each team had one and each day it was driven into the wall at the end of the tunnel. Every day we were set a target, a distance I believed Prig plucked out of his rotten mind each morning. Our shift lasted until we reached that distance, measured from the marker, and if we didn't do it fast enough then Prig would make his displeasure known with the lash of his whip, which is to say he whipped us fucking bloody. There were few jobs more dangerous than holding the marker.

"Right there," Prig said with a smirk, pointing.

I stood next to the wall and sank down onto my knees, holding the marker up against the wall in both hands and leaning as far away as possible. Prig was watching *me*, not the marker. A fat brown tongue licked out over his cracked lips and he hefted the hammer onto his shoulder.

"You know the job." Prig's voice sounded like he spoke through his nose as much as his mouth. "Hold *real* still."

The anticipation of the blow made my blood freeze in my veins and I felt a cold sweat spring onto my brow. Prig knew his stuff, I have to give the slug-fucking bastard that– he made it last. At first, he tapped the flat end of the marker, lining up his strike. Then he drew back the hammer and waited.

I had seen him hit two men with the hammer in my three months down in the Pit. The first I believe was an accident. The entire team watched as the hammer hit the side of the marker and Prig stumbled, the momentum carrying on and crushing skin and bone. I had seen blood before, of course, I had been the cause of injuries far worse, but seeing Ossop's wrist snap, the bone punching through the skin... Ossop's screams are what I remember most sharply. Even now when I think about it, I can't remember his face, but I remember the sound of his pain.

The second man I had seen Prig hit with the hammer was no accident. He did not miss the marker. You can't miss a thing if you were never aiming for it. The rotten bastard changed his swing at the last moment and that solid iron hammer smashed into the man's handsome face. It was brutal fucking murder, plain and simple, for a reason no one but Prig ever knew. There were no screams to remember, only the smell of loosened bowels. Prig made us work with a bloody oozing corpse at our feet. I think it was meant as a message though in a language alien to me. It just made me hate our foreman even more. There was no retribution for it, no justice for the murder of a man. Two days after his death, a new scab arrived to take his place and we all forgot about the handsome man and his crushed skull. I never even knew his name. I think that scared me even more than Ossop's death. I hated the idea that I might die down in the Pit, nameless and forgotten. That my death would be even more meaningless than my life.

Prig spent a long time drawing out that first swing of the hammer, waving it back and forth as though he couldn't quite get the angle right. It was such a blatant show, he might as well have been waving his cock about. I had seen people close their eyes and await the blow, and I had seen others focus on the marker as though that little spike of metal was the most important thing in their world. Well fuck that! I have never been one to hide from my fate, whatever it might be, and I wasn't about to give Prig the satisfaction he craved.

"I am the weapon," I whispered the words so quiet no one else could hear then I turned my head and stared straight at the bastard, holding his malicious gaze. It was foolish. I was daring him to miss the marker, but I couldn't back down from that fight. Prig made my life in the Pit a living hell and not just my life, but all of those on my team and even Josef. Come to think of it I've never been good at backing down from a fight, even the ones I've already lost.

Prig's face crumpled with rage. By watching him, I was defying him. Defying the terror he instilled within us. With a roar he drew back and swung the hammer.

I felt the bones in my arms rattle, pain shooting up and down. I'm a little ashamed to admit, I cried out. It was the first time I had ever held the marker and I was not prepared for the shock of it. But I kept my eyes locked on Prig, watching him as he drew back and swung the hammer again, and again, and again. Each time I felt as though my arms would snap, bones piercing through skin just like they had with Ossop.

After four blows the marker was driven deep into the side tunnel wall. I could feel sweat pouring down my face and I was shaking, still staring wild-eyed at Prig. His little victory stolen, he quickly put us to work and was not shy with the whip that day. It didn't take long for the bruises to show, by the end of the day my hands were brown and yellow, and my teeth hurt from clenching. But I survived. My first time holding the marker, and my first time defying Prig, and I survived.

I think Prig wanted to kill me that day. I could see the rage on his face, the anger at the defiance I showed him. I know now he wasn't allowed to kill me. Not while the overseer still had plans for me.

16

CHAPTER 2

Josef was waiting for me when I returned. I was weary and bruised, exhausted and coated in a new layer of sweat. My clothes, little more than grey, fraying rags were stiff with weeks of filth, but there was nowhere to wash it off and no fresh wardrobe to change into. I might have been ashamed of how I smelled, but we were all living in the same pile of shit and none of us smelled pleasant.

I collapsed next to my oldest friend and let out a sob, glad to be near him again. The lash on his leg from Prig's whip had scabbed over, and I hoped it wouldn't get infected. There was little any of us could do about a fever and the foremen often worked us hard even when we could barely stand. Honestly, it's a fucking miracle any of us survived that place.

"Let me see," Josef said in a quiet voice and I held out my hands, staring into space as he turned them over with a gentle touch. Josef sighed and pulled up my ragged sleeves, seeing the full extent of the yellow-brown bruising already spreading up my arms. "What did you do this time, Eska?"

I lowered my head onto Josef's shoulder and sobbed. I felt like crying, but I was far too exhausted to shed any tears. Dry sobbing is a lot like falling in love, pointless save for the pain.

One of the other scabs on my team, a giant by the name of Hardt was watching us. "She defied him," he said.

I've rarely seen a bigger man than Hardt. He was taller than most, with a bulk that defied the meagre rations we were fed. A true workhorse, he did more of our team's digging in a day than I managed in a week. Both Hardt and his brother, Isen, were Terrelans, though I didn't hold it against them. They both had dark skin and darker hair, which they kept short. I had no idea why they were down in the Pit. I didn't care. I didn't give a shit about anyone but Josef. Besides, we were all criminals no matter how innocent we were.

"Never seen anything like it," Isen said. He was shorter than his brother, though not by much, and not nearly as brawny. He was handsome in a rugged way, even wearing layers of sweat and grime. No one was truly pretty down in the Pit, but Isen made it work. "You just stared at Prig like you were watching *his* death, and all while he was swinging a fucking hammer at you."

"I thought he'd kill you for sure," Hardt agreed.

So did I, at the time. I think a part of me wanted it. They were not the first nor last suicidal thoughts I have entertained in my life. More than once I have considered how much simpler it would be to not be.

The others in my team moved away from the conversation. As though merely talking about Prig might cause him to appear, and they would be spared his wrath simply by not taking part. Bloody fools, all of them. Prig had more than enough wrath to spare even for those who hadn't earned it. Hardt moved forward though, two rolls of cloth in his giant hands. He held them out to Josef and we could both see they were bandages, and mostly clean.

I think I would have refused them, pushed Hardt away and suffered in the sullen silence I was known for. I didn't trust him or his brother. I didn't trust anyone. Not even Josef really. Not since his betrayal on the tower. He was my oldest friend, my only friend, but I couldn't forget it was he who had blindsided me. Luckily for us all, Josef was not me and trust came easier to him. He took the bandages with a smile and a nod and started wrapping my hands and forearms. I sat there, staring at nothing and letting my hate, exhaustion, and pain make me numb inside. There is pleasure in being numb, in retreating from the world and feeling nothing. It is matched only by the agony of emotion returning.

Isen moved closer, picked out a spot on the floor that looked slightly less rocky than the rest, and sat. A small lantern burned away in the corner of the cavern, and in that flickering light I could see his face was bruised and scabbed. The leftovers from a black eye. He was always nursing an injury or two. I thought it made him rugged, mysterious, maybe even a little dangerous.

"So, who are you?" Isen asked.

I realised then that I had never offered my name. In three months down in the belly of the Pit, not once had I so much as uttered my name, and until then no one had asked for it. These days, I couldn't buy that sort of anonymity. My name is known far beyond the limits of this continent. It's known far beyond the reach of the Terran language. These days even gods know my name, and that's not the sort of attention you want. Trust me. But back then, I was no one, and no one knew who I was.

"Josef Yenhelm." Josef extended his hand. Isen took it and they shook and Hardt followed quickly after.

"Isen," said the younger and smaller of the two. "This is my brother, Hardt."

All eyes turned to me as Josef finished wrapping the bandage around my left hand and started on my right. I felt scraped raw and no longer cared who knew my name. I let out a sigh and leaned against Josef's bony shoulder.

"Eskara Helsene," Josef said for me. "Don't let her terseness fool you. She can be quite sweet once you get past the bite."

That bastard! I should have bristled at his words. I certainly do when I think about it now, but I was so tired that it was taking more effort than I could manage just to stay awake. My memory of that conversation is softened by blurred edges and missed words, faded away like a fleeting dream leaving only vague impressions as proof it had ever been.

"What were you?" Isen asked. "Before all of this." He didn't ask what we were there for. It was rude to ask after someone else's crimes.

I grabbed hold of Josef's hands then, despite the pain it caused me. Whatever else they might be, Isen and Hardt were Terrelans. The enemy! Neither they, nor anyone else, needed to know that Josef and I were Sourcerers for the Orran Empire. Looking back now I realise how much easier life might have been if I had trusted the brothers. If I had told them who and what I was. Maybe if I had, we would all still be alive. But no, I was a secretive bitch for whom trust was an increasingly alien concept. And besides, second-guessing the past is no different to predicting the future; it is a fool's game with no winners. Time runs ever forward and not even Chronomancers can change that inextricable fact. Though I do know a few who have tried.

"Soldiers for Orran," Josef said with a shrug, patting my arms to release my clawed grip.

Isen nodded but Hardt frowned. Always the smarter of the two, was Hardt. He saw things that no one else did. Sometimes I wonder if he could see into the hearts of people, to know their intentions before they themselves did. It was a peculiarity of the man and one I came to rely upon time and time again.

"You're a little young to be soldiers," Hardt said, his stare lingering on me. He didn't need to point out that I was still a girl and a slight one at that. It was likely more than a little obvious that I had never before held a sword, let alone swung one in battle. Honestly, I looked about as likely to be a soldier as a goat looks likely to fly.

I almost heard Josef reply. No doubt he said something diplomatic. He was always that way, making others laugh and putting them at ease. When I opened my eyes, I saw Hardt sitting next to his brother, a crude set of dice on the ground between us. I couldn't say how long I had been asleep, certainly long enough to drool on Josef's shoulder and develop a taste in my mouth that suggested I had been chewing on blistered feet. I've never understood how just a few snatched minutes of sleep can produce such a foul taste.

"What..." I struggled away from Josef's shoulder and wiped at my mouth with bandaged arms.

"Here," Josef said, handing me a small clay cup. Water was one thing the Pit had more than enough of, though it was rarely clean. Some of the lower tunnels were flooded and I'd even heard of a giant cavern somewhere on the twenty-fourth level. The other inmates claimed it had massive stalactites that glittered in lantern light. They also claimed there were monsters living in the water that could suck the flesh from bone. I never once visited that cavern, though I sometimes wonder if the entire Pit is filled with those monsters these days, reducing all the people I left down there to bones and bad memories. It was far more likely the monster never even existed. We prisoners had little power, but convincing a person of a lie is a form of power over them. Lies, fear, food, and shoes, the greatest of all currencies down in the dark.

I drank deeply, sediment and all. It didn't so much wash the taste away as replace it with something less foul and more earthy. It's the strangest thing but to this day I sometimes miss the taste of Pit water. I think it made me feel connected to the earth somehow in a way that even a Geomancy Source couldn't.

"What's the game?" I could feel sleep tugging at me again, yet I didn't want it. The food bells would ring soon and I was ravenous enough to fight to be near the front of the line. It was a fight I would lose. The scabs of the Pit were beaten into a submissive lot for the most part, but the promise of food could wake a beast from even the deepest slumber.

"It's called Trust," said Isen with a cheeky grin. "And it's a game about trust. I was just explaining the rules to young Josef here, but I can start again for you."

I nodded and looked down at the dice. Each one was crudely made, carved from black rock with symbols scraped into each of the six sides. They were chipped and scratched and uneven, but then the Pit did that to all of us.

"Each player gets three dice," Isen said, "and each player gets a partner. Partners rotate, first you will play with the man on your left, then the man on his left, and so on. When it comes to your turn to play you select a side from either *Friendship*." Isen held up one of the die and showed me a face with a crude depiction of two men holding hands. They were stick drawings the like of which children were apt to scrawl. "Or *Betrayal*." The second face Isen showed us had another of the stickmen with an equally crude depiction of a knife in his back. I found I could sympathise with the poor stickman.

"You select your side in secret and keep it covered until your partner has also chosen." Isen placed the die on the ground and covered it with his hand. "If both players choose the side of *Friendship* then no dice are lost or exchanged, and the next set of players take their turns. If one player chooses *Friendship* and the other *Betrayal*, then the player who chose *Betrayal* takes the die from the player who chose *Friendship*. If both players choose *Betrayal*, then both players roll one die to determine the outcome."

I could see both the simplicity and the complexity of the game right away. It started with an illusion of truce, all players on equal footing. The first player to betray another would, of course, get an immediate benefit, but the other players would then know their calibre and be more likely to choose betrayal against them. In a room full of murderers, the second person to die is usually the first person to start the killing.

"The roll?" I asked.

"That is just as simple. If you roll *Friendship* you keep your die no matter what. If you roll *Betrayal* you lose your die no matter what. As for the others." Isen held up the die and started turning it to show me all the sides. "*War* beats *Peace*. *Peace* beats *Trade*. *Trade* beats *Coin*. And *Coin* beats *War*. If you roll the winning face you take both dice. If neither player rolls a conflict, both players lose a die."

I struggled then, to consider all the possible outcomes of a single game of Trust. Even now, after hundreds of games played, the complexity staggers me. Every game is different whether the players are new or old. Friendships made and broken over a simple game of dice. And believe me, I have lost friends over games of Trust.

"What if everyone chooses *Friendship* all the time?" I asked, though I already knew the answer.

"Then no one wins, and the game continues," Isen said.

Hardt shook his head. "Someone always picks *Betrayal*." He sent a pointed look at Isen. I thought, at the time, that Isen won games more often than not because he was the first to betray another. The more I think about that look the more I believe it was something else entirely. Something I was simply too damned naive to understand at the time.

"What happens when you run out of dice?" Josef asked.

I pulled back and stared at him. I would not have used that word. Josef assumed he would, at some time, run out of dice. He was already planning on losing. I never plan to lose or fail. I have always played to win.

"Then you fucking lose," I said, already staring at the dice and deciding who I would betray first. It was foolish. A player might go into a game of Trust with a plan, but those plans needed flexibility above all else. Back then I didn't understand that winning was never about the game.

We played a game then. My first game of Trust. Josef lost his dice first, just as he had planned, even if he hadn't realised it. I was the second to go out, playing far too aggressively, betraying more often than extending an olive branch. I watched Hardt and Isen go head to head, eagerly waiting to see what tactics were involved once the game was reduced to just two players. They played only once, both picking *Friendship*, and then shook hands declaring the game a draw. I didn't understand at the time, I thought them idiots. A draw seemed like a loss for all players. They didn't see it that way. To them it was a win.

CHAPTER 3

Long after I stopped trying to keep track of days or time, I could tell a week had passed by my appointment with the overseer. Prig would appear, whip in one hand and a savage grin on his fat fucking mouth. I think he enjoyed parading me to my interrogations, knowing why I kept the attention of the overseer when so many others were forgotten in the depths of the Pit. There were men and women down there who were once mighty. Orran generals, lords of noble houses, legendary brigands of great renown. The Pit made nobodies of us all.

At first, it wasn't just me the overseer sent for. Josef would come back, shaken and cowed, sometimes sobbing and sometimes barely conscious. He never told me what the overseer did to him during those interrogations. Maybe the man used the same tactics to break us both, but I doubt it. My years have taught me that as every person is different from one another, so too are the best methods to break them. Eventually the overseer stopped calling for Josef.

The route Prig led was always the same. We didn't need to go through the main cavern, where food was dished out and new arrivals were inducted into their living hell. But Prig liked the illusion of power it gave him. He was on a mission from the overseer and the overseer was in charge. He liked to think that made him important. What a fucking idiot. Anyone could have done his job, but those of little consequence often mistake convenience for importance.

It took me a while to learn the structure of the Pit. At first it seems like chaos. The Terrelans were in charge, it was true, but there was only a small garrison of soldiers stationed inside the Pit and they took no part in the day to day running of the inmates. They were there so the criminals running things remembered who was really in charge.

The Pit was governed and run by inmates. Deko, the narcissistic psychopath at the very top, ruled over his captains and they, in turn, ruled over the foremen. The rest of the inmates, the scabs as the foremen called us, were the workers. We were the ones who dug the tunnels and fought in the arena. We were the ones who died while Deko and his sycophantic cronies lived a life of relative luxury. I hadn't met Deko yet, but I had seen him from a distance as he toured his little empire of rock and filth. He wasn't particularly tall, but had a girth to him, which is nothing but a nice way of saying he was a fat fucker. The rumours said he would kill another inmate simply for looking at him, and it was one rumour I could well believe was true. There were few people I would agree belonged in the Pit and Deko was one of them.

Being on the overseer's business gave Prig a measure of respect no other inmate could earn, and he made certain to flaunt it every time my appointment was due. I never felt as vulnerable as I did when I was marched through the main cavern. So many eyes watching me, it made my skin itch, although that could have been the lice. It made me glad that Josef thought to hack off my hair. At a distance, covered in grime and sweat, I might have passed for a boy, though closer up there was no mistaking my breasts. Still, when Prig marched me to my interrogation, I was untouchable. No one would dare make me late for my appointment.

Prig led me right through the centre of the main chamber, through the Trough where us scabs were fed, and through the Hill where all Deko's captains and foremen gathered about and congratulated each other on being cunts. It was not truly a hill and not raised in any way, but those in charge named it thus. No scab was allowed to climb to the Hill without permission. I saw the very worst humanity had to offer every time Prig dragged me through the Hill. Deko did not pick his captains based on good nature but on their ability to brutalise and instil terror into his subjects. I learned a lot from Deko even before I had the *pleasure* of meeting him.

There were six wooden lifts around the main cavern and Prig always used the same one. He knew the operator and they chatted and laughed together as I stood meekly by, waiting for my parade to continue. I hated the way Prig's friend looked at me. I was still a girl and he was long since grey, but he stared at me with such lust I felt myself redden, heat making me ashamed. It wasn't lust or desire that brought such heat on in me, but disgust. Disgust that such a loathsome man might be thinking of my body. A thousand painful deaths would never be enough for that arsehole.

"She clearly wants me," Prig's friend said, licking his lips, his nostrils flaring.

There was very little I wanted less, but voicing that opinion wouldn't have earned me anything but a beating, and my arms were still bruised from holding the marker for the fourth day in a row. They felt almost boneless and I was fairly certain the bandages Hardt had given me were the only things holding me together.

"Fuck you!" I spat in defiance of my own decision to say nothing. Prig raised a hand and I scurried back a couple of steps out of reach. I hated myself for showing fear.

"That'd be the point," Prig's friend said, staring at me with a greedy intensity. Arsehole!

"Don't think the *overseer* wants her soiled." Prig liked to mention the overseer whenever he had the chance, and that was often. "Maybe he wants her all for himself." Prig punctuated the statement by grabbing his crotch and both men laughed. I have noticed men often like to touch their cocks for little reason, or draw them on any surface they can find. We lived in a prison, deep underground where the only light was from lanterns, and yet there wasn't a single stretch of tunnel that didn't have at least one crude drawing of a penis scrawled upon it like a signature.

"Lucky bastard," said Prig's friend, still eyeing me in a way that sent a crawling sensation over my skin. There is a way some men can look at a woman such that it makes them feel dirty even when they are clean, uncomfortable in their own skin. Back then I had no choice but to suffer the indignity. I am pleased to admit I no longer suffer such stares.

"Did you see Yorin's fight?" Prig asked.

His friend laughed. "Saw him push in Arst's fucking eyeballs. Never thought I'd hear a man scream like that."

They both had a laugh at that. Two men laughing over the brutal killing of another. I have often wondered if the Pit made them cruel, or simply allowed them to stop hiding their true natures. Are we all just monsters waiting for the opportunity to show it?

"I should go. Don't want to make the *overseer's* fun late," Prig said

His friend grunted. "You coming back for some cards later?"

"You better save me a chair," Prig said even as his friend started working the wheel. The mechanisms began to turn and the lift started rising into the air. It wobbled at first and I almost fell. There were no railings to hold onto and more than one inmate had plummeted to their death since I had been in the Pit. By the end of my time in there I even saw a man thrown from high up on one of the rickety devices, and I also saw the pile of mushy flesh and bone he was reduced to. "I still have to nail that cheating slug, Rekka, to the wall," Prig shouted over the sounds of the mechanism *thunking* as it lifted us into the air.

We were going a long way up, to the third level of the Pit. It was the closest to the surface I would get, though still not close enough to see any sunlight. I didn't even know if it was day or night outside. Inmates functioned on Pit time. I sometimes think part of the point was to make us forget what real light looked like. Perhaps it was about making us forget how to be terran, reduce us to little more than beasts. The lift was not fast and I had plenty of time to watch the great cavern sink below us.

"Ahh!" Prig shouted, stamping a foot towards me. I jumped, startled by the outburst. Prig laughed then, snorting and chuckling to himself as he turned and ignored me once more. I felt my cheeks redden again, ashamed that I had let him scare me so. Shit-gobbling arse-stain! I definitely hated Prig most of all.

With his back turned, Prig could no longer see me. He was staring out at the cavern, hacking up some phlegm to spit down onto anyone passing below, making sport of others' misery. I crept closer to him on silent feet, stilling my breath and keeping my eyes fixed on his back. In just a few steps I was right behind him, close enough to reach out and push. We were a good distance up and the fall would be enough to kill a man. Prig would scream as he plummeted to his death, and I would watch. But I didn't do it.

It was not that I had never killed before. True, the battle of Orran was my first real taste of war, the only time I ever fought for my kingdom, and it was true that the battle had been cut short by Orran's surrender. But I had killed. I summoned hellions to swarm units of soldiers. I rained down fiery death on advancing cavalry. Up on the highest tower of Fort Vernan I froze a woman, a fellow Sourcerer, solid and then shattered her into so many pieces a master puzzologist would need to spend three lifetimes putting her back together.

I had killed before, but this time felt different. It was more personal. The times before, I had not known those I killed. Not their names nor their faces, nor anything about them other than they were fighting for the Terrelans. I knew Prig. I hated Prig, but I knew him. The realisation made me hesitate. Perhaps if I had had longer to come to terms with it, I would have pushed him, sent him screaming to his death. I know for certain that I wouldn't have hesitated even a moment these days. Age has made me more callous in many ways.

I can be quite intense sometimes. I have seen enemies pale from my gaze, friends rally, and I've seen lovers fluster. Never underestimate the power of eye contact.

Prig glanced over his shoulder at me. I was just an arm's reach away and staring so intently. He jumped, fear and shock mingling in his shit-coloured eyes. I saw that fear for just a moment before the back of his hand caught my face. Pain erupted and blood filled my mouth. I found myself on the floor of the lift. Prig was pacing back and forth shouting, though what he said is lost to me. There's little like a good backhand to scatter the senses. He was furious, lashing his leather whip and screaming at me, his face red even beneath the grime. He was still shouting when the lift bumped to a stop at the third level. Prig stormed towards me then, hauling me to my feet and pushing me along in front of him. I had a bruised cheek and bloody lip, but Prig had learned not to turn his back on me. Prig had learned to fear me. I counted it a worthwhile exchange.

There was a distinct change in atmosphere when we entered the small Terrelan garrison on the third level. The general stench of unwashed inmates gave way to something cleaner. Boot polish and fresh air made me feel out of place. Prig was no different. He might be there on the overseer's business, but he knew he didn't belong. Soldiers were stationed at doorways and they eyed us with savage scrutiny. Just a few months ago, I would have considered these soldiers beneath me. Now I hung my head against their gaze and hoped they wouldn't notice me. Fortunes change so quickly with the fall of empires.

The overseer was always in the same room whenever he interrogated me. It was a small cell carved out of the rock. A single table sat in the centre with a chair on either side. Two lanterns hung on the walls and bathed the little cavern in a light so bright it hurt my eyes until they adjusted.

The overseer looked up as Prig stopped me outside the room. The two soldiers on guard outside watched us both, hands on weapons. I could smell the fear dripping off Prig. It smelled sweet and sour all at once, like meat left to rot.

"Right on time, Overseer," Prig said, bowing his head so low he was staring at his own ragged boots. I missed the feel of boots on my feet. They are one of those things I have always taken for granted in my more affluent times. You don't realise how much you need a good pair of boots until you step on something hard and sharp, and the Pit was littered with such mines.

"How would you know?" the overseer asked.

I glanced up to find Prig looking confused. I had to stop myself from grinning. It was often easy to forget that the foremen were inmates as well, and they themselves had as little concept of time as us scabs.

"Go," the overseer ordered in a flat voice. Prig turned and I turned with him. "Not you."

I stopped, again stifling a smile. Prig stopped as well, looking confused and glancing from the nearby soldiers, to the overseer, to me. It felt good to vex the overseer. I knew once I was in that room with the door closed, the tables would quickly turn.

With a nod from the overseer one of the guards stepped forward, grabbed me by my dirty tunic collar and shoved me inside the room. A moment later the door slammed shut behind me and I was alone with the one man in the Pit who tormented me more than Prig.

CHAPTER 4

The overseer was a bastard. A short man, he was of a height with me and I was just fifteen, still growing. He was much older than I, with a face pitted with pockmarks and a neatly trimmed grey beard that stuck to his chin and nowhere else. His skin was pale as milk and his voice as cold as the watery grave.

"Sit, Eskara," he said, pointing to the far chair. It was a show of power using my name. He knew that and much more about me. The Orran Academy of Magic kept meticulous records on all their students, and I later learned that all those records ended up in the Pit. Josef and I were not the only Orran Sourcerers locked up in the dark. I, on the other hand, knew nothing about the overseer, not even his name. I still know nothing about him, even so many years after his death. I sometimes think that might be my greatest victory over the man; I buried him without ever even knowing his name. He knew everything about me and never managed to break me. Well, almost never.

I trudged around the table and sank into a chair, letting my eyes fall on the table in front. It was bare grey wood, save for a small red stain close to me. If I looked carefully I could tell it was blood. The table had seen violence, that much was obvious. I wondered how long it would be before the overseer used violence on me.

"Are you thirsty? Hungry?" the overseer asked. He didn't wait for a reply but turned and knocked on the door. A moment later, it opened. "Bring a bottle of wine and a bowl of stew," he said, never taking his eyes from me. "And some fresh clothing. Boots as well."

The door closed and the overseer stepped forward, sitting on the chair across from me. I looked up into his eyes and saw compassion. It looked real, genuine. I don't think he knew how close that look came to breaking me then and there. To see someone care about me and my situation, someone with the power to change it, was surreal. Part of me longed to break down, to be rescued from the Pit. I squashed that traitorous little part of me down and crushed it. The overseer didn't care about me. No one did, except maybe Josef. Back then I think Josef cared about me more than I did myself, but still not enough to do anything about it.

"How is the foreman treating you?" the overseer asked, concern still written on his face.

I placed my hands on the table so the overseer could see the bandages wrapped around my arms. He ignored them and continued to stare at me. "As well as can be expected," I said. "We dig, he whips us, we dig some more."

The overseer nodded. "And the other Sourcerer? Your friend?"

There was an iron rung underneath my chair, no doubt for chaining unruly prisoners to. I kicked my feet against it, struggling to sit still. Anxiety was making me restless. "He digs sometimes too," I said. "We all dig. One day we might just dig ourselves free."

The overseer smiled and nodded. "Hope is important for people in your situation."

I couldn't decide what he meant then, and I'm still not sure now. On the one hand he might have been genuine. Hope was important down in the Pit. I saw inmates lose hope and I saw the wrecks they became. Some got themselves killed, others stopped living and just existed, working away the rest of their lives in obscurity. Then again, the overseer might have wanted to cultivate hope because having hope would make me easier to break. He could be cruel at times and I've always wondered just how cruel. I sometimes think he wanted to make me hope just so he could see my face the moment he took it away. It was fucking maddening trying to comprehend the man's insidious games.

"What would you hope for?" I asked, suddenly desperate to turn the tables. "If you were in my situation."

The overseer seemed to think about that for a moment. "Freedom, of course," he said with a shrug. "An end to my suffering."

I let a slow smile spread across my face and stared at the man. "I hope one day I can give you both."

He frowned then, fidgeting in his chair under the scrutiny of my stare. A knock at the door broke the tension, and when it opened three soldiers filed into the little room. The first brought chains and a bowl of water, the second brought a tray of food and wine, and the third brought a fresh set of prison clothes with a new pair of boots that looked suspiciously like my size. They each deposited their burdens on the table and then the first soldier set about attaching manacles to my wrists and the chain to the iron rung beneath my chair. After I was firmly secured to the floor, the soldier put the key on the table and all three of them left, leaving me alone with the overseer once more.

I waited for the door to shut and rattled my chains, giving the man a real *fuck you* look.

The overseer smiled and fingered the key on the table, turning it around and around. "It's all part of the process," he said.

When I look back at my time in the Pit now, I see the overseer's plan in its entirety. I see the ingenuity of it. Prig was there to torture me physically, to break me down with pain and exhaustion. The cunt! The overseer was there to torture me psychologically, and he did a better job of it than Prig ever did with his whip. He was also a cunt!

The overseer pushed the bowl of water towards me. I smelled a slight zest, a lemony fragrance. There was a white cloth floating in the liquid.

"I expect you're quite pretty underneath the dirt," he said, still turning the key around and around. My hands could just about reach the lip of the table and no further. Unless he unchained me, I had no way of reaching the bowl, or the food, or the clothes.

I've never thought of myself as pretty or beautiful, though some have some called me such, often in an attempt at flattery. The truth was, my coating of dirt was probably doing quite a bit to keep me safe from the other inmates. No, I didn't care for the washing water, or the clothes. My mouth was watering at the smell of meaty stew, but all of us were fed and I have never been a particularly hale eater despite the hunger that gnaws away inside of me. I would have killed for the boots, though.

"Perhaps you don't realise just what a mess you look," the overseer continued in a voice like the most virulent of patronising arseholes. He reached forwards and lifted a mirror from the table, standing it to face me. At first, I thought to defiantly refuse to look at it, to refuse the sight that would stare back at me. Then I realised refusing to look would be a victory for the overseer as surely as bursting into tears at the sight. It would be all the confirmation he needed that I cared. I really fucking hate no-win situations. So, I glanced at the mirror. And I did not recognise the face staring back at me.

I had never been fleshy but now I was gaunt, skin tight over bones, and pale as snow. Pale as sun bleached bones. A carcass left to rot away to nothing. That's what I found staring back at me, not the girl I knew flushed with health and power, but the ruin I had beaten into. The visage of a corpse unwilling to admit it was dead. My blue eyes were still bright. They were the only bit of the horror staring back at me I recognised.

I couldn't let him win. Couldn't let him see how close I was to breaking, how much it hurt to see the wasted, pitiful, hateful thing I had become. I tested out a smile in the mirror, and swallowed a sob at the corpse smiling back at me. Then I turned it on the overseer. "You don't think I'm pretty?" I said, trying my best to appear manic.

We had been seeing each other for weeks now. In the beginning I counted the number of interrogation sessions, but eventually I stopped. I wondered how, after so many meetings, he still didn't understand me in the slightest. I was such a bloody fool. It was I who didn't understand him. The overseer was playing the long game and I couldn't see the foundation he was laying.

"Food, maybe?" he asked with a wave towards the bowl of stew. He left the mirror where it was. I would like to say I was strong enough not to steal the occasional glance, but there is a streak of vanity running through me I can't quite ignore. I think we all have one to some degree. I will not deny that every time I looked in that mirror I longed for better days. For cleaner days. It was torture every time I saw myself, like picking at scab, lifting it to see the oozing flesh beneath. I couldn't stop myself.

My traitorous stomach gave a rumble at the thought of food. The overseer took it as a victory and leaned back in his chair, still watching me. I glanced down at the bowl to see it steaming. Chunks of brown meat and orange vegetables floated in a watery stock. I licked my lips and tore my eyes away, meeting the overseer's stare.

"All this can be yours, Eskara," the overseer said, sweeping his hand to encompass the table. "You could be clean again. Well-fed. Clothed. I'm not asking you to swear loyalty to Terrelan. I'm certainly not asking you to fight for Terrelan. I'm not asking you to kill for Terrelan." I almost laughed. The Orran empire didn't ask me either; they took me as a child and never gave me a choice. Not that I minded. They might not have given me a choice, but they did give me power.

"All I want from you, Eskara," he continued, "is an answer to a question. Where were you trained?"

I didn't understand. It seemed such an innocuous question. The overseer already knew where I was trained. He had all that and much more in the notes and documentation recovered from the fall of Vernan. I answered almost without hesitation.

"The Orran Academy of Magic," I said slowly, waiting to see the arsehole's trick.

The overseer nodded and stood from his chair. He crossed to the door and pulled it open. A soldier stood on the other side, waiting.

"Unchain her and leave her alone for ten minutes," the overseer said. "After that, she is free to join the rest of the inmates." He turned to look at me, a sly smile on his face. "Thank you for your co-operation, Eskara. I shall see you next week."

I sat stunned as the soldier walked into the room, took the key from the table and unlocked the manacles from my wrists. He took the chain away and closed the door behind him. I found myself alone in the room with the water and mirror, the stew and wine, the clothes and the boots. I found myself alone with my utter confusion.

What a bloody idiot I was. Maybe it was my age, but I didn't understand. I sat there and mulled over what had just happened, replaying it in my mind. I wasted most of my ten minutes trying to figure out the overseer's game and came up with no answer. Eventually I looked down at the table.

The wash water was a trap. I was going straight back down into the Pit. The last thing I wanted was to look clean. The clothes would mark me out amongst the rest of the population. I stared at the boots for a while, wishing I could take them, but good footwear was more valuable than food down in the Pit. The other inmates would happily kill me for a chance at a sturdy pair of boots.

41

That left only the stew and the wine. I can't impress how much I wanted to gulp down the stew. It smelled delicious even over my own stench, and I had eaten nothing but gruel and stale bread for months. I wanted it so much I had the bowl in my hands and most of the way to my lips before my defiant streak kicked in. I didn't know what the overseer was up to, asking me a question he already knew the answer to, nor rewarding me so handsomely for that answer. But I knew it was what he wanted. And I would be fucked before I gave that bastard anything.

With a scream, I dashed the bowl of stew against the far wall. Then I dumped the wash water over the clothes and added the wine in with the mix. Finally, I looked down and saw myself in the mirror. The creature staring back at me was red faced, even underneath the muck, and snarling like a wild animal. I picked up the mirror and launched it at the door, grinning as it smashed. I think I would have turned the table over then, but it was secured to the floor, so I contented myself with kicking over the chairs and screaming again. I was quite surprised when the soldiers didn't open the door and drag me away. From outside that door I heard nothing.

The thing about mirrors is that they are made of glass and glass has a habit of forming sharp edges when smashed. As I waited amidst the mess I had created, I looked down to find a number of those shards shining in the lamplight. I knelt and snatched a smallish shard into my hand, quickly tucking it into the bandages wrapped around my left arm.

When the soldiers finally opened the door to throw me back into the general population, I was sitting on the table, tearing the wine-stained clothing apart at the seams and throwing bits of it onto the floor. They were not gentle as they escorted me from the garrison.

CHAPTER 5

I have said my life started in earnest down in the Pit, but that is not strictly true. Actually, it's a blatant lie and I'm bloody good at telling it. I lived fifteen years of my life before I was incarcerated there, and I would never claim a single year of it was quiet. No, there is far more to my tale. More you need to know. Or maybe I'm just indulging my ego. Chronomancers like to tell us that past and future affect each other in equal measure. The past shapes how we react to things in the future, and the future shapes how we view events of the past. As the past only exists in memories, it is entirely shaped by the lens through which we view it. So, as this is my story, I have decided to digress.

When I was a young girl, maybe just five or six years old, I loved two things more than anything. Well, maybe not as much as my parents, but as most five-year-olds are entirely dependent upon their parents I think it is fair to have loved them most of all. I loved the trees and I loved the sky.

I was raised in a small forest village called Keshin, located on the southern side of Isha and far from the Orran-Terrelan border. Through the eyes of a child who didn't know any better it seemed a busy village, but I look back now and realise it was so small with barely a couple of hundred inhabitants. We traded in lumber and fruit, and my mother weaved baskets that were distributed far and wide, but mostly Keshin kept itself to itself. I had no idea of the world that existed outside those forest borders.

Before I even knew of the Orran empire or their Sourcerers, I used to climb. I would shoot up trees so tall, from the canopy the people below would look like ants scurrying about our tiny village hive. I climbed with wild abandon and took risks as only a young child can. The danger of a fall seemed an abstract risk, at best.

I remember the first time Ro'shan passed overhead. My brother, older than me by three years and working the blacksmith's bellows, came running home covered in sweat and ash. He pointed to the sky and shouted the Rand had come. He had no idea what a Rand was and neither did I. We had heard stories of their power, the miracles they performed, but that was as far as our meagre knowledge went. Those stories did not do the truth justice. Both the Rand and Djinn are as gods to all the peoples of Ovaeris, or at least that's what they'd have us believe. If there's one thing you remember from my story, one lesson you take from it, let it be this: Gods are fucking arseholes. All of them.

After sprinting to the tallest tree in our little forest, bare feet pounding on the detritus, I scurried up the trunk and began climbing the branches. Hand over hand I went, faster than was safe and earning myself a latticework of scrapes and scratches up my arms and face. I suppose it is one of life's great ironies that children heal so fast yet do not appreciate it. It's only when we get older and a shallow bruise sticks around for a few weeks that we miss such swift healing.

The forest canopy was thick in places, with broad-leaved trees that stretched out as far as they dared. It was possible for little ones such as myself to find a place where a few leaves overlapped and sit there above the forest. I had done this before of course, but never to watch a city float by over my little village.

I remember staring up at Ro'shan and marvelling at its size and grace. It looked like a mountain turned upside down gliding through the sky. I knew, from eavesdropping on my elders, that a city larger than any terrans had ever built sat on the topside of that floating mountain, but even from my vantage point, all I could see was rock sailing across the endless blue of the sky.

Freedom. I think that is what Ro'shan signified for me back then. The freedom to go wherever the city willed. Even now I see that city and it awes me. It has no need for the borders of empires. There is no sovereignty of the sky. But these days I know it is far from free. It is as much a prison as the Pit, though a far more elegant one.

Once I was ejected from the garrison the soldiers no longer cared what I did or where I went. They left me kneeling on the rocky ground nursing a couple of new bruises and considering whether I had just done the right thing. My stomach still rumbled and my mouth still watered at the thought of the food I had wasted, and my feet made their own displeasure known at my shunning of the boots. I have been footsore many times in my life, but this was the one and only time I have ever turned down the offer of a good pair of shoes.

I considered heading upwards instead of down. The third floor was not so far from the first. I would never be able to escape, all us scabs knew just how well the entrance to the Pit was guarded, but I might have been able to catch a glimpse of sunlight. I longed to see the sky again. To remember what freedom looked like. Down in the evergloom of the Pit, you quickly forget what it is like to be able to see more than a dozen paces. You forget what the horizon feels like.

In the end, it was sheer defiance that stopped me. I *would* see the sky again. I *would* see sunlight again. But I would not go and stare up at it longingly. I would not try to content myself with stolen glances. I would earn my freedom one way or another and the sky would be my reward. Until then I decided to let my desire drive me, knowing it would only get stronger every time I was this close yet still so far away.

At the time I still held secret hopes I might be rescued. I believed the Orran Emperor was still alive. I thought he would be massing troops in secret somewhere, maybe under a forest canopy, like my home village. I believed they would come for me. Josef and I were the last of Orran's Sourcerers able to hold five Sources at once. All the others had been captured or killed before the siege at Fort Vernan. I was powerful and I was loyal. I thought that would be enough. I was an idiot, still suffering from the idealism the Orran Academy of Magic had burned into me.

I spared only a glance for the wooden lift waiting to take me back down to the main cavern. Prig was gone, but with a pull on the rope I could have signalled his friend to work the contraption and bring me back down. I hated the idea of walking back through the Trough, of skirting the Hill and watching Deko laugh and joke with his syphilitic captains. Yes, I meant sycophantic, but I'd wager both descriptions were equally accurate. I turned away from the lift and headed towards the stairs. There were other ways to reach the little cavern I shared with Josef and my team.

The stairs were not the safest of ways to move between levels. They snaked around and around as they led downward, little tunnels with steps built in. Occasionally they would open out into tunnels or caverns and the stairs would continue elsewhere. It was quiet, save for my footfalls, almost peaceful. The danger rested in the other inmates.

Everybody down in the Pit was a criminal of some sort. Many were war criminals like myself and Josef, others were Terrelans whose crimes should have earned them a tight noose and short drop. Unfortunately, the Terrelans didn't believe in execution, they preferred to sentence their criminals to a lifetime of pointless hacking away at solid rock. There were murderers, thieves, and worse, all living out the remainder of their lives underground, and some of them refused to give up their ways. It was well-known that some of those who felt the need to murder others haunted the tunnels and corridors. Prig himself had suggested never going anywhere alone, not just to me, but to all his scabs. Apparently, the slug-fucker wanted to keep the option of killing us all to himself.

Despite the danger in using the deserted stairways I continued. I think I would have welcomed someone trying to kill me after the overseer's strange compassion. A good old-fashioned struggle to the death seemed so much more straightforward and honest. Of course, I had no doubt I would have lost the struggle. Back then I didn't know how to fight without magic.

The sounds of digging never went away in the Pit. At first it was maddening. I spent many of my first days in the Pit on a knife edge, driven to anger and despair by the endless fucking sounds of metal striking rock. But after a few months, I learned to live with it. It became background noise that I no longer paid any attention to. And in many ways the noise of the constant digging became comforting. Terrans can get used to just about any adversity given long enough to acclimatise to it, but it takes some real seditious shit to make us start relying upon it, craving it. The few times the digging stopped I found my nerves fraying from the relative silence. I don't know how many teams lived down in the hole with us, but it was a lot. No matter where I went, I could hear the faint ring of picks hitting stone and hammers breaking rock. Even in the central cavern, as noisy as that was, I could always hear the digging. Or maybe by then it was just so prevalent that I heard it in my head. Now I think about it, it took quite some time, even after I was out, for the noise of the place to fade.

That was the very first day I saw Tamura. He was already something of a legend down in the Pit and I had heard his name spoken before. Never kindly. But I'd yet to see the old man. These days I know every line and scar on his face. I could sketch that leathery bastard from memory. I have done just that more than once. A person's face tells the story of their life with every crease, mar, and dimple. I've known people able to read a person's past simply by their face— I have never developed that skill, but I enjoy sketching and I have always been one to draw inspiration from those around me. Tamura's face was weather-beaten leather even back in those days. I sometimes wonder what that face had seen. What Tamura's past might tell us? What it might teach us? I know bits and pieces, the little things he can remember. The sad truth of it is, Tamura is as addled as a moonfish dropped on its head far too many times and can barely remember yesterday. He has forgotten more than most of us will ever know.

I was hurrying down a corridor, passing a number of tunnels running off in every direction. I knew the stairs down should be close by, and I still had another four levels to go before I reached my own home. I've always had a good nose for direction and, though I'd never been to that part of the Pit before, I knew where I was headed. Tamura was halfway down an abandoned tunnel. The old man had a small oil lantern burning away on the floor behind him. His skin was dark as night, but his hair was a pattern of whites and greys all clumped together in tight, greasy locks that hung down past his shoulders. He stood there, staring up at the roof of the tunnel. Still and silent. And quite mad.

I thought Tamura was crazy at the start. I still think he's crazy. Maybe it was the rigours of the Pit that shattered his mind or maybe it was something else. It was certainly something. If only I had thought to talk to him that day. If only I had listened to the madness he spewed out. I might have saved us all a lot of pain. But I was angry and confused, and I trusted no one, especially not a half-insane old man who lingered in dark tunnels to pass the time. I heard plenty of horror stories about people like that, and most of them ended with a very clear kernel of advice: Stay the fuck away. I left him there and spared his vigil of the tunnel roof no mind.

Josef was waiting for me back in our cavern. He was always waiting for me after my visits to the overseer. He knew the sorts of things I'd been through, had suffered through similar himself. Josef was always there for me in case I needed to talk or scream, or maybe just lend a shoulder when I needed to cry.

"What did he ask you this time?" Josef said as I slumped down next to him and accepted the heel of stale bread he offered.

"Where we trained," I said. "No. Where I trained. He didn't mention you."

Hardt and Isen were in another corner trading lazy blows. At least that was what I believed at the time. I know now that Hardt was helping Isen train. Pugilism is the art of fist fighting and it was extremely popular in the Pit. A scab could earn extra rations, alcohol, or a host of other rewards just by fighting in the arena below. They didn't even need to win, though losing was not advisable. Some men only fought when it was to the death. Yorin was one of those. The king of the arena, they called him, and he had never lost a fight. Strangely, there was never a shortage of scabs willing to challenge him. I wondered if some saw it as a way out. A final solution to their misery. I can think of a hundred ways less painful than challenging that monster to a fight.

I watched Isen duck and move. Watched him fire off a series of quick blows, staring at the way his muscles moved underneath his skin as they flexed, and I felt myself warm at the sight.

51

"Eska. What did you tell him?" Josef asked and I got the feeling it was not the first time.

"The truth." I saw no reason to lie to the overseer and I saw no reason to lie to Josef. Only after the words were out of my mouth did I realise it was a betrayal. Whether the overseer already knew the answer or not, I was a prisoner of war and it was my responsibility to fight him, no matter what. The truth was staring me in the face, but I had been to bloody stupid to see it. Of course he asked me an asinine question he already knew the answer to. It was never about the answer. The overseer was trying to establish a rapport. He asked a question, I answered, he gave me a reward. The fucker was trying to train me like an animal. Well, I would bloody well show him that this animal has teeth.

"Good," Josef said. He leaned forwards and hugged me. "No sense in angering him. We need to survive, Eska. Both of us. There's no shame in telling the overseer what he already knows."

I saw a strange thing in Josef's eyes then. I saw hope rekindled from embers I had long believed dead. I wondered what sort of power could put a man back together again after being broken for so long. And they had broken Josef the moment Orran surrendered. The answer to that question terrified me when I finally learned the truth, and it haunts my nightmares even to this day.

CHAPTER 6

I was just six years old when the Orran recruiters
came for me. They knew what they had even before they
started my training; the diviners told them I was special, a
powerful Sourcerer in the making. All I knew was that one
moment I was playing in the trees, not a care in the world
as only a child can, then I was sitting on a horse in front of a
woman I didn't know. Larrisa, was her name and she
smelled of wood smoke, always of wood smoke.

When I think back now, I can't remember much else
about Larrisa. I believe she was kind despite having just
ripped me away from my family. I was scared. It was the
first time I had ever really left Keshin, certainly the first
time I had ever left the forest save for climbing above the
canopy. I didn't even have my family for company. That
was quite the shock. We grew up poor, as village folk often
are. We had a small home, barely more than two rooms,
really. We cooked in one of those rooms and slept in the
other, and my parents hung a blanket across that second
room whenever they wanted time for intimacy. My brother
and I huddled together at night on the same pallet. I found
that separation to be one of the most difficult things to deal
with. I both hated and loved my brother. He was both a
bully and a bore in equal measure, but those first few nights
away from Keshin, I struggled to find sleep without the
smell of him beside me. We cling to things, familiar things,

not because they are good for us, but because we are scared that the unknown might be worse.

I cried a lot in those days, but then I've never been afraid to cry. Some people tell me it shows weakness. I have never seen having emotion as a weakness, nor showing them. My emotions have always made me stronger. My hatred and anger give me strength when it should fail. My love and compassion have made me allies that otherwise might have been enemies. I have known emperors who were trained to wear their face like a mask, fall. Yet I have sat on a throne of corpses, and it was my emotions that helped put me here.

It was a long, hard journey from my old home to my new. I remember that much, though not many of the specifics. Memory is a strange thing. I know the journey was a hard one. I know I felt exhausted and scared. I know I ached from long days atop a horse and how mysterious that beast seemed to me at the time. Yet, when I think back on those memories now, I see them as happy. It was my first time out in the world and I saw more in those weeks than in the past six years of my life. I missed my family, and I didn't understand why I had been taken from them, but the distractions of the world outside Keshin kept those fears confined to tears cried into the darkness each night.

We passed fields of red and white; flowers, I now know, but at the time they were just blankets of colour in an otherwise green world. I saw a lake so large I took it for the ocean. I had no idea at the time what lay at the bottom of that lake, no idea of the horrors that haunted those waters when darkness fell. A city ruined and sunk beneath the waters, and thousands of lives lost as casualties of a war between gods who should have fucking known better, all hidden from me at the time. It seemed endless and magical. We stopped at a farm that bred giant trei birds, flightless and vicious as an angry snake. My wonder only increased when I saw men and women riding those birds, wearing full armour and trading blows with blunted swords.

We passed through towns that made Keshin seem tiny. Hundreds of buildings clustered together. I was both shocked and awed. My memories of those towns are a blur of people and noise. I remember Larrisa kept me close, always a hand on my shoulder as she shopped for fresh supplies. We never stopped for long at any of those towns. Larrisa preferred to keep us on the road. I don't think I ever saw her sleep. Each night I drifted off with her staring blankly into the flames of our little fires. Each morning I woke to find breakfast waiting and the camp being struck. Even the most mundane of things, like breakfast, can seem magical to the eyes of a child.

I think it might have been pure chance that a day out from Picarr, where the Orran Academy of Magic stood, we ran into another recruiter, this one escorting a young boy. Larrisa seemed to know the man by name and the two dismounted, leading their horses side by side as that mammoth city grew on the horizon. Picarr was unlike anything I had seen before, a buzzing hive of activity and noise and smells.

For a while we rode in silence, stealing glances at each other. He was a young boy, though a little older than myself, with a muddy face and a black eye. I doubt I looked much better. Larrisa had not given me time to pack any clothing, and I was wearing the same faded tunic and trousers I had been when we left Keshin. Children rarely care about being clean. These days I enjoy bathing every day and have ten wardrobes full of clothes, though I tend to mostly wear my robes. There is a certain freedom in a robe I find quite liberating; I won't begin to list the things and people I have hidden beneath my robes from time to time. Some things are not for impressionable ears.

Josef was the first to introduce himself. Always the more diplomatic and sociable of the two of us, he thrust his hand toward me and all but shouted his name as though it was some great act of defiance. The more I have travelled, the more amazed I have become at the ways people introduce themselves. I have seen people kiss just to say hello, and I have been kissed many times for just that reason, often by complete strangers. The clasping of hands is perhaps one of the most common, at least amongst terrans. It's about forming a physical connection from one person to another. I can get the measure of a man by the firmness of his grip, the moistness of his palms. It's also about trust. To have someone that close, to tie up one hand gripping theirs. Handshakes are a dangerous business in some parts of the world.

I held out my own hand just as Josef did and I said my name. I was a little startled when he lunged closer and grabbed hold of my wrist. It was by pure instinct that I returned the grip rather than fall backwards off the horse. That might have been a rather ignoble end to my life before it even got started. It probably would have saved the world a lot of pain.

There is an innocence in children that is only matched by their cruelty. There is also the rarest form of acceptance and compassion. Only children can go from complete strangers to closest of friends in a moment. Trust and love can take a lifetime to build in adults, but in children it can take just a second. Josef and I were that way. Maybe we were kindred souls, even from the beginning, or maybe we were just two scared children looking for comfort in one another. We were still holding hands as the recruiters marched us up to the academy and presented us to Prince Loran Tow Orran, the man the Terrelans called *The Iron Legion*.

Five months into my time in the Pit and I was starting to feel a change in my arms, as though they were stronger than they had ever been. Prig no longer selected a new scab to hold the marker each day. Ever since my first time it had been my job and mine alone. At first, I think it was punishment for staring at him, an open act of defiance against the fear the fat fucker cultivated within us all. After a while, it simply became part of my workday. We no longer waited for Prig to select me out of the team. Each day when we arrived in our tunnel, I picked up the marker, held it to the wall, and stared at Prig as he lined up the hammer. There was a change in the foreman too, Prig no longer met my stare as he took his swings. The cowardly fuck rarely met my eyes at all, always finding something else to look at.

I still wore the bandages Hardt had given me. I washed them regularly and then bound my hands again soon after. After a while I learned to wrap them around my arms by myself. I think Josef felt shunned by it. Maybe he thought it was me claiming I no longer needed him. He couldn't know it was so I could wrap the shard of mirror tight, hidden, and close to my skin. I kept it with me at all times and told no one about it, let no one see it. It was mine. My secret weapon against the dangers of the Pit. I felt stronger just knowing that I had some sort of defence.

My routine changed as the weeks rolled on. I still woke up and took a few minutes to hate the world, my situation, and everyone I knew, including myself. I still hated Prig most of all for his daily torture, and I dreamed of shoving my little shard of mirror into his fat neck. In those dreams he always died quickly with eyes full of terror, staring into my face, pleading, my name the final thing that ever passed his shit-stained lips. I know now that men like Prig do not die easily, and my little shard was quite small. It would have hurt, but I would have been lucky to kill him with such a weapon. More likely it would just piss him off and earn me a savage beating for the trouble.

I still worked each day away to Prig's schedule. Always digging. Hammers and picks striking stone and the squeal of those bloody rusted wheels as the cart took the rubble away. There are some noises that tear away every nerve you have; we all have those weaknesses. Sometimes, even now, those noises drive me either to cower as though terrified, or lash out in violence. It was no different back then, only I didn't have the power to lash out. Each day I heard those squealing wheels long after they had fallen silent.

Prig grew more violent, both with myself and with Isen. I didn't know why at the time. I didn't know then that Isen regularly fought in the arena, nor how his performance affected Prig's standing with the other foremen. Nor did I understand that his increasing violence against me wasn't just punishment for the daily defiance I showed him. It was also an order from the overseer. Rarely a day went by where I didn't earn a lash across my back, or a bruise if he was brave enough to get close and use his fists. It was fucking torture. The physical kind of torture designed to slowly wear away at a person's sense of safety and defiance, and Prig knew his trade well.

Some people learn to fear the threat of violence. It trains them into obedience just as some people train a dog with a stick rather than table scraps. I am not one of those people. I came to expect the violence. On some level, I thought I deserved it. Instead of fearing it, or trying to please Prig to stop the pain, I taunted him to see how far he would go. Some people flee from danger while others court it. Me? I stare danger right in the face and tell it to take its best fucking shot.

Josef no longer saw the overseer, but my appointments held at once per week. They were always different. Each week he would ask me a new question, some personal, and some not. Once he asked about my family, and if I had any siblings. Another time he asked me how many Orran Sourcerers survived the battle of Fort Vernan. Sometimes I answered his questions without hesitation and other times I refused to answer no matter how innocent that answer might seem. I did it to keep the overseer guessing. Thinking back on it, I really had no other reason. I liked trying to confuse the man. It seems a silly game I was playing now, yet at the time it was so important. I never took the rewards he offered. Not once. More often than not I left the room in chaos, destroying as much of it as I could. It was petty, but I am petty, and I took my acts of rebellion wherever I could.

"You are difficult to play against," Hardt admitted, his hand clamped firmly over one of his Trust die.

"Thank you." I let slip a small smile.

The big Terrelan shook his head. "I didn't say you were good at the game. I said you were difficult to play against. You're too unpredictable."

Again, I smiled. I had chosen my own side long before my turn to play Hardt had rolled around. "I'm taking it as a compliment," I said.

"Don't," Hardt said with a grimace. "Unpredictable to your enemies is good. Unpredictable to your friends is bad. Hard to catch a person when you don't know which way she'll jump."

I shrugged. At the time I still took it as a compliment. I revelled in the fact that no one knew much about me. Even those who did had no idea what I would do from one moment to the next. It took some time, and some loss, before I understood the lesson Hardt was trying to teach me.

"You think we're friends?" I asked. I didn't consider Hardt a friend. Back then I had only one friend and he was a terrible Trust player.

"Allies, at the very least." Hardt's voice was always deep, but also soft. I liken it to the rumble of thunder in the far distance. Even quietly, it demands you stop and listen, and when you do it's almost comforting. But you also know there's violence there, terrible and unrestrained.

Alliances, real alliances, are built from trust. They need it as a foundation if they are to survive. Alliances built from need are doomed to fail just as soon as one no longer needs the other. I didn't trust anyone.

I nodded. "Allies, then," I said. Hardt smiled and I shifted my hand just a little to turn the face of the die over. "Ready?"

We lifted our hands at the same time. Hardt's dice showed *friendship*, mine showed *betrayal*. I reached over and took the man's die, holding his disappointed stare all the way. "I am the weapon," I said quietly.

Eventually Hardt chuckled. "One day, girl, you might learn the point of the game," he said. "Then you really will be dangerous."

I scoffed, thinking myself smart. Thinking myself already more dangerous than Hardt could know. I was a foolish girl. I lost that game on the roll of the dice, but such is the way when everyone knows you'll betray them. I lost far more often than I won, and seethed quietly every time.

Later on, in the evening, and again I call it that only to keep some sense of structure for my time in the Pit, Josef and I were curled up together, the threadbare blanket draped over us. I pressed myself close into his back and felt the heat build between us. It could get bitterly cold in the Pit, or sometimes it could be uncomfortably warm. I never did quite get to grips with the climate down there.

"Hardt was wrong," Josef said quietly. "You're not unpredictable."

"No?" I quite liked the idea of being unpredictable.

Josef started to shift and rolled over until he was facing me. He looked tired; his young face gaunt with lines I hadn't seen before. There was a dusting of hair on his cheeks and chin, and I wondered how I had never before noticed it. He was just seventeen, but the rigours of the Pit made him look at least a decade older.

"No," Josef said with a smile. "You're just terrible at the game."

I punched him in the stomach and he laughed it away.

"I'm serious," he said.

"You're a shit-sniffing liar, is what you are." I've never liked being told I'm bad at a thing; anything really. My tutors at the academy realised this early on. They always expected so much of me but not nearly as much as I expected of myself. I've never been able to decide if I worked so hard to impress them, or simply not to hate myself for failing. "Besides," I said. "If I'm bad at the game, you're worse. For once you're worse at something." I wonder if I sounded as bitter as my memory suggests. "You always lose first."

We were close enough that I could smell Josef's breath. It was as rancid as my own. He grinned and shook his head. "I always lose first. But I'm an excellent player."

I rolled onto my back to stare up at the roof. "I don't understand," I said. It took a lot for me to admit that. The words were hard to push out, and I could never have said them to anyone else. I think I probably sounded sulky as only a young woman can.

"It's not about the game, Eska," Josef said, his voice already light as though he were drifting off. "It's never about the game. It's about the players."

CHAPTER 7

It's easy to look back on my time in the Pit and remember only the bloody digging. It certainly took up enough of each day. But there was more to life underground. There had to be. The foremen, Prig included, worked us scabs hard, that much was undeniable, but they also wanted the work done quickly. The sooner they could ditch their scabs, the sooner they could head off to the arena or the Hill.

For Deko's captains and their foremen, positioning and respect was everything. Prig had a lot of respect, thanks to the overseer's interest in me, but he was never happy with how quickly we got the digging done. He was never happy with his positioning on the Hill. I always wondered why he didn't just have us dig less each day. I had no idea, at the time, that the foremen were handed daily work orders by Deko himself, and Prig's association with the overseer was not something Deko shined upon. My team had to dig further each day than any other, and that was one more thing Prig resented me for.

There were things for us scabs to do as well. The Pit had a thriving trade community. Some items were more easily obtained such as extra food rations, or bandages, while others were far more difficult and needed to be smuggled in by the Terrelan guards. I never found out which guards did the smuggling; all my contraband came from trade and winnings.

Along with any sort of trade community came the gambling. It has always been a mystery to me why people with nothing feel the need to fritter it away on games of chance. The game of choice for most was a simple one, though it required a basic understanding of numbers. Each player took turns pulling a small stone triangle out of a bag and the little stones had a variety of numbers etched onto them. The aim was to get as close to twenty-one as possible without going over. Why the desired number was twenty-one, I still do not understand. Perhaps because it is one more than a terran's digits combined and therefore as high as most of the uneducated masses can count. Perhaps there is a special relevance to the number, laid down by the Rand or Djinn many thousands of years ago. Some significance they would, no doubt, claim no terran could understand. Then again, perhaps it was just someone's favourite number, and they decided to invent a game around it. A sad fact of life and time is that insignificant things often outlive their significance.

There were other games as well and all paled in comparison to the stakes that were traded back and forth over matches in the arena. Rarely a week went by where Isen did not earn a host of new bruises and cuts from fights down on those blood-stained floors. But with the injuries he also earned extra food, bandages, things to gamble away. I often wondered why Hardt didn't fight. He trained his brother, and was stronger by far, but never took part in the combat. Pacifism was a trait I spent long hours training out of Hardt.

It was Josef who finally convinced me to socialise with the other scabs. We had just finished shoving and elbowing our way to the front of the Trough to get our daily rations. The later you got to the front of the line, the more likely you were to get more mould than bread. The freshest bread was gone long before us scabs got anywhere near it. Deko and his lot claimed the best food and the largest portions, the rest of us often got whatever we could fight tooth and nail for. I mean that literally. More than once I left the Trough with a few bite marks from overzealous scabs.

There are advantages to being small and fighting your way to the front of a mass of people is not one of them. At fifteen, I was still growing, and Josef was only a couple of years my senior. Neither of us had the bulk or power to force our way forwards, and for the first few months we contented ourselves with the worst fare scabs could get. Hardt, on the other hand, was a head taller than most people and had an indomitable strength. I remember the first time I saw him wade into the mass, gently shoving people out of his way as he pushed through to the front. Before long, Josef and I learned to trail along in his wake, riding the void he left behind all the way to the front. Of course, once we were there it was nearly as difficult to keep our food. There was never a shortage of scabs willing to snatch a heel of bread or a handful of gruel in the press. Stealing from each other was frowned upon but in that mass of pressed flesh it was nearly impossible to tell where snatching hands came from. That was where my size became an advantage. I was small enough to slip away, beneath the notice of most people as they shouted and pushed their way forward.

Most days I took the opportunity to slip back to our little cavern once I had my food. There I would enjoy the peace and quiet and consider all the people I hated, cataloguing all the reasons why, and simmering in my own anger. A stew of bitter resentment. It was perhaps not the healthiest of choices. I was already a social outcast, shunning others in favour of my own company. Josef's loyalty was dragging him down along with me.

"Not today," Josef said, grabbing hold of my arm before I could slip away. We were just out of the press near the Trough and he started dragging me toward the series of stone tables and stools that were set out for the scabs. I'd passed by the place every day I'd been in the Pit, it was impossible not to unless I was happy not eating, but I always averted my eyes and moved quickly. I didn't want to socialise, didn't want to make friends. I wanted to escape, to be rescued. I also didn't trust the other scabs not to steal my food the moment I sat down.

Hardt and Isen had a table all to themselves, surrounded by other tables, each similarly occupied. I couldn't understand how they looked so comfortable surrounded on all sides by men and women they couldn't trust, but then I suppose when you're as big as Hardt, you're far more likely to be the one causing fear than trapped by it. Josef kept a firm lock on my arm as he dragged me towards them. I could have pulled away, wrenched my arm free, but I didn't want to make a scene nor spill any of my gruel. As foul as it tasted, it was food, and my stomach rarely stopped grumbling at the meagre portions while I was underground. The truth was, my hunger had less to do with the portions and more to do with my desire to feel the power of a Source in my stomach once more. It is a gnawing hunger all Sourcerers know too well.

The brothers looked surprised as Josef sat down and pulled me down onto the stool next to him. I grumbled out a complaint— I won't repeat it, but it was quite insulting and Josef looked at me aghast. I didn't take it back.

Isen was bruised and a little bloody, his bottom lip swollen on the left side and a number of cuts across his face were hastily pulled together with a strip of cloth across them. Isen had a lot of little scars on his face. They only served to make him look rugged to my young eyes. I thought them evidence of his prowess down in the arena, but they were evidence of his mediocrity. People always think those covered in scars are a good bet in a fight, but it often just means they've been punched a lot.

"This is rare," Hardt said in that quiet rumble of his.

"Rare would indicate it has happened before," I said, thinking I was smart. I was already in a bad mood, my daily routine interrupted by Josef's insistence. "This is unprecedented."

Hardt glanced at Isen and the younger brother shrugged.

"She means, there's a first time for everything," Josef said, giving me a shove that very nearly made me spill some gruel. I was angry at him already, but furious at the near miss. I may have growled.

I spooned a mouthful of the paste into my mouth and bit off a chunk of bread, refusing to inspect it lest I find anything furry or wriggling. "You lose a fight?" I said around a mouthful, nodding at Isen.

Isen grinned at me then and I felt my cheeks warm. I was a little thankful that the grime covering my face would hide it. I hate to admit it, but I was young and inexperienced. For years, the only man even close to my age I had any contact with was Josef and the love there was more like to that of a sibling. My tutors at the academy were all in their middling years and most of the other students were much younger than I. This was my first experience of attraction and I was attracted to Isen and oddly ashamed that he made me feel that way.

"This is the face of a winner." Isen smiled and a little gruel slipped out over his swollen lip. He quickly wiped it away. I found myself staring at his lips, wondering what they might feel like. I had seen people kissing; my parents, other students, even a few of the inmates down in the Pit. I wondered what the attraction was, how Isen's lips might feel against my own, how he might taste on my tongue. I was still staring when his tongue poked out from between his lips and wiggled at me. I focused on my gruel to hide my embarrassment and tore off another chunk of bread, chewing as loudly as I could.

I look back now and I can't see why I was so embarrassed. It seemed horrible at the time, Isen catching me looking at him like that. I suppose I should just be glad he couldn't see how I thought of him sometimes when I was alone. The young love hard and they love fast, and they recover from it almost as quickly. The sentiment is doubly true for young lust.

"How did the other guy look?" Josef asked around a mouthful of his own gruel. Manners were something we had been taught back at the academy, but they were useless down in the Pit. It was far safer to eat while you could, whether or not you were talking. The only really safe place to keep your food was in your stomach.

"Unconscious," Isen said, a smug look on his face. It was the sort of expression only the victorious wear. It was one I had worn many a time back at the academy, and I was bloody smug about my victories there. But I couldn't remember the last time I had won anything but a beating.

"You didn't kill him?" I asked. "I would have killed him." It was a boast, and a stupid one. I wanted Isen to think I was more mature than I was. I wanted him to think I was dangerous.

It was Hardt who answered my question. "Killing should never be easy, nor handed out indiscriminately. A person's life is a one-time thing. No one should take that away without good reason." He didn't know. Couldn't know. Life is only a one-time thing for the powerless.

"What if they deserve it?" I asked with a smirk. I thought everyone down in the Pit deserved it. Murderous bloody criminals, the lot of them. That mistake is all mine and I will live with the guilt of those deaths for the rest of my days.

"Especially if they deserve it," Hardt said. "Mercy is the mark of the great."

I snorted. "What a load of slug shit! Mercy is the luxury of the powerful and the mark of the foolish." I was eager for an argument, though in those days I was rarely not in that mood. "Leave an enemy alive and they're most likely to stab you in the back."

"Not everyone is Lesray Alderson, Eska," Josef pitched in, his eyes on the table.

I fucking hate that bitch. Maybe not as much as Prig or the overseer, but her name was definitely high up on my list of people I'd like to see thrown off a cliff. Knowing Lesray as I did, I knew a drop off a cliff probably wouldn't be enough to kill her. She'd likely grow wings or turn the ground to jelly beneath her. I hoped she was dead, that the Terrelans had killed her, but I knew I wouldn't be that lucky. I rubbed at the scar she had left me to remember her by, a rough patch of skin on my side almost as large as a fist.

"You have a bleak outlook on life, little soldier," Hardt said. "You can't have seen that much of war to make you so bitter."

I looked to Josef then and found him staring into his empty bowl. Maybe most wouldn't have seen it underneath the dirt and dust, but I knew the pain on his face. Hardt was right. I hadn't seen much of war at all. I had barely tasted the shock and pain of it. Josef was a different matter. His home had been far closer to the Orran-Terrelan border. Back in the days when the war was just starting, before we were brought to the academy, that border was where the fighting took place and where some of the most horrible atrocities were committed.

"Well," Isen said after the silence became uncomfortable. "I might go gamble away some of my winnings."

"Brother..." Hardt had a way of growling a word that made it sound as dangerous as a cave in.

"Nothing we can't do without," Isen said. He loved to gamble, despite being awful at it. I have long since noticed that those who love to gamble most are those who are worst at it and can't afford to lose. Isen was a man of vices. Sometimes I think he only fought in the arena to have something to throw away at chips or dice.

"I'll tag along," I said after shoving the last of my bread into my mouth. It was partly to spend time close to Isen and partly because I didn't want to be close to Josef and his grief. So many years after it had happened and he still shut down when he thought about it. I had no idea how to deal with him in that state, I never had. He was my best friend, closer than a brother, yet I didn't know how to help him. I think that might be why I truly found it so distasteful, because I simply had no idea how to fix whatever was broken inside of him.

I gave Josef's shoulder a squeeze and quickly followed after Isen, staying close to him as he threaded his way through the maze of stone tables. Near the edge, furthest away from the Trough, there were a number of tables, each crowded with people. The men and women around them were shouting, jostling each other and watching with excitement. Those who sat around the tables were quieter, mostly ignoring the crowd and only paying attention to each other.

Isen greeted a few people in the crowd and then pushed his way towards the table. I followed, meeting any eyes with a fierce hostility I hoped would warn people away. I think it worked, no one paid me much attention at

71

all back then. A young girl following after Isen; they probably thought I was his, and Isen was well-liked amongst the scabs.

"Mind if I play?" Isen asked the gamblers, not waiting for an answer before slipping onto one of the spare stools.

"You got something to stake?" said a broad man with a high voice.

Isen laughed and didn't answer. At the start of the next game, he joined in, slapping down a little cloth bag on the table. One of the other gamblers eyed it suspiciously then picked it up and sniffed. A wide grin spread across the woman's face, showing a set of brown teeth with a few missing. She nodded and the others placed their own stakes in the middle of the table.

The game was one played with small discs of stone. Some of those discs had a variety of symbols carved on both faces, and others left one face blank. The discs were set out in front of each player, though the player chose which face to show the world, and they took turns in trading with each other. I thought about asking the rules to the game, but I didn't want to give away my ignorance to the other scabs, so I contented myself to watch and figure out the rules for myself. It seemed to be a game about matching symbols and scoring pairs, but I'm certain I missed many of the intricacies. Isen won the first game, collecting all the stakes from those who hadn't dropped out. With a few prizes on his side of the table, he was less cautious in the next game and lost his stake to a man with only one eye. I watched the game for a while as stakes were traded back and forth on wins and losses. It seemed to me that few of the gamblers were truly playing to win. There was little of any real value in the stakes, but I think, for most, the attraction was the game itself and the distraction it offered.

After a while I moved away from Isen's table. He was paying me no attention, caught up in his little game, and I was looking for something else. The games were varied, with some tables playing Trust while others simply had men and women testing their strength against each other, each trying to force the other's hand onto the table. I wasn't likely to last a moment in such a game; my arms were like sticks.

I found what I was looking for at a table where the players had split off into pairs. The stakes here seemed more important. The gamblers weren't trading worthless baubles, but things people needed and truly wanted. Food, bandages, even alcohol. I pushed my way close to the table, meeting any stares with my own hostile gaze, and settled in to watch the players.

I watched for a long time. The gaming was more intense. Players growled at each other when they lost, or even threatened violence. I wondered if those scabs watching would intervene should one of the gamblers actually attack another. I wondered, but I already knew the answer. I wouldn't intervene, so why would any of the others. They were here to watch people throw away things they needed on the luck of the draw. There was no value in getting involved in a fight. The Pit made mercenaries of us all.

After picking out my prey, I waited until he had something I wanted: a fresh heel of bread without a spot of mould on it. Then I slipped into the seat opposite him. He was a small man with a bald head, but a chin thick with greasy black hair. He eyed me suspiciously and then shrugged. Oh, I hated him for that. I decided right then to teach the slimy fucker a lesson for underestimating me.

"Gotta have a stake to play, girl," he said in a voice like broken glass underfoot. He cracked his knuckles and looked down at his own winnings. I have to admit, his treasures made him look like a winner. I wasn't cowed.

I glanced at my hands. The only thing I had of any real value was the bandages Hardt had given me. I'd stopped expecting him to ask for them back, they were mine now and sometimes they felt like the only thing keeping my arms attached. More than that, they were where I hid my shard of mirror, my weapon that gave me courage and kept me safe.

"I am the stake," I said. It was a foolish thing to do, but I was a foolish girl. That's putting it lightly, I was an idiot made even more so because I thought I was smart. I didn't really understand the consequences. At the same time how much of what I am, how much of what I have gained, has been down to foolish, impulsive decisions? I was stupid, yes. But I was also fierce, willing to risk anything and everything for what I wanted. I was young.

The man's eyes slipped from my face to my chest and he shrugged as if he didn't give one shit. A moment later he pushed a little tin box between us. "Reckon you might be worth a bit of snuff."

He meant it as an insult, and I certainly took it as one. It wasn't until later I discovered that sniffing tobacco was worth quite a bit down in the Pit, and the little tin box was worth even more.

"You gonna sit there staring at me or are we going to play?" I asked, forcing a self-satisfied grin onto my face and denying the nervous hammering of my heart.

The man picked up the bag with the stones in it and shook hard. Then he placed it on the table between us and gestured. I reached into the bag and picked out a stone, keeping it locked tightly in my fist. After pulling it close to my body so no one else could see, I glanced at it to find just two little marks scratched into it. Two was a low number any way I looked at it. I placed the stone face down on the table and smiled like I'd already won.

He reached into the bag and pulled out his own stone, glancing at it only for a moment before slapping it down onto the table. His face showed me nothing, a blank slate. I felt my stomach turn over and tasted bile in my throat. The last thing I needed was to throw up. I was there to win a second meal, not lose the only one I had.

The next stone I pulled out of the bag was a nine and I placed it on the table next to the first. Eleven was a low number and only one stone in the bag could send me out of the game. The wise way to play the game would be to take another stone and reassess. But I wasn't playing the game. I was playing the fucker opposite me.

I watched him pull a second stone out of the bag and steal a glance. A slight tug at his lip made it clear he had a high number. Then his face went blank again and he gestured back towards the bag. I tapped the table with a single finger and kept my eyes locked on his face.

I had nerves of steel even back in those days and I'm thankful for it. How I managed to play that game without shaking the table to rubble I don't know.

My opponent hesitated, his eyes narrowing. He looked down at the stones in front of him and I knew I had him. I could see in his eyes he wanted to check his numbers again. I couldn't blame him for that. I wanted to check mine as well, even though I knew exactly what I had. It's an odd compulsion, the need to make certain your mind isn't playing tricks on you. I will give you this advice for free, nothing gives away the bluff quite like checking your numbers.

Reaching into the bag for a third time, the man pulled out another stone. "Seven sickly shits," he swore before turning his own stones over to reveal a combined score of twenty-two.

Relief flooded me. I felt I could breathe again and eased my hands open, wincing at the pain my nails had left in my palms. I wanted nothing more than to run away with my meagre winnings and never play the game again. But I had sat down with the intention of winning the man's bread and I wasn't leaving until I had it. I felt the eyes of those watching us, heard them murmuring, but I couldn't make out the words over the noise of my blood rushing through my veins.

I flipped over my stones to show the man my score and saw his face grow red, eyes hard. Eleven wasn't a winning a score, yet I had stuck with it while his own fear of losing had caused him to play himself out of the game.

"Piss-drinking bitch! Again." He slammed a fist onto the table and then pushed a little clay bottle forward.

"What's that?" I asked.

"It's fucking moonshine," he said, still scowling at me.

At the time I had never been drunk, never even touched a drop of alcohol. It was strictly forbidden at the academy. The tutors didn't want it dulling the initiates' senses, and I hadn't even completed my training before they shipped me out to participate in Orran's last ditch defence. I won't lie, I was curious to try it, to see why so many people loved the stuff. It's fair to say my sobriety didn't last much longer. But I was at that table for bread, not booze.

I reached for the little tin of snuff I had just won.

"No!" my opponent shouted. "Same stake as before. I win, I get you."

"Thought I was barely worth the snuff?" I asked and then smiled at him. "But if you get to choose my stake then I get to choose yours." The smile slipped from my face. "The bread."

He didn't hesitate to pull back the moonshine and push forward the bread. I could feel my stomach clenching at the thought of more food. It's always been surprising to me the lengths a person will go to for a little extra food. I had been surviving on my rations for months, but from the moment the overseer had offered me more food... From that moment, I found I was always hungry, always wanting more than my meagre rations allowed. It was as though my body was rebelling at the idea of throwing away food and demanded I win some myself rather than being given it.

This time he went first and we each pulled out our first two starting stones. I had a score of just seven, far too low to gamble a win, and now he was expecting me to bluff. My opponent glanced at his stones and then smiled, tapping the table.

I reached into the bag and pulled out a third stone, bringing my new total to sixteen. It was a good score, maybe even a winning score. I looked up to find him staring at his own stones. After a few moments he tapped the table again and met my eyes.

I didn't credit the man with a lot of intelligence. Perhaps I should have. I had just lost a war, and I suffered regular beatings at the hands of a man I truly believed would happily kill me if not for his orders not to. Despite it all, I still had the arrogance of youth. I still believed myself to be smarter than everyone else down in the Pit. After all, I was a Sourcerer, able to wield magics beyond their understanding. Most of those down in the Pit were common criminals, or so I thought. I was quite wrong on that matter. A lesson you should always take to heart is that while all Sourcerers are powerful, not all Sourcerers are wise. The bard tales might like to make us out as pointy-hat-wearing dispensers of knowledge, but bards are known for one thing above all else. They lie through their fucking teeth. It turns out we Sourcerers do the same.

Reaching into the bag for a fourth time, I pulled out another stone and placed it next to my others without looking at it. I saw the man's jaw clench and this time he hit the table with his hand. I took a steadying breath and tapped the slab of stone.

I noticed then how quiet the crowd around us had become. Those still gathered were silent, leaning in to watch the match between us.

With a flare of nostrils, the man flipped over his stones to reveal a score of eighteen. A good winning score. I flipped over my own stones one at a time, not looking at them, but staring at the man in front of me. I watched his face go from intense scrutiny to seething anger as I flipped over the last stone. The one I hadn't even looked at. Only then did I look down to see I had a score of twenty in front of me. I let out a ragged breath and was a little glad it was drowned out by the chatter of the crowd.

Perhaps if I had been a little more diplomatic I could have avoided the confrontation that followed. But diplomacy has never been one of my strengths. I always left that to Josef. I prefer to rely on raw power and trickery.

I reached out and pulled the stakes to me. I still didn't care for the sniffing tobacco, but the bread was a real prize. Victorious, I stood up and turned to leave.

"Sit down!" my opponent hissed. I turned to find him on his feet, fists planted on the table. It was entirely possible he was not pleased with losing to a young woman. Especially one who had so utterly outplayed him. I think I might have made it worse by not looking at my final stone until it turned. In the eyes of the other scabs it made me look courageous and bold, and him look foolish. In truth, I was the foolish one and my move had been more bravado than real courage. That first round, I played the player. The second round, I let the luck of the game carry me to victory.

"I have my winnings," I said, backing up a step. "You should take your defeat like a man."

"Sit down!" he hissed again. "You'll play another fucking round or I'll beat you senseless and take all the stakes I want."

That didn't go down well with the crowd, not that any of the cowardly fucks moved to intervene. Gambling was one of the few pastimes we scabs had. One of the few that Deko allowed us to have. I didn't know it then, but there was an unspoken rule that fair games of chance were respected. Of course, not many were willing to enforce that.

I glanced around at the crowd, still clutching my winnings to my chest. They were all watching the exchange, but none looked willing to get involved. There was no profit in it for them. All they had to do was watch and they'd at least get some entertainment, though likely at my expense.

I knew I could shout for help. Isen was only a few tables away and both Josef and Hardt would come running if they knew I was in trouble. But I had gotten myself into this mess and I was determined I would get myself out of it. I've never been one to go screaming to the nearest men for help. That being said, I was an antagonistic bitch without a diplomatic bone in my body and had less chance of winning in a fight than I did of learning to fly.

"You," I said, pointing at a big man with a scarred lip and scarred knuckles. "I'll give you half the bread if you beat him unconscious."

"What..." That was about all my opponent managed to say before a scarred knuckle hit him in the side of the head. He stumbled and the big man whose help I had just employed grabbed hold and slammed my opponent's head into the stone table twice, leaving a dark red smear and a broken tooth embedded in the stone. Another lesson to learn, if a job's worth doing, it's worth hiring someone to do it properly.

My opponent slid down to the floor under the table. His eyes were open but unfocused and bloody spittle bubbled between broken lips. He was still conscious, but I counted the big man as having done his job well enough.

"Fair pay for fair work." I tore the heel of bread and tossed one of the halves to the stranger with the scarred and bloody knuckles. It was the smaller half.

CHAPTER 8

My first meeting with the Iron Legion was both awe-inspiring and terrifying in equal measure, and I had no idea who he was at the time. Larissa marched me up to the front gate of the Orran Academy of Magic and kept a firm hand on my shoulder, whether to keep me from running or lend me support, I don't know. I remember thinking the gate was monstrous as it loomed high above us, the walls around the academy grounds blocked sight of anything beyond and all we could see were the barest hints of the tops of buildings and a bruised sky above. It was raining, I think. We were certainly damp. It was cold too, but Josef and I clung to one another, sharing warmth through our rags.

Larissa seemed surprised by the man standing at the front gate. He looked old even then, a heavily lined face and dark hair just starting to grey. A man in his thirtieth year made ancient far before his time. He wore a kind smile as he stared off into the distance, heedless of the rain soaking him through.

I was quite shocked when Larissa went down on one knee in the mud and the other recruiter did the same. Josef and I stood still for a moment. We were too young to know or care about the issue of royalty. Back then I'm not even sure if I knew what the word meant. I know Josef was the first to copy Larissa, sinking down onto a knee and pulling me with him. I hated kneeling in the mud that day, despite the fact that I would happily have rolled in it on most. Children can be so very illogical, and I was no exception.

I remember the moment the man at the gate noticed us. He quit his staring into the distance and startled at our presence, just for a moment, before the smile returned. I thought he looked a lot like my grandfather, though I had lost the man a year earlier and the details of his face escaped me even then. Still, I could remember he had been kind and comforting and never failed to sneak me sweet treats before dinner.

Larissa called the man Prince Loran. I soon came to know him as the Iron Legion, though only in stories about the way he was single-handedly keeping Orran's borders intact. He asked Larissa a few questions I couldn't hear over the rain, and then went down on one knee in front of Josef, heedless of how the mud stained his white robes. I don't think he said anything, just stared at Josef, who stared right back. Then he looked at me and for just a moment I felt — awe. Prince Loran Tow Orran blazed with power. I didn't understand it back then, but I felt it all the same. Meeting his eyes, I could feel the depths of that power ran deep as the bones of Orran itself.

It was only when Josef squeezed my hand that I realised the prince had said something to me. I still to this day cannot remember what it was. I simply wasn't listening. I was lost. The sight of the Iron Legion, the feeling of power he gave off, had shocked me to my core. Then he stood and stepped aside, waving us through the gate.

I looked up to Prince Loran. I'm not ashamed to say it was a touch of hero worship. His name was legend, his deeds were the things bards wrote stories about. I know, I read dozens of them in the academy library. I read accounts of his training with the Golemancers of Polasia, a school of magic all but alien to both the Orrans and the Terrelans. He had convinced them to teach him their arts by impressing the masters so much that it became a mutual exchange of knowledge and ideas rather than an apprenticeship.

There was a tale of his trip to Do'shan, his battle of wits with the Djinn incarcerated there. Some people say no one ever gets the better end of a deal with a Djinn. They are masters of words and loopholes, twisting people's desires upon themselves. The tale was extravagant, I'll give it that, and it claimed the prince answered correctly one riddle for each year he had been alive. In the end, the Djinn relented and gave him a boon. Having since been to Do'shan, I believe very little of that story; only that prince Loran has indeed been there and matched wits with the trapped Djinn.

Years later, I was devastated when word came in that the Iron Legion had fallen to the Terrelan army. Josef was the only one who knew of my infatuation with the prince and he did his best to console me. But I had no time to grieve for the man I idolised, we were too busy fighting a war. Well, we were too busy losing it. I think Prince Loran was my first experience with loss. The first in a long line.

It must have been nearing my sixth month underground when I finally visited the arena. It was located deep within the bowels of the Pit, as far away from the Terrelan garrison as possible. A winding series of tunnels opened out into a large man-made cavern, and the roar of bloodlust filled the space along with the stench of sweat and blood.

Deko created the arena and it was his pride and joy. I heard from the other scabs, those who had been down there for more years than I could imagine, that Deko had ordered teams to work side-by-side excavating the cavern to his exact specifications. It was huge, easily large enough to hold a few hundred inmates with space to spare. Concentric rings, each higher than the last, surrounded a pit carved straight from the rock around us. The pit in the centre was large enough for ten men to fight abreast and the walls surrounding it were high enough to stop any who might try to escape, or to stop any monsters thrown into the pit from getting loose amongst the audience. At the far end of the cavern, furthest from the main entrance, was an area reserved for Deko and his most trusted sycophants. They watched over everything with cudgels in hand to enforce the peace.

Any inmate could sign up for a fight any day. Deko chose the match ups and there was no arguing once it was decided. Nor was there any pulling out of a match once Deko had chosen. That was probably the only reason Yorin still had opponents at all. All the other scabs said he was unbeatable, and he never failed to end with the kill. Some said Yorin fought every day and had since being thrown down there with us. I wondered how much blood his scarred hands were stained with. I still wonder how many men Yorin killed. I'll wager it's fewer than I have.

The more often an inmate chose to fight, the less often they had to dig, especially if they killed their opponent. It was well-known that a scab's performance in the arena directly affected their foreman's standing with Deko, and Deko respected those with a taste for murder. That was why Prig hated Isen so much, because Isen refused to kill.

I picked up the marker and moved towards the end of the tunnel. For months it had been my job. I still feared Prig missing the hammer swing one day, but I faced that fear and I faced the ugly fucker every swing. My arms no longer bruised from it, but I still wore the bandages, regardless. I'm fairly certain I was on my third set of bandages by that point. I wore them partly to hide my little weapon, and partly because it made Prig think that marker duty still hurt me. That way he was less likely to force the job on one of the others.

"Not you, bitch," Prig hissed at me. He was agitated, that much was clear. His whip was out and the bastard kept trailing it along the ground like he was eager to use it.

"I always hold the marker," I said. I might not relish the job, but it was *my* job. Besides, I knew Prig wasn't likely to kill me if he could help it, not while the overseer was still interested. I couldn't say the other members of my team would be so safe.

"You." Prig gave his whip a lazy wave towards Isen.

I tightened my grip around the marker and took a step forward. "I always hold the fucking marker!" I said again. Squaring up to a bully is only advisable when you have a chance of fighting back. If they can beat you without reprisal, then that's all your defiance will earn you. It was an unfortunate fact that, while the majority of us scabs had to be content with wearing sandals cobbled together with strips of leather, the foremen were afforded more solid footwear. Prig's booted foot hit me in the stomach and my legs collapsed. I found myself kneeling on the ground, coughing and fighting for air.

"Not today," the foreman hissed as he reached down and tore the marker from my hands. "Today it's your job." He tossed the marker towards Isen.

Isen caught the marker and grimaced at some pain. He was already bruised and scabbed from his fight in the arena the night before, yet he didn't complain. But neither did he stand up to Prig. I thought him a coward for that. Isen took the marker to the wall and knelt, keeping his eyes on the ground as the foreman lined up the swing. It was the wiser course. Prig wanted to see fear, wanted Isen to know the power he held over him. Unlike me, Isen understood that, and he gave Prig exactly what the bastard wanted. It was the wiser course, but it grated on me to see Isen humble himself like that.

I watched, barely remembering to breathe as I imagined what might happen if Prig missed the swing and killed Isen. I wondered what Hardt might do. What I might do. Try as I might to keep my distance, I had become attached to the two brothers. My attraction to Isen aside, I liked them both, respected them both. I was even starting to trust them. The thought of life in the Pit without one or both of them was something I wasn't even willing to entertain.

I gasped as the first swing connected and Isen let out a cry. It was not easy holding the marker and the shock of it hurt as though your arms were bursting apart. I was used to it, but Isen wasn't. Prig heard me and turned to stare, an ugly grin on his fat fucking face. He knew as well as I that he had finally found a way to scare me. I imagine it was a great victory for him. It was certainly a defeat for me. I knew then I would never hold the marker again. Prig loved to torture me above all others and now he had a way to do it.

After the marker was in the wall, Prig set us to digging. We had a fair way to go that day and I had my weekly interview with the overseer afterwards. Prig wanted some time to relax on the Hill with the other foremen, so he drove us hard. There wasn't a single member of the team who escaped without at least one lash across their back.

Isen got it the worst. Between the rigours of the fight the night before, and Prig's ferocity on the hammer, Isen could barely close his hands. Hardt worked even harder than normal, trying to make up for his brother's slack, but Prig noticed. On the fourth lash, I couldn't take it anymore. I couldn't take seeing Isen whipped bloody knowing that it was my fault, that Prig was doing it to hurt me.

In hindsight I only made things worse.

I threw down my pick and turned to face Prig, stepping between him and Isen. Maybe it was the surprise, or maybe it was the look in my eyes, but he hesitated, just for a moment. Then I saw his face screw up with rage and he lashed out with the whip.

Now, the pain is an abstract thing. I know that it hurt, that it felt like my face had been lit on fire. Thankfully I can't feel it anymore. The whip cracked across my left cheek and I cried out, stumbling backwards into Isen but keeping my feet beneath me.

I still bare the scar of that lash today. I still bear most of the scars that rancid cock-filled arsehole gave me, but that one is a constant reminder of the power that slug-fucking bastard had over us. I have forged a throne out of my determination. I have matched wits and strength with creatures arrogant enough to think themselves gods. I have crushed empires, and watched my own fall to ruin, yet I still bear the scars that pitiful bully gave me underground.

Prig might not have stopped at one lash, he certainly looked willing to deal me another, but Isen shoved me aside so hard I found myself lying on the rocky ground and staring up him, thinking he should be grateful. I did not count on the pride of young men in their prime. Nor the danger of wounding that pride. Honestly, I'm not sure which of us was the bigger idiot. I think we were running neck and neck.

"Don't ever," Isen snarled, his face twisted in rage. I was shocked, blood rushing in my ears and running down my cheek, and my mind reeling. I didn't understand. I still don't. Men can be the most fucking foolish of creatures sometimes. "I don't need some stupid little girl trying to protect me."

Hardt's big hand appeared on his little brother's shoulder and he pulled Isen away. Away from me. The rest of our team stood around, watching and doing nothing. Prig grinned that shit-eating grin of his, anger gone,

replaced by smug victory. He licked his brown lips and
lashed his whip at the ground. "Back to work."

CHAPTER 9

Isen disappeared as soon as Prig announced the work was done. I watched him go, though part of me wanted to run after him. He hadn't spoken a word to me or to anyone since calling me a *stupid little girl*. The insult burned, regardless of how true it was, stinging worse than the gouged flesh on my cheek. I would have hated anyone calling me such, but from Isen... I wanted him to see me as more. I wanted him to see me as a woman.

I didn't know how long I had before my interview with the overseer, but I knew it would roll around sooner than I'd like, and the cut on my face needed tending to. It had stopped bleeding, though it still hurt like a fire burning away at my cheek. Josef always tended to my wounds as I did his, so with that thought in mind, I ignored the other scabs and stormed away to our cavern.

Josef wasn't waiting for me when I arrived and that started a niggling feeling worming its way through my gut. He almost always finished his work before my team. It wasn't unheard of for him to finish later, but... Sometimes I get a feeling. It's like dread and sorrow mixed into one. I knew something bad had happened, I could feel it in my bones, and it scared me.

Hardt arrived shortly after I did, a few of the others in tow. Thinking back, I honestly can't even remember their names. Not a one of them. I'm sure Hardt could though. He probably considered them friends. I wonder if it hurt him when I murdered them all.

"I suppose we better have a look at that cheek," Hardt said in his quiet rumble. In moments he had a bowl of water and strips of cloth in hand. Maybe it was more than moments. I was so worried about Josef I wasn't thinking clearly. I was pacing, hands clenching and unclenching, breath coming fast and ragged.

As Hardt set to cleaning out the wound, I kept my eyes locked on the cavern entrance, waiting for Josef to appear.

"Sorry about my brother," Hardt said. "He had no right to say that to you just for standing up to Prig."

I snorted. "Then why did he?"

"Pride," said Hardt. "He's a man grown and you're just about half his size. You standing up to Prig like that when *he* won't, when none of us will... It shames him. Makes him feel less of a man. He wasn't really angry at you, more at himself."

I winced at the pain in my cheek. "But you're not?" I asked. "Not ashamed for letting Prig beat your brother like that? Not ashamed for acting like a fucking coward?"

Hardt paused. Out of the corner of my eye I could see him staring at me, though his eyes looked unfocused. "There's no shame in surviving," he said. "Prig's a shit-chewer and no mistake, but I don't hurt people anymore. Besides, what would standing up to him get me? You might be safe from real reprisal, little soldier, but me... I could kill Prig. Deko would hear of it soon enough, and then I'd be dead and Isen would be alone. And you'd get a new foreman, one who might be even worse than Prig.

"My dad used to tell me to pick my fights carefully," Hardt continued. "Then he'd punch me about as hard as a grown man can punch a boy and tell me all over again. I spent a good few years taking any fight I could. And spent a good few years learning the lesson he was trying to teach me, in his own way. Now I have."

I thought about his words. On the surface they sounded like cowardice to me, though I now know there was something to them. Unfortunately, it's a lesson I seem incapable of learning. I've never been able to pick my fights. I let them pick me, and then I beat the odds. Or maybe I've just never met a fight I wasn't willing to take.

I was still mulling over Hardt's wisdom when Josef stumbled in through the cavern entrance. I was on my feet in a moment, regardless of whether Hardt had finished cleaning my wound. Josef was cradling his left arm and one eye was swollen shut. A dozen little cuts marred his face and his rags were stained red in places.

"Don't fight," Josef said urgently, shaking his head at me as I ran over to support him.

Prig sauntered into the cavern a few steps behind, that same shit-eating grin all over his face. It didn't take a leap of logic to see how Josef had ended up so badly beaten. My anger raged. My hatred was a fire inside of me, burning away all reason. I have been known to let my anger get the better of me and this was one of those times.

Josef grabbed my arm with his one good one and shook his head at me. "Don't..."

I didn't listen.

Shrugging free of Josef's grip, I ran at Prig and threw a punch. It was a messy haymaker of a strike. These days I'd be embarrassed by such an attack, but back then I didn't know how to fight. I thought my rage would see me through. That my ferocity would overcome any lack of training or brute strength. I was so fucking wrong.

Prig caught my punch, twisted my arm behind my back and shoved me up against the nearest wall. I just about managed to turn my head in time to stop the impact from breaking my nose. Unfortunately, I turned my head to the right and Prig ground my wounded left cheek against the cavern wall. Pain is something one can get used to, and I thought I had, but an open wound pressed against rough stone taught me otherwise and I let out a scream.

"Any of you scabs so much as move my way and I'll put my knife in her and then in you!" Prig roared. He was pressed up close against me, so close I could feel the heat coming off him and feel his breath on my neck. He pushed me harder against the wall and twisted my arm a little further. I'm ashamed to say I squealed from the pain. I think he enjoyed that most of all.

I considered grabbing for my little shard of mirror, but with one arm twisted behind my back I had no way of reaching it.

This is why, in all my life, I have never hated anyone so much as I did Prig. No one else has ever made me feel so helpless. Not even the torturers down in the Red Cells. Not even the emperor with all his fucking knives.

A punch to the kidney is a dangerous thing. It's a vital organ and one that has very little protection when struck from behind. The pain of Prig's punch blotted out the agony in my cheek. My legs collapsed beneath me and I could not even scream. I collapsed against Prig's grip and floundered, lost in the pain. Thought and reason blasted from my mind. Then I was moving, pushed along by the fat bastard, my arm still twisted behind my back.

The caverns and tunnels seemed darker than usual and passed by in a blur. We were on one of the lifts, halfway down to the main cavern floor, when I started thinking again. The pain was all over, as though my body couldn't make sense of what hurt, so everything was agony. I looked down at the cavern floor growing closer and realised how close Prig was holding me to the edge. All he would have to do was let go of my arm and I would fall. It was a strange thing to realise the pain of my arm twisted behind my back was all that was keeping me alive. Strange to think, as much as my shoulder seared with pain, I didn't want Prig to let go. I didn't want to die.

No sooner had the lift bumped to a stop we were moving again. Scabs turned to watch as Prig pushed me onward, my arm still twisted behind my back. None of them helped. Maybe they were too smart to stand up for another scab, or maybe they were just cowards, happy enough to watch someone else in pain as long as they were spared from it. That was the way of the Pit, the way those in charge bred isolation into us all. Nobody was willing to stand up for anyone else in case they found themselves in the same situation. We might have all been in the same shitty, sinking boat, but we were also in it alone.

Prig didn't have to march me through the Hill. I think it was routine that made him. It would have been better for both of us if he'd marched me straight to my interview.

"Prig." Deko had a deep voice and sounded almost lethargic as though sparing any attention at all was a great effort.

"Dipped in goat shit," Prig spat under his breath, and pulled me to a stop. We were deep into the Hill and I could see a number of foremen watching us now. I sagged a little in Prig's grip now that I was stopped again, though he quickly convinced me to stand straighter with a slight raising of my arm. "Don't say a word," he hissed in my ear.

"Come show me what you got there, Priggy," Deko continued. I turned my head to see him sitting on a table with his four most vicious captains lounging nearby. Deko's eyes were fixed on me. I should have looked away. Instead, I stared straight back at him. Defiant. Daring him to take an interest. Refusing to back down no matter how fucked I was.

Prig pushed me forward slowly, it was a meeting neither of us wanted. Deko was a daunting man up close. He wasn't tall, but he made up for that lack in girth. His arms were thick with muscle and his belly bulged. It said a lot that down in the Pit a man could grow so fat. He had black hair, long and matted and streaked with grey. But by far the most striking thing about him were his eyes; they were dark and shone like lamplight reflected off a pool of oil.

"She's got an interview with the overseer," Prig said. It was the first time I had ever heard the man sound humble. It might have made me smile had I not been near crippled with pain, seething with rage, and still very much at the fucker's mercy.

"I don't give a rancid poxy shit," Deko said with a grin. His captains laughed like the good little sycophants they were. Well, all except Horralain, but then I'm fairly certain that monster didn't know how to laugh.

"He don't like her being late," Prig said. As far as I had been able to tell, the overseer barely cared if I was late or not. But then that day was a special day, and Prig knew it.

"Priggy, Priggy, Priggy. Are you arguing with me, little Priggy?" Deko asked. I heard the scuffing of boots on the floor behind us and felt Prig's grip on my arm tighten.

"No, sir."

"Good," Deko said. "Best not speak again unless I ask you to then." He sniffed and scratched at his belly. He wasn't wearing a shirt, but then I had never seen the man wear a shirt. I think he liked people to see all the scars he had. A show to make potential challengers think twice seeing all the attempts he had survived.

"I've seen you around, scab," Deko said, turning his full attention to me. "Who are you?" He looked relaxed, but his captains did not. Behind him, I could see all four of them looking as though they were ready to leap at me and tear both myself and Prig to shreds. I almost thought it would be worth drawing out that violence if it meant Prig died with me. A final fuck you to the man who made my life miserable.

There was Karn, the man the other scabs called *The Butcher*. Poppy, a tall woman with more scars than Deko himself. Rast, who, rumour had it, was an ex-Terrelan soldier sent to the Pit for war crimes even the brass couldn't justify. And finally, Horralain, a mountain of a man who had once wrestled a khark hound down in the arena. I have summoned a few khark hounds in my time. Monsters from the Other World, they are as large as a bear and covered in razor-sharp spikes that grow through their skin. I have seen just one of the Other World beasts tear ten men apart. They are a nightmare of teeth and claws given terrible form, and that said a lot for the man who had wrestled one and survived.

I considered lying to Deko, telling him I was the queen of Polasia just to spite them all. I have since met the queen of Polasia. I have seduced her son and sunk her favourite demonship. It's fair to say our relationship is slightly strained these days, but back then I was nobody and I doubt she would have minded my baseless claim.

"Eskara," I said, still gritting my teeth through the pain of a split cheek and my arm wrenched behind my back. There seemed little point in lying and much more to be gained by telling the truth.

Deko laughed and his captains joined in. I didn't see what was funny, and I could tell by Prig's rapid breath stirring my hair that he was just as unamused.

"How are you liking my little kingdom, Eskara?" Deko asked after a few moments.

I attempted a shrug. It's worth noting that if ever you have your arm twisted behind your back, do not attempt to shrug.

"I wouldn't recommend it to my friends," I managed to growl through the pain.

Again, Deko laughed.

"What's wrong with your eyes?" I asked. Perhaps I could have phrased the question a little better, but I was under some considerable strain.

The laughing stopped and all pretence of a smile slipped from Deko's face. He stood and took a step towards me, bending down so his eyes were level with mine. He had a big face, round, pitted, and covered in a thick mat of oily beard. His eyes shone, an unnerving sight, but I locked my gaze with his all the same, still unwilling to back down.

"What?" Deko goggled his eyes at me and I could see little red streaks snaking out from the edges towards the pupils. "Do my eyes scare you?"

"No." I said. It was a lie of sorts. Of course I was fucking scared. Terror to go right along with the anger burning like a furnace inside, but it wasn't his eyes that scared me. The mystery of why they shone was something I was clinging to. That riddle was perhaps the only thing stopping me from collapsing and sobbing my way out of the situation.

Deko stared at me for a few seconds longer before snorting and backing up to sit on his table again. "There's nothing wrong with my eyes," he said. "It's just carrot juice." Again, his sycophants laughed along with him.

I had heard many times in my youth that carrots granted good night sight, but I dismissed it as an old wives' tale. Of course, I was taking Deko's words literally at the time. I didn't understand the joke. I didn't understand that I was the joke to them.

"Tell me something, Eskara Helsene," Deko said once the laughter had faded. "What do you know about Impomancy?"

Despite the anger burning inside I felt my blood go cold. Deko knew my name— my full name— and he was asking about Sourcery. There was only one explanation. He knew who and what I was. I felt something else as well. Hunger. There was a possibility, slim as it might be, that Deko was asking about Impomancy because he had a Source. I think I would have done anything right then for a Source. Then I would have used it to turn the Pit into a glorious fucking tomb filled with the bodies of every fucking inmate down there.

I felt Prig lift my arm a little and my shoulder blazed in agony. It felt as though it were about to pop from its socket and I have experienced a dislocated shoulder more than once in my lifetime. It is not a pleasant injury.

"I know a little about the school." It was a lie, but I decided it was best to hide the full extent of my knowledge and abilities. Deko might have known I was a Sourcerer, but at the time I wasn't sure he knew just how powerful I was. Or perhaps I should say how powerful I could be. Without Sources I was nothing but a young woman in a precarious situation.

Deko nodded. "Maybe you'll be of some use then," he said. "All manner of nasties down here with us. The last adviser we had perhaps wasn't as smart as he thought. What is it, Prig?" Again, the sycophantic laughing from his captains.

Prig let go of my arm as he stepped beside me to talk to Deko.

I have always had trouble letting go of my anger. It boils inside of me for days and there is no quashing it save

100

for violence or sex. Or sometimes violent sex. But when I was younger I only knew about the violence.

Prig started talking but I couldn't hear him over the rush of blood in my veins. I hated the fucker. I hated all of them, but I hated him so fucking much! For everything he had done to me, all the pain and humiliation. For everything he had done to Josef just for knowing me. For everything he was going to do to Isen just to bloody well get to me. I hated Prig and I wanted to see him hurt. I wanted to see him bleed. I wanted to see him die!

"I am the weapon," the words hissed from my mouth. I reached for the shard of mirror hidden in my bandages, tore it free, and stabbed it into Prig's fat fucking neck.

Prig screamed and I saw blood wash over my hand. All around me Deko's people were moving, some protecting him while others moved towards me. A whirlwind of chaos and violence all moving in slow motion with me at its centre. I saw Prig's fist coming, but I didn't have time to dodge it. He punched me in the face and the world went black.

CHAPTER 10

Induction into the Orran Academy of Magic was the worst time of my life. It only lasted a month, but that month was worse than all my time in the Pit. Worse than my stay in the Red Cells underneath Terrelan's capital city of Juntorrow. Worse than the birth of my second child, Sirileth, the Monster.

Josef and I were inseparable. The tutors at the academy tried, of course, but I have long since discovered it is quite difficult to control a pair of wilful children. Each night they separated us into our dorms and each night one of us would slip out and find the other. Come the morning, they would find us huddled together in one of the bunk beds. This was before they decided to embrace and nurture the relationship. We were always stronger together than apart.

The first few days of induction were not too harrowing. We were introduced to the others who would be in our classes: Lesray Alderson, who I later gave the incredibly clever nickname of bitch-whore, Tammy Oppen, and Barrow Laney. It was not a large induction by any means, and of the five of us, only myself, Josef, and Lesray were deemed to be powerful enough to be suited to war. We were shown around the academy, both the places we were allowed to go and those that were off limits to students. I remember taking note of every door we were told never to open, and I opened almost all of them, and a few they thought well-hidden even from curious children.

We were fed, three meals a day and good food. It was the best I had ever eaten in my young life, and probably better than I eventually ate as a queen. They tested us with our numbers and letters. At the time, I could do simple mathematics, but my parents hadn't thought to teach me what little they knew of letters, there simply wasn't a need for it in our little forest village. Only the elders and merchants had need of reading, and the young daughter of a basket weaver was never intended to be either of those. Josef had a better grasp of both reading and writing, but he was also two years my senior. Still, I remember being a little jealous of him for his ability to make sense out of pages and ink.

I believe it was our third day into induction, just our fourth day at the academy, when the tutors began testing us. Sources are dangerous things to anyone not attuned to the magic they contain. Even after half a lifetime of research I still do not know what affects specific attunements. Even the diviners, those whose sole task it is to find potential Sourcerers, do not know the secrets. I'm certain neither of my parents were attuned to even a single Source and yet there I was, able to wield five at once. Perhaps the Rand know, or even the Djinn, but it's fair to say neither of them will be sharing any more of their secrets with me. I don't just burn bridges, I scorch their foundations and set the water on fire as well.

For young students at the academy the only way to test attunement was with time, pain, and lots of Spiceweed. Trial and error, they called it. I call it fucking torture, and

I've experienced enough of it to be a bloody expert on the subject. I suppose I should be thankful they used small Sources, those no larger than a marble, to test us.

The pain brought on by ingesting a Source you're not attuned with is... Well, it's bloody horrible. Within the first minute, the cramps start. They begin in the stomach, but spread outward, muscles tensing, tendons contracting. They get more severe as it goes on as well. So painful... Nothing else I have ever experienced has come close and I have suffered a great many types of torture. After a couple of minutes vision starts to dim and something tears inside. I am no student of physiology, the Biomancy arts are as foreign to me as the more mundane surgeries, but I believe it is considered a bad thing when people start bleeding from their eyes, ears, and nose.

If the incompatible Source is not regurgitated within a few minutes the Sourcerer will die painfully, and messily. Despite the rather terminal outcome of using an incompatible Source, it remains the only way to test a Sourcerer for their attunement.

One by one, Josef and I were made to ingest a Source and we were monitored for the reaction. As soon as we started to cramp, Spiceweed was administered. The weed might have saved my life time and time again, but it is not without its drawbacks. It feels like vomiting up everything you've eaten in the past week, and the retching doesn't stop just because you're empty. Some people have it worse than others, and I have always been one of the former, though I wish it were otherwise.

Pyromancy was the third Source the tutors at the Orran Academy of Magic tested me with. I had already failed my first two attunements, both Geomancy and Meteomancy, and I remember the trepidation I felt on that third day. People can be trained just like any animal and I had already come to expect the discomfort from swallowing down a Source, the feeling of something hard sticking in my throat on the way down. Then the agony would start, the cramps moving from the gut out toward my limbs, my muscles screaming in pain. It never got any further than that, the moment I showed signs of rejection Tutor Luen would rush forwards with Spiceweed and shove into my mouth. After just two failed attunements I had already come to expect failure, and the consequences scared me shitless.

The tutors never told us what attunement or rejection really meant back then. They never told us it was out of our hands. I had failed twice and I thought it was my fault. I thought I had done something wrong or not tried hard enough. I was terrified of what would happen if I showed no attunements. Just six years old, torn away from my family and forced to swallow shards of magic that hurt on the way down almost as much as on the way back up. Worst was the thought that they might kick me out if I failed too many times; the uncertainty of what I would do, how I would survive on my own was terrifying. Josef stood by me as much as he could, even so early on in our friendship, but he was also going through attunement. Though it didn't affect him as badly as it did me, he was also suffering.

I remember the feeling after swallowing the Pyromancy Source. I winced, expecting the worst. Tutor Luen moved towards me, a small clump of dried

Spiceweed in hand. A Sourcerer can use any Source, any magic, but if they lack attunement it will hurt them, kill them much faster. With the Geomancy Source I felt connected to the ground beneath my feet. I could feel the composition of the earth. I didn't even understand it, but I could feel the lines of power in the earth. Right up until the rejection started and then all I could feel was agony. With the Meteomancy Source I could tell rain was coming even though it was hours away. The Pyromancy Source was different. It felt like a fire had been lit inside my body, but it didn't burn me. It warmed me through. I could have stripped naked and bathed in ice water and not felt the cold. I've done just that since, and I can tell you it's quite refreshing. There are tribes of terrans in the far north who insist it is excellent for the skin and for good health, though few of them can use Pyromancy to keep them warm through the soaking.

I was ecstatic. Not just because of the fire I felt inside and the certain knowledge that I could use it to set the world ablaze, but also because it meant I could stay. Stay at the academy, stay with Josef. Relief was what made me truly happy that day, relief from the fear that had been gnawing inside of me since that first rejection. True, it was only three days, but to a child, three days is a lifetime and also passes in the blink of an eye. I admit I was less happy when Tutor Luen advanced upon me with Spiceweed once again. They had discovered my first attunement, but that didn't mean I was ready to wander around with fire at my beck and call. I can't blame them for that; untrained Sourcerers discovering magic for the first time are dangerous on an entirely different level. And only a fool gives an unsupervised six-year-old a match.

The strange thing is, not all Pyromancers feel the flame inside. It is the magic of temperature rather than fire. When Lesray Alderson was tested for it, the bitch-whore said she felt a ball of ice inside, not burning but freezing instead. Maybe that is why we were always at odds with each other, even from the start. A natural war between fire and ice. Then again, I think it far more likely it's because she's a rampant cunt.

There were, at the time, twenty-two known Sources. I had attunement to only six of them, but I was tested for all of them. I retched so hard I was vomiting blood. After the third day, the tutors stopped sending me back to the dorms and gave me my own bed in the infirmary. I remember looking in a mirror and seeing red dots all around my eyes. The physicians told me I had burst blood vessels, such was the violence of my reaction to Spiceweed. Despite it all, the testing continued. I was just six years old, torn away from my family. It felt like torture. It *was* torture! I cried myself to sleep every night, and every morning I woke to find Josef next to me in my infirmary bed.

CHAPTER 11

I awoke to pain. The coughing fit that racked my body only heightened that agony. I ached everywhere and could barely summon the energy to open my eyes. Instead, I chose to listen. And I heard nothing.

Silence down in the Pit was beyond rare. There was always noise, usually from the digging. I felt my nerves fraying, warring with the pain inside until staying still became a torture all its own. A little part of me dared to hope I was free. That somehow, I had been rescued from the hell of that place. But I felt cold rock beneath me and already I knew the false hope for what it was.

With a groan I started to shift, getting my hands underneath me. I dragged my eyelids open to see grey stone and a puddle of spittle and blood. As I rolled onto my back, I saw a single table bolted to the stone beneath it, and two chairs. I was in the overseer's interrogation room.

My head pounded like the end of a week-long drunk, an unpleasant feeling I have since come to know more than once, and my face felt stiff and swollen. I remembered Prig hitting me, the shard of mirror still embedded in his neck. I tried to smile at that, but my cheek flared with agony like fire running through my flesh. The wound still hadn't been dealt with. Raw flesh still oozing blood.

I struggled to sitting, clutching at my ribs. I'm convinced Prig or the others must have kicked me after I collapsed. It was my first time experiencing the delightful agony of a broken rib, and I was quickly learning just how debilitating it was. It took a lot of effort, and more than a few cries of pain, before I pulled myself up onto one of the chairs. There, sitting in that room, I wondered if I would ever walk properly again. I thought I was crippled from the pain.

"Fuck!" I lowered my head onto the table and cried. The pain in my ribs soon put a stop to the sobbing. I could see my right hand, blood soaked through the bandages. At least that brought a smile to my face, seeing Prig's blood on my hands. It was too much to hope he was dead, so instead I hoped I had taught the filth-licking bastard to fear me.

When the door to the interrogation cell finally opened I didn't even lift my head from the table. I listened to the footsteps as the overseer approached and slid down into the chair across from mine. I heard the door shut again, and I waited for the overseer to say his piece. I didn't have the energy for his games. All I wanted was to curl up into a ball next to Josef and sleep.

I think it was the thought of Josef that strengthened my resolve. I wasn't the only one beaten by Prig, and by stabbing the foreman I had put Josef in even greater danger. I knew there was no way Prig would have sated his anger with a single beating, bullies never do. Everything to them is an escalating series of offences and insufficient retribution. There would be more, I realised. Prig wouldn't stop until one of us was dead, probably me, and even then, he'd just pick someone new to bully. Fuckers like that were never happy unless they were tormenting someone else, as if they could make their own worthless lives better by making someone else's shit.

It took a lot of effort to raise my head and sit up straight in the chair. I look back now, and it seems like it should have been an easy thing, yet at the time it felt a heroic achievement. The overseer watched me, a curious look on his hawkish face. It was the first time I truly felt like a prisoner. I was in rags held together by filth and hope, and bleeding from a dozen different places; and bruised everywhere else. The overseer was in a pristine military uniform. I knew then what he was about to offer me.

"I can make it all stop," he said.

I have to hand it to the fucker, he knew what he was doing. If he had offered me the deal any earlier I would have scoffed and it would have strengthened my resolve, but he waited until I was at my lowest. He waited until I was beaten and bloody, until the only other person I really cared about was in a similar condition. Worst of all was that I knew Prig wasn't going to stop; if anything, he would only get worse from here on out. More vindictive. More brutal. The overseer was the only one who could stop it. He knew it. And I knew it. By all the pox-ridden whore-faced fucks, he had won and we both knew it. He didn't even have the good grace to look smug about it.

"Perhaps you still think some of vestige of the Orran empire will be coming to rescue you?" The overseer paused and shook his head. "There is no Orran empire. The entire Orran bloodline has been wiped out. Your emperor is dead. He died before your armies even laid down their arms."

Truth is a flood, waters rising while we hide inside homes of self-deception. There is a point where water starts gushing in under the door, through the cracks in the windows. You cannot hide from the truth, nor barricade against it. You can only run from it, and I had nowhere to run. It made sense. I'd always wondered why the Orran army had surrendered. We could have fought on. I could have fought on. But the call to lay down arms was given, and now the overseer was telling me why. I knew it for the truth. The doors burst open, the windows cracked, and the water flooded in. And I drowned in the truth.

That was the moment I felt something snap inside. Hope shattered and all I could do was stare at the pieces with no concept of how to put them back together again. At that point I could see my future laid out in front of me. I could read it in the broken bones I would suffer and the scars my flesh would form. How long before Prig took one of the beatings too far? How long before he did something to me or Josef that wouldn't heal? What if he had already?

And the overseer was offering to take me away from it all. I had no hope of rescue from the people who had raised me and trained me. The empire I had sworn to serve was gone. But the overseer *was* the rescue I had been waiting for. He was the answer. He who had only ever asked me questions. He'd tried to help me, offering me food and fresh clothing. I looked up to find him nodding at me, a genuinely concerned look on his face.

"I can make it stop," he said again. "I just need one word from you, Eskara. Just one word, and you don't have to go back down there. I'll send men in to pull out Josef too. Just one word and you can see the sky again."

111

He had me and we both knew it. He was offering everything I wanted. A way out. A reprieve from the constant fear and pain. The sky, my freedom. He was offering too much. He knew too much. How did he know to entice me with the sky? The horizon I longed to see again. The reward I had promised myself for getting out of the Pit. I had never told him that, it was a secret I kept to myself, uttered only in stolen whispers as we slept.

"What word?" I asked through swollen lips. I could almost see the light, natural light. The sun shining down from the sky. I could almost taste it. I don't think I have ever wanted anything so much in all my life.

"*Yes*." The overseer smiled. "I just need you to say *yes*."

I could have said it then. Looking back, I wonder how different the world might be now if I had just agreed then and there. Maybe it would be a better place. Maybe the friends I've lost would still be alive. Maybe my children would never have come to be. I'm certain the world would be a better placed without Sirileth, yet I love her despite all she has done.

"To what?" I asked. Exhausted and broken as I was, I still couldn't agree without knowing the terms.

"To serve the Terrelan Empire," said the overseer, making it sound like the most reasonable price in the world. As if it wasn't a betrayal of everything I had been raised to believe. "You are the last living Orran Sourcerer to agree, Eskara. Join us and both you and Josef can be free. You can have all the luxuries you learned to enjoy from your old life. You can have that life back again, only without the war. Just say *yes*, and the Pit will be a distant memory you can forget."

Sometimes I curse my defiant nature. There I was with the rescue I had hoped for and dreamed of right in front of me, and all I had to do was ask for it. Some prices are too heavy to pay no matter the reward.

"Never." I tried to spit at the overseer. You should never try to spit with swollen lips, all you'll end up doing is dribbling on yourself.

The fake smile slipped from his face, replaced by a deep frown. "I can't guarantee your safety anymore, Eskara," he said. "Nor Josef's. Refuse me now and I'm done with you. No more protection. No more offers. This is your last chance, Eskara."

I leaned forward and sniffed, treating the overseer to the iciest, fuck you stare I could manage with a beaten, swollen face. "I've been done with you since the first time we met."

The overseer stood and shook his head. He pulled open the door and waved to the soldiers outside. "Throw her back into the Pit and make sure she doesn't return. I never want to see her again."

He got his wish. For all the good it did him.

CHAPTER 12

I was a wilful child at the academy, in trouble as often as I earned praise. I was regarded as a bad influence on Josef, who was always much more obedient than I. Doing as I was told was never any fun, adventures always start off the beaten path. We were just one year into our training when I made it through the first of the locked doors that were forbidden to us.

The length of time each Sourcerer can hold a Source in their stomach varies. Even a Source they are attuned to will eventually start to damage them from the inside. I didn't know why, when I was a child, and the tutors at the academy didn't either. It wasn't until I involved myself with the Rand that I learned the truth behind the Sources and behind us Sourcerers too. But that's getting ahead of myself.

A vital part of our training was to learn our limits. Unfortunately, limits are affected not just by the type of Source but also by number of Sources and the frequency of use. I should point out that much of a Sourcerer's training is trial and error. Painful trials with potentially fatal errors.

There are two types of Source that no Sourcerer is advised to sleep with inside their stomachs. Empamancy is the control and manipulation of thoughts and emotions. I thought it a weak school of magic at first, until Lesray Alderson very nearly convinced me to kill myself. I hate

Empamancy! A sleeping Sourcerer with an Empamancy Source inside of them cannot control their magic. There are stories told in the annals of the Orran Academy. Stories of Castle Uoping and of the Sourcerer who forgot to retch up their Source one night. A madness gripped hold of the castle. The few survivors told of walls bleeding in the night and spectres wailing for their lost lives. Men and women went crazy, hacking at themselves with knives or murdering their own kin. The Sourcerer woke to find their mistake writ full. Hundreds dead, and only a handful of survivors all broken beyond repair. It's a lesson well worth learning.

The other Source is Impomancy, the school of summoning and binding monsters from the Other World. It is said that nightmares stalk that world and dreaming of them while holding an Impomancy Source will give them a way to cross over, unbound and uncontrollable.

One of the first things the tutors at the academy pressed upon us was to respect the magic that Sources granted us.

The first Source I tested my limits with was a Portamancy Source. A fairly powerful school for those well-trained in its arts and able to fully utilise the true abilities it offers. I was not well-trained in those arts and have never been. It remains, to this day, one of my weakest attunements.

Most of that first year was spent learning to control our breathing and being drilled with the theory of Source use rather than the practice. It was maddening to be given tastes of power and then kept away from it for so long.

I could create portals, but they were small things, about as large as a fist, and I could project them only a couple of meters at best. It was a far cry from those who could use Portamancy to cross hundreds of miles with a single step. But I was young. My control of portals these days is somewhat more advanced. I once trapped a man in a portal loop, endlessly falling the same couple of meters. There have been times in my life where I have been forced to improvise with methods of torture. I imagine it was as unpleasant as the poor bastard made it sound.

Our tutors had long since stopped trying to keep Josef and I from each other. We were assigned to different dorms, but that was as far as their token attempts went. They knew once we were fully trained we would be almost unstoppable so long as we were side by side.

It was late at night and we had just suffered through a full of day training. Tutor Inilass used to say we were moulding both our minds and our bodies into something strong, but not rigid. A Sourcerer needs to be strong enough to contain powers beyond them, but malleable enough that those same powers don't break them. Looking back now, I think that Tutor Inilass was a fool who barely understood the magic she was teaching us to use. Most of the tutors were fools. Maybe not the Iron Legion, but Prince Loran was something of a special case. I think maybe he understood the Sources better than anyone. Maybe he knew the truth, even then.

Josef groaned as I shook him awake. He was never a quick one to come around from sleep and I gave him a minute to collect himself. I whispered my plan in his ear and he shook his head. What I was planning was against the rules and the tutors indicated that dangers were locked away behind the forbidden doors. Danger just made it all the more exciting. Ignoring Josef, I slipped from the bed and padded across the floor on silent feet towards the dormitory door. No sooner had I opened the door and peered out, then Josef was by my side. He might not agree with my plan, but I knew full well he wouldn't let me go it alone.

Maybe I did pull Josef astray with me. Perhaps, if not for me, he would been a better student; a better Sourcerer. I certainly have a history of pulling people along on capers they would rather choose to leave well alone.

We slipped through the academy corridors like a summer breeze, ducking into alcoves or open doors twice when we heard nearby footsteps. Josef was scared of getting caught, I remember the fear plain on his face, but I was not. To my young mind we were on an adventure and adventures were always exciting, not scary. These days I know that they are usually both; and I still can't resist them.

I knew exactly which door we were going to explore. It was on the second floor of the Academy Archives building. The Archives were full of old treasures and priceless artefacts, or so all the other students said. I believed the older students without question at the time. It wasn't until later on I learned the Archives had a much more sinister purpose.

The door was polished brass with no handle and no keyhole. The hinges were on the room side and there was a not enough gap between it and the floor for a breath of air. I had no idea how the door might open. My imagination ran wild with the possibility of what we might find inside.

Josef followed along, always on the lookout for any tutors we might stumble upon, or any who might stumble upon us. It was against the rules for students of our age to be out of our dorms at night, and even more against the rules for us to be in the Archives building without supervision. Josef never wanted to come on my adventures, but he always enjoyed them once I dragged him along.

We had a short conversation about the door itself. It is possible to enchant items, and nothing holds an enchantment quite like metal, but I got no feeling from the door, no tingling sensation or otherwise. I have travelled the world and I have never found an enchantment that is undetectable. Some leave shimmers in the air, while others make the hairs on my arms stand on end. Some magical traps are almost undetectable, especially to the unwary, but there is always a tell. My sensitivity to enchantments has saved my life on more than one occasion.

Eventually I focused on the Source in my stomach and tapped into its power. I was young and inexperienced, and it took a lot of concentration to summon a portal, even more to sustain it while Josef reached through and fumbled against the other side of the door. Through the portal I caught glimpses of the treasures that lay inside and I felt my heart quicken. I had to calm myself to keep my concentration. I have seen portals snap shut on people before and I did not want to have to explain Josef's severed arm to our tutors.

The door was bolted from the inside and Josef was panting by the time he managed to pull them back. In his defence, he was only eight years old and small for his age. After Josef withdrew his arm, I let the portal snap shut with a sigh of relief. I was quite sweaty and exhausted. Magic wasn't so easy for me in those days. Just carrying a Source in my stomach was uncomfortable enough, but drawing upon the power within left me feeling leaden inside. All thoughts of discomfort left me when we pushed open that door.

The room inside was large and open without a window and no lanterns hanging from the walls. Yet there was light, bright and powerful. Josef hesitated but I stepped quickly over the threshold and gawked in wonder. In the centre of the room, in a glass case on top of a plinth was a crown made of fire. It sat on top of a red cushion, yet the flames did not set its cushion alight. I squinted as I stared at it, longing to reach out and touch it, to see if the flames were hot. I am as fascinated now as I was then by the Crown of Vainfold, and these days I know that the flames are hot as a forge fire but they do not burn. I have worn it only the once, and only then to save my daughter.

To our left, secured to the wall by four steel staples, was a sword almost as long as I was tall. The pummel was a yellow jewel, but as I looked closer I realised it was a small Source, glowing with the power contained within. The blade drew the eye, it bubbled as though the metal were boiling yet also kept its shape. I remember staring at the patterns moving and changing on that blade for a long time. I might still be there now, but for Josef pulling me away, breaking the trance.

Josef dragged me towards the final treasure in the room. From a distance it looked just like any other kite shield polished to a shine, the flames from the crown dancing across its polished surface. But when I stopped in front of it I realised the shield's surface was mirrored. Instead of seeing myself in the reflection, I saw an older woman, scarred and grim, a snarl on her face. She stood in front of rift formed of darkness and terror, and tears of sadness fell from eyes that flashed with the fury of a storm. At the time I thought it was my mother; I wondered what could have happened in the year since I had seen her last to turn her from basket weaver to the hardened warrior I saw before me. The truth, had I realised it then, would have scared me far more. I watched her lips move but could not hear the words. If only I had heard her warning.

I returned to that shield twice more in the years before the academy fell to the Terrelans. In its polished shine I saw many things. I saw myself die at the hands of ruthless killers, beaten to death for the insult I had given. I saw myself leading a great army of monsters and men against a foe that could not be killed. I saw myself standing in a desert, staring up at a great portal, through which a God stared back. The glimpses it gave me of my future saved my life at least once, and may yet do so again, one day.

Tutor Olholm found us. When we finally turned away from the shield the old man was standing in the doorway, watching us. Olholm was never one to get angry, but even young as I was, I could see the disappointment on his face. The other tutors were not nearly so passive.

That fat fuck, Prig had survived and was waiting for me outside the garrison and he wasn't alone. As the soldiers escorted me back into the tunnels, I could see three figures loitering, lit by the flickering of a nearby lantern. The first I recognised as Prig, though he had a swathe of bandages wrapped around his neck. Even from a distance I could see the red that had seeped through. The bastard might have survived, but at least I'd repaid him for the wound on my cheek. I recognised another of the figures as Prig's friend who operated the wooden lifts. I didn't know the final man, though I guessed he had a similar intent to the others. They were waiting for me and I doubted it was to celebrate my defiant stupidity. No, without the overseer's protection they were going to fucking kill me.

There are two options open when confronted with overwhelming odds. The first is to meet those odds head-on with blade, magic, or guile. The second is to show the odds your arse and hope you can run faster and for longer than them. I had no idea how to use a blade. I hadn't so much as tasted a Source in almost half a year. And I was fairly certain no amount of guile would get me out of the beating I had coming. So, I turned and ran.

It has to be said that sprinting down a twisting staircase is not a wise decision under any circumstance, but fear has a way of making people stupid and I am no exception. I ran as though my death were chasing me, snapping at my heels. And it was. Without the protection of the overseer, Prig would kill me for stabbing him. It was a challenge to his authority, far beyond my casual defiance.

I heard shouting coming from behind and up the stairwell. Heavy boots slapping against stone. Curses drifted after me and I heard Prig, already sounding out of breath, threaten me with violence unless I stopped. I laughed at that, shrill and wild. There is nothing quite so liberating as laughter. So, when the axe is falling, you might as well giggle at the executioner. Of course, laughing with broken ribs quickly turns into hissing in pain.

I bounced off the walls of the stairwell, unwilling to slow my headlong decent. It hurt to breathe, hurt to run. I hurt all over just from being alive and yet I didn't slow. I ran into the pain, through it, letting it drive me onward instead of slowing me down.

When that first stairwell ended, I burst into the corridor. There were a few scabs moving to or from their digging tunnel, and I cried out as I bumped into one. I think he shouted after me, an insult or threat no doubt, but it was lost amidst the shouting from Prig and his friends. I glanced back to see the three of them careening out of the stairwell, shoving the scabs aside as they continued the chase. It was too much to hope the fuckers all tripped and broke their necks, but I hoped it anyway as I turned sharply and launched myself down another twisting stairwell.

I had to squeeze by another scab and that slowed me down. The pain in my ribs as I pressed myself against the wall and edged past them was almost unbearable. In some ways it would have been easier to stop, collapse, and let Prig catch me. But the fear of reprisal kept me going. I stumbled down the rest of the stairwell, my vision fuzzy from the agony and my breath coming in short, painful gasps. I knew then I wouldn't outrun them. Maybe I could on a normal day, but I was too injured to keep up my pace. Already I was slowing, my sprint turning to a defiant stumble.

I staggered out of the stairwell into a corridor that was dimly lit even by Pit standards. It was empty of other scabs and stretched away into darkness, only one lantern fixed to the wall and burning low. Everything was looking slightly darker than normal. I think maybe the strain I was putting on my body was too much. I stumbled into the nearest wall and stopped, just for a moment, to breathe. But the deeper the breath the more my chest burned, and it felt as though my ribs were digging into my lungs.

There is a feeling that is hard to explain. It's a feeling that you've been somewhere before, that you've done something before, and you already know the outcome. It was the feeling I got as I dragged myself down that corridor. I could see myself stumbling forwards, Prig and his friends catching up with me. I also had the feeling that it did not end well for me. For a long time, I thought it was just blind luck that the feeling struck me when it did. It was a few years later, thinking back, that I realised I *had* seen that corridor before. I had seen it in the reflection cast by the shield back at the Orran Academy, and I knew it led to my death. Unless I changed things.

I ducked into the nearest tunnel offshoot, the shouts of Prig and his friends close behind me. Tamura was there, staring up at the tunnel ceiling, lit by a small lantern on the floor. I hesitated for only a moment before staggering past him into the darkness beyond and collapsing down against the solid rock at the tunnel's end. I curled into as small a ball as I could manage and tried desperately to calm my breathing, staring out towards Tamura and the tunnel entrance with narrowed eyes.

Prig and his friends stopped at the tunnel and stared towards me. All three were breathing hard and even from a distance I could tell Prig was snarling. The fat cunt's mouth twisting into thing of rage and the promise of violence.

"Hey, old man. You seen a little bitch?" shouted the one who operated the lifts.

I watched as Tamura lowered his gaze from the tunnel roof and glanced towards Prig and the others. He giggled then, high and full of a crazy mirth no one else could ever understand. Tamura was always like that. He saw things no one else did and found humour where no one else could. The more I got to know him, the less I thought him mad, yet the more I thought him crazy.

Prig started down the tunnel, fists clenched. I froze. I wanted to push myself into the wall at my back, but I dared not move lest it gave me away. I was saved by Prig's friends pulling him back. I didn't know it then, but Tamura had a reputation. Not even Deko interfered with the old man.

With an angry curse, Prig turned away and he and his friends moved off, searching for me elsewhere. That was the first time Tamura saved my life, the first of many, and he didn't even realise it. I stayed there for a long time, huddled against the tunnel wall. I stayed there while the footsteps of Prig and his cronies vanished into an echo and then beyond. I stayed there while Tamura let out a content sigh and went back to staring at the ceiling. Until my breathing slowed and the pain in my chest eased. Until it stopped feeling like bony fingers clutching at my heart.

Eventually I pulled myself back to standing, holding onto the wall while my legs wobbled beneath me. Tamura hadn't so much as glanced in my direction. I wondered if he even knew I was there. I approached him slowly and quietly, aiming to move around him without disturbing his strange fascination with the tunnel ceiling.

The tunnel seemed just like any other. As a rule, we dug them with a high ceiling, taller than I could reach, though I could never claim to be the tallest of women. I looked up as I passed and couldn't fathom what he was staring at.

Curiosity, so many people say, killed the cat. Though, curiously, it is a trait far more common to us terrans than it is to the pahht. The pahht I have known would hate me comparing them to cats, but the resemblance is too close to ignore. I sometimes wonder if the Rand created them that way as pets. Though, in truth, the Rand consider all us lesser races as little more than pets or pests. Well, I consider them sanctimonious, smug arseholes.

"Is this the same tunnel as before?" I asked, giving in to my curiosity.

For a long time, Tamura said nothing. So long, I was close to giving up and leaving him in peace. I think we're both a little glad I had more than my usual amount of patience that day.

"No." Tamura has always had a strange way of speaking. Sometimes his voice sounds lethargic, as through it's a struggle to get the words past his lips. Other times he speaks with such excitement, that the words tumble out almost on top of each other. "There are many tunnels," he said slowly.

"That's not what I meant," I said. "I've seen you before, staring up a tunnel ceiling. I don't know this part of the Pit well. Is this the same tunnel as before?"

When Tamura lowered his head to look at me I saw an odd smile on his face. It's frustrating, but he stares through you, rather than at you.

"No," he said slowly. "There are many tunnels. This one is not as promising as the last."

"Promising?" I asked.

"Not very at all," he said. "What do you see when you look up?"

I saw rock, mostly dark grey. Shadows playing across it as the flames of the lantern danced. I told Tamura as much and he laughed at me. I had little time for the old man's games and I very nearly left there and then. Something in his dark eyes stopped me. I thought then it was a glint of madness and I wanted to see how deep it went. I know now it was the opposite side of the coin from madness; it was wisdom and it went deeper than the hole in the ground we stood in.

"You see stone because you are trapped," Tamura said. "Locked in by viewing the world as what is instead of what can be. Trapped. Trapped. Trapped. Or maybe you just don't feel it yet." His speed surprised me. One moment he was staring up at the ceiling prattling away to himself and the next he had me gripped by the shoulders, pulling me to where he had been standing just a moment before. He's a strong man, even ancient as he is now. It wasn't the brute strength of Hardt, but more a wiry power to his emaciated arms.

He manoeuvred me into position and then stood back, staring at me with an expectant look on his face. "Hmm?" He grunted.

126

"What should I be feeling?" I asked. At that point I wasn't sure what scared me more; another round of chase the Eska with Prig or being trapped in a dark tunnel with an old crazy Terrelan.

"Stop talking and listen," Tamura said. "You are trapped down here, seeing only what you think is real. You see rock, stone. Solid. I see possibility. I see stars. Gashes in the sky. Holes where the world pours through."

I have said most people think Tamura to be crazy and there is a good reason for it. He speaks in riddles and ideas more metaphysical than most can grasp. The wisdom is there, for those willing to dig into it and decipher whichever puzzle he chooses to use on that day. But for all the love in the world, he is a pain in the arse.

"Stars?" I asked, grasping onto the only part of his madness I could understand. "Are you saying it's night up above? How do you know? Or do you mean the specks in the rock? The way the lantern light glints off the minerals?"

"No. No. No. Stop talking. Stop thinking. Feel."

I raised my head to the ceiling and pondered his words. Actually, I was deciding how easy it would be to push past him and run. The pain in my ribs did a good job of convincing me to procrastinate a little more.

The slap caught me completely unaware and the pain that blossomed on my wounded cheek made me cry out. Tamura did not soften his blow and caught the oozing wound Prig's whip had left.

"Sand-eating sludge-licking fucker!" I cursed and straightened up, intent on fighting my way clear of the mad man.

127

"Stop thinking." Tamura pointed to his left cheek and then up to the ceiling. "Feeling."

My cheek felt as though it were dipped in fire and I could feel fresh tears welling in my eyes. Despite that pain, the humiliation, and the certainty that Tamura was a mad man trying to make me look a fool– despite it all, I raised my face to the rock above once more and stopped.

There is a technique all first years at the Orran Academy are taught. It's meditation. The act of silencing the mind and listening to the body. Isolating limbs and organs. Biomancers are even able to extend that feeling into another's body, to determine which bits are broken and how they should be put back together. I am not a Biomancer and I have never been good at telling my mind to be silent, but I reached for that meditation then. I listened to my body and it told me it fucking hurt.

I had a cracked rib on the right side of my chest and knew without looking I would be a motley of bruises. It hurt to simply breathe and would for weeks. There is little more painfully annoying than a bruised breast when running is in order, and I had done quite a bit of it. My body informed me it would rather we not attempt any more sprints for a while. I was bruised elsewhere as well, everywhere almost. My muscles were weak from the exertion and exhaustion. My stomach, as always, was an empty pit that never felt full. My bottom lip was swollen and I bled from a hundred tiny cuts and scrapes. My cheek stung like I had recently tried to eat a wasp's nest and it was making my teeth ache too.

But there was something else. Something cool and light brushing across the heat of my cheek. I knew the feeling, though it had been so long since I had felt it last. It was the wind blowing down through the rock, coming out down there in that tunnel right where I was standing. It was so light I would have missed it a thousand times had Tamura not made me *try* to feel it.

I felt something powerful blossom inside of me. It was something the overseer and Prig had torn away from me bit by bit. Something they had worn down with their beatings and the psychological games. I felt hope again. Not hope of rescue, but hope of a way out, all the same.

Most people would look up at the stone above them and see rock trapping them in. Tamura looked up and saw the stars in the night sky. I looked up and saw something else. I saw escape. Freedom. I saw my way out.

CHAPTER 13

"You said this one is not as promising as the last?" I was perhaps a little more agitated than I intended, but the barest taste of freedom will do that to a person after six months trapped underground. "There are others?"

Tamura nodded, gently pushing me away and reclaiming his position underneath the breeze. "One hundred and four so far," he said. "Some breeze, some gust. One drips. Drip. Drip. Drip."

"Which one is the most promising?" I gripped hold of Tamura's arm and he twisted away, dislodging my hand and sending me stumbling backwards with a gentle push. Then he went back to staring at the ceiling.

"Fourteenth level from the top. Not bottom. Tunnel twelve near the mouse-bear intersection. Foreman Polega's team used to dig there, but that was… some years ago. I haven't seen Polega since the new king took over."

It took me a moment to decide which question to ask first. I will admit, I had quite a few. Tamura's ramblings have always had a habit of spawning more questions than they answer. "You memorise every tunnel down here with names and numbers?" I asked. The scope of it is baffling. There were hundreds of tunnels down in the Pit, maybe even thousands. Forty-two levels at least, each one with dozens of tunnels and tunnels branching off from tunnels into yet more tunnels. There was no map of the Pit because to even attempt such a thing would be impossible. And yet Tamura had somehow done it, in his head.

"Of course," Tamura said. "How else would I know where I am?"

This was my first real brush with Tamura's insanity and I thought it to be just that. These days I realise it was a unique way to make sense of a jumbled mind. He babbled like a punch-drunk toddler at times, but there was no one down there who knew the maze of tunnels quite like Tamura.

"Where are we now?"

"Tenth level from the top. Not bottom. Tunnel five along the starfish-spider intersection."

I started to wonder if he named each corridor after animals. "Starfish-spider?"

"A starfish has five legs as a star has five points," he said. "A spider has eight legs like the symbol for infinity after a bad fall." He chuckled. "This intersection has six and a half tunnels."

"Half a tunnel?"

"Yes. Listen." Tamura cupped a hand to his ear and frowned. "Hmm. No digging. Maybe the stars aren't out anymore."

I have never been the most patient of women and with a cracked rib and an oozing cheek, what little patience I had was worn away by pain and exhaustion. "So, if we're on level ten and the most promising crack in the rock is on level fourteen, all we need to do is go down four levels?"

Tamura nodded. "Four levels and half the world away," he said. "First, we go up, to go down. Then, back up."

"Can you take me there?" I wanted to leave the old man's madness to himself. I wanted to go back to my cavern and curl up with Josef. But I couldn't. Prig wouldn't quit looking for me and the next place he'd go would be our cavern. I needed to find a way out or find a way to protect myself.

"Of course." Without another word Tamura started towards the starfish-spider intersection, leaving me hurrying to catch up. I had no idea at that time whether he was leading me to the most promising crack or heading off to find somewhere to sleep. But I followed along all the same. I didn't see I had any other choice. Tamura had become my best chance of getting out of the Pit before Prig killed me.

I kept Tamura talking as he led me upwards. I asked him how long he'd been in the Pit and he responded by asking how long had I been alive. I quizzed him mostly on the cracks and how he found them. I was trying to decipher the code even then, trying to sort the wisdom from the nonsense. So many years later, I still haven't truly managed. Sometimes I think it's like searching for a gem in a quarry, other times I think it's more like searching for a gem in a fucking treasury full of gems.

He led me up to the fifth level and to the lift there. I hesitated, holding back even as Tamura pulled the rope that would let the operator below know someone was waiting. I cursed myself for being afraid. Prig's friend, the lift operator, was one of those chasing me, but he would not be operating the lift now. Even if he was, I shouldn't have been so scared. I was still a child in many ways, small in stature and weak. With a Source in my stomach I could have brought the Pit down around me, but I didn't have a Source. I had no choice but to rely on others to get me through the situation I had created. I wasn't sure I could rely on Tamura, but I already had a plan forming.

We rode down the lift in silence. I will admit, I kept my distance from Tamura. It would take little effort for him to push me over the edge and I didn't yet trust him. Part of that distrust was because I didn't yet know him, and part of it was because he was clearly as crazy as a bucket of razor eels.

I could hear the general buzz of the main cavern before the lift even touched down. It was feeding time at the Trough and I felt my stomach rumble at the thought. Tamura started forward straight away, angling to the right. His direction would take us past the Hill and towards another lift.

"Up, then down, then up again," I said and earned an emphatic nod from the old man. I touched his arm lightly, not wanting him to pivot and send me crashing to the ground. I'm not sure my body could have taken another beating. I was already limping and cradling my ribs with every step.

"Wait for me," I said as Tamura glanced at me. "Stop here." I took a deep breath. "I need to see Deko before we go on."

The old man shrugged and collapsed onto his arse, crossing his legs beneath him. For as long as I've known Tamura he's always had the patience of a glacier. I'm more like the weather. I work to my own schedule and wait for no one, carving my own path through the world.

I approached the Hill at a steady limp, knowing full well I was being watched all the way. Deko was at the centre and I would have to pass through the mass of foremen and his captains to get to him. There was no way of telling if any were loyal to Prig. It wouldn't take much for any one of them to stop me if they chose to.

"Run away, little scab," said one of the foremen, standing up from his stone stool and blocking my path.

It's fair to say I was in no mood to be turned away by a peon with no authority. "Get out of my fucking way, scum sniffer," I said. "I'm here to see Deko and he's going to want to hear what I have to say."

The foreman was tall and broad, yet he couldn't meet my icy stare. I think he might have been angry at my lack of respect, but I didn't give him a chance to act upon it. I stepped to the side and continued into the heart of the Hill.

I didn't know it at the time, but I was doing something no scab had ever done before. Deko had made sure the Hill was a place of terror for us scabs. It was home to all those who tormented us; those who could kill us for less than no reason at all. No scab had ever willingly walked into the Hill without an escort. No other fucker was crazy enough to try. I'm amazed they let me get as far as I did.

The foremen let me thread my way through the throng, but they didn't leave me alone. I was pushed more than once and sent stumbling into tables. I'm ashamed to say I cried out in pain a couple of times, but I didn't let that stop me. It was like walking into a pit of hungry snapbacks; wild animals on every side and if just one of them decided to take a bite they would tear me to pieces. Luckily for me, the wild animals let me pass mostly unharmed. It wasn't until the ring of captains surrounding Deko that I was stopped.

Horralain, perhaps the only man in the Pit larger than Hardt, rose from a nearby table. The murderous arsehole was faster than I gave him credit for. Or maybe I was slower. A meaty hand wrapped around my neck and suddenly I was choking, lifted from the ground. The pain in my ribs might have made me scream but for the hand gripping my throat. I think I have Horralain to thank for the croak that sometimes creeps into my voice even now; the damage he did to me never fully healed. I also have Horralain to thank for the reputation I earned down there. Thanks to him, the whole Pit was watching my confrontation with Deko. The other scabs might not know what I said to him, but they knew I survived it.

My vision was going dark when Deko's voice cut through the whooping and braying. "Put her down. Let's see what the little scab has to say this time."

Horralain did not put me down. The bastard fucking dropped me. My legs hit the stone and crumpled underneath me. I might have been embarrassed at that, but I was far too busy sucking down air and coughing it back up. If you've ever had a coughing fit with a cracked rib you might understand why there were fresh tears in my eyes when finally, I got back to my feet to face Deko.

The ruler of the Pit was at the same table as before. His little court, surrounded by his most trusted and feared captains. He had a bowl of gruel in one hand, and a loaf of

bread fresher than any I'd seen in the past six months in the
other.

"Didn't expect you back so soon," Deko said around
a mouthful of food, showering me with crumbs. That said a
lot. Us scabs wouldn't dare waste food like that. Even
crumbs were valuable. "You haven't got another shiv on
you, have you?"

My first few words were raspy and painful, like my
throat was full of gravel. Being strangled will do that to
you. "You... You said... You needed an Impomancer."

Deko laughed and leaned forward as he dipped his
bread in the bowl of gruel. "Not right now," he said.

I held his gaze. "Not ever." My throat was raw but I
doubted Deko's rotten sycophants were going to offer me a
drink. "Not unless you give me something."

That knocked the smile from his face. The crowd
reacted to Deko's mood so quickly I almost thought him an
Empath, though I knew better than to believe there was an
Empamancy Source down in the Pit. The nearby captains
fell silent and Deko placed his food on the table behind
him. I look back on that moment and feel the trepidation
even now. I was betting everything on his need for
someone with the knowledge of creatures summoned from
the Other World. Walking a razor thin line with death on
either side.

"I don't fucking like ultimatums," Deko said. His
dark eyes shone and I wondered if they would be the last
thing I ever saw. "Or threats. Or requests."

"It's none of them," I croaked. "It's a bloody fact.
Either you protect me from Prig, or I won't be around long
enough to help you."

"Overseer cut you loose, huh?" Deko let out a loud laugh.

I nodded. "He didn't like what I had to say."

I was shaking as Deko considered the proposal. Fear, adrenaline, exhaustion, pain; all mixed into one, and I was trembling from the effort of keeping upright. I knew all of Deko's people were watching, knew the shaking made me seem weak. I might have been angry at that, but I was feeling numb inside. It had been a long fucking day.

"Willet," Deko said eventually. "Priggy is one of yours. Tell him this little bitch is off limits." He leaned forward again. "You belong to me now, Eskara Helsene."

I smiled, or at least I tried to. I have learned that it is quite hard to smile with a swollen face. "This is the Pit," I said, already starting to turn. "We all belong to you." I hated myself for saying it, despite the fact that it was true.

I left the Hill the same way I entered, limping and trembling with dangerous beasts on all sides of me. It wasn't until I cleared the final group of foremen that I realised all the scabs were watching me. Hundreds of faces turned my way. In all my time down in the Pit I had never seen the Trough so quiet at feeding time. I turned away from their eyes and made my way back to Tamura.

CHAPTER 14

Kinemancy was the only attunement Josef and I shared. I remember being so happy the day we were tested for it and neither of us rejected the Source. It was something we could learn together, practice together. Another connection to strengthen the bond that had formed between us. Unfortunately, it didn't take long for Josef's progress with the school to leave me behind. The tutors considered him a genius, a student the likes of which hadn't been seen since Prince Loran. Maybe they were right. Maybe Josef could have been that great, but he didn't have the temperament.

I remember reading about Prince Loran's studies at the academy. He was brilliant, that much was obvious to all the tutors, but he was also driven. The man the Terrelan's named the Iron Legion got that name because he was always willing to push the boundaries of what his magic could do, even at severe cost to his health. He didn't just want to learn, he wanted to pioneer. Now, I know it was more than that though. Prince Loran didn't just want to discover the unknown, he also wanted to rediscover the lost. It was a drive that almost cost us everything. Josef, on the other hand, wanted a quiet life. He might have been brilliant, but he would have been happy being nobody. Whereas I... I have always had the drive, but not the raw talent.

We were just two years into our studies when Josef first started to outpace me. We were training with Kinemancy in the practice yard. It was a large open square with various items of different shapes and weights to pick up and throw around. The walls were reinforced brick, coated with straw, designed to absorb the force of impacts. It is rarely the act of being thrown by psychokinesis that kills a person, and far more likely the impact of hitting something hard and unyielding. Much like gravity; it isn't the fall that kills, but rather the landing.

The art of Kinemancy is generating invisible waves of force. Some people believe it to be moving things with the Sourcerer's mind. They are ignorant idiots. I can throw a psychokinetic blast at a wall, but it requires me to *throw* the blast at the wall. The more experienced, more skilled Kinemancers can hold the wave of force. They are able to pick up and hold things, generate a constant push. Josef was one of those skilled Kinemancers even so early in our training. He excelled at generating pushes of varying strength. Some felt like little more than a strong breeze, some felt like being crushed by the weight of the world. I have never been so skilled even with a lifetime of practice behind me.

The Kinemancy tutors pulled Josef aside at the end of our practice. The rest of us were dismissed. I would have been wise to go about my business, maybe find some food or continue my book studies, maybe even find a quiet space for some much-needed sleep. We were worked hard at the academy, even at eight years old I was rarely afforded more than five hours sleep a day. But I didn't like to leave without Josef. My curiosity may also have had something to do with it. I wanted to know what was being said to him. I wanted to creep closer and listen.

There have been a few times in my life when I wish I was attuned to Vibromancy. With it, a Sourcerer can eavesdrop from a mile away or make sounds carry, to appear as though they have come from somewhere else. It is even possible to create a blanket of silence over an area, or amplify a whisper to a roar. But Vibromancy is not an attunement I can boast of, and even those who do often find themselves going deaf or being driven mad by the noises they work with. Poor Barrow Laney was one of those and I wouldn't wish what happened to that poor sod on anyone. So, I waited while Josef argued, listening to the sharp words, watching the thrown gestures.

When finally, Josef was dismissed he was furious. An angry ten-year-old may look comical to an adult, but to an eight-year-old, Josef looked terrifying. I had never seen my best friend so disgruntled. He stormed past me and I followed along, hurrying to catch up with his longer strides. I remember following in silence for a while, not wanting to anger him further, but eventually my curiosity won out.

The tutors had told Josef he was ready to advance past our basic training. They wanted him to move up a class, to train alongside older students. Josef's argument was that he refused to leave me behind, and the tutors had told him I was holding him back. They ordered him into the higher class. He still didn't go. Josef continued to attend the same class as myself and eventually the tutors relented. He may never have had my drive to be stronger, but Josef more than made up for it with a stubborn streak wider than Aranaen gulf.

The thing I remember most is how fucking guilty I felt over the whole thing. As if it was somehow my fault. That the tutors believed I was holding my best friend back from greatness, was a revelation that stuck with me for many years. Maybe it was his friendship with me that quashed his drive to be better. Maybe Josef could have been the Sourcerer the tutors wanted him to be. The Sourcerer the Orran empire needed him to be. Or maybe he just didn't have the fight in him to excel. All he really wanted was a quiet life away from hardship. But that seemed to be the one thing life refused to hand him.

By the time I returned to my little home cavern my mind was, for lack of any better term, blurry. Between the exhaustion, the pain, and the rumbling pit that my stomach had become, I was a sorry state as I limped in, still clutching at my ribs. I hadn't found time to wash Prig's blood off my right hand, and my cuts and scrapes were scabbed over with blood and grime. Despite it all, I was not defeated. The overseer might have crushed my hopes of rescue, but Tamura had given me a far greater hope in return. The possibility of escape.

Most of my team were asleep, Hardt included, but Isen was missing. Josef watched me enter and tried to stand, before collapsing back against the far wall, clutching at his chest. I wondered if he, too, had cracked a rib. The pain certainly made standing difficult.

I limped onward and Josef struggled to his feet, this time without collapsing. His wounds looked like they'd been tended to; Hardt's work, I didn't doubt. That man should have been a surgeon, but men as big as Hardt are always taught to fight before they are taught to heal. I think he has his father to thank for both skills, not that Hardt would ever thank his father for anything.

As I drew close, Josef lurched forward and wrapped his arms around me. I'm not sure which of us that embrace hurt more. Two peas in a pod of agony. Despite the pain I leaned into him, and for the first time in so long, I relaxed a little. Josef always had a way of calming me, making me feel loved and protected. I hope I provided the same for him. Before I could stop myself, a sob broke free and suddenly I was crying into his shoulder. My legs finally gave out and we sank down to the floor together.

Time is a strange thing, even master Chronomancers agree on that. It flows ever forward, and though its rate never truly changes, our perception of it can make a second last an hour, or a day pass in the blink of an eye. I don't know how long I spent collapsed against Josef, only that I was brought out of that strange trance by Isen.

Hardt was awake, a bowl of water in hand, and Isen had a small clay pot. It was a healing balm made from a moss that grew deep underground. Those who fought in the arena were given a single pot after each fight, as long as they survived the fight. And Isen was giving the balm to me. I'm not so proud I didn't take it, and it's probably a good job that I did. My injuries were quite severe and not a one of them had been looked at.

Isen never spoke of his outburst earlier that day. He'd called me a stupid little girl and at the time he meant it. But as quick as Isen could be to anger, he was just as quick to forget, especially when Hardt was there to talk some sense into him. Or knock some sense into him, when the talking failed. I think I envied him for that. I've never been able to forget my anger, only feed the flames until they have burned everything else away and left me too charred and raw to care anymore. Perhaps if I had been a bit more like Isen I would have more friends and fewer enemies. But I am who I am and fuck trying to pretend otherwise.

"You're wheezing pretty bad," Hardt said, even as Josef pulled away from me and took the bowl of water.

I nodded. "Hurts to breathe."

"Sounds like both of you cracked a rib," Hardt said.

"Prig was kind enough to crack it for me," I said with a grin at them, despite the left side of my face being swollen and ablaze with agony. "He won't be doing that again, the arsehole."

"Which side?" Josef dipped a wad of cloth into the water and started wiping at the gash on my face. The cloth came away brown and red. I think perhaps if I'd had the wound seen to earlier, it wouldn't have left such an obvious scar. Now, it's a jagged line of puckered flesh running from the corner of my mouth, almost to my ear. A reminder of the hell that forged me into who I am. I wear it with a savage pride. That scar is a part of me, a symbol of what I went through. It shows that no fucker can break me no matter how hard they try.

"Right side," I said.

Josef chuckled and winced, tapping his left side.

Hardt shook his head. "The sludge-licker gave you matching injuries," he said. "How kind. Lift your top up. I'll need to wrap it."

It hurt a lot to lift my rags up, but I managed, stopping at my breasts. It would have been easier just to remove my filth-encrusted shirt, I know, but I didn't want Isen to see my breasts, not while they were coated in dust, and sweat, and grime. I turned red at the thought, no matter how fucking foolish that was. No one seemed to notice, or maybe they were just too polite to say anything. Hardt set about wrapping bandages around my chest and I closed my eyes against the pain.

Josef and Hardt continued to tend to my injuries while Isen paced. The others in the cavern did their best not to watch, but I was nearly half-naked, and some of them probably hadn't seen tits in years.

"You stabbed him in the neck," Isen said as he paced. "That won't stop Prig. It'll probably just make him worse. He'll fucking kill you, Eska."

"I made a deal with Deko," I said, my voice croaking out between swollen lips. "Our fat fuck of a foreman won't touch me, so long as I'm useful."

"Useful doing what?" There was an edge to Josef's voice.

"Nothing like that." I punched at his arm but I lacked the energy and missed. "Information about..." Hardt and Isen were watching, listening. They still didn't know I was a Sourcerer, and I found I no longer cared. "About any Other World creatures they find down here."

"You told him?" Josef asked. I was acutely aware that he was still cleaning out an open wound on my face.

144

"He already fucking knew," I said with a sigh.

"Knew what?" Isen asked.

Keeping secrets is tiring work and I was already exhausted. Deko and his captains knew. Prig knew. I no longer saw any reason to hide it, especially not from my allies.

"We're not just soldiers," I said, ignoring Josef's attempt to silence me. "We are... were Sourcerers for the Orran empire."

"Goat-shit," Isen swore. "Guess I owe you my next heel of bread." Hardt just grinned.

"You knew?" I felt relieved at telling them. Secrets aren't just tiring, they weigh heavily on a person's soul. I might have had no secrets from Josef, but together we held so many, I was amazed we didn't sink into the earth. Maybe we had. Maybe that is what the Pit was, a place for those with too many secrets.

"I suspected." Hardt said as he finished wrapping my ribs and took the balm from Isen. "Soldiers don't get sent to the Pit. Takes a real crime to end up here."

"You made a deal with a Djinn." There was a sullenness to Josef's voice, one I hadn't heard since the time I almost got us both killed back at the academy.

"Deko isn't that bad," Isen argued. "As long as you stay on his good side and don't tilt the cart. It's his captains you want to watch out for."

I rubbed at my neck. My voice was still hoarse and the flesh was bruised from where Horralain had strangled me. I wanted to pay the bastard back for that. Unfortunately, that was only the first time the giant slug-sniffer almost killed me.

145

"I heard about that," Hardt said, peeling my hand away from my neck to look at the bruising. By the way he sucked at his teeth I guessed it didn't look good. "Everyone's talking about it. How a lone scab, a young woman, walked into the middle of the Hill and walked out again. I knew it would be you. No one else would have the balls."

I have always found it strange that people equate having testicles with courage. Threatening a man's balls is often the fastest way to make him cower.

"It was the only choice I had left," I said, wincing as Hardt rubbed the balm on my cheek. It is fairly hard to talk when your face is on fire, and mine certainly felt like it was bloody-well burning at the time. "I had to get that arse-sucking fuck, Prig, off my back somehow."

"You should have come to me," Josef said. "We could have figured something else out. Together. Some way that doesn't put you in Deko's eyesight."

I wanted to argue, to tell Josef that together or apart, Deko was the only choice I had. Unfortunately, Hardt chose that moment to push at the wound on my face, trying to force the parted skin closer together. I clenched my jaw and a whine squeezed out from between my swollen lips.

"This is going to hurt," Hardt said.

My eyes were screwed shut against the pain already and I could feel tears welling again. Having angry flesh stitched closed while awake is a precious sort of agony. I'd like to say I endured it with a fierce stoicism, I certainly remember it that way. I have been reliably informed by Hardt that my memory is shit. Apparently, I threatened to kill his entire family. And when he told me Isen was the

146

only family he had left, I threatened to give him a puppy, wait until he'd formed a connection, then fucking drown it. I think I prefer my own recollection.

When it was done, Hardt handed me a fresh bowl of water and told me to drink. I didn't realise just how thirsty I was until I started, and then he had to stop me from draining the bowl in one go. Apparently, it's important to sip, though I struggled to find the patience. It has never been one of my virtues. I'm much more of a *wade in and deal with whatever consequences dare to rear their head* type of person.

As soon as I was feeling up to it, I pulled Josef further into the cavern with me. Hardt and Isen shared a look, then went back to their own pallets. We all knew it would only be a matter of a few hours before Prig arrived to order us to dig our day away again. No one ever asked me *why* I stabbed Prig. I have thought about it many times over the years. It was not his treatment of Isen or even the scar he gave me. It was for what he did to Josef. I would have stabbed a hundred Prigs a hundred times, and taken the beatings that followed, to protect Josef. I honestly believed he would do the same for me. I have been wrong many times in my life.

"I think I have a way out of here," I lowered my voice so no one else in the cavern could hear, but I couldn't hide the excitement. Together there was nothing Josef and I couldn't do.

"The overseer made his offer?" Josef asked.

"No," I said. "Well, yes. But..." I paused. It took a moment for Josef's words to really sink in, and when they did they brought denial with them. I couldn't believe it.

Didn't want to believe it. Hope is an insidious disease, and denial is one of the symptoms. I saw an eager look on his face. I saw hope. The same hope I had held for rescue before the overseer crushed it. "How did you know about that?"

"Because he offered it to me as well," Josef said.

"You turned him down?"

Josef shook his head. "He didn't want me alone," he said. "He told me either we both agreed or we both stayed here. That you had to choose to be free. That you had to..."

"To break?" I spat. Just like a horse, you had to break its spirit before it could be ridden. I had to have my spirit broken before I could be set free. Again, I will point out the overseer knew his business. If he had used Josef against me, if I had known my friend had given up, it would only have galvanised my resistance. It did.

"But it doesn't matter now," Josef said. "We're getting out." I could hear the happiness in his voice, the relief. The almost hysterical hope. Then I crushed it just as the overseer had done to me.

"I turned the fucker down, Josef." My words settled between us like a death knell.

There are times in my life where I have looked upon those I love, searched their faces for the person I know, and realised I didn't recognise them at all. That was the way Josef looked at me then, as though he still saw me as the young girl I had been when we arrived at the Orran Academy, and only at that moment, was he realising I had changed. That young girl was dead, murdered the moment Josef betrayed me and forced me to surrender. Murdered by him! I was now someone else. I was what the Pit had

148

made me, or was making me into. It hadn't finished yet. There was yet more it could do to me. More it could take from me.

"Why?" There was hurt in his voice.

"The cost was too high, Josef," I said. "We can't serve the Terrelans."

"Why not?"

"Because we're fucking Orrans," I hissed at him.

Josef laughed then, a harsh sound that quickly turned to pain as he clutched at his ribs. "There are no Orrans anymore, Eska. We're all Terrelans now."

"I'm fucking-well not."

"Yes, you are," he snapped. "Even if the Orran Emperor was still alive..."

"You knew?" I couldn't fathom how Josef had known of the emperor's death and not told me. How had he hidden something so important from me? Why had he kept it a secret? But the truth was obvious. Because the overseer had told him to. He wanted to save that bit of information to break me when I was at my lowest. And Josef had fucking helped him.

Josef paused. I watched him close his eyes and clench his jaw. I think this was the angriest I had ever seen him, even more than when the bitch-whore put a hole in my side. I pulled back from that anger. I was scared. It was a side of Josef I had so rarely seen before.

"It doesn't matter," he said eventually, his voice sharp. "Even if he were still alive, or any of the Orrans. Their empire is gone. It's all the Terrelan Empire now. And what did we ever owe the Orrans anyway? They kidnapped us from our families. Put us through... It was torture. What we went through at the academy was torture, Eska. Then, when they decided it was time, they made us kill for them."

I saw the anger on Josef's face fade away, and what it left behind was even worse. Guilt. I never really thought about the men and women we killed in battle. It was war. People died on both sides and no fucker emerged from the slaughter clean. I also hadn't realised how heavily it weighed on Josef. Unfortunately for us both, I was angry and I have never made the wisest of choices while angry.

"You knew. And you didn't tell me." There was scorn in my voice. I felt betrayed, and with good reason. I still don't know if Josef even realised it, but he had betrayed me again. Just as he had on the tower of Fort Vernan. Just thinking about it makes me angry all over again. There're so many years between then and now. So many miles travelled, so many friendships made and broken. So many loved ones lost. I find I still cannot forgive him.

"That's not really the point, Eska..." he started.

"How long have you been whispering the overseer's words in my ear, Josef?" I couldn't keep the anger from my voice. Nor did I care to. "How fucking long have you been telling him how to get to me?"

"Don't you want to get out of here, Eska?" Josef asked, tears in his eyes. "What does it matter who we're working for? At least the Terrelans won't be making us murder people."

It took some effort, and the help of the cavern wall, to pull myself back to my feet. Every part of my body protested at the movement, and I could see myself trembling, though whether that was from the exhaustion or the rage, I couldn't tell. Josef just stared up at me, his dark brown eyes wide and pleading. That look almost stopped me. Almost. I was so close to collapsing and curling up next to him. Maybe if I had forgotten my anger just for that night, it wouldn't have festered within me. Maybe I wouldn't have widened the rift forming between us. But that isn't me. I never let things go.

"You. Betrayed. Me." I bit off each word, turning each one into a damning insult. Then I turned and limped out of the cavern. No one followed me.

I found Tamura right where I'd left him, staring up at the breeze gusting from a crack in the rock. He nodded to me as I staggered into the tunnel, and just watched as I collapsed against a nearby wall. I think he was still watching me as I closed my eyes and finally let the darkness claim me.

That was the first time in years I hadn't slept with Josef curled up next to me. And it was the first time since we met, so many years ago, that one of us had chosen not to sleep next to the other. It wasn't until the next day that I realised I hadn't told him about my hope of escape.

CHAPTER 15

When I woke, Tamura was gone. I found myself covered with a patchy blanket. It's a strange sensation, waking up in total darkness. We spend so much of our lives in the light that when it is taken away, we lose all semblance of time. I might have been asleep for a few hours, or a week. All I really knew is that I was still tired. Well, that and I ached all over and my stomach felt like a portal to the Other World trying to devour me from the inside.

I like to think I'm quick to rise, even in my advancing years, but I was not that day. I struggled to stretch out my legs and arms, wincing at the tightness in the muscles. My rib was a special kind of pain and it made every movement feel like it was cracking all over again. After a while, I risked touching my cheek and found it painful and swollen, but it did not burn with new pain at the slightest touch. For that I am grateful. An ugly scar marring my face is one thing, but I imagine it would have been far worse had infection settled in.

I fumbled my way out of the tunnel, leaning against the wall and letting my memory guide me. I tripped a few times, and each time I worried that I might not be able to stand again, such was the effort it was costing me. There was light at the end of the tunnel, a lantern lit and hanging from a wall of the corridor. There were no other scabs about, the area long since abandoned for tunnels further below. I was glad of that.

Like an old hound set in its ways I found myself heading towards my team's tunnel, soon realizing I had no idea what time it was. No idea if our shift had started or not. I arrived to find the tunnel deserted. Instead of turning away, I moved further in. A lantern hanging from the wall bounced light off something wet near the end. Something dark and shiny. I knew it was blood. I knew it! But I had to see it. No matter how much my gut twisted and I wanted to turn and run, I had to see it. I had to know what my defiance had cost. And who had paid the price.

I don't know how long I spent staring down at the pool of blood on the tunnel floor. It was fresh. Still wet. It hadn't been there the day before. The day I stood up to Prig. The day I put a blade in his fat fucking neck. I didn't know whose blood it was, but I knew whose fault it was. I had done this, and it turned all my little victories the day before to ash. Prig could no longer take his anger out on me, but Deko's protection didn't extend far. Just like any bully when robbed of one victim, he took his frustration out on another. There is no give in a bully like Prig, no quit, no words you can say that will reveal some hidden good within them. He was a hateful, spiteful waste of shit, and that was all he was. All he would ever be. It's easy to believe that everyone can be redeemed if only given a chance. It's shit. There are people in this world who are beyond redemption, beyond compassion, and beyond fucking reason. I had fought my way free of Prig, and the bastard had murdered someone to make himself feel better, even if only for a moment. People like that don't even deserve a chance to redeem themselves. Bastards like Prig only deserve death, preferably by the most painful fucking method possible.

I wondered if the blood was Hardt's or Isen's. Which of my two friends were dead? There was no surviving losing that much blood. A new tightness formed in my chest, coiling its way around my heart. One of them was dead and it was my fault. Prig might have wielded the weapon, but I pushed him into it. A traitorous part of me hoped it wasn't Isen, and I hated that part. To wish it wasn't one, was to hope that it was the other. An impossible situation, an impossible choice, but of course my foolish young heart lurched towards the brother I was attracted to.

There was a pick nearby, a length of wood with a metal spike fixed to the end. There was blood on the pick, dried into a rusty-brown smear. I wasn't thinking clearly. It was against the rules to steal tools from a tunnel. But I no longer cared. I grabbed hold of the pick and limped from the tunnel, dragging its point along the floor behind me.

I passed a scab on the way out, an older woman grey of hair and missing most of her teeth. She didn't even seem to notice I was carrying a pick. She stared at me with a smile and nodded as I passed. I didn't know it then, but I was now infamous down in the Pit. The tale of how I walked into the Hill and stood up to Deko was spreading like a plague. No matter how untrue it might be, it was spreading. Rumours are like water spilt onto a flat surface. The more they spread, the bigger they get, and the thinner they become. Before long the other scabs were talking about my epic fight with Horralain and how I knocked him down to get to Deko. I did better in the rumours of that fight than

I did with both our subsequent encounters. Despite it all, I can't hate Horralain. I have too much respect for the evil fucker.

After appropriating a lantern from a wall, I made my way back to the crack. Tamura was still nowhere to be seen. I placed both the pick and the lantern at the far end of the tunnel, blew out the lantern and covered them both with Tamura's blanket. After that, I groped my way from the tunnel and set my feet towards the main cavern. I had no idea if it was feeding time or not, but there would be food for the winning over dice, chips, or cards, and I needed to eat. My stomach was a churning voice of aches and pain.

Feeding time was almost over at the Trough. I heard the whispers as I approached and saw faces turn my way. At the time, I wondered how beaten up I looked. I wondered how it could be any worse than the previous day. But I didn't care. All the staring from all the scabs in the world wouldn't have kept me from my meagre rations of bread and gruel. My stomach rumbled and clenched at the thought of food and I limped forward, not even bothering to wonder why the scant crowd was parting before me.

The captain serving food to the scabs more than made up for my lack of interest in the attitude of the others. He looked at me in disgust, one eyebrow raised and a small smile tugging at his lips. I still didn't care. I reached up, accepted my food, and turned toward the tables.

Isen was standing in front of me, staring at me. In that moment I forgot everything, no longer caring we were standing in line at the Trough or even that every scab in the cavern was watching. I stepped forward and put my arms around him, leaning my head against his chest and holding him tight.

I honestly can't recall which of us pulled away from that embrace, only that I felt Isen begin to stiffen against my hip and then we were apart. He flushed red, and then so did I. I tried to hide my embarrassment by walking past him, as much to get away from the stares and whispers than anything else.

My mouth was already full of stale bread as I sat down at a table across from Hardt. My happiness at seeing both brothers alive was not diminished by the need to devour my rations, but hunger can put even the most powerful of emotions at the back of the mind, and once I had food in front of me I found I couldn't stop. It did not take long to demolish the bread and scoop every last drop of gruel into my mouth. I was still hungry. Always hungry.

The brothers just watched me as I ate. I think Isen was still embarrassed from our embrace. Hardt was clearly impressed with how quickly I could eat when I really wanted to.

"We were worried you might be... gone," Hardt said as I washed down the gruel with a cup of water.

"Dead?" I asked with a shake of my head. "I thought you..." I looked from Hardt to Isen and felt a fresh wave of relief wash over me. Guilt followed quickly, as it usually does. Someone had died in our tunnel. Someone had paid my price. "What happened in our tunnel?"

"You saw the blood?" Hardt asked. I nodded, not willing to tell anyone about the pick just yet.

Try as I might, I can't remember the man's name. Sometimes I think I feel guiltier over that than his death. He died in my place, a vent for Prig's impotent frustration, and I can't even remember his name, nor what he looked like. I can't remember a thing about him other than the fact that Prig, in a fit of rage at my defiance, put the pick through the man's back. Hardt told me he took a while to die, bleeding out on the tunnel floor. Prig made the others work on, despite the man dying at their feet. I honestly can't decide if that death is on my conscience or Prig's. Actually, I don't think Prig ever had a conscience so I suppose I'll shoulder that burden as well. Just one more skull paving the road behind me. I sometimes wonder if anyone in the history of Orran or Terrelan has ever been responsible for half as much death as I am.

There was grief etched plain on the lines of Hardt's face. As sociable as the big man was, he knew everyone on our team and considered them comrades, or friends. It was clear he was hurting, though I believe he placed the blame for the death solely at the feet of Prig. Hardt has always found excuses to not blame me. Sometimes I think he still views me as an innocent little girl, but I left innocence behind long before my time in the Pit.

"Josef was distraught," Isen said, though he wasn't looking at me. I think maybe it was an issue of age that made him so embarrassed. I was just fifteen, barely old enough to call myself a woman. Isen was older. Despite that, there was something between us. I longed to see him naked, to feel his arms around me, run my hands over his skin. Attraction is a dangerous thing for a young girl.

"I don't care," I lied. I just wished I didn't care. I'm very good at holding grudges, though I always found it so hard to stay angry with Josef.

"When he woke and you weren't there, he ran off to look for you," Isen said relentless.

"Let's hope he found a hole to fall into," I said. I can be quite relentless myself when I want. And also a massive bitch.

"I don't know what you two said to each other last night," Isen said. "You might have protection from Prig, but Josef isn't protected from Lurgo, and that pig-tickler is a bastard of a foreman, too." There was true concern in his voice.

"Has he ever killed a scab?" I asked.

"No," Hardt said, his voice a low rumble. "Just likes to beat on them with that little club of his."

"Well, maybe Josef deserves a beating or two. I've got more important things to discuss with you." I lowered my voice. There were plenty of other scabs nearby, some even looking our way, and I didn't want them overhearing. "What if I had a way out of here?"

It has been my experience that there are two ways to get a man's attention. The first is to show them tits, and the second is to show them coins. Down in the Pit, things were a little different. Food was better than any amount of coin, and talk of freedom demanded attention, and the brothers already knew to take me seriously.

"No one has ever escaped the Pit," Isen said. "Everyone knows that. Heard it often enough, even when we were at sea. The other sailors used to say it as a sort of warning to us, uh, gentlemen of fortune."

Hardt nodded. "Deko and his thugs run this place, and even they know they'll never see sunlight again. The Terrelan army puts people down here to forget about them."

I grinned at them both, though it quickly turned to a wince as the wound on my cheek gave a twinge. "They put Josef and I down here to show us the error of our ways. The overseer has spent the last..." I tried to remember how long I'd been underground. Too fucking long. "Months trying to turn us."

"Well, that's good for you." Isen sounded less than pleased. "I don't think he'd be willing to let us tag along."

"I turned him down," I said. "Repeatedly. Seems yesterday he took the hint. That's why I needed Deko's protection from Prig. The overseer has given up on me."

"You have another way out?" Hardt asked.

I explained it to them. I told them about the crack, and Tamura, and the wind gusting in from above. I expected them to jump at the opportunity, to rush off and help me. Instead they looked sceptical.

"Fourteen levels above," Isen said once I had finished. "Fourteen levels of rock. That's a lot of fucking rock."

"But there's a crack..." My voice was a quiet hiss.

"A crack..." Hardt repeated. "I won't fit through a crack. You won't even fit through a crack, and you're tiny."

"So, we widen it," I said.

"With what?" Hardt sounded like he was entertaining the foolish whims of a child and I hated him for it.

I glanced around to make certain no one else was close enough to hear. "I stole a pick. We could steal more."

"And then what?" Isen asked.

"We dig," I said, incredulous the brothers were still not getting it. "Widen the fucking crack so we can fit through."

The younger brother let out an exasperated sigh. "I spend all day digging..."

"So, you'll be real fucking good at it," I hissed.

Hardt was shaking his head again. "Even if we did. It could take years."

I shrugged, and then clutched at my rib as a twinge of pain lanced through me. "Do you have something better to do with your time? Maybe another plan that will get us out?"

They were running out of arguments.

"Tamura is crazy as a two-headed bat." Isen's last ditch attempt to naysay me.

"I'm sure people said that about a scab who walked into the middle of the Hill all alone." I paused and tried out another painful smile. "I hear she came out of it alright."

The brothers shared a look and Isen shrugged. I soon came to realise that Isen almost always deferred to Hardt's judgement. It was obvious the older of the two was in charge.

"Freedom is rarely free," Hardt said. "I guess we could put in a bit of work to earn it. Wouldn't mind sleeping in a real bed again."

"A pint of ale would be nice," Isen agreed.

"A meal that isn't half blue and furry."

"Bury my face in a pair of tits." Isen froze and looked at me for the first time since we hugged back at the Trough. "Sorry."

I'd like to say the thought of Isen face deep in a pair of breasts didn't bother me. He'd certainly never have managed it with mine. However, I felt a strange pang of jealousy over the idea. I covered it with false indifference.

"Don't apologise. I'm sure a nice big pair would make for a comfortable pillow." There was more of an edge to my voice than I intended and the silence that fell across us was awkward and uncomfortable. It was a fucking stupid thing to say. Luckily, Hardt was there to break the tension.

"The least we can do is go and take a look," he said. "What about Josef?"

"I'll tell him about it next time I see him."

I didn't.

CHAPTER 16

Time's slow advance waged on. I didn't know it at the time, but the new year rolled around while we were underground. Year six hundred and twelve on the Orran calendar, not that the Orran calendar existed anymore. The year of the Blind Hammer Crab. I have no idea who named the years on our calendar, but they were certainly inventive. A hammer crab is a wonderful little beasty able to pulverise bones with a single punch of its claws. I can only imagine a blind hammer crab would be a true menace for all its underwater brethren.

Maybe I should have noticed a change in the temperature, the weather growing colder as the seasons moved onward, but deep down in the Pit, even the most severe changes were muted. You might think the deeper underground you dig, the colder it gets, away from the warmth of the sun. It's quite the opposite. In the bowels of the Pit was where it was warmest. Some of the deeper tunnels even filled with steam from time to time. Rather than feel the chill of winter, it was often uncomfortably warm and cloying down there.

For two weeks Isen, Hardt, myself, and Tamura all worked at the crack. We took it in turns, in groups of two. One person watching the intersection while the other hacked away to increase the size of the crack. I was always watching the intersection. I hated making the others do all the hard work, but I could barely lift the pick with my rib still healing, let alone swing it at something overhead. It galled me to feel so fucking useless, but I had to leave the labour to the men this time.

There was a strange tension between Tamura and the brothers. It went deeper than their inability to understand most of what he said. I was starting to get a grip of his madness, and even I found myself lost half of the time. But Hardt didn't entirely trust Tamura, and if Hardt didn't trust the old man, neither did Isen. I was not very good at fostering trust between them and at the time, I didn't care. As long as they continued to work together, as long as the digging was done, they could outright hate each other and I'd be happy enough.

For two weeks neither Josef or I had spoken one word to each other. We still slept in the same little cavern, still saw each other every day, but I couldn't swallow the betrayal, or my anger. I think Josef kept his peace because he was frustrated with me. Maybe he saw *my* actions as a betrayal. He had his hopes of getting out of the Pit and I dashed them by refusing to dance to the overseer's sadistic, bloody tune. Josef should have known me well enough to know I would never have worked for the overseer. Defiance has always been written into my very nature. Nothing brings it out of me quite like authority.

I took to sleeping with Hardt instead. I could have slept alone. Looking back, I think we'd all have been better off if I had started sleeping alone. But I was so used to sleeping curled up with someone else, sharing warmth, and feeling safe with someone I trusted at my back. In my entire life I had never slept alone and doing so just felt strange. I

163

was also quite aware that it twisted whatever wound Josef believed I had given to him, and I was more than happy to do just that. I admit, his betrayal had made me quite bitter and I have always been one to lash out, rather than capitulate. I think it might have made Isen a little jealous too and that was something else I enjoyed. I may have been naive in many ways, but I saw the way the younger brother looked at me. I wonder if he saw the way I looked at him. Or, more often, the way I didn't look at him.

There is very little in this world as cruel as children on the cusp of adulthood and girls are usually worse than boys. At the time, I thought myself clever, manipulating other's feelings to my own ends. But after many long years, some of which were spent with children, I look back with a different perspective and realise that I was a bitch.

My fame amongst the other scabs continued to grow and I did very little to stop it. I even helped it along a couple of times by planting new stories once the others had gotten stale. I made a point of stating quite loudly that no one had seen the overseer since our last appointment. Before long the scabs were spreading my rumour for me. Some went so far as to suggest I killed him and was hiding out down in the Pit. That rumour eventually blossomed into one about my stay in the Pit being my choice. That I had broken through the garrison and was hiding from the Terrelan military. The scabs had little love for the military, despite mostly consisting of Terrelans, and at least two young men congratulated me on my decision to *fight the power*. I wonder if those two men were still down in the Pit when I eventually returned. I probably murdered them.

164

We still had to dig each day in our little tunnel, ever under the watchful eyes of Prig. He reigned in the violence, at least where I was concerned, and no others died in my place. Both Isen and Hardt suffered regular beatings and even the occasional lash, but they made me promise not to get involved and that was one promise I kept, though it pained me to do so. I always found it so strange when Prig set to beating Hardt. The bigger man never fought back, just covered up his head and let the fat arsehole punch away. Some days I wondered if it even hurt Hardt or if he just pretended to be in pain to appease our foreman. I have no doubt he could have twisted Prig's shit-filled head from his fat fucking neck, but he never did.

I was down in the Trough when Deko finally found a use for me. I took to gambling daily, playing at dice and chips mostly, as I found the card games they played to be far too random for my liking. I was better at games of strategy, where I could outplay the opponent rather than the game. I lost far more than I won, especially early on, and went hungry more times than I cared to count. The only stakes I had to put up where the food I was given from the Trough. I fared better once I had the measure of the opponent, once I understood why they played and what they were willing to bet and bet on. Gambling is such a strange vice. We so often bet things we need for things we can so happily do without. But then it isn't really about the stakes, it's about the thrill.

On this day, the other scabs hushed around me and I knew something was amiss. For a moment I thought I was about to be attacked, blind-sided while sitting at a table. No matter who it was, it would be a short fight face to face, even shorter if they jumped me while I wasn't looking. My strength lay in the allies I chose and the reputation I built for myself, not in the strength of arms. I think that was when I made the decision to change that. I realised I couldn't always rely on others to help me. Nor would I always be able to talk my way out of a situation. I needed to know how to fight.

"Time to make yourself useful, scab." I craned my neck to see Poppy standing behind me. There was a severe look on her pitted face and her scarred arms were crossed as she stared down at me. My audience drifted away from the table, deciding to put some distance between themselves and one of Deko's most brutal captains.

I thought about finishing my game, telling Poppy to wait. But I was not so stupid as to believe I'd get away with it. I picked my stakes from the table and stood.

"You forfeit the game, you forfeit your stake." My opponent was a wrinkled old man grey in hair and always grinning. I liked the old bastard, even if I can't remember his name.

I glanced down at my stake. A small bag of snuff. Worthless to me apart from the price others put upon it. Worthless, but mine. I pocketed it and fixed the man with a stare.

"You're welcome to try to take it from me," I said. "Or you can try to win it again later. Count yourself bloody lucky. You were about to lose." Another lie on my part. I was one turn away from giving away the last bloody thing I owned to that shrewd old man. The thing about bluffing is you need to be able to understand when the bluff has failed. You need to know when to get out and admit defeat.

Perhaps you have noticed, I am not good at admitting defeat. I really shouldn't be allowed to bluff.

The old man laughed as I turned and waved for Poppy to lead the way. "Later then," he called after me. I was on good terms with most of the scabs by then. If they'd known what I had in mind for them, things would have been quite different.

Poppy was ever the quiet one of Deko's captains, even more so than Horralain, who communicated mainly in grunts. I knew a little about her, rumours of her past, whispered by the scabs when she walked by. All were bloody, and all painted Poppy in a grim light. But rumours were shit as often as not, I should know, I started enough of them. Still, I always wondered where she got all of her scars. History was written plain on her skin in the ridges and discoloured flesh. She didn't lead me to the Hill, though we passed by it. It was hard to see through the press of bodies, but I didn't see Deko presiding over his empire.

We stopped at one of the lifts where Prig's friend waited. He leered as we approached but stepped to the mechanism all the same. I hated the way that fucker stared at me, but I refused to let it show. I had protection from Prig, and that extended to the other foremen as well, but I was still a scab. I imagined waiting until he raised the lift and then pushing him down the hole, listening to his screams as he fell and waiting for the fleshy thud as he hit the bottom. I imagined myself as being quite triumphant. I still didn't know how hard it is to look a person in the eyes as you kill them. These days, I don't even blink. That probably says a lot about my eventual reign as queen.

"Down." Poppy's voice never really matched her grim visage. She looked a right bloody horror, but her voice was sweet as honey.

"How far?" asked Prig's friend.

"All the way," said Poppy.

I felt a nervous flutter in my stomach. I had never been to the bottom of the Pit before. Back then, I didn't even really know how many levels there were. The furthest I had been was the twenty-sixth level where the arena was located, but that was only halfway to the bottom of the Pit.

Just four days before Deko first put me to work, I went to see Isen fight. I had thought it would be a bare-knuckle bout of pugilism with the combatants taking turns to thump at each other. I was quite wrong on that. I watched on with Hardt as Isen, bare chested with wiry muscles straining, clashed with his opponent. There was a brief exchange of blows and then Isen threw the other man to the floor and leapt on him, wrapping his legs around the midsection and pushing the man's arms away from his head as he rained down blow after blow, his knuckles painted red. Isen never killed his opponents, and he left the man bleeding on the ground.

Hardt had said it was a clean win. It looked messy to me. Both men scrabbling on the floor, wrestling for dominance over the other. Since then, I have been in a few fights of my own and I have never won any as cleanly as Isen did that match.

I noticed Poppy was watching me as the lift ground its way down. Her eyes were bright despite the gloom and she had a slight smile on her face. She did not look away when I noticed. It was the same way Prig's friend looked at me. I have never been one to shy away from a staring contest, and went to it with a passion, meeting her hungry stare with a cold one all of my own. Most people couldn't weather too long under the scrutiny of my pale eyes, but Poppy managed it. Her smile deepened. I will admit that was one of the few contests I have ever lost. I looked away, strangely embarrassed and unsure why. Some people might have laughed, gloated at the little victory. But Poppy said nothing. Even when the lift bumped to a halt at the very bottom of the Pit, she said nothing.

I sometimes wonder if Poppy saw something in me even then that I didn't. Perhaps I wasn't ready to see it.

Even down at the bottom of the Pit I could hear digging. That constant bloody echoing tap of metal on stone floated along the stale air, reassuring and maddening both at the same time. I didn't know it then, but down at the bottom was where the real digging took place. Further up was where us scabs worked our life away and that was the face Deko showed to his Terrelan masters. But down in the belly of the beast, his best workers, craftsmen and artisans, worked at turning the Pit into a palace sunk deep underground. The scabs that worked on Deko's palace were treated far better than those of us that toiled above, but they weren't allowed to mingle with us. Deko wasn't willing to risk word of his endeavour leaking out. Part of me is still amazed he let me return above, knowing what I did. But then I wasn't just any other worker. I was useful.

We found Deko along with Horralain waiting at the mouth of a cavern that opened out into an inky darkness. Deko watched me approach with a smile that made my

169

skin crawl and I felt my hatred of him stoked hot. He might have been my protection, but I hated that he owned me.

"It's about time my little Sourcerer arrived," he said with a sneer. "I finally have something for you to do. A way to earn your fucking keep." Deko liked to do that, remind me that my protection was entirely dependent upon him. Bastard! He liked to remind everyone just what they owed him. I have always hated him for that. I hated myself almost as much, when the time came for me to copy his tactics.

"What happened to your last Impomancy expert?" I asked, acutely aware that I was surrounded by Deko and six of his captains. I was the only scab nearby, and quite a bit smaller than all of them. I was vulnerable and afraid, and determined to survive whatever they were about to throw at me. After hatching my plan to escape, I found I no longer harboured any suicidal thoughts. I wanted to live again. I wanted to live, and I wanted to escape, and I wanted to rub those victories in the faces of every fucker who had tried to keep me from them.

"He mistook a ghoul for a ghast." Deko grinned at me. "But you know the difference, right?"

I let out a dramatic sigh and rolled my eyes before answering. "One is a mostly harmless incorporeal horror that feeds off fear and can do little more than scare us. The other is a monster of sharp teeth, razor claws, and a lust for dead flesh. Not easily mistaken. Your last expert was a fucking idiot."

Deko shrugged and laughed. Most of the others joined in but both Poppy and Horralain remained silent. "He's a dead idiot now," Deko said. "Let's hope you don't repeat his mistakes. I like you, girl. Poppy does too. I hope you don't die in there."

A hooded lantern was pushed into one hand and then Horralain gave me a hefty shove that sent me stumbling into the dark cavern. My heart raced, trying to beat its way out of my chest and I turned to find Horralain's giant body almost blocking the entrance.

"Don't even think of coming back until you've figured out what the fuck it is." Deko's voice drifted around his captain and was followed by a nasty laugh.

I turned back to the dark cavern and tried to calm myself. That was when I realised the laugh wasn't coming from Deko or his captains. It was coming from the cavern.

CHAPTER 17

I was twelve when the academy started training me in the school of Impomancy. Even so I think I was too damned young for the horrors I faced. I'm not sure there's ever a good time to learn those arts. The Other World is a dark place without sun, moons, or stars. There's nothing above but fathomless black. It's no wonder so many of the creatures summoned by Impomancers ended up down in the Pit. Horrors and monsters looking for familiar ground.

I had seen pictures of many of the creatures found in the Other World; the Orran Academy kept detailed records on each and every one of the monsters they found over there. But some of those things should never be brought over to our world. Some should remain forever trapped in their dark home.

Tutor Windlass was the foremost expert on Impomancy at the time, though in truth she was a bloody fool whose knowledge was rudimentary at best. She worked with each student privately, however, I was the only one of my age group to have an attunement to the school. I think this made it worse somehow. I could talk to Josef, or even Barrow or Tammy, but none of them could understand the feeling of being connected to the Other World, the constant draw into the darkness within. There is something oddly addictive about that place. None of them could understand the nightmares that plagued me every time I closed my eyes. The dreams of creatures too horrifying for most to even believe exist. And none could understand the strange compulsion I had to visit those nightmares again and again like picking at scab and refusing to let the wound heal.

It's a strange sensation bringing something over. Tutor Windlass ordered me to start small, and I thought I did. It's not like opening a portal. There's no shimmering disc of light showing the other place. An Impomancer uses themselves as the conduit, to drag the monster from the Other World. Their own body becomes the portal. And the creatures of the Other World don't always come willingly.

One thing I will say for the Other World: it's a beautiful place full of grand cities that shine in the darkness. Wonders that boggle the mind. I have seen a waterfall that flows upwards, vast mountain ranges far too ordered to be natural, a forest with trees of clutching skeletal hands. I understand now why the Other World is that way. I know how the things there came to be as they are, but to a child's inexperienced eye, I was awed by the beauty and scope of that world just as I was repulsed by the things that inhabit it. I remember wondering how such monsters could build those things. But of course, they didn't. They merely claimed what was already there. We are all living in a world built by ancients. And just as we do, they often struggle to comprehend the meaning of their world.

The creature I selected to bring forth into our world was a tiny thing. It looked like a slug no larger than a mouse. Its skin was grey and membranous, and it slithered along the ground leaving a thick, viscous slime. I watched it for a while. To be an Impomancer in the Other World is to be a disembodied spirit. We can float around, seeing all there is, but we're not really there, and the creatures of that world don't see us. Well, most of them don't see us. And trust me when I say, you would rather not garner the attention of those that can.

I reached out with my spirit and touched the little slime and it quickly faded from the Other World. Then I began to gag.

Tutor Windlass panicked and called for help. I remember not being able to breathe. Feeling something deep inside slithering up my throat. I tasted bile and something far worse and retched as a grey tentacle reached out from inside my mouth. The thing was larger than I had thought with tentacles thrashing as I vomited it up. It was already as large as a cat once it was out and the thought of it inside of me, the taste of it as I brought it up, made my stomach turn. I stumbled away from it, retching and gagging while it thrashed around the floor, growing larger and larger until it occupied more of the small room than I did.

That was when I noticed I was no longer connected to the Other World. The little monster stole my Impomancy Source as it slithered its way up and out of me. Once an Impomancer's connection to the Source is severed, so too is the command they hold over whatever they have summoned, and that command can never be regained.

Tutor Windlass' assistant picked me up and carried me from the training hall even as I watched the thing continue to grow, thrashing about as more tentacles erupted out of the pallid, membranous flesh.

The monster I summoned continued to grow until the training hall was nothing but rubble and debris beneath it. My mistake that day cost two people their lives, and another six were injured before they killed it. As far as I know I am still the only Sourcerer to have ever summoned an Abomination. The first and last. It was quickly put on the banned list and the Orrans and Terrelans both respected that list for good reason. To this day, I sometimes dream of that disgusting monster and I always wake up retching, the foul taste of it strong in my mouth.

Not all the things from the Other World are mindless animals, though hellions and khark hounds might give that impression. Many, like the Abomination, have a strange intelligence to them. It knew I would use the Source to control it and it dragged the shard of magic from my belly as it passed into our world. Others have an even greater intelligence and some few can even speak our languages. But it's important to remember that they are still fucking monsters.

My hooded lantern cast a beam of light into the cavern. It was a poor source of illumination and I wondered why Deko hadn't ordered the room filled with torches to keep the darkness at bay. Glancing back, I saw nothing but Horralain staring at me from the doorway and knew I'd get no answer. Whatever had taken residence in the cavern was mine to deal with. It dawned on me then, how foolish a situation I had gotten myself into. I was a Sourcerer without any Sources. I didn't know how to fight, even if I had a weapon. The creatures of the Other World were called monsters and horrors for a good reason. Even a mostly mindless hellion would tear me apart and there was nothing I could do to stop it but tell it to fuck off.

I took each step slowly, cautiously, shining my meagre light around me. The cavern was empty, save for rubble strewn about the floor. It was hewn straight from the rock that surrounded us, but even in the darkness I could see the walls were too straight and uniform. The craftsmen Deko kept down in the belly of the Pit had been carving the cavern with greater skill than us normal scabs could ever have managed. We were blunt instruments, not fine tools. As I ventured further in, I soon found there was a throne at the far end. The Pit boss had created a throne room for his palace and some unnatural beasty from the Other World had claimed it for itself. The thought brought a chuckle to my lips. The laugh that echoed back at me was mocking and harsh and most definitely not mine.

I almost tripped over the first body. I was too busy looking up and around, not at the ground. The rags made it obvious he was a scab, though I had rarely seen clothing bloodier. The man was covered in thin gashes all over his arms, face, and chest. He might have had a look of fear frozen on his face, but it was hard to tell under the wounds and blood. The one eye that was still intact stared up at me, pale and sightless. In short, the poor bastard was a right bloody mess.

It was the first time I had truly seen the handiwork of a creature from the Other World. I had summoned creatures and set them on my enemies, or lost control of monsters so that they escaped into our world, unbound. Yet I had never seen up close what those creatures could do to a person. I saw it now and I didn't look away. I deserved to know what sort of horrors my callousness was visiting upon the world.

I realised the dark was closing in around me and looked down to see my lantern as bright as before. The darkness was a thick, cloying thing that drank up the light and left only black behind. I wanted to scream, panic and fear mixing into an unbearable energy. But I couldn't. I couldn't scream, couldn't move. All I could do was watch as the darkness swallowed me up until it was complete. Then came the icy cold fingers of a real monster.

Terror froze me to the spot, made me rigid. I was so scared, I couldn't even tremble. There is a strange response in animals when confronted with something terrifying and beyond their capability to understand. They just stop, as though if they remain entirely still nothing can see them. I learned that day that terrans have the same response. I have the same response. It was a revelation and not a welcome one.

I could feel the lantern in my hand still, yet there was no light or heat. Trails of ice drew up and down my skin, leaving frozen pain in their wake. I remembered the dead man on the ground and the wounds he had, hundreds of thin slices all over him.

Fear and terror are strange things. They can paralyse the body, yes, but they also often paralyse the mind. I've known people far smarter than I, turn into babbling fools once fear sets in. I have used the trick many times to my advantage. I may not be an Empamancer, but these days, I know how to instil fear into people.

I closed my eyes and swallowed down the lump in my throat, trying desperately to ignore the icy trails along my skin. The creeping sensation of the grave yawning open to swallow me whole. It dawned on me then just how fucked I was.

I am the weapon. That thought, that mantra drilled into me by the tutors at the academy lit a spark of anger in me. Anger that I was in a situation so far beyond my control all I could do was wait for death. Anger, not at the arsehole of a monster trying to eat me alive, but at myself for not being bloody-well strong enough to fight back. "ENOUGH!" The word erupted as a broken scream torn from my mouth. I was quite surprised when the trails of ice stopped. For a few moments, silence held. Then I heard something move behind me. It sounded quite big.

"What are you?" I asked of the darkness. I thought myself quite knowledgeable back then. I thought I knew most of the secrets the Other World held. I know now just how much of a bloody fool I was. I knew nothing.

There was no reply, only a noise like metal tapping against stone. "You're no ghast," I said. Now the icy trails were gone from my skin I could feel hot, wet blood oozing out along the little cuts. My arms, chest, and legs all stung from the wounds. A ghast couldn't have done that to me; those horrors have no physical form.

Most of the things from the Other World don't have names other than those we give them. Some, however, are quite different. Some are older than the others. Old even as the world they come from.

"Ssserakis." The word whispered along the ground in front of me like snakes slithering closer before finally hissing out in front of my face. I felt an icy claw close around my chin, the cold of it burning my cheeks. I opened my eyes again, but still there was only darkness. I wonder if that is how blind people live their lives. Feeling a foreign touch upon their skin, and not having the ability to see who or what it is. The thought of that scares me more than I care to admit.

I shook my face free of the hand and it vanished, like smoke on a breeze. It was strange, but knowing the horror could speak, hearing its voice like glass shattering, I was free from the paralysis. I craned my head around, towards the door out of the cavern.

The horror laughed, a croaking sound like old men wheezing out their last breath. "They can't hear you. Can't see you. No one can help you now."

"Good." I put as much iron into my voice as possible and stared straight ahead. I knew the thing could kill me like it had the workers lying at my feet, but I wasn't about to go out mewling in fear and crying for mercy like those poor bastards. "You're not like the others. You're not some mindless beast an Impomancer can control. You're..."

"Older," whispered the voice. "In a world of nightmares, I am what the darkness fears." I felt a rush of air and knew the monster was moving around me, studying me from different angles. I had intrigued it by breaking its hold. That, and I think it may have grown bored with murdering terrans. We were too easy a prey for it.

It was my first encounter with one of the ancient horrors and I was inexperienced. I believe I danced to Ssserakis' tune like a puppet with her strings pulled.

"Are you corporeal?" I asked and in response I felt a glacial air breeze through me. Not around me, but through me. I have to say it was a fucking unpleasant feeling and chilled me to my core.

Most of the horrors have bodies. Bodies make them easy to kill, they give us something to aim at with magic or steel. Some are more like illusions, ghosts drifting through the world. Some are stranger still. Ssserakis is one of the latter.

"How did you get here?" I asked. "Who summoned you?"

"Questions. Questions. Questions." I heard the slither of something fat and wet behind me, writhing on the ground. It took a lot of willpower not to turn and stare into the darkness towards the sound. But that is how Ssserakis works. Distractions and fear, killing its prey inch by inch, second by second. A thousand shallow cuts all designed to make us piss ourselves in terror. "Perhaps I've always been here. Perhaps you summoned me."

Again, I felt an icy razor leave a trail along my skin, this time it started on my neck and trailed around my jaw and up to my ear. I felt blood leak down into the collar of my rags.

"Fine." I gritted my teeth against the stinging pain. I was still scared, but the terror had left me and, in its wake, it left a blazing determination. "You can answer in your fucking riddle all you want. Or you can tell me what do you want."

The trail of ice stopped again and I felt Ssserakis drift away from me. While the horror considered my words, I lifted the lantern up and felt the warmth coming from it. The flame was still burning, but the light was gone.

"Home." The voice was a whispered wail of longing and despair. "Where the light doesn't burn. Where I don't have to hide underground. Home. Where I was strong."

"I can help," I said quickly. I think I wanted to get the words out before I realised what I was saying. "If I can find an Impomancy Source I can send you back." I sounded very confident. Yet I didn't even know if such a thing was possible. Impomancers could send back the horrors they summoned themselves, so long as the Source was still inside of them and control had never been broken. I had never heard of a Sourcerer sending back another's summoned creature.

For a long time, all I heard was the darkness swirling around me. I felt myself trembling, the cold of Ssserakis' presence seeping in bone deep.

"Why?" Came the voice from behind, so close it was only a whisper though sounded like a thunderclap.

I decided truth was probably the wisest of options. "Because I need you to leave this place," I said. "Either you kill me here, or the others kill me out there when I can't get rid of you. Either way I'm fucked." I knew it was true. Deko would either murder me himself or hand me over to Prig the moment I stopped being useful and this was my very first chance to prove I had any use at all. Talk about setting the bar high. It's like being told to go catch a fish and landing a whale. There would be nowhere to go but down from there.

"You have seen my world?" Ssserakis asked. I felt icy hands close around my head, sapping the heat from me, driving icy spikes of agony into my mind.

"Yes," I said through chattering teeth. I couldn't stop the trembling. Couldn't stop the cold seeping into my limbs. I honestly thought I was dying, that I'd said the wrong thing and that ancient horror was tearing apart my soul.

"You will carry me there?" I could hear the hunger in its voice. The longing so deep it made my own heart ache.

"Yes." It's fair to say that was an agreement I came to regret making. Yet I would make it again a hundred times over.

I felt the cold rush into me again, but this time it didn't pass through. It wrapped itself around my heart and mind and stayed there. The unnatural darkness lifted in an instant and I could see the cavern again, lighter than before. There were three bodies scattered about the stone floor and one more draped over the rock-hewn throne. My lantern cast a hazy beam of light forward and I stood alone in the cavern. Ssserakis was gone. Even as I thought it I knew it wasn't true, but we terrans are good of convincing ourselves of convenient lies when the truths are too hard.

"Hey. You done, girl?" Deko sounded impatient.

I turned, shining my lantern back towards the entrance where Deko and Horralain waited. Apparently, the darkness had fallen like a blanket almost as soon as I entered the cavern. Now it was lifted they could see me again. I approached slowly, my limbs feeling numb from the cold.

"Slithering shit," Deko cursed as I drew close, his eyes widening. "What happened to you?"

I was covered in hundreds of tiny cuts, each bleeding only a trickle. It was Ssserakis' way and the first of so many injuries the horror dealt me.

"I fixed your problem." My voice came out as stammer and I very nearly collapsed. I was weak and weary beyond belief. Worse than the pain or the exhaustion, though, was that I could feel something foreign and terrible inside of me. Something living inside, feeding off me as it waited for a chance to escape home.

"Yeah?" Deko asked, taking the lantern from my trembling hands. "What was it?"

I just shook my head at the man. Maybe it was the look in my eyes, or the blood leaking from so many cuts, maybe he just didn't care, but Deko never asked again, and I never told anyone of the ancient horror I kept inside.

CHAPTER 18

In our second year at the academy we made a game of getting each in trouble with the tutors. They were harmless little pranks for the most part. It was a foolish thing, but children can be both foolish and wise in equal measure. I always tended towards the former.

One time, while learning letters I created a small portal behind Josef's head, reached through and flicked his ear hard enough to make him yelp. Tutor Ein was furious at the interruption and made Josef stand in the corner, facing the wall for the rest of the class.

The next day, in retaliation, Josef used Kinemancy while we were out for the morning run. Tutor Gellop was a taskmaster when it came to exercise and anyone who fell behind was punished with a second run all on their own. It was hard not to fall behind with a constant psychokinetic push against my chest. I remember it felt like trying to run through water.

But there was one time, Josef took it too far. Empamancy is a subtle school of magic. That's probably why Josef found an attunement for it and I did not. I am rarely subtle. I much prefer grand gestures. Empamancy is as much about reading a person as it is about manipulating their emotions. Josef always excelled at reading me.

It was during a meditation exercise by Tutor Bell. She taught us to breathe properly, drawing in strength and exhaling weakness. She taught us to centre ourselves, to let go of physical needs and focus. Each day, Tutor Bell would lead us all through a complex series of movements, often instructing us to hold a position for so long I would start to sweat and tremble. I still move myself through those positions sometimes to keep both body and mind limber. Only down in the Pit, during my darkest times, did I forget them entirely.

After the series of movements, the tutor would get us to sit and clear our minds. There, we would meditate, concentrating on breathing and letting the subconscious take over. One time, Josef used his Empamancy on me. I remember a great sadness washed over me and dragged me out to sea. So much pain and sorrow, I thought I was drowning in it. Before I knew it, I was crying, bent over and sobbing into my hands. My eyes blurred as tears rained onto the mat beneath me. I had no focus for the emotion, no memory within which to ground it. I drowned in it, unable to find the surface, unable to breathe. Then Tutor Bell was there, gathering me up into her arms and holding me tight. The wave of emotion passed and left me feeling raw inside. I could remember the sorrow; even now I can remember it, but I no longer felt it. That was worse. The absence of it left a pit inside of me that couldn't be filled, a yawning void of… nothing.

Tutor Bell never spoke of it, never even realised it was Josef's fault. She just called an early end to the session and hugged me again before I left. I went from feeling a sadness so profound I struggled to breathe, to feeling comforted and safe. I burst into tears again at that. Strange how pain and relief can cause such a similar reaction.

Afterwards, Josef admitted what he had done, and I was angry. How could I not be? Empamancy is the manipulation of thoughts and emotions within a person. It's an intrusion, a violation of a person's mind and heart. And Josef, the person I trusted and loved most, had been the one to violate me. It was a betrayal. His first betrayal. I should have known then that it would only be the first of many.

I stayed angry for two days. Seething silently while echoes of the emotion he had inflicted upon me drove me to fits of tears. But I am a determined woman and I wanted to find a way to protect myself from Empamancers. By then, the library was open to us and I stole every minute I could to research the school of magic. I found no way to shield myself, but I did learn something important. Empamancers cannot create emotion from nothing. They can impress their own emotions on others, and they can amplify emotions. That is when I realised the sorrow I felt was not my own. It was Josef's sorrow over the things he had seen before coming to the academy, and over the loss of his family at the hands of the Terrelans. He might have amplified it as he pressed those emotions upon me, but they were his. The pain and sorrow were his. I forgave him there and then. I simply couldn't stay angry after knowing how much pain he was in.

When we made up, Josef promised never to use Empamancy on me again and he almost kept that promise. Of course, he had, unfortunately, shown the bitch-whore a way to get to me, and Lesray Alderson was more than happy to violate my emotions. I've said it before and I'll say it again; I fucking hate Empamancy.

I was always cold with Ssserakis inside of me. It was a chill that went deeper than the skin, down to my bones. Perhaps even further than that. It was a coldness that infected my very soul. I could be standing beside a fire, so close the flames could reach out and lick at me, but still I would shiver.

The nightmares were also a gift from the horror. I dreamed of things that had me waking up in cold sweats, or sometimes I screamed myself awake. Those close to me never learned the whole truth of what had happened to me down in Deko's palace, or the deal I had struck with Ssserakis. They only knew what they had to. I showed no fear while I was awake, but the things that horror showed me in my dreams were the very essence of terror. I learned about the Other World in those dreams. Maybe too much.

I stopped digging. I stopped going with my team to our tunnel. Prig no longer had any power over me, not while Deko's protection was in place, and I had secured that protection. He called upon my knowledge two more times, but Deko no longer sent me to deal with the monsters alone. I identified the creatures and told Horralain and his thugs how best to kill or capture them. The rest was up to the giant.

I didn't forget the day Horralain strangled me, almost killed me. I've never forgotten it. But I learned to live with the anger of it. I learned to respect his strength and skill. No amount of respect could stop me from hating him, though. I've always been one to nurse my hatred, feed it on the fires of past wrongs and forgotten slights. While others might let a thing go, I hold on tight. My grudges are mine, they are a part of me, and I don't let anything that is mine go without a fight.

Each day I would wake next to Hardt and be gone from the cavern before Prig arrived to corral his team. I hated that he might think I was scared of him, but the old saying *out of sight, out of mind* holds some truth. Prig was less likely to take his anger over me out on the others if I didn't shove my protection in his face. So, I chose to avoid him for the sake of my friends.

I spent my days watching the tunnel as Tamura widened the crack that I hoped would lead us to our freedom. Crazy, the old man surely was, but he's never been one to shy away from work. Sometimes I think he understands others perfectly, but words get jumbled between his brain and mouth. Maybe not. Maybe he thinks in the same codes and similes that he speaks in.

A few weeks after Prig cracked my rib, I thought myself strong enough to wield the pick without doubling over in pain. Unfortunately, by that time the widening crack was too high up for me to reach. I have never been the tallest of women, and I was just fifteen at the time, and still growing. The truth of that was apparent every time I looked down at my rags and saw my ankles. There was, of course, a constant stream of new clothing being sent down, but most of that went to Deko and his captains. I could have asked for some, and Deko might have obliged, but I didn't want to owe the bastard any more than I already did. I've always hated owing people or asking for things. Pride is a damned thing that stops us from doing so much that is good for both us, and for the world. It's also something I have in spades, and believe me when I tell you sometimes I wish I didn't.

I heard the pick strike stone and a crumble as rocks dropped to the ground below. I turned to find Tamura shaking rock dust out of his hair. He looked at me and smiled.

"Like Ro'shan passing." Tamura laughed and went back to studying the crack.

It was growing daily as Tamura and the brothers worked at it. An inky darkness leading upwards into the rock. It was already large enough that I could start the climb and as we shined a lantern up above, I could see that the crack opened into a crevice. The urge to start climbing, to see how far I could get was almost overwhelming. My desire was only furthered by the strong breeze blowing into my face. I grinned and closed my eyes.

"Listen." Tamura's voice was a whisper.

I cocked my head to the side, trying to block out my other senses, to concentrate on whatever sound the old man could hear. I was quite amazed I hadn't heard it myself. A constant, muted roar echoed out from the crack.

"What is it?" I asked.

Tamura giggled. "Blow through your lips."

I did as he bid.

"Tighter." Tamura ordered. "Tighter." He reached out and put fingers above and below my lips, squashing them together until the sound I was making was a breathy whistle.

I shook the old man's hand away. "It's wind gusting through a small opening," I said, more confident than ever it would lead to our way out.

"Grass beneath my feet," Tamura said, and did a little dance, lifting each foot in turn and spinning around on the spot. So childlike at times. So much innocence. It is somewhat ironic to me that someone so steeped in guilt could also be the most innocent of us all.

"You and I might fit through, but Isen and Hardt don't stand a chance," I said. "We need to make the crack wider still. I think it opens out further up, so we just need to widen it a little more here."

Tamura shot me a quizzical look and held the pick up at arm's length. The metal only barely touched the roof of the tunnel. I nodded my understanding and Tamura gave me a shrug.

"We're going to need rope," I said, but the old man gave no sign he was still listening to me. He was staring up at the crack, feeling the breeze on his face. I left him there and made my way towards the main cavern. We were so close to freedom I could almost taste it. I imagined the sky; giant and blue, glorious and endless. Freedom and my reward.

What if there is no way out? All that crack leads to is a stone coffin. A cold grave. The thought made me stumble, set an unspoken fear coursing through me. It was the first time I had even considered the possibility. Now that I was, it seemed all too real.

I almost bumped into Josef on my way to the Trough. Part of me still thinks I was so distracted I didn't notice him coming towards me. I know the truth though, he stepped into my path. He wanted the conversation. I can't blame him for it. I wanted to talk to him too. Josef wasn't just a friend, our bond went deeper than that, deeper than if we had been true siblings. We were a pair. Two of a kind. The academy raised and trained us that way, to rely on each other for everything. Despite that bond it had been almost a month since we had spoken. We saw each other every day, yet neither of us could find the humility to swallow our pride and mend the rift that was growing larger day by day. Why? Because he had fucking betrayed me *again*! Despite the blinders of love for him that I wore, despite the hope of reconciliation inside of me, I was starting to see the pattern.

We stared at each other for a while. I honestly don't think I've ever felt more awkward in my life. Eventually I stepped to the side, determined to move past him and the situation. Josef didn't let me.

"It's been a while," he said. I realised then just how much I'd missed the sound of his voice. It almost broke me. I felt cracks snaking their way through my will. I wanted nothing more than to hear his voice tell me it would be all right and to lean my head on his shoulder and feel the closeness we had always shared.

"I saw you just this morning," I said. Pride is a terrible thing constantly pushing us into mistakes. Regardless of what I wanted, I couldn't help but remember all the betrayals Josef had stacked against me. At that moment, I wanted to both wrap my arms around him and kick him off a cliff. We could both fall together, die together. I would have saved the world so much pain.

"Well... I mean..." Josef stammered to a stop. "I mean, I miss you, Eska."

He'll betray you again. I couldn't shake the thought. It echoed in my mind and every time I pushed it down, it started up again. I missed Josef like a part of myself had disappeared and it itched at me all the time. But he had betrayed me, time and time again. I had the pattern, I could see it. It was there and I couldn't ignore it. Josef claimed he held love for me, I knew it was true. He did. But that had never stopped him betraying me to get what *he* wanted. *He* wanted to surrender at Fort Vernan, not *I*. *He* wanted the overseer to set us free, not *I*. *He* would fucking betray me again!

"Why wouldn't you?" I said with a scoff. It was terse and harsh and when I look back now, I wish I hadn't listened to the voice in my head. I wish we had made up then. I wanted to tell him about my hope, about the escape plan. I wanted to be friends again.

He'll tell the overseer. It sounded so reasonable. It sounded like truth. Fear is speculation more often than it is truth. The truth is almost never as terrifying as imagination makes it seem. Almost never.

"I have to go," I said coldly, and made to move past him again. Josef stepped backwards and in front of me.

"Please, Eska," he said. "Talk to me. I'm sorry. I'm sorry about everything. Just… don't push me away. We've been through too much to let whatever this is break us."

He'll say anything, and report everything. From your mouth to his ears to the overseer. Fear. Fucking fear. Sometimes it makes us wise, other times it makes us bloody idiots.

"Goodbye, Josef." I pushed past him and we both hissed from the pain in our ribs, but I kept going.

"Eska, wait," Josef called after me. "I'm sorry. I'm sorry I hurt you. I didn't mean to betray you. I just wanted... I just want to get out. I'd do anything to see the sun again and the overseer offered me that. He offered us both a way out. But I don't get out unless you do. Like it or not, we're together on this. And I don't like life without you in it. Please..."

I wiped the tears from my eyes and kept walking, refusing to listen to either Josef or the voice in my head telling me everything he said was lies.

CHAPTER 19

When I was nine years old, still a student at the Orran Academy of Magic, I first learned to fight. Sparring was required teaching. There were dozens of fields of study and research, and many Sourcerers spent their lives furthering Orran's agriculture or blacksmithing. There is truly no end to the possibilities in the ways magic can be applied to help everyday life. But all Sourcerers who attended the academy needed to know how to fight. It wasn't just because of the war with Terrelan, but the prospect of any war. The Orran Empire kept track of its Sourcerers and was prepared to put them to work in military efforts wherever they were needed. Josef and I were different. We were trained to be weapons against the Terrelans. We were trained to fight with our magic. That was an oversight, I think. They should have also trained us to fight without.

There were rules to the sparring, of course. The first and foremost, was that we were never allowed to bring our full strength to bear against our opponents. They too, were Sourcerers and Orrans just like us. They too, were weapons being trained to rain destruction down upon the Terrelans. There was simply no sense in going overboard and killing our classmates. That never seemed to stop the bitch-whore from trying though.

Lesray and I were often pitted against each other. The tutors soon realised that Josef and I would never attack the other. We always worked far too well together, and that was a dynamic the tutors wished to endorse and nurture rather than break. I think the tutors believed we would keep each other strong and dedicated to the Orran cause. Looking back, I think they were right. Josef didn't have my loyalty to Orran, and I kept him true. I didn't have his power or wisdom and he kept me alive.

But Lesray hated me. I had no idea why. We were paired against each other because the tutors of the academy considered us of nearly equal strength. I was attuned to six Sources and Lesray to five. That we both could use Pyromancy and Portamancy was another reason. The tutors deemed it important that we learn to fight using magic that the enemy could also control. In a battle of magic, countering an opponent is often as important as striking a blow.

We were in our third year of training when Lesray first tried to kill me. She claimed otherwise, of course, but I know the truth of it even if the tutors believed her.

Pyromancy is not, as many believe, the magic of controlling fire, but temperature. A well-trained Pyromancer can burn a city to the ground or freeze a lake. We were trained to fight with both fire and ice, trading fire balls and freezing the ground beneath us. I have always found myself to be strongly attuned to the magic, and especially to the flames. Despite that, Lesray was stronger. Or maybe just better. Or maybe just more ruthless. Whichever one it was, she was also a cunt.

I have always preferred to tint my fire green, for no other reason than I can, and I like the colour. Lesray preferred an icy blue, I think to confuse her opponents. It made it harder to tell if she was trying to freeze or burn me. Though in truth it was usually both.

The sparring ground lit with the light of flames crashing against each other. The sandstone walls were blasted with so much heat the rock had long since turned black. Even the ground underfoot was brittle from so much fire and ice. I don't remember the fight as clearly as I'd like; the memory is blurred by the pain that followed it. I remember we spent some time trading flame, turning each other's attacks upon themselves. Footwork is important, as it is in any form of combat, and we circled each other, always on the move. Always watching for an opening.

The bitch-whore attacked me with a plume of fire that rippled across the ground towards me like a wave. I was about to leap over it, only my foot wouldn't move. I didn't even notice when she had frozen it to the ground. It was all I could do to throw up my arms and block the wave of fire with my own raw power, which obscured my vision. That should have been it, a victory claimed by academy rules. I never saw the icicle coming, only felt the frozen agony in my side.

I remember dropping to my knees, screaming. As the flames died down, I saw the icicle melt away and looked up to see Lesray wearing a nasty grin, knowing she had won. Knowing she had killed me. It was short lived as Josef hit her with a psychokinetic blast that crumpled her against the far wall. It was still too late though. I collapsed onto the ground, bleeding out from a hole in my side as large as a fist.

Josef reached me first. I remember feeling his magic flood into me as he tried to heal me with his Biomancy. Just twelve years old and he knew more about the terran anatomy than most of the tutors. I remember those tutors arriving and feeling other people's magic inside of me. I remember the pain. Then I blacked out. Josef liked to tell me how scared he was when I stopped screaming. He could feel my heart beating through his Biomancy and he later told me he was certain he felt it stop.

When I woke, my head was pounding and my side felt like it was on fire. The irony was not lost on me. Josef was asleep in a chair next to my cot, his face pale and drawn. His skin waxy and sunken. I'm told the tutors tried to remove him but he fought them. You might think a twelve-year-old is mostly harmless. You would be very wrong. Eventually they let him stay, and I don't think he stopped healing me with his magic even for a moment. I lost five days of life in that attempt, and a few weeks spent recovering. Josef spent almost as long regaining the health he had poured into me. All magic takes a toll on the Sourcerer, and Biomancy is no exception. As far as I'm aware, Lesray was never even punished. At least not by the academy tutors. I, however, have a long memory and a passion for holding grudges.

Rope was something of a rare possession down in the Pit. Not because there was no rope to be found, it was everywhere from buckets to carts to lifts. It was rare because all the rope that was delivered to the Pit was needed. Deko was a thug and ran the Pit like a criminal empire, but he had people keeping track of every resource that was brought in, and things like rope were allocated sparingly. That wasn't to say there was none to be found for scabs like me. You just had to know where to look.

I knew the man I was after and had a good idea of where he might be. Lepold was a tall, gangly scab who had peculiar habit of taking old rope worn beyond use, peeling it apart and then braiding it back together. I think he somehow found the mind-numbing tedium of it fun, or relaxing. The Pit had no shortage of madmen. He carried a number of lengths around with him and used them as stakes for particularly valuable games of chance. I was confident I could best Lepold in most of the games he liked to play, but I was less confident that I had something valuable enough to entice him to put any of his precious rope on the line.

Given my soaring infamy amongst the scabs, I probably could have jumped ahead of the people waiting to sit at the table. Everywhere I went I drew stares and whispers, and every time Deko summoned me, the rumours grew. I think the scars and healing wounds helped as well. I was fairly certain I looked like a feral crag cat, and a vicious one at that. Yet I waited my turn, and watched the game unfold, studying Lepold and the other players for their tells.

When a spot opened up on the table I slipped onto the stool and smiled at the others. I had something of a reputation on the tables as well as off, and two players laughed and packed away their stakes when I sat down. Luckily, Lepold wasn't one of them.

He gave me a nod of respect and I returned it. "I was hoping to get a chance at some rope," I said quickly, before anyone could decide on their stakes.

"Not trading on your name, I hope." The gangly rope braider replied. "I'll want something of equal value up for stake."

I reached into a pocket and pulled out a small box, setting it on the table.

"A snuff box?" Lepold asked. "With respect..."

"It doesn't have fucking snuff in it," I said with a knowing smile then let the silence hang between us.

"Uh, so what's in it?" Lepold asked.

I tapped the lid of the box. "You'll have to win it to find out."

I saw the other two players look to Lepold, and I saw Lepold bite at his lip. From the games I'd watched him play I discovered he always liked to see the other players' chips even after he'd gone out of the game. He was curious by nature, and I was going make him hang himself on that curiosity. After a few moments, he pulled a length of rope from his belt and laid it on the table. It wasn't a long braid, maybe as tall as Hardt, but it would be enough; we'd make it work. The other two players put up their own stakes. I had to admit I'd be a rich woman if I won the game. Well, rich in Pit standards, which is to say a fucking pauper anywhere else.

"Mind if I play?" Josef slipped into the last remaining seat. I bit back a curse. The voice in my head warned me he was trying to derail all my plans, and at the time it seemed like truth.

"I fucking mind," I growled.

"Anyone can join if they've got a stake," Lepold replied and it was true. The rules of the gaming tables didn't care for personal feuds.

Josef pulled a half loaf of brown bread from inside his rags. It earned a few gasps and a lot of hungry eyes. The bread looked as fresh as any of us had seen in months, and brown bread was rare as gold down in the dark. I knew I wasn't the only one wondering where he had got it. I could have asked him. I wanted to ask him. I wanted to know what he'd been doing for the past month.

He obviously got it from the overseer. Payment for all your secrets.

"I'd say that's good enough," Lepold saying, licking his lips at the sight of the bread. The other players seemed to agree. "Highest stake chooses the game."

Josef looked at me and I knew what he was about to fucking say. I was already shaking my even as he said it. "Trust."

It was a new experience for me. Until that day I had only ever played Trust with both Hardt and Isen at the table. They knew me well enough to know I was far more treacherous than the roll of the dice could ever be. This group of players were different. They played differently. And they didn't know me. Josef, on the other hand, was trying to make amends. We both knew he was on my side and every time we were pitted against each other he picked *friendship*. The first time I took a dice off him. The second time, we both chose to shake hands though I railed at the false nicety.

One by one, the other players went out. I was ruthless where I needed to be, and unpredictable as well. More than once, I gave a dice away to confuse my opponents. There is a temptation in Trust to always pick *betrayal*, to leave fate up to the dice. Those players usually lose fast and hard, bested by their savvier opponents who are willing to wait out the aggression. For the first time I was one of the savvy ones. Josef, too, played a smart game. He was already friends with a couple of the other players and he used that friendship to his advantage.

Lepold was the last of the others to go out, losing his dice to Josef on a roll. By that point Josef had dice to throw away and he was more than happy to bully the rope maker out of the game. I had just one dice left myself, but Trust changes when there are only two players remaining. It no longer matters how many dice a player has accrued. Only one round is ever played where two players are concerned.

The other players didn't leave the table. They knew better than to forfeit their stakes by walking away. If both Joseph and I picked *betrayal*, then the game was reset for all to play again. If we both picked *friendship* then we would split the stakes, and there was only one item I really cared about. Though Josef's loaf of bread was tempting.

I stared across the table at Josef and he smiled back at me. I hated that smile, almost as much as I'd missed it. I knew then that he would pick *friendship*. He didn't care about the stakes, he just wanted us to be friends again. To be like we were.

You're not playing against Josef. You're playing against the overseer. He's trying to take it from you. He wants you to fail

*so you have no choice but to crawl back to the overseer and beg
the Terrelans to let you be one of them.*

I tried to ignore the thought, but it repeated itself
again and again. Fear is a powerful motivator. Sometimes it
motivates us to good, to run from danger or shy away from
a flame. Other times it motivates us to evil, to take before it
is taken, or to attack first. To mistrust those who are closest
to us. Ssserakis fed on fear, nurtured it and drew strength
from it. In me, it found a feast never-ending.

We each chose our faces and hid the dice with
hands. For a long time, we watched each other. I had
known Josef for most of my life, all of it that really
mattered, yet I couldn't be sure what he was about to do. I
knew him as well as I knew myself. I trusted him with my
life. Or at least, I used to. I was no longer so sure. I wasn't
certain if I trusted him with my life or my hope. I
considered the possibilities again. Even if he did betray me
again and took the rope I needed, I would have another
chance. He might have even given me the rope. All I had to
do was pick *friendship* and my victory was assured. One
way or another I would get the rope. I had almost talked
myself into it as well.

"Ready?" Josef asked, still smiling at me. I looked at
that smile and didn't recognise it. I didn't even recognise
the face he was showing me. A voice in my head whispered
deception and I didn't know to ignore it.

I nodded and we both took our hands away. Josef's
dice showed *friendship* and I breathed a sigh of relief. I
glanced only once at his face too see the hurt there, but I
couldn't bear more than a glance. With some empty

platitudes about *luck* and *next time,* I gathered my winnings
and fled before Josef could find his tongue.

CHAPTER 20

I found Hardt pacing back and forth near the crack. Tamura waved at me as I approached and I saw his eyes goggle at the rope, a grin lighting his face.

"Chains with which the moons are anchored to the world," Tamura said. "Lokar would be proud." Those words have stuck with me for some reason, and I have puzzled over them many times. I still cannot fathom their meaning. There are many tales of how our two moons became one, but I have always preferred the story of the Chase.

Millennia ago we had two moons. Lokar and Lursa. They were lovers, sharing everything but flesh. They passed through the night sky watching over us all so far below. Until one day Lursa broke away. The bards call her capricious, fleeing Lokar at a whim for no offence at all. I believe she wanted to strike out on her own, away from her lover for a time. Lokar gave chase, as jilted lovers often do. For a long time Lursa ran and Lokar followed, always gaining on his smaller counterpart. I have often wondered what it might have been like to look up into the sky and see two moons so close together and yet so far apart. Eventually, Lokar caught up with Lursa. The stories say he gathered her up into his arms, an embrace so strong they began to merge into one, and that is how they remain. Two moons slowly becoming one, spinning through the sky above our world. Some think it romantic, some think it a marvel. Personally, I think those people hopeless. They have clearly never stood on the ground amidst a moonshower, hoping not to be squashed by falling rocks.

Tamura snatched the rope from me and started tying knots into it. I stopped Hardt from pacing. He glanced up at me and I saw anguish on his face. Hardt was never one for undue worry.

Prig has killed Isen. The thought paralysed me, fear scaring me away from asking for the truth. I didn't just think it possible, but probable. In that moment I imagined never seeing Isen's cheeky smile again, never seeing the green of his eyes, or the brown flecks dotted throughout. I imagined never hearing his voice again, never hearing him say my name again. Never getting to feel his arms around me. Yes, I was a foolish girl who believed herself in love, but that is what we do when we are young, before life has ground the optimism out of us. We love hard and love easily, and then we turn the feelings of loss and rejection into sickening melodrama.

"...Eska?" Hardt's voice snapped me out of my daydream and I shook the lingering images away.

"What happened?" I asked.

Hardt shook his head. "Isen signed up to fight today," he said. "I tried to talk him out of it, pointed out we're getting close." The big man pointed to the crack in the ceiling. "We need him hale, not wounded. He signed up regardless, something about keeping up appearances."

I shrugged. "So? Isen fights all the time." I decided to go and watch him. If for no other reason than to shake the fears of his death from my mind. More than that.

though, I wanted to see him fight. There was something brutal and passionate about the dance of combat, and seeing Isen move like that always warmed me up, and I felt like I needed warming. I felt like a cold had frozen the marrow in my bones.

Hardt grabbed hold of my shoulders and I almost shook him away. The look in his eyes stopped me. An intense fear that bordered on panic. "Deko matched him with Yorin," he said through gritted teeth.

Fear hit again, and I felt even colder than before. No one fought against Yorin and won. No one even survived. "Can he win?" I asked.

Hardt growled and stalked away, bunching his shoulders like he was about to throw a punch. "No one ever has."

"No one else has been trained by you," I said.

"He's not as good as I was." Hardt set to pacing again. "Isen has the speed but he lacks power, and his technique gets sloppy when he tires. Yorin..."

"Could you take him?" I had yet to see Hardt fight and didn't know the truth of it. It is a sight to behold, even more so when the man is in a rage. There is little as terrifying in this world, or the other, as an angry Hardt. Even now just thinking about it gives me chills.

"I don't fight," he said. I have rarely seen Hardt look more pained than he did then, and the other times I have, have been entirely my doing.

"But you could," I pressed him. "The rules of the arena say a scab can't back out, but they also say someone else can take their place." *Sending one brother to die in the other's stead.*

"It is the curse of the living to mourn the dead," Tamura said as he crouched against the wall, still tying knots in the rope by the flickering lantern light. "It is the curse of the dead not to care. They're dead." It put a haunted look into Hardt's eyes. I knew then, he wouldn't take Isen's place. I thought him a coward. I didn't know why at the time, but Hardt was willing to let his brother die rather than throw a punch.

"He's not fucking dead yet!" I all but screamed, storming out the tunnel and leaving the two men behind to wallow in their premature grief.

I was in a rage as I stormed out of the tunnel. I kept going despite not knowing where I would find either Isen, or Yorin. I wasn't even sure of what I'd do when I did find one of them. I couldn't stop the fight, and I certainly couldn't take Isen's place. The horrid truth was that I had no way to stop Isen from dying but I couldn't just let it happen. I was a fucking fool. I thought I loved him. I thought I could save him, and if I did, he would love me back.

It can't be a coincidence. The thought struck me like a hammer blow. The timing was too perfect to be coincidental. We were so close to making our attempt, a week or two at most. Isen signed up for one fight and now, unlike every other time, he gets assigned to fight Yorin. It had to be planned, by Deko or maybe even the overseer. It couldn't just be chance.

I think I might have been talking to myself, muttering maybe. I have been known to curse and insult under my breath when in a rage, though I rarely remember anything said. Scabs backed away from me, staring as I passed. Some even trailed after me, no doubt hopeful they were about to see me perform another spectacle. I didn't disappoint.

Riding the lift down to the Trough I braved standing close to the edge so I could look down on the main cavern. From high up, even Deko and his captains looked small. There's a lesson to be learned there about power and perspective.

You might fall. It doesn't take much to plant the seed of fear in a person. Just a few days earlier I had seen a man leap from a lift— at least we were told he leapt. He screamed on the way down and the sound as he hit the rock below was sickening. A long way to go for a quick way to die. I ignored the thought and crept closer still to the edge. I have ever been one to court danger when angry.

"Well look who it is." The foreman, I never bothered to learn his name, who operated the lift was a fat man with a patchy black beard. I ignored him and started towards the Trough, already looking for Isen amongst the scabs.

Many of the scabs around the tables greeted me as I passed through, searching their faces. They knew me by name and reputation both, and I even stopped to ask a few of them if they had seen either man. Yorin, I was informed, never bothered to visit the Trough and was rarely seen outside of the arena. None of them had seen Isen.

The fat foreman was watching me as I made my way back to the lift. My reputation wasn't just with the scabs. The foremen tended to hate most of us anyway, but Prig was very vocal about me. He knew he could no longer touch me, but that didn't stop the mangy bastard spreading disgusting rumours amongst his friends. Most of the foremen thought me a slut, screwing my way through the ranks of scabs. I'd even heard one or two claim I'd bent over for Deko and all his captains. I'd like to say I let the rumours wash over me and ignored them all, perhaps these days I would simply laugh them away. But I was young and angry and didn't want the lies getting back to Isen.

"Send me down to the arena," I said. The man was leering at me. I didn't have time for him or whatever rumours he believed in. I stepped onto the lift platform and waited. It didn't start to move.

"How about I get a taste of what Deko gets?" he said.

Contempt, anger, and loathing were all things I had to spare. I took a couple of steps closer to the man and glared up at him. I think he saw the rage in my eyes. He may have been close to twice my size, but he paled and took a step back all the same.

"How about I go tell Horralain you're possessed by a bloody horror?" I said. "Have you seen what he does to those things? How do you think it feels to have your intestines pulled out through your nose, you fat, ignorant cunt?"

There was shock and fear on the foreman's face. I doubt any scab had ever talked to him like that. A part of me, deep inside, grew stronger as it drank that fear in. I saw him shiver and take a step back. It broke whatever rage-fuelled trance I was in and I stepped backwards onto the lift. Looking down at my arms I saw the little scars Ssserakis had given me standing proud and white amidst the goosebumps. I was cold to my core and the anger made me colder still. I longed for a Pyromancy Source, they sit like little flames inside the stomach and I have always enjoyed the warmth of them.

"Send me down to the arena," I repeated and this time the foreman leapt to the task without so much as a word. He never spoke to me again and I was more than glad for it.

I'm not too proud to admit that I spent some time brooding on the way down. I cracked my knuckles, paced back and forth, and ground my teeth. My anger was lending me a nervous energy and standing still only let that energy build. I never once stopped to consider why I was angry. I think if I had, I might have tried to find another solution. Maybe if I had, all my friends would still be alive.

I was off the lift and moving before it even bumped to a halt. There were a few scabs in the nearby corridors and the sounds of digging echoed all around me. Deko had work crews fashioning a second arena to expand his underground empire. The other scabs watched me go but said nothing. I think maybe the look on my face convinced them silence was the best option. I was still just a girl and already feared by my peers. I was not to be fucked with.

I found Yorin in the arena antechamber. It was only the second time I had ever seen him, and the first time that he was not speckled with another man's blood. Yorin was tall, maybe a couple of fingers taller than Isen, and thick with muscle. He shaved his head completely clear of all hair and his life's story was written all over his body in scars. He had a strange sense of peace around him. I don't think I ever saw him angry. Most of the time he was cold, distant. That was probably why the other scabs gave him such space. Well, that and his proficiency with killing people.

Yorin didn't notice me at first, or maybe he just didn't care to spare me any attention. The antechamber had a number of benches where fighters waited for their turn and Yorin was sitting on one, waiting despite the fights being hours away. There were scabs nearby as well. Some were signing themselves up to fight, while others were the audience, turning up early to debate the matches and secure themselves the best spots to watch.

After a while of being ignored, my anger got the better of me. Yorin knew I was there, and my pride and arrogance wouldn't allow him to pretend I wasn't. I was flush with the energy and anger of scaring a foreman. It made me bold. It made me a bloody idiot.

"Get up," I hissed. Looking back, I could have handled that first encounter somewhat more diplomatically.

Yorin raised his head slowly and locked eyes with me. He stood then, rising to his feet with a fluidity that belied his size, and towered over me.

Now that I had the man in front of me, I struggled to think of something to say. Yorin was as much a monster as any I had encountered in the Other World. He killed one scab a night down in the arena and all while the rest of the Pit watched. He was a murderer and a damned good one. I sometimes think back over the encounter and imagine how it might have happened had I a Source in my stomach. With only a small Kinemancy Source I could have picked Yorin up with a burst of psychokinetic force and dashed his head against the wall.

"I know who you are," Yorin said, his voice flat. Just the memory of that man's voice makes me so angry I want to burn the world to ash. "I have no wish to deal with one of Deko's pets." And like that I was dismissed.

Yorin didn't dig. He didn't abide by Deko's rules and laws. He spent his days either fighting in the arena or wandering the Pit. I think maybe Yorin could have challenged Deko for control and won, but he didn't want control over the foremen or scabs. All Yorin ever wanted was to fight and kill. He told me as much once, tried to convince me I was no different. I scoffed at the idea at the time. Now I'm not so sure he was wrong.

I treated Yorin to the full fury of my icy glare. It was arrogance to think that it might cow him like it had the foreman. I barely saw the strike coming. A flash of pain lit up my cheek along my still-healing scar and I was on my hands and knees, spitting blood onto the stone beneath me. Scabs started to gather to watch. I had a reputation, and I was even liked by many, but none were going to stand up for me against Yorin. Besides, there was little the inhabitants of the Pit liked more than to watch people fight.

After shaking the spots from my eyes, I lurched back to my feet to find Yorin still standing there, watching me. I think he was curious. I would have been, in his stead. Yorin was a pit fighter. The best I have ever seen, and there I was, a young girl with the fire of anger in my eyes, treating him with as little respect as he was giving to me. These days if someone came to me like that, I would hear them out just to see what they had to say. Then, I would probably put them where they deserved; on their knees or in the dirt. I see now just how thin the edge was on which I walked.

"You're fighting Isen Fallow tonight." My voice was an ugly hiss even to my own ears, and I've always quite liked the sound of my voice.

"One dead scab is as good as another," Yorin said with a shrug. I realised that he meant it. It was not a plot to bury my plans of escape. Neither Deko, nor the overseer, nor Josef were trying to kill Isen. It was sheer chance, bad luck, that Yorin had been picked to fight Isen so close to our attempt at escape. Some of the fire went out of me at that realisation, but it let some clarity seep in instead.

"Don't kill him," I said. I couldn't stop the fight. Neither man could change their mind and back out, the rules forbade it. But the loser didn't have to die. Yorin didn't have to kill.

"Go away." Yorin sank back onto the bench behind him, took a deep breath, and let it out as a sigh.

I couldn't let it go. I couldn't let Isen die. I couldn't let Yorin kill him. My infatuation with the younger of the two brothers had grown into something I thought I couldn't live without. In my most private moments, I dreamed of Isen, of our skin touching, hot breath tickling each other. In my defence, I was still young and naive. The closest I had come to a sexual encounter was in the pages of a book. I thought myself romantic, fighting for the life of the man I loved. I was a desperate little girl clinging to the idea of something I didn't even understand. Desperate, but also determined.

"What do you fucking want?" I asked, a note of despair in my voice. I dared a step closer so the other scabs couldn't hear. "For his life. I have food, a half loaf of bread. Snuff. Bandages, balm, dice..." Quite a fortune I had amassed, at least down in the Pit, up in the sunlight it was all as good as worthless. Trinkets and baubles for the most part.

Yorin's eyes flicked to mine then down and back up again. "You have nothing I want," he said flatly. "There is nothing I want. The only thing down in this hell is death, and digging, and I will not dig. I kill because I can. Because in the circle of stone and blood, I am free again. So. Go away."

"Freedom?" I asked, latching on to the one thing I had to offer. "You want to be free?"

Yorin didn't answer. There was a sullenness to him, like a caged animal that remembered what it was like to run wild. I knew that feeling all too well. Yorin wanted to be free, but he had given up the hope of it. In the arena he found a different freedom of sorts. I think the need to kill was something else, though. I think that was about power. The need to feel powerful by holding another's life in his hands and snuffing it out. I've always wondered what Yorin felt in those moments where he took another's life. Even more so, I've always wondered what he felt afterwards. Did he feel the disgust and regret like I do? Or was it all just nothing to him?

"I can get you out." I leaned in even closer, so close I could smell the sweat on him. "I'm getting out. I can take you with me."

There is a point in all relationships where the power shifts. Countless little points, small changes in the dynamic between two people. This was one of them. The change

214

from me wanting something from him, to him needing something from me. He didn't believe me, not really. But he wanted to.

"How?" Yorin asked.

I shook my head. "Not here," I said. "I have a small group. We're getting out. Soon. It doesn't happen without Isen."

"How do I know this is real?" he asked.

The answer seemed obvious to me. "You don't. But you have nothing to lose and everything to gain. I'm giving you a chance at getting out of here, and all you have to do is *not* fucking kill someone. How hard is that? I'm not asking you to lose, just don't kill him. Please."

Yorin leaned back against the wall and crossed his arms. For a while we just stared at each other. Maybe he was trying to decide if I was telling the truth, or just playing for time. Maybe he was flipping a coin in his head about whether to kill me there and then. I had nothing else to offer, no other cards to play. All I had was the hope that he would see the truth; that it cost him nothing yet gained him everything he wanted. "Five days. Five fights," he said. He leaned forward and the look in his eyes convinced me of the truth behind his next words. "If I'm not out of here in five days. I'll kill your boy, and then I'll kill you."

There seemed little else to say after that. I might have bartered for more time, but I had the feeling it would just have weakened my argument. Whether I liked it or not, I had just put us on a timer.

I stayed to watch the fight even though it hurt me. It sounds strange to say it hurt me. I'll wager it hurt Isen much more. As fast and strong as he was, he didn't stand a chance against Yorin.

Hardt didn't show up, so I watched alone, silent amidst the hoard of screaming scabs and foremen.

By the time it was over, Isen was a bloody mess, still struggling to stand despite the beating. He didn't land a single solid blow. The crowd shouted, roared. They knew what was coming next. A lot of scabs shunned the arena, those who didn't like watching people die for sport, but those who turned up to watch wanted to see the death. I robbed them of that pleasure that night.

As far as I am aware, Isen was the only person ever to fight Yorin and live. I suppose that might have been a grand accolade to some, but he still marked it as a loss. Even worse, he knew the only reason he was alive was because I had convinced Yorin not to kill him. Everyone knew that was the only reason Isen survived his fight. For all the damage it might have done to our friendship, it did so much more for my reputation down in the Pit.

216

CHAPTER 21

I was just four years old when the Orran-Terrelan war broke out. I've read around the subject and I now know the truth, as told by both sides. The Orrans started the war, but it was already coming long before the first troops crossed the border.

The Orran lands were craggy, full or rocks and forests and the indomitable Kinei range of mountains. Where the land started to turn flat and arable was where the Terrelans staked their borders. Our little continent of Isha has always been lush, rich in valuable minerals and farmland. They had the land, we had the mines. But that wasn't why the war started.

For almost a century before I was born, both Orran and Terrelan had been gobbling up smaller kingdoms until only the two remained on Isha. They drew up lines in the dirt and our soldiers stared at theirs, who stared right back. The history books call that time peace, but I'd wager it was anything but peaceful. Sanctioned raids on border towns saw families on both sides caught up in the conflict before it even officially began. Josef was one of those. He was an orphan even before the war started, yet he still blamed Orran for making the first official declaration.

At the time, I didn't even know what a war was, let alone that I was part of the Orran Empire and they were fighting one. My little forest village was far from the front. I think the closest Keshin ever came to the war was when the recruiters took me from my parents.

Years later, after a decade of training in the academy, Josef and I were sent to the front lines. By then, the Orran Empire was losing. So many Sourcerers were dead already. Not to mention the soldiers tasked with waging the front lines of the battles. So many lives lost over lines on a map.

Our tutors argued we weren't ready. Those in charge argued that readiness no longer mattered. The Terrelans were just a few day's march from the capital and if they reached it, the war was all but lost. Looking over reports and maps of the time, I could have told them the war was already lost, and two young Sourcerers couldn't have made a difference. All we managed to do was slow down the advancing tide of flesh and metal and magic. But, like the tide, the Terrelan advance was unstoppable.

They sent us out with the best scouts the Orran army had left. I remember a woman by the name of Aranet; she was tall and lithe and had face like old leather, all tough and wrinkled. Aranet didn't care that we were Sourcerers. She didn't care that we held the effective rank of a captain and therefore outranked her. Aranet kept us alive as we moved through the besieged Orran lands, harrying the advancing Terrelan army. Without her, I have no doubt we'd have been captured or killed long before the final battle.

Under the watchful eyes of the scouts we snuck into the Terrelan camps. Josef used Biomancy to spoil food supplies, speeding decay and planting illness. I used Impomancy to summon monsters from the Other World to savage the horses. We caused as much chaos as we could and vanished before the soldiers thought to look for us. It was like a game to us. I thought myself untouchable in those days.

We never saw the carnage we caused. Aranet was quick to pull us away once the job was done. We never saw the illness or starvation Josef caused. Never saw the mutilated corpses of so many horses. It's quite surprising how much damage a small pack of khark hounds can do in a short time, and they were a favourite summon of mine. Nearly mindless and easy to control, I could happily summon five or six of the beasts and barely break a sweat. It turns out, the stronger willed the creature summoned, the harder it is to control. They don't want to be commanded. The lesser monsters fight it because it goes against the freedom they're so used to. The greater horrors fight it because it is slavery. Ssserakis eventually taught me that. It had a rage that almost rivalled my own.

We slept irregularly and for only a few hours at a time. Grabbing some shuteye is somewhat different for a Sourcerer than it is a soldier. The scouts had the luxury of leaning back, closing their eyes, and drifting off. I admit, it may not have been quite that easy given all the things they had seen, but some of them seemed able to find sleep within moments. For Josef and I, things were a little more difficult. We each kept five Sources in our stomachs, a heavy load no matter how small the Sources might be. Josef couldn't sleep with an Empamancy Source inside and I couldn't with an Impomancy Source, lest our magic go out of control and lay waste to those around us. Each time we tried to steal even a little sleep we would have to suck on

Spiceweed and vomit up everything in our stomachs. Life
for a Sourcerer can be quite wretched at times. Even so, I
wouldn't trade my magic for all the meals and sleep in the
world. I love the power far too much.

The Terrelans caught up to us in a barn outside the
village of Cartswold. I think they were scouts, tracking us
as we harried the main force. They were inside the
building, killing us before I had chance to wipe the sleep
from my eyes. Josef was faster to grasp the situation than I,
he was already swallowing down Sources while I was still
trying to stretch out a yawn.

It is not easy to swallow down a Source. A sad fact
of Sourcery is the larger the Source, the more powerful it is.
Some are the size of a marble and can be forced down with
a little effort and little more pain. Some are the size of a
grape. Some are the size of a small orange and take
considerable force to ingest, they are even worse on the
way up, coated in bile. Some are even larger still. I have
seen Sources as large as a fist and I have seen Sourcerers
able to somehow swallow them. I will admit I have always
wondered how such a thing is even possible. The largest
Source I have ever seen was the size of a melon. I've always
been fascinated by what sort of power a Source so large
might grant, but alas, even a garn couldn't swallow such a
thing, and those monstrous slugs have no Sourcerers so no
reason to try. It is probably the most powerful Source in the
world, and the last time I saw it, it was being used as a
doorstop.

We were on the balcony in the barn and the fighting
was taking place below us. I could hear metal clashing
against metal, the screams of the injured, and sickening

thuds I didn't understand at the time. Now I know all too well the sound of a sword or axe sinking into flesh. It is no less sickening, nor is the sucking *squelch* flesh makes as metal is pulled free.

I shoved my Pyromancy Source into my mouth and tensed as I forced it down. It was a larger Source than I was used to and had a sharp edge. I bled a lot back then. It was not uncommon for me to vomit up blood each night. Despite that, I hated every moment I wasn't carrying at least one Source in my stomach. For as long as I can remember, I have felt incomplete without magic inside of me.

As soon as the Source was sitting inside, I dragged on its power and ignited my right hand with a burst of green flame. Josef stopped me with a hand on my shoulder. I could see he was struggling to swallow down a second Source. I remember seeing him shake his head and after a few moments he simply told me not to use fire. He was right, of course. We were in a barn, surrounded by straw and dried wood. I could have turned the entire building into a pyre in mere moments, but it would have been for our funeral.

As Josef leapt off the balcony and floated down to the ground floor, using Kinemancy to slow his decent, I shoved my Portamancy Source down my throat. It was easier to swallow but still uncomfortable on the way down. Below, I could see Josef was using psychokinesis to throw dropped weapons at the soldiers pouring in through the open doorway. I opened a portal to the ground floor, stepped through, and snapped it shut behind me.

It was my first taste of real battle. The first time I had ever seen death and carnage up close. There were already bodies on the floor, both Orran and Terrelan. I hesitated to join the fight. I knew I had used my magic to kill before, but it was different when I could see the people I was trying to murder. Aranet paid the price for my hesitation.

The weathered scout turned and shouted at Josef and I to run. I remember seeing a soldier rise up behind her. I could have stopped it, but fear of killing the man paralysed me just for a moment, and that moment was all it took for him to bury his sword in Aranet's head. Josef blasted the soldier away with a kinetic burst, but it was too late. I will always remember the sight of Aranet's face half separated on the left side with a length of steel embedded in her skull. Shattered bone, pulverised flesh, and pulsing blood. I will always remember the look in her eyes. It wasn't fear. It wasn't even pain. Surprise and confusion were the last things Aranet ever felt. It was sickening. I had known Aranet. Maybe I would never have called her a friend, but I respected her. She dropped to the ground a ruin of what she had once been. I would probably have vomited but for my body's stubborn refusal to relinquish the Sources I had inside of me.

We were losing, outnumbered and most of the scouts were dead already. Josef and I might have been able to fight them off, but neither of us had time to swallow the rest of our Sources and neither of us was prepared for a close quarters fight.

I opened a portal behind us, one emptying out just a few hundred paces away. With just two scouts left to protect us, one severely injured, the fight was lost. I helped the injured scout to her feet and pushed her through the portal. She cried out in pain, her right arm almost severed at the elbow. The last scout was holding three soldiers at bay and I could see more forcing their way through the door in front. I grabbed hold of Joseph and threw us both through the portal, snapping it shut behind us. For a long time, I wondered if I might have been able to save that final scout. Probably. One more skull on the road behind me.

Josef was the first to his feet and he pointed back towards the barn. I didn't need him to tell me. I drew on my Pyromancy Source and created a flaming ball in each hand. They grew as I launched them towards the barn and impacted against the wood, engulfing it. Within moments the entire structure was ablaze. The ground rumbled beneath us as Josef used Geomancy to crack the earth and sink the barn in a crash of noise, splintered timbers, and burning embers. I remember the screams of the people trapped inside, burning to death. The blaze of that barn lit up the darkness.

I watched and listened for a long time, bearing witness to the carnage. Josef forced his Biomancy Source down and set to saving the last remaining scout's life. Her name was Lilth and, though Josef couldn't save the arm, I know for a fact that she survived long after that battle and long after the war ended. My road might be paved with skulls, but Josef's, I think, was paved with lives he saved.

I have always considered Aranet's death to be my fault. The first of the skulls I could name littering my wake. If only I hadn't hesitated. If only I had been stronger, faster, better I might have saved her. The morning after Isen and Yorin's fight I woke from a nightmare of the scout's rent face. I didn't realise it at the time, but it was Ssserakis toying with my sleeping mind, drawing out fear to feed upon.

I found myself coated in a cold sweat, crouched above Josef. I saw my friend's eyes flick open and felt my heart break a little at the terror I saw there. Josef scrambled backwards, scooting along the ground until he was pressed up against the wall. I froze and for the first time I realised my right arm was raised and I was clutching something. It was a small rock, no larger than my own fist.

"Why?" Josef asked, his voice quiet, quivering slightly.

You are the weapon.

It wasn't until I opened my mouth to speak that I realised I had no answer. The rock was in my hand and I was still poised to strike. Yet I couldn't understand how I had gotten there. An odd strength flooded through me. The fear coming off Josef was an ecstasy I couldn't compare at the time. These days I've tasted more than a few ecstasies, and I think I would still put that fear fairly high up on the list. I might have realised it was Ssserakis there and then, but every time I caused such fear the horror receded into whatever part of me it hid in, sated for a time.

The rock dropped from my hand and I fell backwards onto my arse. I sat there for a while, staring down at my hands and trying to reason out my actions. I had none. I thought myself a monster. A fucking monster! Mere moments away from murdering my best friend. The hatred I feel for myself has never been stronger.

"What is wrong with you, Eska?" Josef asked, still huddled against the wall. I saw Hardt stir from the corner of my eye, but no one else had seen my attempt to kill Josef. It took a long time for me to admit the truth of that night to Hardt. "First you push me away, and now you try to kill me?"

"I didn't..." My words stumbled to a halt. "It wasn't me. Or I didn't mean to..." Shame burned in me.

"To what?" Josef looked hurt, truly hurt. "Kill me? Why, Eska? Why?"

I floundered for an answer and couldn't fucking find one. I was crying again. I think I ran out of tears down in the Pit. At least for a time. There will always be more tears, and more reasons to shed them.

"I get it," Josef said, lurching to his feet, his eyes flicking briefly towards Isen. The other scabs in our cavern were all awake now. All watching. True privacy was hard down in the Pit. "Easier to move on if I'm dead. Maybe I just remind you of what you were."

Josef was breathing hard and there were tears in his eyes as well, yet still I couldn't find my voice. I think maybe this was the moment our friendship ended. I look back at it, and I wonder what I could have said to change things. Hardt likes to tell me there was nothing I could have done. He's wrong. So damned wrong. I could have fixed things. I just didn't know how. I never know how.

With a shake of his head Josef started to walk away. He kicked a little stone and it hit my knee. I barely felt it, yet I hissed in pain and for just a moment Josef stopped, the hard expression he wore crumbling away to concern. Then he shook his head and stormed out of the cavern.

I should have gone after him. Maybe... I like to blame Ssserakis some days for putting the fear in me, for telling me chasing after Josef wouldn't have helped. Another lie I tell myself. I just didn't know what to say. I had no way to fix what was broken between us. What I had broken.

Josef never returned to our cavern and I never looked for him. I left him there. I left my best friend, someone closer to me than my own blood had ever been, the other half of me, to live and die in a miserable existence deep underground. Even worse, I knew Prig and Deko would torture him to find where I had gone.

CHAPTER 22

It's easy to look back at my years at the academy and remember only the most harrowing bits, but that's not the whole truth. There were plenty of good times as well. Josef and I grew up thick as thieves living privileged lives. We were fed and clothed and treated to the finest education the Orran Empire could throw at us. Josef took to the lessons with a passion, but I took to books like no other.

We were in our second year of classes when the tutors started teaching us letters and words. As with most people my age I can barely remember the time I spent learning to read, and I'm sure I've forgotten half the books I've read, but I do remember the joy of being able to read. The academy library was quite extensive, and I had almost full access, barring some of the texts the tutors considered to be too dangerous for young students. Unlike some of the others in my class I did not restrict myself to factual texts regarding magic and history, but spent almost as much time reading bards' tales and depictions of folklore.

I remember one story about a warrior of great renown who travelled the world fighting monsters. Most of the creatures he encountered were crude depictions, giant beasts with multiple heads or fire breathers. In truth, they were rather tame, given that I was already learning the basics of Impomancy. What really fascinated me about those stories were the hero's travels through exotic lands where few terrans ever set foot. I think that was when I realised how small my world was.

History books tell us that the Orran and Terrelan empires were all that was left of a hundred smaller kingdoms. Terrans fighting terrans for control over the lands they deemed theirs. After the fall of Orran only the Terrelan Empire remained. Still, I considered myself Orran for a long time even after the empire was nothing but memory and unmarked graves.

Most folk from Orran or Terrelan never even considered that the world contained other peoples. We all knew of the Rand and the Djinn, it was hard not to with the great cities, Ro'shan and Do'shan floating around the skies. But most terrans on Isha went their entire lives without seeing a pahht or tahren, let alone those who lived even further away. It wasn't until later in my life I discovered why, that the other races shunned Terrelan. I changed that. For the better or worse.

The stories I read made me want to see the world outside the empire, but they also made me realise, and appreciate, how old the world was. It was through those stories I first realised that there are things, secrets buried deep in the earth and rock beneath us. Some of those things are precious and valuable, things of wonder. Others are better left buried and forgotten. I was fool enough to dig them all up.

Isen ignored me the next day. And I was fucking furious. I saved his life and he sulked about it. It was a slight to his pride that, once again, I stood between him and death. As though it were far manlier to roll over and die than to let a woman save him. But Isen was quick to forgive and forget. Not that anything I'd done for him really required forgiving.

I didn't tell the others about my deal with Yorin. It was a distraction they didn't need. I just pressed upon them how little time we had left to escape. The rest of the digging was done by Hardt and Tamura. I was too short and not strong enough for the work, and Isen could barely stand, let alone swing a pick. That didn't stop Prig from lashing him for slacking.

The whispered rumours about me grew and grew. The other scabs started bowing their heads to me as I passed by, and some even came to me with gifts, currying my favour. My fame had grown due to confrontations with the most powerful people in the Pit. I knew it couldn't last. I wasn't just living on borrowed time from Yorin. Soon, the rumours would be too much for Deko to ignore and he would have to make an example of me. It's the way arseholes like him work. As useful as I was to him alive, I would serve just as great a use as a broken corpse strung up near the Trough. Reputation is a blade with no hilt, it cuts both ways.

By the fourth day we had opened the crack enough that even Hardt could start to climb up into the dark crevice above. We were so close I liked to think I could smell freedom as well as hear it. Tamura agreed with me, I think. He said, *"Fresh rain on the ground."* and I took it to mean it was a pleasant smell. What a load of shit that was. Nothing down in the Pit smelled pleasant.

Nobody wanted to say it, but we had no idea if it would lead to the surface. For all we knew the crevice would close just a dozen meters above leaving us trapped with no way, but back down. We could keep digging, of course, but I believed Yorin's threat was real. I had just one day left to give the man freedom or both Isen and myself would pay the price.

"I'm going up," I said, staring into the darkness.

Trapped with the rock closing in. Crushing in the darkness. I shook the thought away and buried it.

Tamura nodded. "First to flee, first to fall," he said.

Hardt just stared at the crazy old man for a moment before turning to me. "You sure? Maybe I should go."

"Chivalry now of all times, Hardt?" I said. "The last thing I'm afraid of, is the dark." It was true enough. I had faced down the darkness and accepted it inside of me, even if I wasn't yet sure of what that meant.

"I was thinking there might still be some digging to be done." Hardt was ever the practical one. "It might require a bit more strength than you have."

I thought Hardt might be surprised by my strength, but he meant strength of arm and he wasn't entirely wrong there, but I hated being called weak in any sense of the word. "It might require a bit more space than you'll have." I replied and patted my belly to insinuate he was fat. It was a harsh insult and unjust, but I really was a bitch. I plucked the little hammer from the ground. "Can't swing it if you're wedged in tight."

Hardt made a sour face and nodded, and the discussion was over. I just wanted to be the first up into the crack and the first to taste the freedom above. I wonder if I would have gone back down to fetch the others if I had found my way out.

Hardt gave me a boost up, shoving me towards the crack and I reached for a handhold, pulling myself up into the waiting darkness. I could see the crack opening up and the crevice beyond seemed to stretch out forever. I wedged my feet against the wall and pushed my back against the other. Tamura handed me the little hammer and a small lantern to hang from the rope tied around my waist, acting as a belt.

What if the lantern breaks? A blazing corpse wedged between rock.

I'd be lying if the thought didn't cause me fear. But fear was what Ssserakis wanted. I eventually learned that feeding the horror was a good way to shut it up for a time.

Now I was up in the crack I could hear the wind whistling above, feel the cool breeze on my skin. It would probably have put a chill in me if not for the permanent cold I felt inside. Besides, spelunking is not an easy sport and the effort will soon warm a body up.

I inched my way upwards, squeezing myself against the rock and reaching for handholds. The light from the lantern helped a little, but I was feeling my way up more often than not. It was hard going, and I earned more than a few scrapes, but I was used to little injuries by then. Cuts and grazes were nothing new, the pain kept my mind sharp. Strange to say it, but it's quite easy to let your mind wander crawling through the darkness. You start to see shapes, black against black, images the mind tries to decipher. That, I think, is why so many people fear the darkness; their minds trick them into seeing things that simply aren't there. That is what I thought I was seeing when I looked up and saw two yellow eyes staring at me from the darkness.

I glanced up, seeing the yellow dots, then squeezed my eyes shut. I could hear myself breathing hard, the hammering of my blood rushing through my ears. I could feel the closeness of the rock around me. Fear made me indecisive. When I opened my eyes again the yellow lights were still there glinting back at me. I froze, staring up at them. It's hard to say how long I waited there, not moving. Hoping that they hadn't seen me. Hoping if I didn't move, they wouldn't notice. Long enough that I heard Hardt call up to me.

The lights didn't move, nor blink out. They just sat there in the darkness above.

"I'm alright," I shouted without taking my eyes from the lights. Fear paralyses, makes us weak. I hated weakness and I hated being afraid, and I knew the best way to overcome fear is to face it head on. I started to crawl upwards. Still the lights didn't move. I could hear the whistling of the wind, closer now, and feel the breeze.

At some point I realised what it was I was looking at. They weren't eyes in the dark or even lights. They were reflections from the lantern hanging at my side. I reached out towards them, and my hand met rock, hard and unyielding above me. I scratched at it with broken nails and pulled free a small gemstone that held the reflected lantern light within even when I cupped my hands around it, cradling it in complete darkness.

I let out a short laugh and pocketed the gem before prying the second one free as well. Only then did I let the reality of the situation dawn on me. The way above me was solid stone. The crevice we had opened up ended and I was fairly certain we were still far from the surface. I unhooked the lantern from my belt and held it up to be sure, but all I could see was rough rock.

Well that's the escape plan over. All that's left is to wait for Yorin to finish the job. The thought brought on a nervous type of fear that niggled at me. I almost dropped the lantern as I tried to fix it back onto my belt, and only then did I let frustration take over. You might think that deep underground there is no one to hear you scream, but sound carries.

"Are you all right?" I heard Hardt shout. "I'm coming up."

"No." I shouted back down before lowering my voice again. "Then we'd both just be up here fucking sulking in the dark."

"What's the matter?" he shouted.

I shifted to the side a little so I could look down and see Hardt's face, lit by a lantern, staring up from so far below.

"The crevice ends. There's no way out." I felt like screaming again. I very nearly did.

Tamura's face appeared below me, shoving Hardt out of the way. "Nothing from nothing," said the crazy old man. "Even the sea begins somewhere."

"Right." I rolled my eyes though I knew he couldn't see it. "Really fucking useful. Thank you, Tamura."

He whistled up at me before Hardt shoved him out of the way again. "Can we dig the rest of the way?"

Looking down I knew I hadn't moved more than four levels up, maybe less. We'd have to dig through close to sixty feet of rock to reach the surface. I tried to think of a witty response that would make Hardt feel as stupid as the question he asked. I was feeling a bit too frustrated and exhausted to be witty.

"No," I shouted back, my shoulders slumping. "No," I repeated to myself so quietly my words were drowned out by the whistling of the wind around me.

There is a point where inspiration hits. It's strange. Almost like having an idea, but not knowing what the idea is. I floundered for a moment, desperately searching for the reason that hope was flaring within me again. Then it dawned on me. The whistling of the wind. Everything had to have a beginning. A strong breeze didn't just come from nowhere, and it was a strong breeze.

I started feeling around, placing my hands on the rock all around me until I felt where the wind was whistling into the crevice. After raising the lantern once more, I could finally see a small hole in the rock just in front of me. Another crack to dig away at. Swapping the lantern for the little hammer I started smashing away at the rock, trying to widen the hole. Rubble rained down around my feet and I heard Hardt shout, asking what I was doing. I didn't bother to answer. I was far too busy smashing away, tearing rock free from the wall in front of me. I hoped the big man had the sense to back away from the falling debris.

Fresh sweat dripped into my rags as I hammered away at the wall. Before long there was an opening large enough to shove my hand through. After a couple of inches of rock, I felt empty air all around, a gentle breeze cooling my sweaty skin. I pulled my arm back in and shifted until I could peer into the hole. I saw little yellow lights shining back at me, dozens of gemstones like the ones in my pocket. A grin spread across my face as I realised all was not lost.

The lights beyond were not bright but they showed flat walls, a carved roof and ceiling above. The hole didn't just open into another crevice. There was a room the other side of the wall. For just a moment I wondered if it was a part of the Pit, sealed off and forgotten about, but the walls were too flat and uniform to be hewn from the rock by us scabs.

Just before I pulled away from peering through the hole, I saw something move against the darkness and then it was gone. I ignored it, believing my eyes were playing tricks on me. I was wrong about that.

I hammered away at the wall some more until the hole was large enough I could put a leg through it. By then I was coated in a layer of sweat and feeling every bit of the exhaustion. I realised then I couldn't do it alone.

Crawling back down the crevice took far too long. My excitement filled me with nervous energy and I almost fell a couple of times before I finally felt open air beneath me, my legs dangling. A moment later strong arms wrap around me and Hardt lifted me from the crevice to the ground.

I grinned up at the big man and wrapped my arms as far around him as possible, squeezing him tight. I found him smiling back at me and Tamura too was giggling, as though my excitement were somehow contagious.

"I thought you said there was no way up?" Hardt asked.

"Not up." I was breathless from the climb and the excitement. "But out maybe. I found a hole in the wall of the crevice where the air was whistling through. Just like you said." Tamura nodded back at me. "It opens out into a room. A room. Carved and everything. A proper room."

Hardt nodded slowly. "Just a room?" he asked.

"Well I think there was a door leading out of it," I said as if the question were a stupid thing to ask. "There must be."

Hardt didn't look convinced. "Leading where?"

"I don't fucking know," I said. "But if there's a room then there has to be more. Carved walls and a ceiling don't just appear in the middle of solid fucking rock."

Hardt still didn't look convinced. He glanced at Tamura and then back at me. "Better than nothing," he said. "So how do we go about exploring? Two people through at a time until we find a way out?"

I shook my head. "I was thinking we'd open the hole wide enough so we can all fit through and then get out of the Pit for good."

Hardt let out a sigh. "We'd only have whatever food we could scrounge together. Oil too. We'd be better exploring for a day or so at a time. Maybe you and Tamura. You two don't need to dig."

"We don't have time," I said. I knew it was about time I came clean. "I didn't so much save Isen's life as give it an extension." I let out a sigh and hoped Hardt would understand. "I told Yorin I'd get him out as well." I saw the look on Hardt's face and decided to plough on before he could argue. "And if I don't help him escape by tomorrow, he's going to kill me and Isen."

For a while Hardt just stared at me. I'm still not sure if it was anger, disappointment, or something else he was feeling, but whatever it was, he swallowed it. Hardt was always good at that. I, on the other hand, have always struggled to hide my feelings.

With a shrug, Tamura grabbed the lantern and hammer from my belt and leapt up into the hole. He was far more spry than a man his age ought to be. Within moments all I could see of him was a shaking light shining down from the crack above.

"Do you think he'll come back?" I asked, attempting to lighten the mood.

Hardt nodded. "Tamura is crazy, but he's reliable. He won't go running off making decisions without us."

It was hard to miss the intonation. "That decision saved your brother's life," I spat. "Something you seemed unwilling to do." I regretted saying that the moment it burst from my lips. I still regret saying it, even now. I saw how much it hurt Hardt. The words were mine, but the fault was his. His pesky pacifism was what almost killed Isen.

Silence settled between us, broken only by the scrabbling of Tamura up in the crevice above. I couldn't help but wonder if I'd just destroyed another friendship. I was fast running out them to burn. I've never been very good at repairing things, relationships least of all. I've always been so much better at doubling down and laying waste to everything around me. Luckily, Hardt doesn't share that trait with me and he's never been one to hold a grudge, though I have given many opportunities to in our time together.

"Thank you, Eska." I saw the big man swallow back the lump in his throat. "Isen won't say it and I think someone needs to." I'm not sure which of us felt more awkward then. It was probably me. I wasn't used to being thanked for things.

The sound of metal striking rock started to echo down from above and rock dust cascaded around us.

"We'll need some food then?" I asked.

"For a start." Hardt began pacing. "Lanterns as well. We have two but we'll need more. One each would be best, and oil to fill them."

"We won't get that but for the storeroom and Deko keeps that guarded. Can you and Isen get in?" I knew it was unfair of me to ask but I couldn't do it all myself and I already knew where I would be needed.

Hardt shook his head. "Isen is still in a bad way and..."

"Hardt," I interrupted him. "I need you and Isen to do this. I'll take Tamura and get as much food as we can carry."

"How?"

"I don't know yet." It was a lie. But I didn't want Hardt knowing what I was going to do. He wouldn't agree with it. I don't think he'd have let me go through with it. These days I've done far worse things of course, and Hardt has helped me. I wonder if I corrupted him somewhere along the line.

"We still have a problem with Deko and Prig," Hardt said. "If none of us are there to dig, Prig will start looking for us. Enough people have seen us around this area. It won't take long before Deko has a full search for us. They'll find the crack." He paused and I could see him struggling with something. "I want to get out, Eska, but we can't help Deko and his thugs escape as well. They're criminals. Real bloody criminals. They're here for good reason. Bad enough we're helping that murderous snake-kisser Yorin escape."

"Don't worry about Deko," I said. I could see Hardt was about to argue. "And don't ask why not. Just leave it. Please."

Hardt drew in a deep breath and nodded. Some things are better left unknown and he didn't want to know my plan. "What about Prig?" he asked. "We could do with taking him out."

"I'll see if our murderous snake-kisser can help," I said. "Get him to earn his freedom."

"Tomorrow then?" Hardt asked.

"Tomorrow," I agreed. "We each do our part and meet back here."

With that our plan was made. More rock dust and rubble fell from the crack above and I heard Tamura give a giggle. I was so nervous. A hundred different things could go wrong and Ssserakis whispered each of them to me. I tried to ignore it, but the horror knew how to scare me, and the fear I fed it made it bolder.

Worse than the fear, though, was the guilt at leaving Josef behind. I knew I could have looked for him still. I knew I should have. Maybe I would have found him, repaired the rift between us. But, as I have said, I am not very good at repairing things. I've always been so much better at breaking them and setting fire to the remains.

CHAPTER 23

Photomancy is one of the strangest schools of
Sourcery for it involves the manipulation of something
most of us can only barely perceive. It is the power to wield
light, or so the tutors said. In terms of practical applications,
the uses are many and powerful. With it, a Sourcerer can
create a powerful flash of light so bright it blinds all those
who aren't swift enough to shield their eyes, or bring about
a darkness so complete one would think the world had
simply stopped being.

Barrow Laney was a Photomancer. He entered the
academy around the same time as Josef and I, and we both
counted Barrow as a friend. He was always quick with a
smile and knew jokes that could even make the tutors
blush. There was an easy charm to Barrow, yet I have never
known anyone so devoted to their studies. Perhaps it was
because he was the only son of a merchant and had been
expected to learn the business before the academy took
him, so studying came easy to him. Or perhaps it was
because he knew from the start that his particular
attunements would eventually drive him insane, and he
wanted to fight it. He was a master of Photomancy even at
a young age, took to it like water to a sponge. Barrow could
make you see things that weren't there. Illusions crafted by
his imagination and brought into existence by his magic.
He once handed me a bouquet of flowers so red they shone

like blood. But they weren't real, and when I tried to take them my hand passed through the stems and the petals burst apart to become butterflies that flitted about my head and landed on my shoulders. I was only eight or nine at the time and I giggled as only a child can, truly and utterly lost in the joy.

Of course, the tutors had a much more sinister use for Photomancy.

The academy was there to teach Sourcerers, all schools of Sourcery. Well, most of them. Some schools were deemed too useless to bother learning, or too dangerous to teach. But the Orran Empire was at war, it needed Sourcerers trained for battle, and Lesray, Josef, and I were the newest batch of recruits. It wasn't enough that we knew how to use our magic to bring death and destruction to our enemies, we needed to be willing to use it. We needed to be able to see what we had done, what we were doing, and not balk. Not waver. We needed to be weapons. Orran's weapons. The Emperor's weapons.

The three of us were separated from the others twice a week, taken aside. They started slow, I suppose. The academy Photomancers showed us things, wove the light into illusions. Perhaps they were things from the imagination, or perhaps the horrors they showed us were from memory. Bodies. Hundreds of them. Thousands. An ocean of blood, thick with corpses like islands. Scavengers picking at dead flesh. Crows ripping out eyeballs, dogs fighting over a leg torn free in a ragged, wet squelch. This was what they called starting off slowly, adjusting us to the things we would see. After all, it wouldn't do if they newest little soldiers broke down at the horror of their first battle.

Bastards! They started off slowly, but it was only the beginning.

Twice a week, every week, they took us three aside and showed us things, made us do things. All in the aim of desensitising us to the violence, to the pain, and to the death. All in the aim of removing us from the consequences of our actions. We were just the weapons, and a dagger does not feel guilt over the flesh it parts.

Twice a week for ten years.

All those times they told us Terrelans were animals, not people. All those times they told us Terrelans would murder and rape their way across our kingdom, slaughtering good, honest Orrans. When they told us we were heroes, bringing justice to the world by killing monsters. It was not our responsibility, that others would shoulder the burden of conscience. All those times they told us we were just weapons. We were arrows, the tutors and generals we would serve were the bows, and the Emperor was the archer. I believed them. I believed all the lies. I believed them because I wanted to. I wanted to stay in the academy, stay with Josef. I wanted to be useful, to the tutors, to the Emperor, to the Iron Legion. I believed the lies because I looked up to the tutors. I thought they had our interests at heart because we were children, and they were adults, and I trusted them. I believed them because I didn't know any better.

I am the weapon. They drilled that into us over and over.

See the horrors of war. It doesn't matter. The victims aren't people, Terrelans deserved to die. *I am the weapon.*

Kill an ant. Its life was meaningless, nothing. *I am the weapon*.

Kill a mouse. It was an animal, not really alive. Mindless and soulless. *I am the weapon*.

The corpse of a man, peeled open, innards on display, the smell of death nauseating. It was only a Terrelan, as numerous and worthless as the mouse. *I am the weapon*.

I am the weapon.

I am the weapon.

Twice a week, for ten years. A day of death, of pain, of punishment. A day of being forced to see and do things no child should endure. I don't know if I was ever truly innocent, but what little I might have had, they stripped from me.

I found Yorin where he slept in a small, private cavern on the nineteenth floor. It took quite a bit of asking around, and a few incentives, but it was useful information to know. I had already considered sneaking up to him in his sleep and putting an end to the uneasy partnership. Unfortunately, I wasn't sure I could kill him quick enough to get out with my own life. That, and I needed him.

Despite the danger of creeping up on a known murderer, I did it anyway. Crouching down in front of him, I wondered how easy it might be to kill a man while he slept. I had certainly been close to trying with Josef. Nobody wanted Yorin along, but we didn't have a choice. Unless we did. One swift rock to the head was all it would take. Put him out of all our miseries.

I was still considering how easy it might have been to kill him when Yorin's eyes flicked open. He was quicker than I, muscles practised to instant motion. Yorin leapt up and his hand closed around my neck, bearing me down onto the ground. I didn't fight back. I doubt I could have squirmed free even if I had tried, and I had no weapon with which to defend myself, only the icy blue of my eyes and the knowledge that Yorin wanted freedom as much as I did. That, and I was his only chance of that freedom he desired. Without me, he would rot down in the Pit for the rest of his dwindling days.

When his hand eased from around my neck I sucked in a deep breath and coughed, rubbing at the tender flesh he left there. You would think I would have learned my lesson about sneaking up on people long ago, but I still haven't. I think I like to see the shock and sudden fear in their eyes. At least these days I am better able to defend myself from retribution.

"Are we ready?" Yorin asked, standing up and crossing his arms. I surged to my feet and stared up at him with a slight smile tugging at my lips. Yorin scared me. Hardt wasn't wrong in calling him a murderer. I knew full well there was little between me and a painful death. But I refused to show Yorin that fear. Another man might have taken offence at that, but not Yorin. He didn't seem to care one way or the other. A true pragmatist. Along with a murderer. It made for a dangerous combination.

"Later today," I said "We have the way out, just collecting supplies."

"When?"

"After feeding down at the Trough. There's a tunnel on level ten, far side. Use the stairwells. The lifts won't be working." I took a deep breath. "I need you to do something first."

"I've already not killed someone for you, girl. What more do you want?" There was an edge to Yorin's voice. He always had an edge to his voice.

"I want you to not kill someone else," I said it with a grin, as though it might make the request more reasonable.

"Done. Can we go?" I think that was the closest I ever heard Yorin come to a joke. I gave it a smile at least.

"Fuck you. There's a foreman called Prig," I said. "I need you to beat him up. Badly."

Yorin raised an eyebrow at that. "You want your foreman out of the way so he doesn't search for us? Why not just kill him?"

I might have lied. I could have said his death would cause too many questions asked and we didn't want Deko looking too closely into it until we were long gone. Sometimes a lie is necessary. Sometimes a truth is better. "Because one day I'm going to return, and I want to kill the fat fucking slug-licker myself." It's just as important to tailor a truth to the audience, as it is a lie.

I expected him to smile, but Yorin just nodded at that, not a trace of emotion. "Done."

Gruel was carried to the Trough in vats. The bread was carried down in sacks. It was all handled by the foremen and Deko's captains. Hard work was usually done by the scabs, but Deko was wise enough not to trust any of us with the food. We were kept hungry for a reason and food was the highest form of currency to us down in the Pit. Deko wanted it that way because he controlled the food. One more way to keep the scabs in line. It was fucking diabolical.

I dragged Tamura down to the Trough with me, and we waited for the food to be delivered. A raised dais where the gruel could be spooned into bowls and handed to us. Where mouldering bread could be thrown into starving hands.

There were two captains manning the Trough. Burly men hand-picked by Deko for their ability to knock heads. I realised then where my plan was so likely to fail. *I* was the weakest link. I was small and not nearly strong enough, and I didn't know how to fight. I needed the captains out of the way and I wasn't strong enough to remove them.

I was still hesitating even as the first bowls of gruel were handed out. I was running out of time. I needed the scabs hungry.

"Calm before it breaks," Tamura said, his voice knowing and sage.

"I'm hesitating, I know." I ground my teeth in frustration. "I just... I need..." I trailed off as Tamura started forward with a giggle. We were to the side of Trough and I watched him skirt around it, leap up onto the dais, and strike.

The first of the captains went down to a punch to spine before they knew Tamura was there. The second turned, brandishing a ladle. In a move so quick I couldn't follow it, Tamura disarmed the man and chased him away with his own ladle. I'm not sure if I was more surprised

246

than the scabs watching, but I leapt into the opening Tamura had bought me.

Climbing the dais behind the food I caught the scabs' attention easily. Some laughed, a few cheered, most watched with eager eyes, wondering what I was about to do next. They had come to expect momentous events from me, and I didn't plan on disappointing them. If only they knew the price.

There is a secret to working a crowd, especially a crowd of underfed workers living their lives in the worst conditions imaginable. First, tell them the truth. Just a little bit of it. Just enough for them to swallow the lies that follow.

"Deko uses food to control us," I shouted. Out of the corner of my eye I could already see his thugs over at the Hill standing and staring my way. It would be only moments before they got order to remove me. I had just set in motion something I couldn't undo. Either I got the scabs to listen, to respond, or Deko would kill me. The rumours and fame were something he could ignore, but this was not. This was inciting rebellion. Luckily, there were far more scabs than foremen, and at feeding time almost all of us were down at the Trough; a churning crowd of flesh and sweat they would need to push through to get to me. "They dish out meagre portions for a lifetime of endless bloody digging. And all the while they keep the best bits for themselves.

"Fresh bread, more than most of us see in a week." The crowd was nodding along, but I needed them to do more than just agree. I needed them whipped into a frenzy. "They don't want us to know it, but they don't just get this shit." I kicked at the gruel to make my point. "The Terrelans give us broth. Real meat. Real food. Deko didn't get that fucking fat by accident. They steal the food that is meant for all of us." I can be quite compelling when I try and the crowd bought my lie without hesitation. In all fairness, it was easy to believe.

The foremen reached the crowd of scabs in front of me, trying to push their way through, but the scabs were pushing back. It wasn't just that I was speaking, of course, they didn't want to lose their place in line for food.

"It's not just the food, either," I continued while I could. "Clothes. Bedding. They steal everything meant for us." I was almost screaming to be heard over the noise of the crowd. I've always found it quite surprising how loud a crowd can be even when all they're doing is listening. "We're prisoners, not slaves!"

The first of the foremen to push his way through, reached the dais and leapt up. Tamura appeared behind the man and, with a twist, sent him tumbling away into the crowd. I didn't see him rise again.

"They make us fight in the arena for extra scraps." The crowd shouted at that. There were still foremen trying to push their way towards me, but there were others, captains included, at the edge of the crowd who started to back away. There was a charged sense in the air. I didn't realise until then how close Deko kept the scabs to revolt. Walking the knife edge between open revolt and resigned destitution. It must have been a tough balancing act for him, but he managed it with such brutal skill.

"Down below he is using us to build a palace underground. Deko thinks he's a fucking king. But he's not.

He's nothing. Just another prisoner like us." Another cheer and the foremen struggling to push their way through the crowd suddenly found themselves being dragged down. I saw little circles open up in the scabs where the more violent started to kick at the downed foremen. More deaths on my conscience. More skulls paving my way.

"We outnumber them!" I screamed myself hoarse that day. It was worth it. "They keep us down with fear. But I am not afraid. We are not afraid. This isn't fear. This is unity. This is strength." The crowd screamed with me. "Let's take back what is fucking ours!"

I finished by pointing towards the Hill where Deko and his captains were massing. It was hard not to see the glint of steel in hands. Shivs and clubs. Harder still not to see the snarl of rage on Deko's face. As I have said, burning bridges is a speciality of mine. If I didn't escape, I would have half the Pit tearing me to pieces by the end of the day, and the other half cheering them on.

Watching a crowd turn is terrifying when you're behind it. A shift in momentum, the damn breaking and flood waters rushing out in a wave that is all destruction and no reason. It's even worse when you're in front of it, and I have to give respect to Deko and his thugs. They held their ground against numbers that could have crushed them. They didn't. The rebellion lasted only an hour at most before Deko regained control. I have no idea how many scabs died that day, but I am the weapon, and it is not for the weapon to count the lives it has taken.

No sooner had the crowd turned, then I dropped back down behind the dais, and hurried away with Tamura, clutching two sacks of bread each. Even as we reached the closest stairwell, I could hear the sounds of fighting and the sounds of dying. I had just started my very first rebellion. It would not be my last.

CHAPTER 24

We are insular creatures. We rarely consider, truly contemplate how our actions affect others, affect the world around us. It is not selfishness or arrogance, it is simply a matter of perspective. Drop a pebble in a lake and the ripples will reach every bank. We cannot track every ripple, we cannot see every outcome. Consequence is defined by perspective. That same pebble dropped in the lake, affects a bird resting on the surface, and a fish swimming underneath in entirely different ways. And we cannot be expected to consider them all. Then again, maybe I'm just making excuses for my actions. For the violence I caused.

I tried to forget that I had just traded away hundreds of lives for a chance at freedom. I can't forget. Nor can I justify it. I did what I did, and I would be lying if I said I wouldn't do it again. Maybe that makes me a monster, yet it is far from the most monstrous thing I have done.

We found Yorin pacing a tunnel intersection near our escape route. He reminded me of a caged animal left hungry too long. Short steps, balled fists, muscles tight as though he were just waiting to pounce on something. When we got closer, I noticed fresh blood on his knuckles. Yorin seemed to calm when he saw us, standing up to his full, considerable height and taking a deep breath.

"Is it done?" My first words were all business. Yorin never did pleasantries.

"I don't like leaving them alive," he said. "Especially not a foreman. If you don't get me out and Deko hears of this..."

"We're getting out," I hissed and pushed past him towards our tunnel. "Besides, Deko has enough to worry about. If we don't get out, he won't care a rat's blistering arse about you when he has me."

Tamura let out a giggle. "Winter winds." He twirled a finger around in the air then clapped his hands together with a loud crack. "Churning waters. The mountain meets the storm."

"What does that mean?" Yorin asked.

I shook my head and glanced back at Tamura. He looked happy enough, despite the gibberish he had just spewed forth. "Sometimes I just don't know," I said.

When we reached the crack, Tamura collected my food sacks and placed them with his own against the far wall. He took a length of rope and tied them all together, leaving enough of the hemp to tie around his own waist so he could haul the food up and out.

A nervous energy filled my veins, and not just due to the prospect of escape. I didn't realise it at the time, only through looking back do I see why. There was a sense of fear, far greater than any I had ever felt, flowing through the Pit. It moved through rock and empty air alike. Hundreds of people fighting and dying below. Ssserakis fed on the terror and I felt it.

"Up there?" Yorin asked, staring into the darkness of the crack above.

"Yes."

"It leads out? I don't see any light."

I picked a lantern from the ground and stood next to him, shining it upwards to reveal cold stone above. "It leads to a way out," I said. "A buried building or something." One way or another, Yorin would have to learn the truth. "We haven't had time to explore it."

I saw him turn to me out of the corner of my eye. I chose not to look back.

"You don't know it leads out?" he asked. "Are you saying we could be trading one prison for another."

"Fuck you." I glanced to find his face unreadable. "Ask yourself this, Yorin. Down here there is nothing but death for you. A lifetime of fighting and killing before you have a bad day and someone beats you. Or maybe you survive long enough you just can't keep up any more. Or maybe Deko gets bored of you always winning. One way or another, you stay down here, and you will fucking die down here.

"Up there is a chance at freedom," I continued. "Maybe we just find more rock. Maybe we find a way out." I found myself becoming more heated as I spoke, anger and passion both slipping out through my voice. "I'm willing to take that chance because I can't stand another day down in this shitting hole waiting for Prig, or Deko, or the overseer or *you* to decide it's time I die."

I found Yorin nodding. "That's a good point." It's fair to say I was a little surprised. I had misunderstood Yorin. He was a murderer, that much was true, but he was also pragmatic. "So, what now?"

"What is that pig sticker doing here?" Isen's shout announced his presence and made me cringe. A part of me had hoped Hardt would have told his brother. It was foolish wish, really. Hardt has always supported me once I made a decision, but that doesn't mean he takes the hard parts off my hands.

I desperately tried to think of a way to calm Isen. I didn't want him angry at me when we were so close to freedom. A part of me still imagined our escape to be romantic. Once we were out, we would give in to our urges and come together in glorious union. I have mentioned my naivety before. It didn't take long before I was cured of that.

"Maybe she wants a real man along for the trip," Yorin said, still staring up into the crack. I saw Isen bristle.

"Maybe I should rid us all of you here and now." Isen was angry but I knew posturing when I saw it. So did Hardt. The older brother moved past the confrontation with a frustrated look sent my way.

"Take your shot," Yorin continued, still not even glancing towards Isen. "I doubt you'll get a better opportunity."

"HEY!" I stepped in between the two men and shouted so loudly both turned their attention to me. "Good. No one fucking cares. So bury it down here and follow me to freedom."

Yorin just shrugged. Isen deflated and pushed past me. I'd like to say I held my ground, but I was quite a bit smaller than Isen and I stumbled a step. I suppose it was my own fault. I felt I handled it all quite well at the time, but I was ignorant of the pride of men and the cost of disturbing that pride. The truth is, they were both fucking idiots and I should have known it was far from over. I stifled a hiss of pain as Isen jostled me, clutching at my still healing ribs, and he didn't even ask if I was alright.

"You going first then?" Hardt was packing supplies into as few bags as possible and following Tamura's lead by tying them together so he could haul them up after him.

I grinned at Hardt, all teeth and hungry eyes, finally feeling some of the victory I had achieved by pulling this escape together. "You're damned right I am..." Even as I finished saying it Tamura leapt up towards the crack and disappeared into the darkness. A few moments later the bags tied to him started off the floor and slowly rose up out of sight. I just stared after them for a few moments. "Fine. But I'm going second!"

I crawled, climbed, squeezed, and scraped my way up the crevice and breathed a sigh of relief when I finally felt hands reach through the hole in the wall as Tamura helped pull me through. If the climb had taxed him at all, he showed no sign of it despite his advanced years. Tamura's hair might have been greying with age and rock dust, and his skin was wrinkled, yet he possessed the strength and stamina of a much younger man. Though I occasionally caught him nursing an aching back, but then, don't we all?

The room was lit with a single lantern in the centre of the floor. Now there was real light I could see it for all its glory. The rubble on the ground was both stone and even some coloured glass. Bits of crumbling debris near the edges looked like they might once have been wood. It took me a moment to realise that the gemstones, the ones that held light, weren't just spaced randomly on the ceiling and walls. They were arranged into shapes, patterns that couldn't just be chance. Art is a subjective experience and often one better appreciated by age. I saw shapes of light and thought them pretty at the time. Later in my life, I wondered at such depictions and the creatures that made them. What meaning did they hold? Did artists make them or were they predetermined designs? History is often just another word for mystery.

I had little time to explore as I heard a grunt from the wall and moved closer to see a shape clawing its way up. Yorin was no climber, using brute strength where many would opt for skill. He pulled himself up, arm over arm, and ignored the grazes it earned him.

Stepping back, I reached out to help pull Yorin through into the room and he shrugged me away, struggling through the gap and flopping onto the floor. He grunted in pain as he fell onto a shard of stone. It was his own damned fault and I hoped it hurt. I was elated to be on the path to freedom, but it made me no more magnanimous.

I heard a curse from inside the crevice, something so inventive it could only be Hardt, and the grunting that followed confirmed it.

"I'm bloody stuck," he said with a lethargic sigh.

I poked my head back through the hole and held two light gems in front of me. I could see Hardt wedged just a few feet below. His shoulders were a just a little too broad and he was struggling to get past the thinnest section of the climb. It was terrifying for him. I could feel the fear, taste it. I giggled, and then burst out laughing. Hardt stared up at me, incredulous, for a few seconds, and then he started to laugh. It shouldn't have been funny. I don't really see the humour in it when I look back, but at the time I couldn't stop laughing. We were so close to freedom and Hardt was stuck because his shoulders were just a finger's width too broad.

It was the laughter that saved us in the end. With both of us giggling so hard, Hardt found the shaking pushed him through the tight space and suddenly he was climbing again, still chuckling as I helped Tamura pull the big man through the hole in the wall. The crazy old man joined in with the laughter. I'm not sure he really knew what we found so funny, but I've noticed many times in my life that Tamura doesn't need to know. He just enjoys laughing, and it's an act that's always more fun with a group.

Only Yorin didn't laugh. He was standing by the doorway, peering out into the darkness, a brooding shadow.

Isen was the last one out of the crevice, hauling the final bag of supplies with him. He sank down against the wall once he was through and let out a sigh. Even covered in muck and rock dust the man was handsome and never more so than when he smiled. I moved closer and sank down next to him. For a moment I think he forgot his damaged pride and we leaned into each other. I don't know if he was breathing heavily from the climb or from being close to me. I like to think, even now, that it was me. Actually, now I'm almost certain it was. A man who hasn't stuck his cock in anything for a while can get aroused by just about anything. I was scarred and dirty, and I wore it both on the inside as well as out, but I was also still pretty. Back then, such a trivial detail seemed so important.

We leaned into each other for a while and I enjoyed the smell of him. There was stale sweat, true enough, but we all boasted that smell. Isen also smelled, of Isen, and that was something I quite liked. I looked up at him and found him looking back. I ached for Isen to lean in and give me my first kiss. I could see nothing but his cracked lips and the blue of his eyes. Then Tamura giggled and we both turned to find the crazy old man squatting on his haunches and staring at us all too close and all too knowingly.

No one can embarrass quite like the young, and I was still very young. I felt my cheeks flush, a strange sensation considering I was still chilled to the bone, and pushed Isen away from me. Launching to my feet I stalked past Tamura and headed to where Yorin and Hardt were peering into the darkness beyond the doorway.

"...probably just rats," Hardt said. I pushed past them both into the dim light beyond.

The corridor connecting to the doorway stretched out into the darkness. A few light gems embedded in the walls nearby gave off a slight illumination, but it appeared they only glowed after being exposed to light and the halls had no doubt sat in complete darkness for more years than any of us had been alive. The air hung heavy, a slight breeze barely perceptible.

I stopped a few paces in and glanced one way, then the other. The corridor extended into darkness in both directions with a number of visible doorways. A few stone benches lined the walls along with some pedestals. Whatever had occupied those pedestals was long smashed or rotted. A few benches had been reduced to nothing but rubble. An ancient helmet rested nearby, too small for anything but a child and dented in the forehead. Something seemed off. Something I couldn't quite place at the time. I felt as though I had seen the architecture before.

"It's so dark, I can barely see you. Eska?" Hardt's voice from the doorway.

I am the darkness. Said the voice inside my head and I repeated it out loud.

"All the same, I think we'll light a couple of lanterns." I turned to see Hardt disappearing back inside the doorway. It was odd, but I could see him so clearly despite the dark. Yorin remained, leaning against the wall and squinting towards me.

"Feel the breeze?" I asked. "That means there's a way out."

Yorin just nodded.

More likely we've just traded a prison for a tomb.

CHAPTER 25

We should have tried to collapse the wall behind us, or maybe even the crevice. I'm not sure which would have been easier, but we should have tried to conceal our escape route. That, at least, might have slowed our pursuers. But we foolishly believed we had gotten away with it. I thought my distraction would provide sufficient chaos to cover our disappearance. I thought Deko would have his hands too full to search the Pit for me, and I thought Prig would be too injured to care. I was right about that. The one person I did not count on was the overseer.

After lighting two lanterns and distributing the supplies so we were all carrying our fair share, we set out in the dark corridor. We followed the breeze as best we could and checked in each room we came across. It was slow going but it was fascinating seeing a ruined city long since buried beneath the earth. I wished Josef was with me. He would have been as fascinated as I, wanting to stop and pick through the remains. I have always loved adventure, reading stories of grand quests through buried tombs, but Josef loved history and spent almost as much time reading the annals. But I had left him behind. I had made the choice to leave him behind. Oh, how I wished I could take it back.

The architecture continued to tug at a memory I couldn't quite recall. The walls sloped outward for the first two feet from the ground and then inward at a slighter gradient all the way to a high ceiling. They were patterned, designs carved into the rock from which they were built. Some of the patterns seemed eloquent shapes and nothing more, while others looked like they might be lettering in some foreign language none of us knew. I wasn't sure if any of the others could read any known languages, though I guessed Tamura probably could. Whether or not his addled brain made sense of the words was another matter. I realised then how little I knew about my companions' pasts. But I didn't need to know who they had been or what they had done. I knew who they were, and that was what was important. Well, except for Yorin. I knew nothing about him other than his skill at killing things.

Every now and then, along the walls, an alcove showed remnants of statues. Every one, without fail, was little more than rubble laying around shattered remains. The others didn't seem to think anything of it, but it had me worried. Time laid waste to all things, but some things decayed more swiftly than others. Some of the stone benches were rubble, it was true, but those were far outnumbered by those left mostly intact. I pondered over the question of why stone benches might stand the test of time, yet stone statues did not. The voice in my head, the one I mistook for my own thoughts, suggested time and time again that we might not be alone in those endless halls of darkness. And they did seem endless.

At first, I thought we might have somehow gone in a circle and doubled back upon ourselves. It's hard to judge how straight a corridor is when you can only see a dozen feet in front of you. That first day we walked for hours, checking every room along the way, ignoring stairwells that led up or down. Isen argued we should be going up whenever the opportunity presented itself and it sounded sane enough, but Tamura and I had other ideas. We were following the breeze. The slight taste of fresh air was more certain to lead us to freedom than a stairwell leading to even more darkness. At least, that's what we thought.

We walked in silence for the most part, each of us listening to the sounds echoing around us. Or sometimes we just listened to Tamura humming away to a tune only he could hear. No matter which, there seemed little to say to each other. I think the tension between Isen and Yorin had something to do with the silence. The two had settled into a quiet disdain for each other and I feared any attempt at conversation might bring an argument between them. I doubted Isen would resort to violence, he knew Yorin would win, but if Yorin decided to fight, I wasn't certain any of us could stop him from killing Isen.

That first night we slept in a mostly empty room. I think it might have been a kitchen once, a small stone stove in the corner sat dusty and dead. We were all exhausted, even Yorin was starting to drag his heels, and there was little else to do but clear away patches of rubble and collapse into sleep. I wanted to curl up with Isen. Our impending freedom gave whatever was between us a growing urgency I couldn't ignore. But we were surrounded by the others, all close together in a small room. Of all the things I have done and seen in the world, nothing is quite so confusing as young lust. In the end I curled up with Hardt, as I had for weeks. I think I saw a pang of jealousy on Isen's face before I closed my eyes and dropped off to slumber.

I dreamed that night. Vivid dreams of eyes watching us in the dark, dozens of them. Beady little yellow lights that never blinked, staring at me while I lay there, paralysed. I still don't know if that dream was real or a product of Ssserakis playing with my subconscious to feed on my fear.

I woke in a cold sweat to find the lantern had gone out and darkness had settled in. A few of the light gems still glowed with a dim yellow hue, just enough for me to roll away from Hardt and refill the lantern. I was already gnawing at a heel of stale bread when the others started to rouse.

Our supplies were limited and we had no idea how long it would be before we found a way to the surface, so we ate sparingly. All of us were used to small rations but I wished my stomach would stop growling. It seemed like forever since I had properly sated my hunger.

When we started walking again, I decided I could no longer take the silence. "Does anyone have any idea what this place is?" I asked. "We've been walking for... I don't know, a long fucking time, and it's just one corridor with rooms either side."

"And stairwells," Yorin pointed out. He was fairly vocal on the desire to start heading up.

"Old," said Hardt.

"Older than old," said Tamura. I heard Hardt let out a weary sigh. Some men did not like riddles and that was all Tamura spoke in.

"The crazy old man is right," Isen said before his brother could round on Tamura. "Look at the walls, Hardt. We've seen this before. It's a Djinn city."

I honestly couldn't say what surprised me more; that we were walking through the corridors of a dead city that had once belonged to a Djinn, or that, of all the people in our little group, Isen was the one to realise it first.

Hardt let out a bitter sigh. "Not again."

"It might not be like last time." Isen said. He was ever quick to forget anger and with Yorin walking behind us all and not speaking, it seemed his sour mood evaporated.

"What happened last time?" Someone had to ask, and I thought it might as well be me. Especially as Tamura would likely spout some riddle that would frustrate Hardt, and Yorin's very presence annoyed Isen.

The brothers shared a quick look and then Isen launched into the story. "Before we were thrown in the Pit, we were gentlemen of fortune."

I admit it was a term I had not heard before. Yorin clearly had, by the merry laugh he let loose. "You were brigands," the pit fighter said. Like it or not, Yorin always had a way of cutting to the heart of the matter.

"Buccaneers," Hardt said with a shrug. I tried to step between Isen and Yorin and the younger brother's scowl faded a little.

"That's why you were down in the Pit?" I was eager to learn as much about Isen as possible. Infatuation has a way of making every little detail fascinating, and pirates were fascinating enough already.

Yorin laughed again. "You don't get thrown in the Pit for pirating," he said. "You get hanged."

I was tempted to ask then why the brothers were down in the Pit, but both lapsed into a sullen silence and I doubted I would get an answer though I longed to know the truth. Curiosity and all that. "So, about this other city." I said. "It was like this?"

"Not quite," Isen said with a snort. "For a start it was underwater."

I have since been to the city the brothers talked about. Everything they told me was true. What Ro'shan and Do'shan are to the sky, Ol'shen is to the seas. An underwater city that dwarfs any the terrans have ever built, but it does not float on rock. Ol'shen sits inside the largest jellyfish the world has ever known. A true wonder designed by the Gods, or at least by the Rand and Djinn, and they certainly liked to portray themselves as gods.

"We weren't just pirates," Hardt started the story, his deep voice echoing in the empty tunnel around us. "We were commissioned by the Terrelan navy to harry merchant vessels across the Sea of Whispers."

Yorin laughed. "And you call me a bloody monster."

I didn't understand at the time. My life had been the academy and the Pit. I knew nothing of the wider world. I didn't understand that the Terrelans were hiring pirates to attack the other peoples of Ovaeris. I had never seen a pahht or a garn. I think most of the other races came to hate us because of the Terrelans. It turns out prejudice breeds more prejudice. I hope I have done some small part in my life to healing the wounds the Terrelan Empire caused.

"You *are* a monster," Isen growled. "How many people have you murdered?"

"None," Yorin said. "I've killed hundreds. Never murdered anyone."

"Little fucking difference," Isen argued.

"All the difference," Yorin said, his voice remaining calm where Isen was getting heated. "Everyone I've killed, I've done in a fight. Maybe not a fair fight, but every one of them signed up for it, just like you did. I beat every single one with my own fists or the weapons they agreed to. I've never attacked a man who weren't ready for it. I certainly didn't sail around an ocean murdering other people because they were different."

That seemed to bring an end to the argument. I think Isen and Hardt knew what they had done. They struggled to come to terms with it. Hardt still does.

I'd had enough of the arguing. "Any chance we could stop attacking each other, and one of you could tell me about this other city?" Diplomacy is overrated. Sometimes people just need beating into line.

"We found it by accident," Hardt said. "After boarding a pahht ship and stealing the most valuable cargo. We thought it was another job well done, and we were in the clear. Sailors like to have a drink after a successful spot of buccaneering, and a good few of us were drunk. That's probably why we woke up to find both our navigator and captain dead. Our charts were missing, most likely thrown overboard."

Isen grimaced. "And we had no idea where we were, only that one of the damned cats had stowed away and steered the ship so far off course I barely recognised the colour of the sea."

"Sounds like you had a run in with a chaakan," Tamura said. I thought it was gibberish but the brothers nodded. I later learned the chaakan are the most elite pahht saboteurs, spies, and assassins. Rumours say they are trained from birth and are nearly invisible when they want to be. They strike from the shadows and leave no trace behind, not even a hair. I consider that quite the feat, given that they are covered ear to claw in fur.

In truth the pahht have always held a fascination for me. The ancient Rand used to treat them as pets, though at the height of their power both the Rand and the Djinn used to think of all us lesser peoples as such. But the Rand favoured the pahht for their cat-like appearance and gave them secrets they guard with the utmost jealousy.

"We never found the fucking cat," Isen continued. "Some of the others didn't think there ever was one. They blamed the death on ghosts or something."

"Ghasts," I said, eager to show off some of my own knowledge. Every other member of the group had so much more life experience than I. They had seen things I had only read about in books and many of the things they were discussing I had never heard of, not that I was willing to reveal that ignorance. One thing I did know, though, was magic. And I was foolish enough to advertise the fact.

"Is there a difference?" Yorin asked.

"Ghosts are fragments of the dead raised by Necromancy," I said with a casual shrug. "Unless there was a Sourcerer nearby with a Necromancy Source it couldn't have been a ghost. They can't exist except that a Necromancer summons them and maintains them. Ghasts are disembodied horrors from the Other World. If an Impomancer has summoned one and lost control, they are free to roam our world until someone destroys them. Either way, neither can really affect the living, other to scare them and cause some pretty vivid hallucinations."

Isen was staring at me, a slight smile on his face. "You really are a Sourcerer," he said.

I nodded and smiled back, quite giddy that he looked at me like that. It sent a warm tingle across my skin. The feeling didn't last. Ssserakis saw to that by planting thoughts of betrayal in my head.

"We sailed for days," Hardt continued, "trying to follow the stars, but with the navigator dead we had no idea where we were going." His face looked drawn out, etched with grief. "And more of us kept dying. It got to a point where it wasn't safe to be alone, nor in groups. Each time the shifts changed we'd find another couple of bodies. No one ever saw what was doing it, but I think by then most of us knew it was a chaakan. Eventually there wasn't enough of us left to sail the ship, nor search for whatever was killing us. We lowered the skiffs and piled into them both, scuttled the ship and watched it sink."

"Never did see the cat." Isen had real venom in his voice. I didn't see it at the time, but when I look back, I think maybe Isen was a true Terrelan. He only ever seemed to speak of the other peoples of Ovaeris with derision. Then again, maybe he had good reason to hate those he did, the chaakan had murdered his crewmates, and he no doubt considered some of them friends. "Hope the bastard drowned."

"Right," Yorin scoffed. "The pahht was the bastard for taking a small measure of revenge against the people who boarded their ship and killed their people. On that ship you boarded, how many of *them* did *you* leave alive?"

Isen was furious, I could see that. I'd wager Yorin could see it too. The younger brother was red faced even in the gloom, and his muscles stood out around his jaw as he ground his teeth together.

"None," Hardt admitted, his voice soft and laced with guilt. "We never left anyone alive. Those were our orders."

I heard Yorin laugh, but didn't bother turning to look at him. "Monstrous," he said. He wasn't wrong.

Hardt shook his head and continued the story. "If you've ever been stranded at sea, no water or food... Madness sets in. Dehydration, sun exposure. I don't know the cause of it. But... Madness. We were pretty close to the end, no land in sight, and Isen leans out and stares down into the water, saying he sees something. Before I could stop him he just overboards and disappeared beneath the surface."

"Because I did see something," Isen said, a sullen tone in his voice. "Saved both our lives."

Hardt nodded. "You did. I jumped in after him and could just about make him out, swimming straight down. I followed, trying to pull him back. I didn't even see the thing until I was on it. It was..." He ran out of words.

"Have you ever seen a jellyfish?" Isen asked.

I hadn't, though again, I hated to admit my naivety to them. I think it was just Isen I didn't want to admit it to. I didn't want him to think me inexperienced. It was foolish really. Everyone in our little group could see how inexperienced I was. I might have been leading them, but only because no one else wanted the damned job, and Tamura is too bloody crazy to lead himself in a dance.

Isen continued at the silence. "It's not a fish at all, it's more like a big... um..." He stopped and looked to Hardt.

"It's a jelly. Slimy skin, no real substance to it at all." His explanation of the creature gave me no real insight into how it looked. I nodded all the same and he forged on.

"Couldn't have been too far from the surface and when I touched it. I just sort of passed through the skin of it." Again, Isen looked to Hardt and again the older brother shrugged. "I could see something vast below me. Couldn't really make it out, given the water blurs everything. There were smaller things too, swimming through the water. Fishes and such, I guess."

"Mur," Hardt said. "The mur are what saved us, Isen. You started drowning and I wasn't far off it either. I saw them come and take you, drag you down. And then one had me too, tentacles wrapped around my arms."

"What's a mur?" Yorin asked and I was glad he did. It saved me the question, and I was loathe to ask it.

"Body a bit like a terran, I guess," Hardt said, gesticulating towards his arms. "They have a face and arms, though the skin looks, uh, stretchy? Rubbery. The bottom half, past the gut is all a writhing mass of tentacles. I've seen them swim, they suck water into their chest, inflating, and then push it out through..."

"Through their arse," Isen said.

"Well, yeah, sort of," Hardt agreed. "But they don't have an arse."

Isen only nodded at that. The truth is mur don't look anything terran, but they can morph their skin to give the appearance of a face. I have spoken to a few. They do it in an attempt to not alarm us terrans. I found their true form to be far less disconcerting.

"Strangest people I've ever seen," Hardt continued. "But they saved us. Dragged us down to the city and threw us out into a room filled with air."

"Underwater?" I asked. "The city is underwater, but not?"

"Some of it is," Hardt said, sounding uncertain. "Well the whole thing, submerged in that jellyfish creature, but not all of it is flooded. Maybe half the city is water and the other half is air."

"The corridors looked just like this," Isen said. "The way they slope out and in. The same carvings. Only it wasn't deserted. All sorts of things living there."

"People," Hardt said. "They weren't things, Isen. They were people. Just... different people. Mur and pahht, even a few garn. We even found a small group of terrans living there. Orrans who found the place by accident. A bit like us only they decided they liked it there. They're probably still there now."

Isen pulled a face, his lips pinching together. I was too blind to see the truth then. I think everyone else saw it though.

"How did you escape?" Yorin asked.

"We didn't," Hardt continued the story. "The city surfaces every now and then and the creature half... I don't know, spits it out? Luckily for us, it was just a couple of miles off the Terrelan coast. We said our goodbyes and swam it."

"Good riddance," Isen grumbled.

Tamura, walking ahead of us, stopped. He cocked his head one way and then the other, before turning around in a full circle. His eyes were wild, darting every direction and I wondered what he had seen.

"Dead end," Yorin said as he ignored us all and continued walking. He was carrying one of the lanterns and held it up to show the corridor in front of us just stopped, a flat wall blocking our path. "So much for following the breeze."

Tamura was still turning around and around, like a strange dance. I realised I hadn't been paying attention to the breeze for quite a while. Whether the crazy old man was moving about in an attempt to find it again or if he had just lost his mind completely, I couldn't tell.

"Once before and once again," Tamura said.

"Wonderful," Yorin said. He shone the lantern straight at me. "Now what?"

I shrugged. "Now, I guess we find the nearest stairwell and go up." It seemed the most logical course of action. Tamura apparently had other plans.

"Treasure!" the crazy old man shouted and then he was off, running towards a nearby stairwell. I barely had time to react before I saw him vanish into the darkness.

CHAPTER 26

I've always liked to run. Maybe my training at the academy put that in me, or maybe it was already there before. There is something about a good sprint with legs pumping, carrying me as fast as possible under my own power. It's close to freedom, in a way. Not running from or to anything, but just running for the sheer bloody joy of it. I had fallen out of practice with my time in the Pit, and Tamura was faster than his old bones should have allowed.

I didn't wait for the others to decide what they were doing but took off after him. I could see flickering light fading away down the stairwell and wasted no time in launching myself down the steps. Only Tamura and Yorin carried lanterns, and the stairwell was almost full dark around me, yet I could see. Somehow, I could see the steps outlined in the darkness. I didn't spare it a second thought then. Maybe it was because the darkness inside of me was a shade darker than anything else the world might throw at me.

The steps led down for a while before stopping on a small landing and then doubling back on themselves, always leading further and further down into the bowels of the dead city. I could see Tamura's light bouncing away far below me. The crazy old man was moving faster than I. Youth, apparently, only counts for so much. After every few sets of steps, there was a landing which had a doorway opening out into even deeper darkness. I couldn't see much past those portals, but some had little yellow lights watching me pass.

I lost track of how much deeper Tamura led us into that place. Level after level sped past me in a blur. I heard the others shouting somewhere behind but ignored them. I can't really say why. It might have been wiser just to let the old man run off, disappear into the darkness. Maybe we should have counted him lost and made our way up, looking for a way out. But I couldn't just let Tamura go. I liked him. He spoke in riddles and I'm fairly certain he had fleas, but something about him comforted me. Tamura has always been part friend, part mentor, and more a father to me than any other I can remember.

I wondered how deep into the earth that city went. What secrets it might hold once it was explored fully. It would take a lifetime just to excavate the areas long since buried. I do know that stairwell continued down even after Tamura left it. He was following something, a memory, and it led into a new corridor. I trailed after, breathing heavily as I followed the light that bounced along in his wake. I didn't bother shouting after him, he wouldn't have stopped. For a crazy old man with a splintered reality he can be quite single minded when a compulsion takes him.

I stopped at the doorway to the corridor, partly to catch my breath and partly so the others, still coming behind me, knew we had left the stairwell. No sooner had Isen appeared around the corner, before I was off again, ignoring the burning in my limbs and launching back into a sprint before Tamura's light disappeared and we lost him in the darkness.

It was a strange feeling pushing my body like that. I could feel sweat breaking out all over my skin, yet I still felt cold inside. Cold, and hungry, and lost, but I couldn't share those feelings with anyone. I knew none would understand. Maybe Josef would have. He certainly knew the hunger. I think he knew the feeling of being lost as well. That was something we shared. But he was gone. Behind me. Left to fend for himself against the monsters I abandoned him to. And how I hated myself for abandoning him. No matter what he had done, how he had betrayed me, I missed him so much.

Tamura's light disappeared, stray beams bouncing around to the left of the corridor for a moment and then gone. I skidded to a halt at the doorway he had used. My feet ached as though the bones in my heels were about to shatter from the relentless pounding. My threadbare shoes were disintegrating and I was almost barefoot.

I started through the doorway and stopped, very nearly pitching off a cliff to my death. The sight ahead of me was bloody awe inspiring. A crumbling set of stairs to my left ended after just two steps and opened out into a grand hall so large it put the great cavern of the Pit to shame. Giant pillars stretched from ground to ceiling in columns, each so large it would take two dozen of me to ring it. The walls, much like those of the corridors, sloped outwards before inwards and stretched nearly a hundred feet above me, I found this more than a little amazing, considering the floor was maybe fifty feet below. Oddest of all was how well lit the hall was. Each of the two dozen pillars had spiral veins of glowing blue mineral snaking through it, casting the whole hall in an ethereal hue.

Tamura wasted no time with the view, he was already scrambling down what remained of the staircase, the lantern swinging from his belt. I was still standing there, awestruck, when the others finally caught us up.

"Huh..." Yorin's voice, and for the first time since we had met he sounded cowed. Grandeur on that sort of scale has a way of making even the most egocentric of us realise just how small we are. It was the same sort of reaction people give the first time they see Ro'shan and Do'shan floating through the sky. Or in Do'shan's case floating in the sky, secured firmly in place by massive chains buried deep into the earth.

"Looks just like that underwater city," Hardt said between deep gasping breaths.

"Except... more dead," Isen agreed.

"The other city had a hall just like this?" I asked, unable to take my eyes off the sight in front of me. I hesitate to admit it, but I was acting like a simpleton, staring all around the grand hall and wondering at what could have built it. It is humbling to see such things. To know we walk in the footsteps of giants, and to realise those same giants could crush us without even noticing.

"More than one," Hardt said. I could hear him moving about behind me, scuffing the stone as he leaned out to see Tamura clambering down to the floor. "We saw one completely flooded. Full of mur doing... uh. They said it was where they spawned. The other was dry enough. Had a roaring fire that didn't need any wood to burn, kept the whole place nice and warm. The pahht were using it as a marketplace. Some of the things they sold..."

"Remember the one that offered me a child?" Isen asked. "What would I do with a little cat anyway? Would just be a furry mouth to feed. It would probably just have stolen my purse and run back to its mum."

Yorin snorted and pushed passed towards the edge. It took him only a few moments to lower himself over and then he was following Tamura down to the ground.

"Where are you going?" Isen's voice was a snarl.

"Following the only one of you who has a lick of fucking sense," Yorin said, his voice strained as he concentrated on the climb down. Before long all three of us were scrambling down, side by side, after Yorin.

Tamura was waiting for us at the bottom of the climb. The crazy old man shifted from foot to foot and repeatedly counted the pillars in the giant hall. Yorin was kneeling, poking at something on the ground.

"Nice of you to wait." Isen was breathing hard and scowling. I thought it made him look dark and handsome in a brooding sort of way. I think back now, and he sounded petulant, and if there is a less attractive trait in a person, I don't know it.

"Nobody else is going to say it, so I will," Yorin started. "What happened here?" He stood up and was holding an old sword in his hand, rusted beyond use. The blade was already disintegrating into a red brown mist of dust. "There's weapons like this scattered all around; all old and crap, but used. Helms too."

"Not to mention the scarring," Hardt agreed. "Walls with rents slashed through them. Benches caved in. Statues defaced."

Isen snorted. "It's just time. These places are old..."

"Older than old," Tamura said.

"Right," Isen said. "Older than old. You know that, Hardt. We saw it in the other one. The creatures there said they'd been there hundreds of years if not more.

"This..." Isen picked up another rusted old sword and slapped it against the nearby wall. The blade burst into dust. "This is what happens when good metal is left to rot for that long. What I wouldn't give for a real sword in my hand." The look he gave Yorin was vicious, and I knew then that their fight was far from over.

Tamura giggled and we all looked his way. "This is what happens when magic and monsters..." He clapped his hands together so fast and hard that the slap echoed around the emptiness of the hall.

We all stood there for a while in silence, listening to the clap echo and straining to hear anything else. Thankfully, the world around us fell silent once again and I let out a sigh of relief.

Tamura was still grinning as he turned and struck off towards one of the pillars. I watched him go for a moment and then followed, ignoring the battered and broken swords and armour that littered the ground along with other bits of rubble and debris. We should have listened to Yorin.

Tamura stopped at the first pillar and started poking it, walking all around it and running his hands over the seams in the rock. I moved in for a closer look at the glowing blue mineral. It looked almost crystalline. It twisted and snaked through the pillar in strange designs. I reached out, scratching against the seam with a fingernail but it was as hard as the rock it was sunk into.

"It's warm," I said idly as I lay a palm against the pillar. "What is it?"

"Blood of the earth." Tamura was still moving around the pillar, tapping at bits and running his hands over the rock. Hardt and Isen had retrieved a third lantern and moved off to the side of the hall, checking inside one of the many doorways. Yorin wandered off, and I turned away as he pulled out his cock to piss against one of the pillars.

"I thought people called lava blood of the earth?" As soon as the words were out of my mouth Tamura stopped searching the pillar and reached out, grabbing my left hand. I tried to pull away but the old man's grip was iron. He turned my hand over and traced a fingernail along one of my veins. I think I was caught between anger, shock, and indignation. Despite the look on my face Tamura just stared at me with a smile. "Blood is red, and blood is blue." He let go of my arm and went back to the pillar.

I am no Biomancer, but all students at the academy were taught some rudimentary physiology. The Orran Academy did a lot of bad in its time, but it also gave me an excellent education.

"Blood is only red when exposed to air," I said slowly. "Are you saying this is lava without air?"

Tamura laughed, blowing out air in a snort. "No. Foolish girl."

I'd be lying if I said I wasn't fairly angry at being called a fool. I felt my cheeks flush red and my hands clenched into fists. Despite the anger coming from me, and the heat coming from the pillar, I still felt cold inside. I fought to master my frustration and managed to push it down.

"That's what you get for expecting wisdom from a crazy old man," Yorin said from nearby.

"So, you think my question was stupid?" I asked.

"No such thing as a stupid question," Tamura answered from the other side of the pillar.

"What about stupid people?" I asked with a savage grin at Yorin.

"Oh yes." Tamura's head poked around the side of the pillar and he nodded at me, then glanced at Yorin. "There are most certainly those. They are usually the ones who don't ask questions for fear of them being stupid."

The old man sighed and shook his head emphatically. "This. Is the wrong one." With that Tamura left the pillar and struck off towards the next one before circling it, searching with eyes and hands.

I glanced at Yorin and found him staring at me. "Crazy old man," he said.

I ground my teeth in annoyance and leapt to Tamura's defence. "That crazy old man is the only reason we're free. He found our escape route."

"We're not free," Yorin said. "This isn't free. It's all just another part of the Pit. It's the illusion of freedom. Chances are, we die down here. You and me. Probably not the old fool. The brothers definitely will. Either we starve before we find a way out, or those things get bored of waiting and eat us." He said it so matter of factly, I almost missed it.

"What things?" I asked.

"Eyes in the dark," Yorin said with a grimace. "Like the little light gems in the walls. But they're not. They watched us sleep last night. All night."

"You saw them too?" I asked. I was more than a little glad it wasn't just me. At the same time, I realised that meant there really were things down in the dark with us.

Yorin nodded at me. His face was so impassive, as though he didn't care one way or another.

"Fuck them! They won't follow us out and there is a way out." I said with force. I wanted Yorin to believe me. I think, perhaps, if I could have convinced the most sceptical of our group then maybe I could have started believing it myself. "There is, and we'll find it."

Yorin sniffed and shrugged. "The old man has found something." He pointed to where Tamura had his face pressed up against one of the pillars.

"Treasure!" Tamura grinned at us as we drew near. The way the blue light lit his face and the rows of hair on his head made him look manic.

I looked at the pillar. Unlike the others, this one had a white X scraped across it, each line as big as my arm. Some of the more fanciful books I read back at the academy, tales of adventure and peril and buried treasure often mentioned a similar mark. Between bard stories and real life, I find it is truly worrying how many times X marks the spot.

"Looks just like all the others to me," Yorin said.

Tamura set to scraping at the stone pillar with his fingers. "One and the same, all the same. Just like all the others. On the outside. All boxes look the same. Cases. Bags. A closed fist."

Tamura turned to us and held out both his hands as fists. He turned his hands over and opened the first. It was empty. He opened his second fist and on the palm of his hand was small sphere, no larger than a marble. "But inside..." he said.

Yorin looked at the open hand and sighed. "Another gem. We're surrounded by fucking gems, old man. Worth a fortune on the surface, no doubt. But down here I'd rather have a bowl of gruel."

Tamura ignored Yorin, his eyes locked on my own.

"It's not a gemstone," I said slowly, almost reverently. Already, I could feel my stomach rumbling and I ached to snatch it from Tamura's hand. "It's a Source."

CHAPTER 27

In our third year at the academy, the Iron Legion himself came to see our class. Josef was regarded as the star pupil and already the tutors were grooming me to support him. It wasn't just because we refused to leave each other's side. Josef was supposed to be one of Orran's most powerful weapons against the Terrelans and I was there to help him, to protect him and keep him loyal. We were both attuned to six Sources and able to hold five at once. Yet Josef was special. A genius with the use of magic, in both practical and impractical practises. Everything he tried, he took to like a bird to the wing. That is to say, with lots of trepidation, some panicked flapping, followed swiftly by glorious soaring above the heads of all his fellow students. He was leagues ahead of me in our studies, but it was not something he ever lauded over me, or any of us. He was that rarest of creatures, with power, knowledge, and humility all wrapped up in one. Not many of us can claim that. I know I can't. I have often wielded great power in my life, and it has ever made me anything but humble.

But if Josef was special, then the Iron Legion was extraordinary. Prince Loran Tow Orran, the greatest of Orran Sourcerers. Generations of breeding and experimentation resulted in a Sourcerer attuned to ten Sources, and rumour had it he could hold seven in his stomach at a time. Not only that, he could hold them for far longer than most.

It's a sad fact that the more Sources a Sourcerer holds onto, the more quickly those Sources start to kill them. I realised this around my third year, that all Sources killed the wielder. Some just got around to it faster. Attunement just meant a Sourcerer could withstand the pressures on their body for a little longer. But the magic would still kill them. We were simply not meant to wield it.

We were lined up in front of the Iron Legion and he looked at each of us. I remember him as being tall, regal-looking with a scholarly baring that belied his apparent ferocity in the war. It wasn't the first time I had seen the prince, but it was the first time since our arrival at the academy. I don't think he was impressed with me. He was certainly interested in Josef, and perhaps even more so, in the bitch-whore.

I thought the prince was going to give us a lecture or maybe even a demonstration of his powers. We had all heard the rumours in the mess hall and common areas. Students talked about the man as though he were the true emperor. Some said he was the most powerful Sourcerer who had ever lived. Others claimed to have seen the way he was able to combine magic from different schools. No one else could combine different magics, to even try always resulted in a rather dramatic and fatal explosion. A magical explosion is not like a physical one, it sends out wild, uncontrolled magic in all directions. It can tear the world asunder, rip holes in the very fabric of existence. No other Sourcerer was fool enough to even try what the Iron Legion could do at a whim.

I was already deep into my theoretical studies of Impomancy and I had seen many of the beasts and monsters it was possible to summon. Khark hounds held a peculiar fascination for me back then. They look just like wolves, only instead of hair they are covered in sharp spines. That, and they are also roughly three times the size of a wolf. I remember wondering how it would be possible to fight one of them. Then I heard students talking about the Iron Legion using Impomancy and Ingomancy together to coat a razorback in iron, protecting the few vulnerable areas the beast had. That was a crude combination of magics, but a potent one. I have since seen the ways Prince Loran combines the schools of magic in far more nuanced methods. His imagination and resourcefulness have long terrified me. And there is not much that truly scares me.

As the Iron Legion stared down at us, even the oldest of us still a child, I thought him ancient. He was tall and straight-backed, but his skin hung on his bones and his hair was grey and brittle. All but his eyes seemed old. Those eyes were bright and full of life and youth. I asked Josef, after the prince was gone, how old the Iron Legion really was. I thought Josef was lying to me, making me the butt of his joke. He told me Prince Loran was, even then, just nearing his thirtieth year.

Chronomancy does strange things to the body, speeding up and slowing down time within the natural processes. I am glad it is an attunement I do not have. Even now as I look down at wrinkled hands, I think I have had too little time afforded me. I often think about making my way back to Ro'shan and asking the Rand to turn back my years. I know she can. I just don't think I could pay the price.

You might wonder just how deep the need to swallow that Source went. The feel of magic inside, sitting heavy in the stomach is not quite an addiction, but in some ways it is far worse. Imagine waking up one day and finding you are unable to walk. You would soon miss the power your legs had once given you. You would soon miss the simple ability of being able to move from one end of a room to another. The knowledge that you no longer have that ability is only made worse by the memories of once having it. As time goes on you might start to cope with the lack, but you would always remember what it was like to be able to walk, and you would miss it. The feeling is much like that. I remembered what it was like to hold fire in my hands, to cross miles in a single step through a portal, to hurl rocks through the sky with a wave of my hand. I remembered it all, but I no longer had the power. And I fucking missed it!

"That's a Source?" Yorin asked. Tamura was still holding it in his hand. Even with a layer of rock dust I could feel the power inside of it. My stomach gave another rumble.

"Doesn't look like much, does it?" I said, my voice distant to my ears.

"First time I've ever seen one, I think," Yorin said with a shrug. "Unless the kids down in the Yarters were playing with magic marbles." It was the first snippet of personal information Yorin had ever volunteered. Yarters was the name given to the poorer section of Terrelan's capital city, Juntorrow. Another time I might have pressed, asked for more, but I was too busy staring at the power in Tamura's hand.

"They come in all shapes and sizes." I spared Yorin a grin. "The smaller round ones tend to be easier to swallow." My smile turned to a grimace. "Easier to bring up again as well."

Tamura was still holding the Source out towards me, his eyes locked on mine with a disturbing intensity.

"So, with that you can... what?" Yorin asked.

"I don't know," I said. "I have no idea what type of Source it is. It might give me the power to create us all a portal out of here. Or it could make my brain melt out of my nose. The only way to determine what sort of Source it is, would be to swallow it, and there's a good chance it would kill me. Actually, it will kill me no matter what. It's just a question of how fast it will go about it."

Yorin shook his head. "What?"

"Sources are magic in a sort of crystalline form," I continued. "We don't know where they come from or how they are made, but what we do know is that they clearly were not designed to be ingested. They give Sourcerers the ability to use magic, but they also damage the Sourcerer's body. If it's a Source I'm attuned to, I might be able to keep it inside for ten days before the magic starts to act on my body. If I'm not attuned, I would have minutes at best."

"The magic starts to act on your body?" Yorin asked, sceptical.

I nodded. "A Pyromancy Source would start to melt and freeze my insides. A Geomancy Source would start to turn my limbs to stone. An Empamancy Source would

287

make me fade away so nothing was left but disembodied emotions."

"That's possible?" You would think such a thought might scare even Yorin, but he just sounded curious.

"Have you ever walked through an emotion?" I asked. "A place that made you feel fear or joy without any reason why."

Yorin sniffed. "My mother used to say that was ghosts passing through."

I snorted. "Your mother was as stupid as most people then."

I didn't see him coming. I should have, especially after insulting his mother, but I was too focused on the Source in front of me. Before I knew what was happening, Yorin spun me around and shoved me up against the pillar. Tamura watched on. Whether the old man cared or not I'll never know.

"HEY!" Isen's shout echoed about the hall. "What are you doing?"

Yorin stared at me and I stared back. I could feel my heart thumping, but I still felt cold. Eventually the pit fighter let me go and stepped back. Some threats don't need words.

"Get the fuck away from her!" Isen snarled as he skidded to a halt beside me. I saw bright steel in his hands and wondered where he had found a sword. Yorin saw the weapon too and backed up another step.

"Got a bit of metal in your hands and suddenly you think we're equal?" Yorin asked.

"Are you alright?" Hardt said. I just nodded and turned my attention back to Isen and Yorin.

"I have had enough of you," Isen snarled. His face twisted in a way that should have made him seem ugly, but infatuation dulls even the most obvious signs. "Sure, you beat me in a fist fight, but I've always been better with a sword." Isen dropped into a ready stance, sword held out in front of him, ready to attack.

I realised then that no one was going to stop the fight. Isen had been itching for a real chance ever since Yorin beat him in the arena and left him bruised, bloody, and alive. Yorin wouldn't stop it, though I had yet to fathom his reasons. Hardt was too passive, despite his size, and I think he believed Isen could win. I think he believed we were better off without Yorin. Just a day ago I would have agreed, but I was starting to think otherwise. There were things watching us from the dark, and Yorin could fight.

Tamura closed in again, still holding out his hand. I knew he was offering me the Source. My stomach growled at the thought of it. My limbs tingled with the possibility of power. I found myself reaching for it and clenched my fist.

"ENOUGH!" I screamed, inserting myself between Isen and Yorin.

Both men stopped. I often wonder how strange we looked to the things watching us from the dark. Both men were far larger than me and muscled as those who were used to fighting. Yet there I was, barely a woman, standing between them and neither one moved. A part of me realised the hall had grown darker, the lights from the pillars and lanterns seemed less bright. The others realised it too.

"I understand you two don't like each other." My voice was edged with anger. I have always thought I sound rather commanding when angry. "But I. Don't. Fucking. Care! Right now, I need you both. Because one way or another I am getting out of here and seeing the sky again, and both of you are coming with me even if I have to knock you bloody senseless and drag you the rest of the way."

Yorin shrugged and stood up straight. Maybe it was his lofty attitude that Isen hated so much. Isen, for his part, held his sword up for a few moment's longer, his hands twisting around the hilt and his jaw clenching. Then he let the blade drop and shook his head.

"I saw him attack you," Isen hissed. Yorin snorted and walked away.

"What you saw was a man telling me not to insult his mother," I said. "I think it was actually quite polite in a Yorin sort of way."

Now that the threat of the conflict was over, I felt my emotions warring inside. A part of me was happy that Isen cared, happy that he ran to my protection. Another part of me wanted to swallow the Source and use its magic to teach Isen just how little protection I needed. In the end, I settled for a compromise and ignored the issue completely.

"Where did you find a sword?" I asked.

"We found an armoury." Isen smiled, much of his anger already forgotten. "Everything in there is completely intact. Cupboards, chairs, weapons."

"There's enough there for us all to arm ourselves," Hardt said. I noticed the big man carried no weapons himself.

"It wouldn't be much use for me. I don't know how to fight." It was hard for me to admit that to Isen.

"I could teach you." He smiled at me and I felt a strange flutter in my stomach at the thought of being so close, working and sweating together. I nodded, not trusting myself to say anything. That was when Tamura approached again, still holding the Source. I felt my eyes drawn to it and let out a ragged breath.

"Is that..." Hardt started.

"Magic," Tamura finished. His other hand shot out and grabbed mine, pulling it up and turning it over. He dropped the Source into my waiting hand and let go.

"How did you find it?" I asked. Staring down at the Source, I could feel my palm tingling. I think I imagined that. It had been a long time since I had last felt magic inside of me and I longed for it even more than I did for Isen's touch. It took a considerable act of will not to throw the little thing in my mouth and swallow, even knowing it was likely to kill me. Certain to kill me. "You knew it was there."

Tamura nodded. "I put it there. Like rain falling on the ocean, it comes back. I've been here before." He turned around. "I think. Maybe another life, another time. I hid my treasure. Found it again. Dogs bury bones."

"Does that mean you can use magic again?" Hardt asked, ignoring Tamura's ramblings completely.

I closed my fist around the Source and slipped it into the little leather snuff pouch tied at my belt. I imagined I could still feel it there, the pouch suddenly weighing heavily against the rope around my waist. It was all in my head, but it felt real.

"No," I said, morose. "Without Spiceweed to make me throw it back up again it's just a fancy way of killing myself. Each Source acts on the body in a different way. There are over twenty known Sources and I am attuned to just six. I don't like my odds." I was rambling, ranting. I wiped cold sweat from my forehead and tried desperately to concentrate on something else.

"You said you could teach me to fight?" I asked Isen. "How about we start now?"

CHAPTER 28

We spent two days camped out in that great hall. The delay grated on Yorin, that much was obvious, but he accepted the logic behind it. We were lost. Even if we could backtrack the way we had come, find our way back to the corridor with the breeze, we had no guarantee it would lead us out. Tamura claimed he had been to the city before, to the very hall we stood in, but he could answer no questions about a way in or out. His mind has always been a fragile thing and mostly so with memories.

With the great hall as a base to explore from, we had a plan, though our dwindling supplies would not sustain us forever. I visited the armoury Isen and Hardt found, and I felt the tingle on my skin. There was magic at play, a Sourcery lasting the test of time and keeping that time from decaying everything within. I am no Chronomancer, and even now I can't fathom how that magic worked. But I was grateful it did.

Yorin chose a pair of daggers from the armoury. He preferred to fight close where a sword would be next to useless. Hardt found some metal knuckles and claimed them at Isen's request. The big man still insisted he wouldn't use them. Tamura refused the offer of any weaponry. At least I think he refused. His reply to the suggestion was to laugh and say *"Does a river need a shovel?"*. I have never seen Tamura so much as hold a weapon, other than the ladle back in the Trough, and nor has he ever needed to. His skill with an open hand made him something of legend after I built my empire. Even that skill couldn't stop it crumbling all around me, though.

    None of us took armour. We hoped we wouldn't need it and that much metal would only serve to slow us down. There was also the fact that most of it did not look like it was intended to fit a terran body.

    Isen preferred to fight with a sword. He liked the reach it gave him, but I was ill-suited for the weight of it at that age. We trained with shorter swords, wrapped in layers cloth. After two days, I was bruised all over and not certain of any improvement. Isen's training regime appeared to be telling me to attack and then hitting me with the flat of the blade after brushing aside my clumsy attempts. Still, I relished the chance to be close to him and basked in the false praise he threw my way. We were both fools. I for my infatuation, and he for pretending I was improving. I know now how much time and effort it takes to learn to fight, and two days is far from enough. It also requires a proper tutor, and Isen was anything but.

    As the others ranged further and further, exploring the catacombs around the hall, Isen and I indulged the heat between us. The first time I ended up in his arms was a merry accident. I swung my little sword, expecting it to connect and Isen stepped backwards. I was not yet used to the weight of the steel and I overbalanced, pitching forwards. Isen caught me and laughed, and I laughed with him. I lingered there for longer than was necessary, enjoying the feel of his arms around me and the smell of him.

I thought myself quite clever the next two times I overbalanced and pitched forwards into him, each time slumping against his body and enjoying the feel of his warmth. I look back now and cringe at my foolish attempts to seduce Isen. A blind woman could have seen his interest in me, and these days I know all too well all I really needed to do was flash my tits and Isen would have had me on my back in moments.

There's an old saying about the third time being the charm, and we proved it. That third time as I lingered in Isen's arms, I titled back my head to look up at him and then his lips were on mine. As first kisses go it was pleasant enough. I felt the tingle of energy and the contact certainly had the right effect further down my body. We both tasted foul but that didn't stop Isen's tongue slipping into my mouth like a leathery slug slapping at my teeth.

All the stories I had read, and things I had been told made me think a first time should be special. Nobody ever told me the truth of it. Isen pushed me up against a nearby pillar and we pulled the rags off each other. What followed was painful, messy, awkward, and embarrassing. At least for me. Isen seemed to enjoy it well enough, and that just made it all worse.

I clutched at the pillar with one hand and Isen's back with the other, grimacing against the pain and wishing it was over. Luckily it didn't take too long, and soon Isen was panting and leaning in, crushing me against the stone. I let out a low whine from the pain between my legs. I think Isen thought it was pleasure by the noises he made in my ear.

No sooner had our bodies parted I collapsed to the ground, wiping at the blood and seed between my legs and shuddering at the pain of it. Isen lowered himself down next to me and let out a great sigh. I glanced sideways and saw him smiling, his eyes closed. It was all so fucking disgusting.

I thought it was my fault. For a long time, I thought I must have done something wrong. Everything I had read, and the few people I had spoken to, told me that sex was supposed to be enjoyable, pleasurable. But I hated it. The fact that Isen so clearly enjoyed it only made me more certain I was in the wrong. My inexperience had ruined it.

The others will know. They'll see the blood.

The voice in my head sent panicked fear coursing through me. I pulled out a bandage, bundled it up and shoved it between my legs. It was not yet time for my cycle, but I couldn't stand the idea of the others knowing what I had done. It was a foolish fear made all the more foolish when I later realised Isen was not nearly so discreet.

I felt a hand on my leg and startled, my breath catching in my throat, my skin crawling beneath the touch. Isen didn't seem to notice. He rubbed a hand up and down my thigh. It was so strange; just a few minutes earlier I couldn't wait for him to touch me, yet once it was over the thought of his hand on my skin made me feel sick.

"I've been wanting to do that for a long time," Isen mumbled, sighing again.

"Me too." I tried to hide it, but my voice was laced with disgust.

Isen chuckled, I think more to himself than anything else. "Give me a few minutes and we can do it again."

The thought of him inside me again sent a shiver through me. I pulled away, moving his hand and hauling myself to my feet. I pulled up my trousers and had to steady myself against the pillar, clenching my teeth against the pain.

"The others will be back soon," I said, hating how broken my voice sounded. Thinking back, I still hate it.

"Plenty of rooms for us to use." I looked back to see Isen staring at me with a hunger on his face. I forced a smile to my own and bit back the pain.

"Maybe later," I said. "I have to pee." I limped away towards one of the little rooms to the side of the great hall. It seemed to take a painful age before I was out of sight. I hadn't lied to Isen, I really did need to pee. I just didn't tell him that I also needed to vomit and sob silent tears into my hands.

I have hated myself many times in my life, and more than once I have considered that the world might be better off without me in it. This was one of those times. I thought I had done something wrong. I thought something was wrong with me. Neither were true. And I hate that I let him make me feel that way. I have since learned that Isen was neither a gentle, nor a considerate lover. I have since learned that sex can be pleasurable, but not from Isen. Silva taught me that.

I was still crouching alone in the empty room, comfortable in the darkness, when I heard voices echo in the hall. I wiped my eyes, checked the bandage between my legs was secure, and limped out to see what the others had found.

They knew right away, I'm certain of it now. Tamura watched with me concern and Yorin with an amused smile. I think Hardt knew from the way his little brother was grinning and strutting like a fucking fool. An awkwardness settled onto the group and it was one more thing I blamed myself for.

"Did you find anything?" I asked, stopping a good distance away from Isen and avoiding the look he sent my way.

Yorin laughed. "Aye, we found something while you two were fucking– training."

"Hey!" Isen growled, but he didn't move to confront Yorin. He moved to stand behind me and put his hands on my shoulders. "Eska's coming along well. I'll have her ready to fight in no time."

I felt him step close. It no longer gave me the yearning and comfort it had. I stepped forwards, shrugging my shoulders clear of him and hating the way everyone was staring at me. Again, Yorin laughed.

"What did you find?" I asked.

"Whispers of the sky," Tamura said. He wasn't smiling. I noticed that and it seemed strange. Grinning always came so easy to the old man.

"Tamura picked up a breeze again." Hardt wasn't smiling either. He had a severe look pointed right at his younger brother. "Only problem is, it comes from a collapsed tunnel. We tried going up a few levels, down a few levels. Every corridor that leads that way is collapsed. I think we can clear it, but it's going to take time."

"And effort," Yorin put in. "Unless you two are too busy *training*."

I fixed the murderer with a stare but he just shrugged and walked over to our campsite, collapsing his legs beneath him and reaching into the bag with our dwindling supply of bread.

"So, let's go," I said. "Clear it and move on." I was eager. Perhaps a little over eager. I wanted to be out, to be free. To be away from that place. I wanted to distract myself from the guilt and shame, and I wanted to distract Isen from staring at me the way he was, making me uncomfortable in my own skin.

Hardt held up a big hand and let out a sigh. "It's a fair way." He too started towards our campsite. "I hate to agree with Yorin here, but I think a meal and a few hours of shuteye would be best."

The delay ground against my nerves but I nodded all the same, not wanting to seem unreasonable. Isen followed me to the others and sat close by, always watching me. I hated it and I hated myself for causing it, but I refused to make a scene in front of the others.

We shouldn't have delayed. We should have left there and then. That was the night the eyes in the dark stopped just watching us and made their presence known.

CHAPTER 29

We should have set a watch. Yorin and I both knew we were being watched. The others thought we were safe, alone in the ruined city of the Djinn. It's a lesson I have taken to heart. I have since spent many days out in the wilderness, or sleeping alongside a road, or delving deep into forgotten ruins. These days I always set a watch.

I woke to the sounds of Isen shouting and found he had crawled close to me in the night. Hardt had pushed me away, yet more evidence he knew what I had done. I had drifted off to sleep feeling rejected, hurt. I hated myself enough already, and I began to think I had ruined my friendship with Hardt as well. Maybe that was why my sleep was plagued with horrid dreams. Or maybe it was Ssserakis, playing on my fears to sustain itself.

I was the last one on my feet. Isen already had his sword drawn and Yorin was in a ready crouch, knives in hand. Even Hardt had his fists clenched as though ready to finally throw a punch. Only Tamura seemed unconcerned, staring into the darkness and scratching at the patchy hair on his cheeks.

The little yellow eyes were all around us, but in the dim blue light of the pillars we could see what they belonged to. Each of the creatures stood close to three feet with a stoop. They almost looked like children, only their heads were overly large and their arms too long to be terran. That and they had no noses. Maybe you've never seen a terran face with no nose, I assure you it's fucking creepy. They wore no clothes of any sort and if they had genitalia it certainly wasn't between their legs. Some of the little creatures had a single tail, some had two, and a few of them had three; all swishing back and forth in the gloom.

There were hundreds of them surrounding us. But all they did was watch. Glowing yellow eyes fixed on our little group.

"What are they doing?" Isen asked, a note of panic in his voice.

There was no answer any of us could give. I scrambled to my feet, ignoring my aches and the need to pee. Like a wave extending outward the creatures bowed their overly large heads. Some even collapsed onto their knees.

"Now what are they doing?" Isen's voice rose again.

"Bowing," Hardt said and glanced sideways at me. "To you."

They were imps, creatures from the Other World. I thought they must recognise me, my power. I was a Sourcerer, an Impomancer, though I had no Source to prove it. It was only right they would recognise one of their masters. And they did, it just wasn't me. I didn't realise it at the time. I still didn't understand the truth of what I carried inside of me. They weren't bowing down to me. They were bowing down to the ancient horror that possessed me. I felt pride at their obeisance. Only it wasn't *my* pride at all. I think things would have turned out quite differently if I had realised from the start just how closely Ssserakis and I were entwined.

"Why?" Isen still held his sword ready, his head darting about to keep track of as many of the creatures as possible. "And what the fuck are they?"

"Imps," I said. Isen's panic was grating on my nerves and I wished he'd bloody well shut up. The strange thing was I was more embarrassed at myself than angry with him. I have taken a lot of time to sort through my feelings, and I have decided that I was embarrassed that the first man I chose to have sex with was a coward and a xenophobe. I have since come to terms with it, but I was just sixteen at the time, and confused. "Lesser creatures from the Other World. They're useless for war, but many Sourcerers use them as a form of slave labour. They're docile, near tireless, and easy to command." I shook my head and scoffed in disgust. "Perfect slaves." The others might be afraid but I was not. I knew the imps wouldn't attack. All Impomancers at the Orran Academy were given a copy of the Encyclopaedia Otheria. It detailed everything the tutors had discovered about the denizens of the Other World, and it dismissed all forms of imps as beasts of burden only.

Despite my claims I was still wary of them. I had never seen so many imps in one place before. I wondered if there was a Sourcerer nearby, one with an Impomancy Source I could steal. The thought of that power made my mouth water.

"Is that why they're bowing to you?" Yorin was tense and I couldn't blame him, but if the imps did attack us there was no other person in our little group I'd rather have at my side. "Because you're a Sourcerer?"

I shrugged. "I guess so."

"You guess?" Isen's voice was still high and panicky.

"Well, I can't exactly ask them," I said testily. "In case you haven't fucking noticed, imps don't have ears."

"How do they hear each other?" he asked.

Tamura let out a chuckle. "Silence down in the dark."

"What?" Isen squeaked.

I let out a sigh. "They don't hear each other," I said. "They don't speak. They must communicate in some other way."

"You don't know?" Isen asked, on the edge of panic. "I thought you were a Sourcerer." That was the last straw! I was angry at myself, that much was true, but I had anger enough to spare for Isen, and the idea that he might question my attunement to magic was a step too far. Such is the pride of youth. I was a Sourcerer and I wanted everyone to know it. To respect it. To respect me.

I turned on Isen and fixed him with a savage glare. I thought it another trick of the mind, but the hall seemed to grow darker around us, as though my anger was sucking the light from the space. Isen shivered, his breath misting as the temperature dropped. I was just about to open my mouth and let loose a torrent of rage on the man when I noticed the imps moving away, scurrying backward while keeping their heads down.

Isen was staring at me, fear plain on his face. I wonder if he knew then what he had screwed the day before. If he saw the horror inside of me before I did. Another relationship I ruined. As quick as he was to forget and forgive, I don't think he ever forgave me for scaring him like that down in the dark.

"They're coming back." Hardt was tense. Well, we were all tense, but with muscles like his, it really showed.

One of the imps crawled forwards, its head bowed and knees scraping on the rough stone beneath. It stopped just a few paces from us, heedless of the sharp steel pointed its way, and held up its hands to me. Imps have strange hands; three fingers and a thumb, all shorter than a terrran's and each ending in small claw. In those strange hands the imp held a shroom with a grey stem and a yellow cap.

"That explains the eyes," Hardt said as he took a hesitant step forward to stand next to me. "That shroom is a shiner. We had them back in the Pit, but Deko kept them all for his lot."

"The drug he uses?" I asked. I had heard of Shine, of course, and knew it gave a feeling of euphoria and excellent night vision. A side effect was the eerie way it made eyes shine, even in dim light.

Hardt nodded, keeping his eyes on the imp in front. "It's all in the way he prepares it. Grinds it into a paste and mixes it with something. But if you eat them, it just gives the night sight and makes eyes glow yellow a bit. Looks like these things have been living off them for years."

"I think it wants me to take it," I said. I stepped forward and reached out, plucking the shroom from the imp's hands. No sooner had I taken it, the little creature scurried away, still keeping its head down. A moment later another one moved forward to take its place, another shiner held up to me like some sort of offering.

I think each and every imp came forward to give me a shroom and before long we had a pile of hundreds of the little fungi. It probably shouldn't have surprised me. Just like our life in the Pit, food was the most valuable thing to the imps of the ruined Djinn city.

"At least we're not running out of food anymore," Yorin said, already chewing on a shroom. "Tastes like arse though."

After the tributes stopped, the imps backed away, waiting out in the gloom. I could see them still, hundreds of them just watching us. I thought them mindless back then. They were a poorly studied inhabitant of the Other World. Most Impomancers ignored them, preferring monsters, beasts, or horrors; things that could be used to fight. At least, most terran Impomancers did. The pahht have done extensive studies into the more docile inhabitants of the Other World, but that information was not given to the Orran Academy. I knew little about imps at the time, though. I now wish I had known more. Perhaps I might have noticed the warning signs. Perhaps I could have communicated with them, asked them to show us a safer way out.

We gathered up the shrooms, filling two bags and our stomachs with the things. I have rarely tasted anything worse, but Hardt assured us they were edible. He has always been very good at knowing which things we can eat, and which will likely kill us. Though he has gotten it wrong a couple of times and we have all paid the price.

The imps continued to watch us from a distance. They didn't seem the least bit concerned by naked steel, yet my movements were marked no matter how small they might be. More than once the whole chittering crowd shifted just because I turned my head. Eventually, one of them dared to come close again. It plodded forwards with its eyes down and both hands held above its head, palms up towards me. That imp looked different than the rest; older somehow, though I couldn't say how I knew it.

"What does the little monster want now?" Isen asked. I ignored him. I think I was already getting quite good at that. It was easier to ignore Isen, than confront him and the mistake I had made.

The imp was still there, silent and patient while the others behind it chattered to each other despite having no ears. To this day I'm still not sure why I did it, but I reached out and touched the upturned palms of the imp. Just one finger and so light a brush I was almost surprised the creature had felt it over its callouses.

The older imp immediately pulled its hands away and began nodding its big head, stepping backwards and keeping its eyes on the ground.

"What did you do?" Yorin asked.

Before I could answer another imp approached. This one was smaller than the last. It too kept its eyes on the ground and held its hands up above its head. I could see a large fleshy sac dangling underneath each of its armpits and both appeared to be wriggling slightly. I admit, at the time I felt disgusted by the sight, thinking the sacs to be some sort of growth or tumour. In truth that was simply how imp's nurture their young until they are large enough to walk and eat for themselves. I knew very little of the creatures at the time. These days I have three full tomes on my bookshelves dedicated to the various species of imp.

Again, I reached out and touched the upturned palms and again the imp backed away into the anonymity of its brethren. And another stepped forwards. This went on for some time. I lost track of the number of imp palms I *graced* with a touch, but I'd wager it was most of those gathered around us. Isen obviously balked at the delay and also because while the little ritual was taking place the imps remained nearby. They scared him, I think. But that was likely because he was a coward. The others were more patient, even Yorin, though I think he soon bored of it all.

It was some years before I learned the true significance of what I had done there. All I really knew at the time was that the imps had given me some shrooms and I had touched a few palms. I think Ssserakis found my ignorance amusing. The horror knew exactly what had just happened. I had given them a blessing of sorts. The blessing of an overlord, one made to rule them. In touching their palms I had granted them leave to continue living their lives, accepting that the tribute they had paid was sufficient. Imps are used as slaves in the Other World just as they are in Ovaeris, but these creatures were free. And I had just given them my blessing to remain so.

Eventually we made the decision to leave. Isen refused to put his sword away even as we struck out from the great hall. The imps cleared away from us, shielding their eyes from the lantern light, and followed in our wake, keeping a good distance. It put us all a little on edge, but I think we were safe enough from them. Even if they were violent, they would never have tried to harm me. Not while I was carrying Ssserakis inside.

Tamura led the way, ever our guide. His sense of direction is almost as good as my own. I have always been able to feel which way I am facing. It was important back then, to know where we were in relation to the Pit. The last thing we needed, once we were finally above ground and free, was to walk straight back to the prison from which we had just escaped. The Terrelan garrison stationed there would either kill us on sight or throw us right back, at which point, Deko would have certainly killed us on sight.

I found myself stroking the pouch at my belt. Even with a stomach full of shrooms I still felt hungry. It wasn't food I was craving. I wanted power. Unfortunately, Spiceweed needs plenty of sunlight to grow and there was no chance of me finding any deep underground. The Source was simply too dangerous for me to swallow.

Tamura led us up a stairwell and the imps followed behind. It was strange hearing the soft slap of so many feet echo around us. Yorin took the rear on the stairs. He was steadier than Isen and more willing to violence than Hardt. The best rear guard we had. Isen grumbled all the way, mostly under his breath but with the odd outburst to his brother. I ground my teeth and closed my eyes to it. To say my feelings had soured would have been an understatement. Lust is a flame that burns everything it comes in contact with. It consumes until there is nothing left to feed it, and then all that's left behind is ashes and scars on all those it touched.

Just before we arrived at the collapsed corridor Tamura had selected, I noticed the imps becoming agitated. They were still following behind us, far enough back to stay out of the lantern light, but they started making a loud noise for the first time. It's strange to think of creatures with mouths but no ears speaking. They can form words but not hear them, like a terran born deaf. I wondered if they knew

what sort of noise they were making. They seethed as well.
A tide of pallid flesh surging forwards and retreating over
and over again as they made *clicking* noises with whatever
passed for a tongue in their mouths.

"The path to freedom," Tamura announced, pitching
his voice to be heard over the noise of the imps.

The corridor ended in a mountain of rocks and
stones. It was quite clear that no cave-in had caused the
blockade. The ceiling was intact. No one wanted to mention
it though. We were too focused on getting free to care about
what we might be unearthing.

"Do you get the feeling they don't want us here?"
Yorin asked me as he passed by. He put his knives away
and set to helping Tamura and Hardt shift the rocks,
clearing enough space for us to squeeze through.

I stood next to Isen, watching the imps chatter and
move behind us. He held his sword in hand. I left my own
sheathed at my side. None of the little creatures dared come
within the lantern light or meet my eyes. I knew they
wouldn't attack. Or maybe I just hoped.

"Get away, you little beasts!" Isen shouted, waving
his sword and stepping forwards, holding up the lantern he
carried. The imps retreated but only for a moment. Only
while the light was close.

"Shut the fuck up! They can't hear you." My voice
was perhaps a bit more severe than I intended. I wanted
Isen to shut up and leave the poor creatures alone. "Help
dig. I'll watch them."

Isen snorted. "If they attack, you'll need someone
who knows how to fight by your side."

I sighed and relented, ignoring his repeated attempts to make the imps flee by waving things at them and shouting. I think Isen did it more to reassure himself that they were scared of him than anything else.

Hardt cursed, something about improper use of a goat's mother, and then the grating of rock against rock. The imps turned as one and fled into the darkness.

"I knew it would work," Isen said triumphantly, as though it were his shouting that had scared the imps away. I sent a glare his way then turned to the others. They were still pulling rocks out of the way, but I could see an opening at the top of the rubble large enough that I could crawl through.

"Stop! Stop." I rushed forwards, touching each of the diggers on the shoulder. They all paused and waited. I turned my head to the side, straining my hearing.

"What..." Yorin started, but I hissed at him and he fell silent.

"I hear... something," I said.

Tamura nodded. "The wind."

It was true I could hear the howl of wind echoing from a distance, but I was certain there was something else. A noise carried on the wind. A different howl. For once I was glad of the cold I felt inside, it stopped that noise from chilling my blood.

"It's just the wind, Eska," Hardt said. I realised he was holding a rock as large as my head and could see his arms straining with the effort. I stepped back and let them continue digging.

There're worse things than imps down here. The thought sent tingles up and down my spine. It's a strange

310

thing feeling yourself grow stronger as though feeding on your own fear. That should have given me pause, an indication that the ancient horror I thought I had pacified was inside. It should have told me just how closely we were now linked.

Once the gap at the top was large enough Hardt scrambled up and through the blockade. Tamura passed a lantern through and followed. I made Isen go through and then Yorin. Yorin stopped next to me before climbing through. He gave me an odd look for a moment.

"Those things," he pointed back down the corridor where the imps had fled, "were scared of something through here. I'm willing to bet *they* blocked it off, and for good reason."

I shrugged at him. "You want to find that way out or not?"

Yorin just smiled and scrambled up and through the opening. I followed, but not before a final glance backwards. I wondered whether the imps were waiting back there in the darkness, or if they had fled, leaving us to whatever fate we encountered.

Once we were all through the barricade, we started forward, following the feel and sound of the wind. Tamura and Hardt led, holding a lantern each, and Isen and Yorin followed behind, weapons drawn. I was no longer angry at Isen for his bared steel. It was strange, but the corridor seemed darker there, as though the gloom was even more oppressive. It took a while to realise there were no light gems embedded in the walls. They had all been gouged out.

We were only a few dozen steps in when we heard sounds behind us. Isen snatched a lantern from his brother and ran back to the barricade. Already some of the rocks we had moved were back in place. I heard imps scatter the other side.

"Little slug kissing fuckers are sealing us in!" Isen shouted.

I took the lantern from him and handed it back to Hardt, fixing the younger brother with a stare. "If they do, they do. No way we can stop them, and no bloody reason to try."

"We could kill them," Isen said, indignant.

I ignored that. We all did.

We continued on, and again heard the sounds of the imps sealing us in behind.

CHAPTER 30

We crept along, lanterns held high in front of us and behind. The wind howled from somewhere far ahead, yet all we felt was a breeze. There was something wrong about the situation, like an itch I just couldn't scratch. I had never seen a wind trap before, nor even heard of one at that time of my life. And as far as magic went, Aeromancy was as alien to me as Empamancy, though I had seen the things a Sourcerer could do with nothing but thin air. I just couldn't understand how the wind could be so loud and yet we barely felt it.

The others were scared, of the noise and of the oppressive darkness that seemed to close in around the lanterns unnaturally. I suppose I couldn't blame them, the howling had me on edge. Isen fished our third lantern out of the bag and lit it before anyone could stop him. Hardt hissed at his brother, but Isen backed away, clutching at the lantern as though the light were the only thing keeping him alive. He really was a coward.

"We don't have any more fuel." Hardt's voice came out as a harsh whisper. It's an oddity, but people tend to lower their voices in the dark. A natural instinct to be as discreet as possible, maybe.

"Then we should get out of here quickly." There was real panic in Isen's voice. It can happen to people who live too long in fear. Their mind loses the ability to reason. Isen

was acting out of irrationality and terror. Part of me wanted
to knock him senseless and leave him there in the dark. I
think the only thing that stopped me from telling Yorin to
do just that was that I knew Hardt would never leave his
brother.

Tamura stopped and cocked his head to the side,
holding up his own lantern.

"Do you see something?" I asked, pushing past Isen
and letting the older brother deal with the younger.

Tamura cocked an eyebrow at me. "The walls have
eyes," he said.

Yorin let out a grunt. "He's not wrong."

That was when I realised he meant it literally. With
lantern light spilling out around us, I could see dozens of
crude faces carved into the walls. Each was different, but
the same, and each had piercing eyes staring straight ahead.

"Balls of a crag cat," Isen cursed and drew in a
ragged breath.

I stepped close to one of the walls and inspected the
faces watching us. Whatever had carved them had no real
artistic skill and the faces were misshapen and ugly. But the
eyes... The eyes were piercing, watchful. I would be lying if
I said I wasn't unnerved by it all. They were bloody creepy.

We continued down the corridor. It was hard to
ignore the faces carved into the walls once I knew they
were there. Every step we took revealed more and more of
them watching us. They weren't part of the architecture. It
was obvious something, or someone, had added them long
after the city had fallen. Back then, I wondered at what
might have carved them and whether they marred every
wall in every corridor. These days I wonder more at their

significance. Why so many faces and why such a focus on the eyes?

We followed the breeze, ignoring the doorways and stairwells to either side, eager to escape. It felt as though we were close to an exit. I could feel it in every part of me. Freedom was calling to me. The sky was calling to me, and I was so close I could taste it on the wind. Perhaps we should have checked some of the rooms. Perhaps if we had, we might have had a better idea of what was coming for us.

It seemed to take forever creeping through the gloom until the corridor ended. The wind was stronger there, louder. We could feel it gusting through the open doorway in front of us. I was the first to step through and found another great hall on the other side of that doorway. Unlike the last hall this one had steps leading both up and down, with doorways above and below us. Eleven great pillars, each with the glowing blue mineral snaking through it, stretched all the way from the floor to the ceiling. The twelfth pillar had collapsed and the rubble of it littered the ground. Strangely, the blue mineral seemed to have stopped glowing in that pillar. Wind whipped and howled around the hall like a wild animal snarling at everything. I could feel the bite of it on my skin.

"The wind must be coming from somewhere." I had to raise my voice, almost shout to be heard over the noise. Tamura was next through, standing behind me, and he nodded, pointing upwards.

"It's about time we started going up." Yorin was already starting up the steps to our left. He stopped and shrugged. "Steps just end on this side. Nothing but rubble a couple of flights up." He trudged back down towards us. "I hate this place." I didn't hear hate in his voice though. He said it as a fact and nothing more.

We started down, Yorin in the lead with a lantern. I followed close behind. I could just about make out the staircase leading upwards on the other side of the hall, but even with my vision, I couldn't see if it was intact or not.

Yorin paused at the bottom of the steps, a knife in his hand and the lantern held out in front of him. I froze when I saw it too. I think we all did. All except Tamura, maybe, but then he has never been good at staying still. The great hall was strewn with rubble, some from the collapsed pillar, some from elsewhere. Only it wasn't all rubble. There were bodies. Dozens of bodies with skin the same dark grey as the rock around us. Each one was huddled into a small ball and lying alone on the ground.

"Well, now we know why those little monsters didn't want us coming this way," Isen said. "It's a fucking burial chamber."

I ground my teeth at Isen's stupidity. He really was an idiot. I don't know how I hadn't seen it earlier. Well, that's not strictly true. I know exactly how. Lust made me blind, made me stupid. But like any emotion so intense it couldn't last, it had burned itself out and faded away to leave a cold clarity in its place. Now I saw Isen for exactly what he was; a coward and a fool. And a Terrelan. There are three classes of Other World inhabitant. Imps are classed as creatures, mostly harmless and suited to labour and little else. Monsters would truly scare him. I wondered what he would do if he ever encountered a hellion or a khark hound, let alone a yurthammer. Yurthammers are on the banned list of summons for a good reason. I eventually used them to great effect in my crusade against the Terrelan Empire. Isen claimed that anything he didn't understand was a monster. It was that fucking ignorance that lay at the very heart of Terrelan xenophobia.

The light of our lanterns illuminated the closest of the bodies, and they did look dead. Lifeless and colourless. I noticed something different about them right away. The lack of tails, the smaller heads. Patchy hair where the imps were completely bald. I didn't say anything. Isen was near enough to panic already. I think the truth would have pushed him over the edge.

We picked our way through the bodies, trying not to disturb any, while the howling wind tugged at us. It had a bitter chill to it, and I found myself feeling frozen inside and out. It is an unfortunate fact that patchy rags do little to keep a body warm. I clutched at the little leather pouch hanging from my belt, thinking that if it was a Pyromancy Source I would be able to light a fire inside that could keep my body warm through even the most frigid of winds. But I couldn't risk it. I have often harboured thoughts of ending my life, and never so often as when I was trapped underground, but I have always known I would never willingly act on them. I wanted to live. I wanted to escape. I wanted to see the sky again and then exact bloody vengeance on every one of the bastards who had put me in the Pit, and everyone who had kept me there. Anger works almost as well as Pyromancy for keeping a body warm.

We were so close to the stairs when the howl turned to a scream above us. I looked up to see a creature clinging to one of the pillars just a few feet above. Its flesh was the same grey as the others, but it was certainly not dead. It had two arms and two legs, five digits on each. Its teeth were yellow but I could see they were mostly flat with just a couple of canines, and the creature had a nose. I knew then what we were up against. They weren't imps. They were terrans.

CHAPTER 31

The grey bodies littering the ground moved. They were not as dead as we believed. Dozens upon dozens of the things stretched out their arms and legs and slowly began to rise. Our group backed towards the stairs; Yorin, Isen, and Tamura spreading out as Hardt pushed me behind them. As though I was a child who needed protecting.

"Die, beast!" Isen shouted and stabbed his sword through the back of one of the bodies. Blood welled up and the creature let out a howl of pain before darting away, almost ripping Isen's sword from his hands. It collapsed a short distance away and some of the other beasts moved towards their fallen comrade. A wave of nausea washed over me as I watched them fell upon the downed one, tearing it apart with teeth and nail. Eating their own wounded.

"I knew we couldn't trust those scum-sniffing monsters!" Isen continued, pointing his bloody sword towards the group of cannibals. I thought about correcting him, but I doubted it would do much good for any of them to know the things we were about to be eaten by were terran. Or at least far closer to a terran than an imp.

The first of the cannibals looked up at us, blood ringing its mouth, bright blue eyes staring at us. Eyes that glowed in the gloom. The gaze was as piercing as my own, but there was no intelligence there, only hunger. It screamed, a shriek that made me cringe. The others looked up from their gruesome meal and joined in and soon the howl of the wind was drowned out by dozens of screaming voices.

They were terran, or had been once, maybe. I'm not sure what we should call them after so long trapped underground, feeding on rats and imps and breeding only with each other. I certainly wasn't about to stop one and ask for details on their culture. I have come to refer to them as the Damned. The tallest of them was shorter than even I, and they wore no clothes, not even rags. The females had grey breasts hanging low, while the males had shrivelled balls between their legs. It appeared modesty was the least of their concerns. They were primitive and savage, and they wanted to eat us. None of us was about to let that fucking happen.

They came on at a run, little legs pumping and hands outstretched as though they had no regard for their own safety. Isen screamed something, but there was already so much screaming I couldn't make out the words. The first few of the creatures went down, running headlong onto Isen and Yorin's steel. Tamura stepped into one of them, grabbing its arms and twisting them about with a *crack* before shoving the creature into some of its comrades. They were a bit more cautious after that, circling us and keeping their distance, pulling away the wounded to tear apart and devour. There seemed to be no question about whether or not to treat their injured.

I struggled to pull my little sword free and Hardt's arm fell across me, forcing me backwards towards the stairs.

"Stay behind me," the big man rumbled. In truth it was wise advice, but I bristled all the same. I didn't like the idea of needing anyone to protect me. I had a sword and the barest knowledge of how to use it. I wasn't about to let others fight and die while I cowered behind them just because I was younger than them, and a woman.

"Why the fuck should I?" I shouted back at Hardt. "I'm more use than you. Or are you going to put those big bloody fists to use for once?" It hurt him, I could see that. Unfortunately, we didn't have time for me to cuddle his feelings, nor for him to hide behind the rest of us as we fought for our lives. If we were going to survive, we needed to use our greatest weapon. We needed to unleash the monster within Hardt.

I stepped forwards, planning to fight alongside Yorin, but Hardt dragged me back again. His strength has always been legendary and I had no chance to resist it. "Stay out of this," he said. "You'll only get in the way."

He was right, of course, but it stung all the same. I wasn't trained to fight. Isen had barely finished telling me how to hold a sword properly before I ruined that for us both. Fighting is like any skill, it requires knowledge and practice, and I had neither. Still, I drew my sword and waited behind the others, my back to the stairs, as they held off the horde.

For all his flaws, and all his damned cowardice, Isen could fight. I watched him, thinking how slow his sword work had been while we played at training. Side by side, he and Yorin looked untouchable. Nothing breeds trust quite like the mutual threat of being eaten alive. It's a lesson I've learned to be true more than twice over.

The creatures darted in again and again, baring teeth and sharpened nails. The others held a semi-circle of protection with me at the rear, driving them back and dealing wounds wherever possible. Even Hardt threw the odd punch, though I could see he was more trying to deter our foes than kill them. Tamura proved his mastery time and time again. Whatever martial art he knew, it resulted in a lot of broken limbs.

The battle stretched on forever. Hardt tells me it was quick, but then his judgement of time is as skewed as my own. He lost track of almost everything in the bloody mess he created in that hall. I think maybe it was because I was forced to watch that time dragged so.

Again, I felt my hand drop to the pouch at my belt. Again, I wished it to be a Pyromancy Source. I have always had an affinity to fire. I'd wager it's because fire is so destructive, and I am far better as destroying things than creating. Evidenced by the fact that I have a lot more dead enemies, than living friends. With a Pyromancy Source I could have sent a wave of flame through the hall searing flesh from bone. I could have ended the fight in moments. I could have fucking killed all of them!

I felt a prickle between my shoulder, a feeling, like knowing that someone is watching, and looked up. One of the Damned was crouching on the stairs behind me. It leapt and we went down together, rolling on the ground and scrabbling for purchase. I felt hot, rancid breath on my face and heard the snap of teeth so close to my neck. Sharp nails dug into my arms and the pain was intense.

Luckily for me, I was scared, terrified even. Up close the things looked even more terran, and also strangely less. Its grey skin was dry and cracked in places, oozing a yellow fluid. Its eyes were a bright blue and bloodshot. I didn't have time to consider what had made them that way, and neither did I understand where the new strength flooding into my limbs came from. Ssserakis was feeding off my terror and, linked as we were, that gave me power.

"I am the weapon!" I screamed at the thing, a guttural sound torn from my lips as I rose up and shoved it hard against the stairs. I held it in place with a hand around its neck, ignoring the flailing arms and tearing nails. And I drove my little sword into its gut over and over again. The thick blood that dripped out of its wounds looked more black than red.

I staggered away from the broken creature. It all felt more like a dream. Or a nightmare at least. Soldiers call it a battle haze. The world feels fuzzy around the edges, distant, almost. It is a place of raw emotion, easy to get lost in. I wasn't the only one in that hazy world.

When I turned back to the others, I saw Isen was down, bleeding from a gash down his leg. Yorin was close by, dancing back and forth as he stabbed at the creatures around him. Tamura stood over the downed brother, his legs apart and his hands ready to catch any attack that came. But Hardt... Hardt was violence incarnate.

He was solid muscle, tempered by skill, driven by blood lust, and topped with steel knuckles. Every punch broke bones and pulverised flesh, and he was throwing them out in generous helpings. My own haze broke as I watched the big man fight. I collapsed backwards on one of the stairs, caught between awe and disgust. I had done this. I had pushed so hard to unleash this. And now that it was free, I couldn't help but wonder... What had I done?

Hardt's rags had torn free. He was topless, covered in little bleeding cuts, and I could see, for the first time, just how muscled he really was. I've seen the sight many times since, and I still marvel at the man's strength. I suppose he was fairly well built before being sentenced to the Pit, and day upon day of digging has a habit of making you stronger.

Eventually the remaining creatures turned and fled from the giant threatening to make them extinct. It wasn't that they couldn't get close, or even land a blow, but more that Hardt didn't seem to feel it. I know now he felt every cut, scrape, and bruise, but in that state, pain just drives him forward, makes him stronger. He was tearing them to pieces and even as primitive as the Damned are, they could see they were losing the fight.

I went to him once it was all over. He had knelt amidst a pile of corpses, drawing in ragged breath after ragged breath and staring at nothing. His eyes were wide and his face looked longer than normal. Unchecked tears ran down the lines of his face, dripping from his chin and mixing with the blood on the ground.

It's always the same for Hardt. When the rage takes him, he says it's almost like watching through someone else's eyes. But he sees it all. Feels it all. Afterwards the sadness strikes him hard. Unfortunately, we had neither the time, nor the alcohol to help him drown his sorrow. We needed to leave before the creatures regrouped and came back.

Sometimes a lie is worth a thousand truths, and I would tell a thousand lies to spare Hardt a single moment of pain. He's earned that and more for sticking with me through the years. I have a habit of turning people into monsters and Hardt is probably my greatest creation. Well, after my own daughter.

"They were imps," I said. "Mindless, soulless creatures from the Other World. I doubt they even felt it." Sometimes a lie can go too far, exposing it for what it is.

Hardt looked up at me and I felt tears well up in my own eyes. Emotion can be like that. It's contagious. Even without Empamancy I felt a little taste of Hardt's turmoil and it nearly broke me. It's a wonder to me he ever manages to come back from the depths of his despair.

"They felt it," he whispered. "I know pain. They fucking felt it." His voice broke on the words.

I gave him a moment with that grief. But only a moment. "Isen is hurt," I said. "And we need to leave, before they come back."

I heard the *clang* of metal hitting rock as Hardt let the steel knuckles drop from his hands. I could see blood and worse on those knuckles, on his hands too. He stood then and it looked a struggle to get his body moving. I collected the steel knuckles and followed, surprised by the weight of those weapons. But as heavy as they were to me, I knew for Hardt, they were much heavier.

Despite his anguish, Hardt saw to his brother's wounds. We had only one small pot of balm and he used it all, binding Isen's leg with the few bandages we had with us. There was no wood to use as a splint and no time to stitch it closed. We needed to escape, find a way above ground, and quickly.

Hardt's own wounds looked superficial and he refused to let anyone look at them. His arms and torso were covered in little scratches, but I could tell he was no stranger to scars. How had I slept next to him for weeks, often curled up in those arms, and not known about the old wounds? I think, perhaps, I was too busy staring at the younger brother to truly notice the older.

When we set off up the stairs it was with Tamura in the lead and Yorin protecting our backs. The two wounded brothers helped support each other up the stairs and I followed them. I don't know if the others could see it, but we were watched all the way.

CHAPTER 32

By the time the war came to Lanfall it was already lost. The Orran army was all but crushed while the Terrelans were busy supplementing their ranks with mercenaries from Polasia. Fort Vernan was the last real bastion of defence. The city of Lanfall didn't even have a wall to protect it. In strategic terms, they call it being fucked.

Most telling of all was the number of Sourcerers we had left. Prince Loran had fallen just a few days earlier. There were no reports, at least not any accurate ones, but they weren't needed. The Iron Legion marched to meet the Terrelans head on, a sizeable force of soldiers and even a few Sourcerers to back him up. Not one person returned, and the Terrelans marched on. That scared me far more than seeing the army surrounding Lanfall. The idea that the Terrelans had the power to defeat the Iron Legion was unthinkable.

The bitch-whore was gone too. Lesray Alderson didn't die though, she never gave the Terrelans the chance to kill her. I think perhaps she was the smart one. Lesray knew to cut herself free from a dying empire and run. She was assigned to another unit, harassing the enemy approach to Lanfall. Two members of her unit made it back to tell us the bitch-whore had burned most of her soldiers alive, before fleeing through a portal. It was many years before anyone heard of Lesray Alderson again. Many years before she crowned herself the Queen of Fire and Ice.

Of my other classmates, Tammy, was dead, and Barrow never made it out of the academy. He was not the first, nor the last Sourcerer to be driven insane by a combination of Photomancy and Vibromancy. I'm told it's all about the strain both schools put on the senses. As for the academy itself… well, it was gone, looted and burned to the ground as the Terrelans advanced. The history books cover it up as well as they can, but I've heard first-hand accounts of that sacking. The tutors I had grown up learning from were slaughtered, every one of them. But they put up a fight and no mistake. The battlefield they created turned the city of Picarr into a ruin, forever haunted by the ghosts of all those who died there. Thousands of innocent Orran citizens who wanted nothing of the war. That is, perhaps, the greatest tragedy of war; the innocent always pay the highest price.

All in all, the Orrans had lost far too many Sourcerers in far too short a time. There were some left, of course, but only two attuned to more than three Sources. Only Josef and I. We carried the weight of an empire on our shoulders and we were both so young. It's probably no wonder we lost that battle and the war. Josef never wanted to fight it in the first place.

It was the only time I ever met Emperor Serazan Orran. While the Terrelans arranged their army outside the city and made their plans of assault, the emperor visited Josef and I on the top of the tallest tower of Fort Vernan. He told us we were the last hope. The last hope of the entire empire, and he assured us we could win. It was a rousing speech, and it certainly lit a fire underneath me, but it was nothing but damned lies. There was no hope and we had no chance of winning. They were pretty words though.

I remember watching the Terrelans approach. Fort Vernan was built with defending Sourcerers in mind, and we were placed on top of its highest tower. The wind whipped at my clothes, tugging at my hair. The bite of cold on my skin was refreshing and it went no deeper than that. I kept myself warm with magic from my Pyromancy. I sat on the edge of that large tower, dangling my legs over the side and feeling the nervous energy as I waited for the fight of my life to begin.

Josef paced behind me. I think he knew it was a lost cause. I think I knew it too, but I also knew I would fight even so. I believed in the Orran empire. And I believed I owed them for all they had given and done for me. I suppose it all boils down to one word; *all they had done for* or *all they had done to*. Josef would have quit the field there and then if not for me. The tutors were right to keep us together. I kept him loyal long past his tipping point.

The Terrelans weren't stupid; they would not have won the war if they were. Their spies knew Josef and I were the most powerful weapon the Orrans had left, and they knew where we would be. We were too valuable to risk down on the battlefield where a stray arrow could spell the end of the resistance. They knew we'd be up on the tower, the most commanding view of the battle for us to rain down death on our enemies. If only I knew how to use Sources then as I do now. That battle, and maybe even the war, might have turned out quite differently. But I only knew what I had been taught at the academy, and the tutors themselves were so ignorant of their true potential.

Before the first horns of battle even sounded, I heard a portal snap open behind us. There is a sound to a portal opening, like a whip cracking. Probably not surprising given that a portal is a tear in the fabric of the world.

We were not alone up on that tower top. The emperor had seen fit to give us twelve of his royal guard to protect us. They were trained in combat both against other soldiers and against Sourcerers. They wore enchanted armour to ward against Sourcery and wielded blades designed to dispel. I have seen one of those blades at work, it severs magical connections. Before the first of our guards could shut the portal, a Terrelan leapt through. Josef was always quite ruthless when his life, or mine, was at stake. That first soldier died screaming, hit with a psychokinetic blast that threw him off the tower to fall to his death. It's quite sickening what the ground can do to a person when gravity has its way.

I turned away from the battle on the tower top, trusting Josef to protect me, to be my shield while I did what I did best; attack. Reaching out to the Other World I brought hellions back with me. Five winged monsters travelled through me and burst out of my chest. Once they were through, I gripped at my tunic and gasped, breathing through the pain. But it was only pain. It felt like they had ripped their way free of my rib cage, but it was an illusion. No magic comes without a price, and the price for Impomancy is pain. I gave my hellions a target and ordered them to attack. With claws that can shred armour and spittle that hardens as strong as solid rock, hellions are quite well-suited to war.

When I turned back to the tower top, I saw two of our guard were down already. They were hard pressed to deal with the portals that kept snapping open and Josef was better suited to a true battle than to that sort of fight.

We didn't know it at the time, but it was all a distraction, really. The Terrelan forces were already inside the fort, making their way to the war room to kill the emperor.

I remember seeing a portal open above us and arrows flew through it. Josef, always faster than I, brushed them aside with a wave of his hand. The portal closed and then another opened behind us. This time I was ready. I snapped open a portal of my own and rained the enemy's own arrows down upon their heads. I'll wager they didn't see that coming.

It was a losing battle from the start. We were two Sourcerers and a handful of soldiers against an army of both. Josef and I were strong, especially side by side, but there were only two of us, and in truth we were still all but children. The Orran Academy gave us all the training they could, but the tutors themselves knew so little about Sources and how to use them. The Terrelans didn't know much better, but they didn't need to; they had numbers.

Josef and I took turns throwing destruction down upon the ranks of the enemy, but we spent more time looking to our own defence. Our guards soon found themselves overly taxed and they fell quickly. Time is hard to keep track of during a battle, but it did not feel like long before Josef and I were surrounded by Terrelans. They were a mixture of Sourcerers and those trained to fight us.

I would have fought them to the death, if not for Josef. He saved my life by betraying me. And I hated him for it. I look back now, and I love him for that same betrayal.

We struggled up the steps at the side of that great hall, moving as fast as Hardt could drag Isen. The younger brother's leg hurt too much for him to put pressure on it, and the steps were barely wide enough for two to walk abreast, especially when one of them was as broad as Hardt. I have seen the man struggle to fit through doorways before, and I have seen the scars on the crown of his head also. The man has faced down armies with nothing but his fists, yet he is constantly defeated by low ceilings.

After following the stairs as far as they went, we ducked through into yet another corridor. The wind was weaker there and I asked Tamura if perhaps we should find another way. He laughed and shook his head.

"Many streams make a river," the crazy old Terrelan said. "All lead back to the mountain." It was about as much of an answer as I expected, and even better that it was one I understood.

After a while of listening to Isen grunt with every step, I called a halt. We ducked into one of the nearby rooms and backed into the corner. Yorin and Tamura watched the corridor while Hardt took another look at his brother's leg.

"We need to sew it and splint it," Hardt said. I have been on the business end of his needles many times and I know now how skilful he is. Doesn't stop the surgery from hurting like a bitch, though.

"I don't see any handy sticks nearby," Isen growled through the obvious pain.

"Then we'll use your sword." Hardt was already undoing his brother's belt to take the weapon. It was sheaved in soft leather and was easily long enough for the job.

"I'll need that if those little monsters come back." Isen argued, but there didn't seem to be much conviction in his voice.

"You can use mine." I pulled my short sword free and laid it by Isen's side. The dark blood of the Damned I had slain was still slick on the blade. "We both know I'm no good with it yet. I'll do just as well with the knife." It was another little weapon I picked up from the armoury, though in truth I think it is better served to carve apples than flesh. I still have that knife. One of my few keepsakes from a time I've often considered trying to forget.

Hardt pulled down his brother's trousers and Isen covered himself with his hands. I think I blushed. Strange to think of it now, and not just because these days it would take far more than the sight of cock and balls to make me colour. I caught a glimpse of it, my first, if truth be told, and couldn't help but think that not too long ago it had been inside of me. I think I covered it well, but honestly it made me queasy to imagine it.

"Over here, Eska," Hardt said as he began unwrapping bloody bandages. "I'm going to need you to hold the wound closed while I sew. It's going to be slippery." He paused and looked at his brother. "And it's going to hurt."

I moved around to kneel next to Hardt and got a good look at the wound. At the academy, I had done my required studies into anatomy and I remember seeing pictures of muscle in the books, but this was the first time I saw some standing out in an open wound. I swallowed back bile. The flesh was ripped open and jagged, and bloody muscle seemed to be trying to push its way outward. I was reminded of a sausage, the skin torn and the meat inside trying to escape its confines.

Isen glanced down at his leg. "Oh, bouncing goat sucker."

"It could be worse," Hardt rumbled. I wonder if he felt as confident as he made those words sound. I've seen him fix up worse wounds since, but I suppose things are different when it's your brother you're trying to save.

"Seen wounds like this make people lose legs, brother," Isen said, gritting his teeth. He took his hands away from his cock, and gripped hold of the hilt of my sword hard. Some men find it reassuring to hold a weapon in their hands.

"On a ship, sure," Hardt said. "If we sew it up. Keep it dry. You'll be fine, little brother."

Isen groaned. "Get on with it then."

I found myself staring at his cock. I've never liked the sight of them, but it was preferable to staring at the wound.

"Here." Hardt pointed at the red flesh surrounding the wound. "Grip here and here and pull it together. Don't be gentle. Try to ignore the screams."

"I won't scream." Isen proved himself a liar with that statement.

"He'll slow us down," Yorin said from the doorway. "He's slowing us down right now. We leave him to the imps, maybe he'll slow them down instead." There was no emotion in his voice. I knew he wasn't saying it out of malice or any desire to see Isen dead. He simply stated it as an option.

"Go fuck a slug," Isen growled. He was sweating and pale. I wondered if maybe Yorin was right. I wasn't certain Hardt could even save his brother. But I was certain he'd try. "Wish we had something stronger than water," Isen said, fear plain in his voice.

"Are you ready?" Hardt asked. I think the question was directed at both of us. I nodded and gripped hold of Isen's leg, pulling the wound closed.

Many years later, down in the Red Cells, the Terrelan Emperor once told me that a ruler needs to be savage. Needs to enjoy the screams of their fellow man. He said there were twenty-one different screams a person could make depending on the stimuli. I lost count of the number he drew from me. I have never been partial to screaming myself. I find it to be an assault on my hearing. Isen screamed. As Hardt sewed his leg back together, Isen screamed himself raw, and I wondered if the Source in my little pouch was a Vibromancy Source. It would have killed me in minutes, of course, but I thought it probably worthwhile just to create a bubble of silence around myself. To block the hideous noise out, even for a few moments.

There was a lull in the sewing when Hardt snapped off the hair and took a minute to set up another. I wiped sweat from my forehead and left a smear of Isen's blood in its place. I was shaking. It's so strange that Isen was wounded and Hardt was doing all the work to fix him, and yet, I was the only one trembling.

"You said you weren't going to do that anymore," Isen said. I think it was a wonder he was still conscious.

Hardt didn't pause as he threaded a new hair through the needle. "I didn't want to. Didn't have a choice."

Isen stared at his brother, eyes red from tears and sweat standing out on his face. "It's always a choice to kill, Hardt. Your words, not mine." They shared a look then. I was more than a little curious to know what passed between them. I managed to drag the story free years later, though not without a fair amount of social lubricant. But that one isn't my story to share.

"Again, Eska," Hardt said. I pulled the flesh together once more.

By the time Hardt was finished, we were all exhausted. I've often thought it takes as much effort and energy to heal a person as it does to be the one healed. I have developed a great respect for Biomancers over the years, and an even greater respect for physicians who rely on skill and knowledge alone.

We let Isen sleep and Hardt drifted off as well. Our position was as secure as it could be with only one way into the empty room. Yorin and Tamura continued to watch the hallway. Yorin wasn't pleased, but he kept quiet about it. Tamura had a grave look on his face and said nothing; I think that scared me more than the amount of Isen's blood on the floor, and on my hands. I considered trying to sleep, but I knew I wouldn't. Couldn't.

We were close to the surface, close to freedom. I could feel it. I had no proof, but I knew it all the same. I itched to move on. More than once I glanced at Isen as he slept and part of me, a horrible insidious part of me hoped he'd die.

CHAPTER 33

There were rumours about Josef and I at the academy. Not to begin with, we were both too young, but after a few years they started to surface. I would bet every fortune I've won and lost over the years on the bitch-whore starting those rumours. Lesray took every opportunity to make my life harder.

Josef and I spent almost every moment together. We trained together. We ate together. We slept together. I suppose it was inevitable that, once puberty kicked in, people would start to question our relationship. The tutors didn't care. No, that's not true, I think the tutors did care. I think they approved, as they did of anything that would strengthen the bond between us. They were always so scared Josef might defect, especially given his outspoken views about the war. I think it might also have been because of how close he grew up to the border. He knew just how little difference there really was between the Orrans and the Terrelans, which is to say nothing but the name.

Josef was always angry about the war. It's not really surprising given the things he had lost, and the things he had seen. He told me about them once, stony-faced and seething with rage. Of the parents that had loved him and treated him like a little miracle. Of the big sister who tormented him in a hundred playful ways and was always

338

there to protect him when he needed her. Of the village that worked the swampland close to the nearby river and were as poor as the mud they sifted through. And he told me of their deaths at the hands of the first Terrelans to cross the border. I cried for him, even as he refused to cry for himself.

He blamed the Orrans for the war, claiming it was all their fault. I've always thought war more of a mutual effort. If one side didn't want to fight, they would have used more words and fewer swords.

At the academy, I heard the rumours. We both did. At first, we laughed at them, maybe even adding fuel to the fires by holding hands and showing more public affection. But those rumours and innuendo soon outlived my patience. It became a chore watching people whisper as we walked past, seeing sly eyes glance our way. I always got the rougher end of those rumours. I caught the odd word whispered behind my back; *harlot* and *slut*. While Josef was praised, more often than not, for *years of hard work finally paying off*. I was just twelve years old and innocent, but the rumours branded me a whore and made me a pariah amongst my peers. Only Josef didn't seem to care what was said about me. He was praised for that *generosity*.

No matter what the rumours said there was never any romantic feelings between us. We were siblings in everything but blood. Closer than siblings, even. The pahht call it *soul bonded*. Two people linked together by their very essence. Two halves only ever whole when they're together. I felt that way down in the ruined Djinn city. I felt broken in two, a part of me missing. I couldn't help but feel I'd pushed Josef away to pursue my infatuation with Isen, and now that that was ended, I wanted my best friend back. I wanted to tell him I was sorry and feel the comfort and solace in his compassion. I wanted to feel whole again.

The Damned didn't attack again. Yorin claimed he heard noises, the scuff of feet on stone in the distance, yet we saw nothing. We all hoped they had learned their lesson. I don't think any of us were prepared for another fight.

When Hardt woke he checked on Isen again and the younger brother started to come around. He was alive, but his pain was obvious and I caught Hardt looking worried more than once. I silently wondered if Isen would ever walk without a limp again, and I discovered a hard truth about myself. I didn't care. We stuffed ourselves with shrooms and picked Isen off the ground. Hardt half carried his brother as we moved on.

We were out of oil, so we left the lanterns behind. One more thing we didn't need to carry. Luckily, we were all eating shiners and the shrooms gave us passable night vision even in such darkness. Tamura led the way again, following the breeze against his skin.

Anticipation can be a horrible thing and I was nervous with it. We were moving slowly, both because of the darkness, and because of Isen. Every step was torture. Every pause was even more torturous and we paused often for Isen to rest. I found Yorin watching me more than once during those breaks, and every time his gaze flicked to the younger brother. There was an unspoken question there; Yorin was asking if we should leave them. Move ahead and find our own way out. I don't know when or why Yorin had come to rely on my opinion, maybe because I took the lead when no one else would, but I wasn't about to argue with the decision. We needed Yorin. We needed someone willing and able to kill. I didn't think Hardt had it in him to go on another murderous rampage. Or perhaps it was that he didn't have it in him to pull himself out of it once more.

Wandering down those ruined halls became a drudgery, all of us moving along with exhaustion and determination in equal measure. We were all so fucking tired. We almost missed the hole in the wall. Perhaps the others thought it just another doorway leading to the wreckage of a room that had once served a purpose, but not me. I dragged my eyes from the floor in front of me and saw a crack in the wall, leading out into broken rock beyond. I felt my heart beat faster and hope sprang alive inside of me anew. It was the way out. I knew it, and I didn't need the wind or Tamura to tell me. I knew it was the final stretch to freedom.

Isen groaned as Hardt lowered him to the ground in a nearby room. The cave opened out from a hole in the wall. It sloped upwards slowly, barely large enough for us to walk single file. The walls were rough and looked as though they had been scraped away. The breeze was stronger and it carried something on it, a fresh smell like the first rains of spring. The scent of life rallying to take back what had been stolen by a harsh winter.

I stared up into the darkness of the cave and smiled, drawing in deep breaths through my nose and enjoying a scent that almost covered the rancid odour of our unwashed bodies. You learn to forget the pleasure of being clean when trapped underground in a prison surrounded by others who barely remember the feeling. But it soon comes flooding back when the prospect of finally ridding filth from skin presents itself.

"We should send someone ahead to explore," Hardt said. "Make certain it's the way out."

"I'll go." Yorin's offer sounded genuine enough. I think we all knew he wouldn't come back if the cave led to the surface.

"We'll all go," I said. "Together. It is the way out. Tamura agrees." The crazy old man nodded.

Hardt drew in a deep breath before arguing. "Isen is..."

"Isen can make it," Isen said, interrupting his brother. "He just needs a quick rest. And the last thing Isen wants is to be left down here in the dark while the rest of you go and see the sun."

It was settled. We decided to wait for Isen to be ready. I'm not going to say it was a pleasant delay, and I longed to charge headlong into the passageway, but I swallowed down my impatience. Isen wanted to be free as much as the rest of us, I knew he wouldn't delay us any longer than he had to. Also, I had to admit to myself that, as sure as I was the cave was the right way, we had no idea of how long a journey it might be to the surface.

There is an art to doing something foolish. It often involves deciding upon the smart choice, the safest choice, and then doing the opposite. In my case it often involves believing myself to be safer than I am, or untouchable. That is why I snuck away from the others to relieve myself. Privacy was a notion the Pit quickly scraped away from its prisoners, but so close to the surface and with Isen's gaze still lingering on me, I felt the need to take myself away from them.

I found a large room, stone and other debris scattered all over the floor. There were two doors, one leading back to the corridor and the other to a connecting room. I think the rubble on the floor might have been a stove once, I saw a metal grill rusted almost to dust. The gloom was thick enough that from the back of the room I could barely see to the doorway. I crouched down in the corner and pulled down my trousers. I was still sore and the bandages were bloody, but I had stopped bleeding. I was just starting to pull my trousers up when the mistakes of my past caught up with me.

I stood up and saw a figure in the doorway. I startled, tripping in the legs of my trousers as I struggled to pull them up, and landing heavily on the floor. I'm afraid to say, there are very few things quite like falling arse first onto a rock. I yelped; hard not to with sudden pain like that, and scrambled back to my feet. The figure in the doorway just watched for a moment longer. I thought it might be Tamura or Yorin come to fetch me. Then I realised that they were carrying a hooded lantern, shining my way.

"Eska," Josef said, stepping into the room and lowering the lantern so I could see him.

I ignored the grave look on his face and the harsh tone to his voice. It simply didn't matter. I had no idea how he had found me. I had no idea how he had followed me. I was just so damned happy at seeing him again. I was finally reunited with the other half of my soul. I knew then whatever hurt we had visited upon each other no longer mattered. Even I couldn't hold onto that grudge any more.

That wasn't strictly true of course. I know now just how easy it is to hold onto grudges. I still hold plenty of them, even towards people I buried decades ago. It's hard to let go of grudges; the longer you keep them the more they seem like a part of you, something so fundamental, releasing them would be like chopping off a toe.

I crossed the gap between us, limping quickly through the rubble, and hugged Josef, squeezing him tight and barely noticing that he wasn't holding me back. He smelled cleaner than I expected, and not just his skin. He was wearing some sort of uniform complete with oiled buckles, worked leather, and polished boots, though all were a bit dusty.

My memory fails me a little. I'm not certain if I pulled away or Josef pushed me away. One moment I was hugging him, trying to ignore the doubts prying their way into my mind, and revelling in the elation of our reunion. The next moment we were apart again, and I no longer recognised the man standing in front of me.

CHAPTER 34

Sometimes I look back at the moment Josef and I parted down in the ruined Djinn city. I look back and think I made a mistake. I still had my knife at my belt and we were close enough. I could have stabbed him there and then, saved us all the pain and trouble. The consequences of that mistake shaped so much of my life and of everyone's around me. But at the time I didn't see it as a mistake. At the time I refused to see what Josef had become.

"You followed me." I'll admit it was a fairly obvious thing to say. Shock and denial can make even the smartest of us sound like an idiot. "How?"

"The gems," Josef said. "All we had to do was turn out our lights and they told us which way you had gone. Things were more difficult after the hall, but we followed the carnage and the blood, and it led straight to you." It is telling how many times people have found me by following the death I leave in my wake.

"We?" I backed a couple of steps further into the room. The evidence was there in front of me, but I didn't want to believe it. Josef followed me in, placing the lantern on the ground. "What the fuck have you done, Josef?"

My best friend was clean-shaven and his hair was cut. His face was stony, so far from the smile I had etched in my memory. He was wearing a military uniform. Blue on black with red trim. I had seen the exact uniform before. I had fought people wearing that uniform before. Sometimes I feel like I've been fighting people in that uniform my whole life. It was a Terrelan Sourcerer uniform.

Josef drew in a deep breath and nodded. He didn't look like my friend anymore. Grief had etched new lines in his face, making him seem older. I think he struggled with the decisions he had made in my absence. Yet he made them all the same. "I'm here to take you back, Eska."

"Take me back?" I asked. "To the Pit?"

"Yes."

"Fuck you!" I shook my head and took another step backwards, tripping on small rock. "Why?"

"Because it's my way out." Josef said, sounding tired. A hard decision can do that to a person. It weighs heavily, dragging them down into pits of despair. "I bring..."

"*We* have a way out here, Josef," I said urgently. "A way up. To the surface. We can see the sky again. Nail the slug-fucking Terrelans! You're here now. Let's just go. Together..."

"And what?" There was a hard edge to his voice. A stubborn edge. "What would you have us do once we're free, Eska?"

"Fight back." I bit the words off.

"Against who?" Josef's voice hissed out between his teeth. He didn't shout but I could hear the frustration there. "You're such a stubborn idiot, Eska. You want to pick up a fight, a war we already lost. The Orran Empire is gone! The Terrelans won. It is over."

I shook my head. "So what? We just bend down and kiss the boots of our captors?" Josef might not have been shouting, but I was. I have never been able to reign in my emotions, and I was feeling quite emotional. I probably should have realised something was wrong then. We were not so far away that the others wouldn't be able to hear my shouting yet none of them came.

"Why do you love the Orrans so much anyway?" Josef asked. "All they ever did was kidnap a couple of scared children and turn us into weapons for a war *they started*."

Again, I shook my head. "They took us in and gave us more than we would have ever had otherwise," I said. "What do you think would have happened to you out there if not for the Orrans taking you? You would have died, Josef. A young boy out on a battlefield as the Terrelan army advanced? They would have squashed you and moved on. Forgotten and dead to decay in the mud. Me? I'd still be in Keshin, weaving baskets and dreaming of a better life.

"The Orrans took us, but they gave us food, beds, an education. They taught us to use a power we were born to use." I took a deep shuddering breath. Josef didn't take the chance to argue, so I forged on. "We weren't meant to be forgotten, Josef. We were meant to be powerful. The Orrans gave us that chance."

"They started a war that killed my family." Josef sounded cold and hard. "They kidnapped us. Tortured us. Maybe you've forgotten just how many times the training they put us through almost killed you, Eska. Maybe you've forgotten how many times I sat by your sick bed. It wasn't just because I didn't want to leave you." There were unshed tears in his eyes. "I spent all those times speeding your recovery with Biomancy. The physicians would have left you to die. The Orrans would have left you to die. They didn't care about you. They didn't care about us. The Terrelans..."

"PUT US IN THE FUCKING PIT!" There are few times in my life I can say I have truly screamed at someone but this was one of them. "Look at me, Josef." I took a step forwards into the light. "I have been beaten. Bones broken. Look at my face. You know how I got the scar." I ran a finger across the tender, ragged flesh on my left cheek. "This is what the Terrelans have done. This is how much *they* care."

In the silence that followed I heard the sounds of steel on steel. Blades clashing together in a chaotic song. I glanced towards the second doorway, hoping my friends were faring well against whoever Josef had brought with him.

"You brought soldiers?" I asked quietly.

Josef nodded. "The others don't matter."

"They matter to me!"

Josef sighed. "I only need to bring you back."

"And then what?" I said. "I spend the rest of my life in the Pit and you get to go free." I wiped tears from my eyes. It was an unfair accusation. I had been willing to condemn Josef to just that.

"They're still willing to accept us both, Eska. Swear fealty..."

"Obedience," I said bitterly.

Josef let out a sigh, deflating. He looked exhausted. "The war is bloody well over, Eska. We won't need to fight anyone anymore. Swear fealty and we can leave together. We can be together again, Eska. Just you and me."

348

I decided to counter his offer. "Take off that uniform and we can leave together right now," I said. "We don't need the Terrelans and their offer, Josef. We'll run."

"They'd chase us." Josef shook his head and I could see he was beaten. Not by me. The Terrelans had beaten him into submission, and he no longer had the strength to fight them, or the lies they told. "If I don't come back, they'll send others. I don't want to fight or run. The Terrelans have their own academy. We could teach others. A life of peace."

We stood there, staring at each other for a while. We both knew the truth, though neither of us was willing to admit it. We wanted different things. Josef wanted a quiet life away from fighting and war. I wanted revenge on everyone who had put me in the Pit, everyone who had kept me in the Pit. I wanted revenge on everyone who had taken my life from me and destroyed everything I knew. The academy was gone. Orran was gone. And now Josef was gone. All I had left was my anger, my hatred. I didn't want peace, I wanted to watch the world burn.

I saw it then. The Josef I knew, the young boy who had shared so much of my life, the young man I trusted and loved more than even myself... was gone. I don't think he realised how much he had changed. I still wonder if the Pit did that, or if it was me. I think it was probably me. I've always been a danger to those I love.

"Eska!" I turned to see Isen standing in the second doorway, my little sword in his hand, the blade dripping red. "Josef?"

"Is it because of him?" Josef asked.

Before I could answer, Josef flicked out a hand. Isen was picked up by an invisible force and crushed against the roof. Josef flicked his hand down and Isen's body hit the floor with a squelch. Even in the dim light of the lantern I could see a pool of red spreading out beneath the body.

I think I was in shock. I didn't move. Couldn't move. I just stood there staring at the body of crushed flesh that had, only a moment ago, been Isen. Hardt shouted, a noise with no words only pain, and a moment later the older brother was there beside the corpse of the younger. He was distraught, babbling with tears streaking down his face.

"Or him?" Josef asked.

The threat to Hardt is what moved me. I had always known Josef could be brutal. He never hesitated to kill when we fought against the Terrelans. He understood, long before I did, that war is harsh, and the winners are often those who strike first. But I had never seen him kill someone we knew. I had never imagined he could so casually murder someone we both called a friend.

I stepped forward, hands up. "Stop it, Josef."

Being hit by a psychokinetic blast of energy is never pleasant. It feels like a wall slamming into every bit of your body all at once. I suppose I should be grateful that he was gentle. One moment I was moving forward, and the next I hit the far wall and crumpled. I might have screamed from the pain but the breath was driven from my lungs by the impact.

"You did this?" Hardt stood from the corpse of his brother. His body blocked the doorway behind him, and the light from the lantern made the grief on his face so plain. I struggled against tears of my own.

But I had no time for tears. I had no time to grieve; I wasn't even certain I would for Isen. I knew Josef. With a

Kinemancy Source in his stomach he would kill everyone and drag me back to the Pit, and there was nothing anyone could do to stop him. Well, there was nothing anyone but *I* could do to stop him.

While Josef was watching Hardt, I snatched the pouch from my belt, took the Source from inside and popped it into my mouth, swallowing hard. It took only moments for me to discover I had just killed myself.

CHAPTER 35

My vision sharpened, as though everything I had ever seen before had been blurred without me knowing it. My heart began to race so fast I thought it would burst inside my chest. I felt power flooding through me from the Source in my stomach. Josef started to turn his head towards me, but he was moving so slowly, a determined look etched onto the lines of his face.

I knew then I had about a minute to live.

Every Source affects a person differently. Most take about five minutes to kill the unattuned. Chronomancy speeds up the body, makes everything faster. It makes the Sourcerer faster. It also kills them faster. Even someone attuned to Chronomancy can only hold a Source for a few hours before it starts to age them unnaturally.

I felt the cramps hit even as I rose to my feet. Pain blossomed in my limbs and in my stomach. I fought it, swallowed down the agony and lurched forward.

"Look at me, Josef," I said. My voice sounded strange as the Chronomancy slowed down the world around me.

"Eska," Josef said, his voice a lethargic drawl. "What have you done?"

There was a lesson Josef tried to teach me early on in our incarceration. A lesson Hardt and Isen tried to teach me also. Even the overseer and Deko knew it long before I did. When the odds are stacked against you, when you look down at your cards and realise you have been dealt a shitty hand and have no way to win, you have two options. You can give up, but if you've learned one thing from my story so far it should be that I never fucking give up! Your other option is to damn the cards, and damn the odds, and damn the game. Play the player. Beat the player. Do that, and it doesn't matter what the rules of the game are, nor how unlikely you are to win.

I couldn't use this magic I had attained to beat Josef in a fight. I had no idea how to use Chronomancy and the pain was so intense it was taking everything I had not to curl into a ball and cry myself to death. I screamed in pain and coughed up blood. The effects of the Source were taking hold so quick. Something inside of me was bleeding. The cramps were agonizing, and I could feel blood leaking from my eyes, ears, and nose. All Josef had to do was nothing, and I would die before him. If he wanted it, he had already beaten me. But I wasn't playing that game. I was betting on him, my best friend, my brother, my soul bonded. I was betting my life on the love we shared. Just like every time he had betrayed me, I knew he wouldn't let me die. I knew it! Even if I no longer knew who he was.

"I can't survive this, Josef," I said through chattering teeth. My whole body was trembling uncontrollably, blood oozed from my eyes, running as crimson tears down my cheeks. "You can stop it. You have Spiceweed." He must. He had to. He wouldn't have swallowed a Source without the guarantee that he could bring it back up. The overseer wouldn't have given him a Source without Spiceweed to stop it from killing him. Or so I hoped.

"Here," Josef shouted. He pulled a small pouch from an inside jacket pocket and pinched a bit of weed between thumb and forefinger. With a flick of his wrist he floated it over to me with Kinemancy. That was how far our relationship had fallen, how damaged our friendship had become. Even weak and dying, wracked by pain I couldn't describe, and being ripped apart by wild magic, he wouldn't come to me. He wouldn't risk himself by getting close to me.

I grabbed hold of the floating Spiceweed and crushed it in a fist, still staring at Josef through bleeding eyes. I had to lock my knees to stop myself from collapsing. "You first," I said, fighting the oncoming seizures.

Josef took a single step forward, pain and fear mixing into a hideous mask on his face. "Eska, that magic is killing you! Take the Spiceweed. Please. I know what Lesray did to you, and I know you still suffer, but please don't kill yourself." There were tears in my best friend's eyes. The grief of watching someone you love take their own life. Not quietly. Not easily. But in agony and blood. "Please!"

He still thought I was bluffing. He thought I was doing this because of Lesray's Empamantic command, that even six years and hundreds of miles removed, the bitch-whore was still whispering in my ear, trying to make me kill myself. Josef didn't understand. "You. First." The words were stilted things, but I was dealing with a mouthful of blood at the time.

Josef stared at me for a few moments, disbelief plain. I saw that change to defeat, and then to acceptance. Josef was many things, a Sourcerer, a murderer, a best

354

friend. A young boy still struggling with the adult world he had been thrust into. A young man taken by enemies and thrown into a prison designed to break people's spirits. He had a ruthless side to him that scared me, and more compassion and love than I was deserving of. But one thing he never had that I always have, was an unbreakable defiance, commitment to a cause, the willingness to bet everything, *everything* to win.

Without a word, Josef took another pinch of Spiceweed and placed it in his mouth. I was shaking, convulsing, bleeding from everywhere and I could feel my body consuming itself as the Chronomancy Source began to age me. Still, I waited until Josef collapsed, bent over, the uncontrollable retching taking hold. Only then did I shove the Spiceweed into my own mouth.

It took only moments, yet for me it felt like hours of agony before the Spiceweed took effect. I retched up everything. I looked down at half-digested shrooms and blood dripping onto the ground. So much blood. I was shaking, trembling so much I was amazed I could see anything. My stomach convulsed and pushed the Chronomancy Source up and out, coated in blood and bile. I wanted to collapse, to roll away and let the cold oblivion of unconsciousness take me. But I wouldn't. Instead I crawled towards Josef. I needed to be close to him. I needed to see him. I needed to know he was all right, and that he didn't hate me.

Josef was on his knees, coughing and retching. I saw him bring up the Kinemancy Source. He snatched it from the ground quickly. Spiceweed always affected me more severely than him. It wouldn't matter though, it would be a while before he could force the Source back down. His uniform wasn't pristine anymore. A strange thing to notice, but I did. It was covered in dust, bile. He met my eyes for just a moment as I reached out for him. I don't know what I saw there; hatred, anger, love, happiness? I'll never know.

I tried to rise. Tried to stop it. But I was too late. Even my own fear feeding Ssserakis, lending me strength, wasn't enough. I could only watch as Yorin stepped up behind Josef and drew a knife across his throat.

CHAPTER 36

It takes a while for a person to bleed to death, even with a wound as severe as a cut throat. Josef gagged on his own blood and convulsed as he collapsed. I watched him claw at the wound on his neck. I could see the fear in his eyes. I could feel the fear pulsing off him in waves. It was so strange to watch my friend die, knowing there was nothing I could do about it, and growing stronger even as he faded.

I reached out and took his hand, squeezing it. I think he tried to squeeze back, but he had no strength. In that brief moment we were truly reunited, regardless of our differences and betrayals. I sometimes wonder if it was peaceful for Josef after the fear was gone. Those final few moments as he drifted off. I could barely see him by then, my vision was so blurred with tears.

Then he was gone. My friend. My brother. The other half of me. Gone.

Getting to my feet was easy. I felt stronger than I had in days, despite the battering my body had taken. Like there was new life flooding into my limbs. I saw Hardt, cradling his arm and leaning against the second doorway. He soon faded as the light in the room grew dimmer, and dimmer still, until Yorin was all I could see. My rage boiled inside of me. In that one moment, I fucking hated Yorin more than Prig or the overseer. More than the Terrelan

Emperor. More than myself. More than Josef. I was rage incarnate and all of it was focused on him!

He stood there in front of me, knives in hand and both still dripping with blood. It wasn't all Josef's. I wondered who else Yorin had killed. It didn't matter. He backed up a step. It was the only time I ever saw fear on Yorin's face. The only time I ever felt it oozing from him. I advanced slowly, flexing my hands and already imagining tearing him apart bit by bit, drinking down his terror. Ripping him into pieces and smearing him over the walls as a monument to my pain.

"What are you?" Yorin hissed.

A simple question, and it should have had a simple answer. But it didn't. It made me confront the truth. In that moment, I recognised the unnatural darkness around us. I recognised the cold and the fear. It was the first time I looked inside myself and I recognised Ssserakis.

Strange to say, but I heard the ancient horror laugh. *You are the weapon.* A voice in my head mocking my stupidity that I hadn't seen it earlier.

The darkness faded, the light of the lantern flooding back in, and I collapsed to my knees. Yorin could have killed me then. I was weak and barely conscious. I think, perhaps, he should have. Maybe he could have saved the world all the pain I have since visited upon it. I would have died there next to Josef. Together again, forever.

Self-reflection is a personal thing. The act of looking inside oneself and shedding light on all the bits you would rather left hidden. Only there was no light inside of me. As I knelt there, amidst the rubble, and the blood of my best friend, I looked inside and saw darkness. And the darkness stared back at me.

I have since had many conversations with Ssserakis. I know the horror almost as well as I know myself. Back then it felt alien and cold. Like a part of myself I didn't recognise. A festering wound inside my mind, coiled around my soul. And Ssserakis just laughed, amused that it had taken me so long to realise the horror wasn't just along for the ride. It was a part of me. Possession, it turns out, is a complicated matter where horrors from the Other World are concerned. That, too, I have discussed at length with Ssserakis.

It's hard to say how long I spent looking inside myself. When eventually I came out of my daze, it was to a hand on my shoulder. I looked up to find Hardt kneeling in front of me. He looked tired. Grief, exhaustion, and pain all mixed together in the lines of his face. In that moment I wanted nothing more than to feel his arms around, crushed in his embrace and told that everything was going to be alright. But he held me at arm's length and I could see something in his eyes, a wariness. Fear. Maybe a little disgust. I couldn't take it. I dropped my eyes to the ground, anything to not see how he looked at me.

"Are you alright, Eska?" I cannot count the number of times I have caused Hardt to ask that question. "You look..."

"Older," Tamura finished.

They weren't wrong. It was a while before I caught a glimpse of my reflection, but I didn't need to. I felt older. I don't know how long I had the Chronomancy Source inside, maybe only a minute, but I believe it aged me a decade in that time. Some of the prime years of my life stolen from me. Even now I hope it had no lasting effect on the little life that was growing inside of me. Time will tell.

"We should get you out of here." Hardt pulled me to my feet with his good arm and I let him lead me from the room. I think it's quite telling about the strength of the man. He had just seen his brother, a broken mess of a corpse, and yet he was more concerned for me. But I know Hardt has grieved for his brother. We have spent many nights drinking to his memory. And the stories I have been told... The brothers lived an eventful life, even before they met me.

Tamura lingered, gathering up the two Sources before following us. There were bodies out in the corridor, soldiers wearing Terrelan uniforms. It appeared Josef had not come after us alone. Whether it was to protect him, or ensure his cooperation, the overseer had sent others along. They were all dead now. Some had the broad cuts of a sword, while others had shallow stabs from knives. I have often wondered if Hardt used his fists to beat any of them to death. It is a question I have never asked him. None of us really want reminding of that day. Some things are best left to gather dust as half-forgotten memories.

I regret leaving the bodies of our friends down there. I regret many things about that day.

CHAPTER 37

In our fourth year at the academy, I was just ten years old and Josef was twelve. We were progressing well, though all the tutors seemed to agree that my own studies could have been better. According to them, I spent too much time reading fictional accounts of heroes and monsters, bards' tales full of danger, action, and romance. They even tried banning me from the library for a while. I enlisted Josef to bring me copies of the stories I wanted to read.

I have long since learned that heroes only exist on the pages of books, and the lips of bards. Out in the world there are only choices. Those choices might appear heroic to some and villainous to others. I often wonder how my own people look at my choices, how my daughters look at my choices. I think I have played the villain far more than the hero.

Josef and the bitch-whore were well into their studies of Empamancy. It was a tough time for Josef, having to use Spiceweed every day so he didn't fall asleep with an Empamancy Source inside. I hate Empamancy. I really fucking hate it. Some people think it the weakest of the biological schools, but I know better. Empamancy is the magic of forcing emotions upon people. It's a violation of the mind. And it can be used to plant suggestions.

I was excelling at Pyromancy, top of the students of a similar age. Lesray didn't like that. Like me, she has always had an affinity to fire and ice. I wonder who she hated more; me for being better than her, or herself for not being better than me. I'll wager it was the latter, given the punishment she dished out.

The tutors had just given me back my library privileges and I was making my way there. I have always loved libraries. I find it peaceful to sit amongst so much knowledge. I find it humbling to think on how many lifetimes of experience and wisdom rest upon the shelves. I find it empowering to know I could burn it all to the ground and render all those lifetimes mute. I should admit I have never set fire to a library, I just like to know that I could.

I never saw Lesray, but I know it was her. She gloated afterwards and it wasn't the last time I felt the touch of her magic. I came to recognise it all too well. I remember I had just sat down with a book on Impomancy, studying the monsters that could be summoned. Then a wave of despair washed over me and dragged me out into a sea of hopelessness and self-loathing.

I should probably feel sorry for the bitch-whore. An Empamancer doesn't create emotion. They can dig it up from within a person and amplify it. They can project their own emotions onto others, but they cannot create an emotion out of nothing. I had never felt such despair or self-loathing before. I never felt like ending it all before. That came from her. At some point, Lesray had wanted to kill herself and she projected that emotion into me. I should probably feel sorry for her, but I can't because I hate her too much. That was the very first time I felt like ending my own life, and every time since, I can't help but think it was all because of her. I can't help but wonder if that magic she used to invade my mind planted a seed I can never be rid of. All wounds leave scars and not all wounds are physical. She made me want to kill myself… And I still do.

As the wave of despair crashed over me, I found it hard to breathe, as though my throat had closed up. I went hot and cold all at the same time. I remember my fingernails digging gouges into the desk, breaking on the wood. I knew, at that moment, that I couldn't take it. It was just too much. I felt the weight of the world bearing down on me; the weight of expectation, the sure knowledge that I would fail and it would hurt those I loved. I knew I couldn't take it, and I knew there was only one way to make it stop.

I stood, leaving my books and my notes. My copy of the Encyclopaedia Otheria was on page two hundred and twelve, depicting a ghoul with detailed explanations of sexual dimorphism within the species. Strange that I remember that so clearly, as though what page the book was on is etched in my mind when so much else around the event is a blur.

The library roof was flat, a full five storeys above ground. I opened the door and walked out into a pleasant summer breeze. It should have lifted have my spirits, yet I barely noticed. My eyes were fixed on the edge of the rooftop; on a drop that I knew ended in flagstones. A short drop, headfirst, and it would all be over. The pain, the despair, the crushing feeling of not being good enough.

They were not my feelings. But it all felt so real, and I knew the only thing that could release me from it all was death.

I was all but falling when Josef caught up to me. He had followed me all the way from the library, calling out and I hadn't heard him. I hadn't even heard him running to catch me. One moment I was leaning into my end, and the next I was tumbling backwards into his arms.

We never talked about it, not really, but I think he knew what had happened. I think he knew it wasn't really me. I just remember him holding me tight, not saying a word, and using his own Empamancy to flood me with feelings of love. The whirl of emotions was too much. I burst into tears and lay there in Josef's arms, shaking, sobbing, senseless.

I should feel grateful. I do feel grateful, even now, for him pulling me back from the brink. But just like Lesray planted a seed of despair and self-loathing that I don't think I can ever truly purge from myself, I wonder if Josef planted a seed of love. I miss him every day more than anyone I have ever met, and I can't help but wonder if those feelings are truly mine. If they ever were. Do I look back on my life through the tinted vision of glasses he forced me to wear?

CHAPTER 38

Yorin was waiting for us by the cave entrance. He had a new lantern beside him casting light on our way out. I should probably have been glad that he waited for us, but all I felt towards him was hatred. That hate has waned over the years, but never vanished. I don't blame Yorin; he had no idea the Terrelan soldier he was killing was my best friend. No, I don't blame him. I blame myself. That doesn't mean I forgive him.

He was wary of me as we approached. I have come to recognise the signs, and a hand on a knife hilt is a fairly obvious one. I think Tamura was the only one of us who didn't look exhausted, though he was starting to look his age. We had all suffered in one way or another.

Without a word, Yorin picked up the lantern and edged his way into the cave mouth. I let Hardt follow and trudged along after him, trusting Tamura to our rear guard. I didn't think anything or anyone would be coming after us, nor did I care. I was feeling raw. Like leather stretched too thin and starting to show holes.

The cave wound back and forth through the rock, but always upwards. It had a low roof so Hardt had to stoop the entire way and I saw him bump his head on more than one occasion. I don't know how long we spent in that cave, squeezing our way between rough walls. I know the breeze continued to grow stronger and I could feel the bite of it on my skin. It was winter after all.

I walked along in such a daze, too numb to feel anything. It was a surprise when Hardt disappeared from in front of me. I looked up and wondered when the tunnel had gotten so bright. It took me a moment to realise the tunnel was gone, nothing but a small crack in a cliff face behind me. What lay in front was a craggy landscape of rocks, heather, and the edge of a forest stretching into the horizon all covered in a blanket of white.

I dropped to my knees in the powdery snow and looking up to a washed-out sky. A blue I thought I had forgotten. I couldn't stop the tears. I didn't try to. I had equated the sky to freedom for so long and now I could see it again. I was free. A deep, genuine laugh bubbled up from inside and burst out. It sounded strange, alien, and I wondered how long it had been since I had really laughed.

Tamura joined in. He has always loved to laugh and rarely even bothers to look for a reason. Some people think him mad because of it and, while they're not wrong, it is not madness that allows him to find laughter at any situation. It is wisdom. I turned to find him lying in the snow moving his arms and legs up and down. I didn't bother to ask what he was doing, only marvelled at the grime that was staining the snow beneath him.

"We made it," Hardt said, his voice soft, heavy with suppressed grief.

I'm not sure if it was shock or disbelief, but I kept expecting it to be some sort of trick. I felt like any moment I would realise the sky was just a cavern roof painted blue. I found myself holding my breath, scared that to breathe in would somehow break the illusion.

Yorin dropped the lantern on the ground, drew in a deep breath, and started walking.

"Where are you going?" Hardt asked.

"Anywhere away from her." Yorin stopped for a moment and glanced back. "I followed you down there because you were my best shot at getting out. But there's something fucking wrong with you, girl." He turned his back on me again and started walking.

I think I scared him. Well, Ssserakis scared him, but he didn't know that. I got to my feet and stared at Yorin's back as he walked away. My emotions a whirl.

"I'm surprised," Hardt said. "I didn't think you'd just let him go after what he did to Josef."

I waited a while, long enough to be certain an errant breeze couldn't carry my words to Yorin's ears. Long enough that his silhouette was a thin black line against the white of the snow around him. Then I let loose a savage smile. "Fuck him! He's walking straight back towards the Pit," I said. "I don't need to kill him. They'll do it for me."

Tamura stepped in front of me, blocking my view. "Ancient eyes," he said. "Past lives lived long but not forgotten. So much pain."

Silva once told me there was an infinite well of sadness inside of me. That even when smiling, she could see the endless sorrow in my eyes. I think maybe she was right, and Tamura saw it too. I keep the sadness coiled inside of me. It is mine and mine alone. I wonder if it started underground, in the Pit or the buried Djinn city.

Maybe it started even earlier. Maybe it has always been inside of me.

I looked up at the sky, at my freedom, and felt a grin spread across my face. I had finally escaped my captors, but it was far from over. They were still alive. The overseer, Prig, Deko. The Terrelan Emperor. They were all still alive, and I had sworn vengeance on them all. My escape was only the beginning of my legacy. Now it was time to set the world ablaze and watch my enemies burn.

Acknowledgements

Where to start? I'd like give thanks to…

My better half, Vicki, who kept me sane throughout writing this book and series. Without you, I would have given up in book 2.

Korra T. BeagleFace, for consistently dragging me away from the computer for walks every day. And for all the occasional attack snuggles she launches.

Felix Ortiz, whose artwork is simply stunning and who knew what I wanted on the covers long before I had figured it out. And to Shawn King for sitting through the previous versions with stoic patience.

Sarah Chorn, who was not afraid in her edits to tell me when to dig deeper and make her really feel Eska's pain and joy and fear.

The alpha squad: Fiona, Rhian, and Mihir. I'm really sorry for that first version of book 2! Thanks for not giving up.

The Grimdarklings. I'm not going to mention you all by name, for you are legion, but you all know who you are. Thank you for being the most welcoming and supportive group of online vagabonds an author could wish for!

And finally a MASSIVE thank you to my readers, both those who are new to my feverish words, and those who have read them all. Thank you!!! Seriously, just thank you!

Books by Rob J. Hayes

<u>The War Eternal</u>
Along the Razor's Edge
The Lessons Never Learned
From Cold Ashes Risen

Never Die

<u>The Ties that Bind</u>
The Heresy Within
The Colour of Vengeance
The Price of Faith

City of Kings

<u>Best Laid Plans</u>
Where Loyalties Lie
The Fifth Empire of Man

<u>It Takes a Thief…</u>
It Takes a Thief to Catch a Sunrise
It Takes a Thief to Start a Fire

<u>Science Fiction</u>
Drones